CHRISTMAS WITH HER DAREDEVIL DOC

&

THEIR PREGNANCY GIFT

BY
KATE HARDY

MILLS
BOON

Miracles at Muswell Hill Hospital

Christmas is a time for healing broken hearts!

Medical marvels occur every day
at Muswell Hill Hospital—but two friends
who work there, Dr Hayley Clark and
Dr Danielle (Dani) Owens, are deserving of
some special Christmas miracles. Bonded by recent
traumatic life events, they've helped
each other recover with their year-long pact
of saying yes to everything!

As Christmas draws near—ready or not—
they are about to meet two gorgeous guys
who, if they will just let them in,
can finally mend their broken hearts!

Hayley and Sam's story
Christmas with Her Daredevil Doc

Sam and Hayley had one incredible week in Iceland—
but when Sam appears for work at Muswell Hill
Hospital, they struggle to keep their 'temporary'
romance in the past. Can their holiday fling
become so much more?

And Dani and Alex's story
Their Pregnancy Gift

Alex is determined never to have children—
but Danielle is irresistible. And after one
night of passion they must face the shocking
and wonderful consequences!

Both available now!

CHRISTMAS WITH HER DAREDEVIL DOC

BY
KATE HARDY

MILLS & BOON

Published in Great Britain 2017
By Mills & Boon, an imprint of HarperCollins*Publishers*
1 London Bridge Street, London, SE1 9GF

© 2017 Pamela Brooks

ISBN: 978-0-263-92675-0

Printed and bound in Spain
by CPI, Barcelona

Dear Reader,

How do you pick yourself up, dust yourself off and start all over again when your life implodes? That's partly why my heroine Hayley has a pact with her best friend to have a 'Year of Saying Yes'—agreeing to opportunities that will make their lives happier. And going to Iceland means that she's met someone who might just change her life for ever…

But Sam has his own issues to work through—and the way he deals with the fallout from his own life is to take risks to remind himself that he's still alive and kicking. Which makes him the worst possible man that Hayley can fall for.

How can he teach her to trust that risk-taking won't lead to another disaster in her life? And how can she teach him to trust that she won't let him down the way his ex did?

I hope you enjoy their story—and definitely the romance of their wedding!

With love,

Kate Hardy

To Gerard, Chris and Chloe, who shared Iceland
with me and fell in love with it as much as I did.

Kate Hardy has always loved books, and could read
before she went to school. She discovered Mills & Boon
books when she was twelve and decided this was what
she wanted to do. When she isn't writing, Kate enjoys
reading, cinema, ballroom dancing and the gym. You
can contact her via her website: katehardy.com.

PROLOGUE

HAYLEY DID A double take as her best friend hobbled into the hospital canteen on crutches, with a full-length walking cast up to her right knee.

'What happened, Dani?' she asked as Danielle heaved herself into the seat opposite hers and rested the crutches against the wall so they wouldn't be in the way of anyone else in the canteen. 'Did you break your ankle?'

'It's not quite that bad—it's a second and third metatarsal stress fracture,' Danielle said, grimacing.

Hayley frowned. They'd been out to their usual dance aerobics class, two nights ago, and Danielle had seemed fine then. 'When did it happen?'

'According to the orthopods, three or four weeks ago, because the fracture shows up on the X-ray and looks as if it's been trying to heal for some time—but the actual diagnosis was this morning.' Danielle sighed. 'I suppose my foot had been aching for a bit.'

And Dani, being Dani, had no doubt ignored it because she was too busy. 'Why didn't you say something, the other night?' Hayley asked. 'We could've missed class to let you rest your foot.'

Danielle flapped a dismissive hand. 'It was fine.'

Hayley raised an eyebrow. 'Fine enough for you to be wearing a walking cast right now?'

Danielle sighed. 'OK, OK. I thought it wasn't anything major and resting it for a day or two would be enough to sort it out, but it felt a bit worse yesterday so I thought I'd better get it checked out. I was pretty sure my doctor was going to roll his eyes at me and say it was just because I still needed to get used to my new running shoes. Except he sent me for an X-ray instead. And apparently almost everyone with a metatarsal stress fracture says the same thing as I did—they don't remember doing anything different or they've just got new shoes.'

'Ouch. So how long are you going to have the cast?' Hayley asked.

'They said it'll take between one and three months to heal,' Danielle said. 'So it's crutches this week and then I have to wear the cast and rest my foot as much as possible.'

'Rest' wasn't in Danielle's vocabulary, Hayley knew. It would drive her best friend crazy to have to sit with her foot up.

'And they said if I don't rest it properly and for long enough, I'll risk making it worse and then I'll end up needing surgery to fix it—which will take even longer to heal, so obviously I'd rather avoid that.' Danielle pulled a face. 'Bang goes finishing my training for that charity run in October. I won't even be able to *walk* the course, let alone run it. I'll have to return all the sponsor money.'

And the run was close to Dani's heart because she

was raising money to buy an MRI scanner for newborns on the maternity unit. 'Unless the organisers will let me run in your place,' Hayley said thoughtfully.

Danielle stared at her in surprise. 'I can't ask you to do that. You hate running.'

'Yes, but it's for a good cause. I can run it for you. Remember, we agreed, this is the Year of Saying Yes. We've both had a horrible year.' Hayley's own life had imploded just over a year ago, when Evan, her fiancé, had been killed while trying to rescue someone from an industrial fire; and Danielle's husband Leo had left her unexpectedly for someone else, nine months ago. They'd supported each other through the wreckage of their lives and, the previous month, when Danielle's decree nisi had come through and the anniversary of Evan's death had passed, they'd agreed that they'd spend the next year saying yes to every opportunity that came their way. The theory was, it would help them both to move on and live life to the full. Or, as Dani had put it, living well was the best revenge and she wasn't going to spend the rest of her life crying over someone who didn't love her any more.

'We agreed we'd make the most out of life and say yes to every opportunity,' Haley reminded her. 'So you have to say yes to me taking your place, and we'll talk the organisers into bending the rules slightly if they have to. They can't expect you to run with a broken foot—and surely it's better to have a substitute so the hospital can keep the sponsor money towards the scanner?'

'If you're really sure,' Danielle said, 'then thank you.' She bit her lip. 'But that's not the worst bit.' She dragged in a breath. 'I'm so sorry, but I'm not going to be able to go to Iceland with you next week. The orthopods tried to sign me off work. I said I can do a lot of my job sitting down—which I can, so don't argue,' she said, holding up one hand to stop Hayley protesting. 'They've agreed to let me have the walking cast, provided I agreed to rest my foot as much as possible. But they said that hiking round Iceland for a week is totally out of the question. And, with the kind of walks we were planning to do, there's no way you could push me round in a chair—not when there's loads of rough ground, volcanic sand, and a fair bit of clambering about on slippery boulders. It's just not doable.'

'Then we'll talk to the travel agent and reschedule,' Hayley said.

Danielle shook her head. 'You wanted to go in the summer so you'd get to see the midnight sun. If we reschedule, then it'll be another year before we can go away—and you really, really need a break. Especially as you're taking up your new job in a couple of weeks.'

Her promotion to senior registrar, which was bittersweet because Evan wasn't here to be pleased that her hard work had paid off. 'I'm fine,' Hayley said.

'This is supposed to be the Year of Saying Yes, remember,' Danielle said. 'We said we'd do it so we'd have fun instead of being miserable.'

'I'm not so sure it'll be much fun, going to Iceland on my own,' Hayley said.

'But you'll still get to see the whales and the geyser and the glacier—tick all those things off your bucket list. You need a break, Haze. Go and have a wonderful time. And I'll talk to the travel agent to sort everything out this end.'

'It's not fair that you're missing out,' Hayley said.

'We can plan something else when my foot's healed,' Danielle said. 'We could maybe go to Vienna in November for the Christmas markets. We can eat lots of gingerbread and drink the best hot chocolate in the world.'

'Maybe,' Hayley said.

'Definitely,' Danielle insisted. 'And you can send me a ton of photos from Iceland.' She smiled. 'If I were you, I'd stock up on the fun now—if you were serious about running that charity race for me, you'll be in strict training for the next two months.'

'Two and a half months, less my week in Iceland,' Hayley pointed out.

'The couch to 10K running programme is supposed to take about twelve weeks,' Danielle said thoughtfully, 'but you do dance aerobics twice a week, so you're not really starting from couch level.'

Hayley did dance aerobics simply because Dani had pushed her into it two weeks after Evan's funeral, making her leave her flat instead of hiding within the four walls and wishing that her fiancé had never, ever become a firefighter. And Hayley had to admit that the combination of the music and the movement *had* made her feel better, if only for a little while. For the same reason, she'd forced Dani to keep coming to the class with her after Leo had walked out on her.

'OK. You sort out the training programme and I'll do it.'

'You,' Danielle said, reaching over to squeeze her hand, 'are the best friend ever.'

'No, that would be you,' Hayley said. 'And you can sit still while I sort out some lunch for you. Even *you* can't juggle a tray and hot coffee with crutches.'

'Try me?' Danielle said.

'Behave,' Hayley ordered with a grin.

'Yes, ma'am. And you're right—I can't hold coffee with crutches,' Danielle admitted, and fished in her purse for some money. 'Thanks, Haze. Just grab the first sandwich you come to—I don't mind what it is.' She paused. 'So you promise me you won't cancel the trip?'

'It's the Year of Saying Yes,' Hayley said. 'So I'll go.' Even though a solo trip felt daunting, Hayley knew that her best friend was right. She did need a break. And maybe ticking some things off her bucket list would help her move on.

She'd always miss Evan, but she knew he wouldn't have wanted her to spend the rest of her life on her own. So she was going to say yes. And, in accordance with their agreement, she was going to date the next man who asked her out.

CHAPTER ONE

THE LAND OF the Midnight Sun. Hayley had been stunned by the sheer quality of the light from the moment she'd arrived at the airport; everything seemed brighter in Reykjavik.

Evan would've loved this, she thought with a pang. Especially the whale-watching trip she'd chosen to do this morning. Now the boat was out in the middle of the open sea, the temperature had dropped quite sharply, but the sun was bright and she leaned against the railing at the side of the boat, listening to the guide and trying to spot the tiny puffins with their bright orange beaks.

'There are lots of birds just above the water ahead of us, and that often indicates cetacean activity—they'll be picking up bits of fish the whales have left behind,' the guide said. And then, a couple of minutes later, she called, 'Spout at nine o'clock!'

Hayley could actually see the spout of warm, moist air blown up by the whale; to her amazement, it really was like you saw in TV documentaries. A perfect misty funnel.

'And here's our minke!' the guide said.

The ship drew to a standstill, and Hayley could see just the dark back of the whale, like a slight hump above the surface of the sea. And then a fin appeared, bright white against the sea and the sky, almost as if the whale was waving to them.

This was magical.

She took a few shots on her camera, hoping they'd come out. And then, to her sheer joy, the whale breached, its snout coming up out of the water and then its body performing a perfect arc, revealing its white belly before the whale splashed back into the sea.

She'd never seen anything so awe-inspiring. The whale's snout came up again, and then a fin; then she saw the divided end of the tail as the whale dived down again.

'I'm sure you could all see the flukes then—that's the whale's tail—and this usually indicates that the whale's diving more deeply,' the guide said. 'So we're going to move on.'

This was a truly humbling experience, Hayley thought; it made her feel glad to be alive.

But then, a few minutes later, the guide called, 'Do we have a doctor on board?'

Her heart skipped a beat. When a tour guide put out that kind of call, it could mean a true emergency, and right now they were almost an hour's sail away from Reykjavik. She had no idea how the emergency services worked here. Would they send out a helicopter to the ship, or would the tour guide have to cut the trip short and they'd have to sail straight back to the city?

She made her way to the guide's post. 'I'm Hayley Clark, a doctor from England. Can I help?'

'My husband's having an asthma attack,' an American woman said, looking anxious and wringing her hands. 'And we don't have his inhaler with us.'

Just as well she worked in the emergency department, Hayley thought. 'Can you put out a call to see if anyone has a reliever inhaler we could borrow, please?' she asked the guide. 'Even a preventer inhaler would help.'

'Will do,' the guide said.

She turned to the woman. 'Would you like to take me to your husband? My name's Hayley and I work in the emergency department of a London hospital.'

'I'm Lulu Adams and thank God you're on board,' the woman said, leading her towards the next deck down. 'I can't believe Milton's having an attack out here. Normally it's pollen and cat hair that sets him off.'

'Cold can set off asthma, too, and the air's quite cool out here,' Hayley said, 'so it's always a good idea to keep a reliever inhaler with you—even if you don't think you're going to come across your usual triggers. Does your husband take his preventer inhaler regularly?'

'He's a man. You can't tell him *anything*,' the woman said with a sigh.

So this was probably an attack that had been brewing for a while, Hayley thought, with a patient who didn't bother taking his preventer inhaler that often. Milton Adams's doctor definitely needed to talk to him about the importance of asthma control. She just hoped she could keep him stable until they managed to get some proper bronchodilator medication for him. 'Does he have any other medical conditions?' she asked.

'Just the asthma.'

Which was tricky enough to deal with, by the sound of things. 'OK. Thanks.'

Do we have a doctor on board?

There were maybe a couple of hundred other people on the boat. The chances were, Sam was the only doctor. Plus this would be a test. Had he done the right thing in accepting the job at a London hospital, or had his experience in Manchester soured his love affair with medicine to the point where he really didn't want to go back to it?

He made his way to the bridge to talk to the guide, and on the way he heard her ask if anyone had an asthma inhaler that another passenger could borrow.

'My name's Sam Price, and I'm an emergency doctor from England. It sounds as if you have a passenger who's having an asthma attack and doesn't have an inhaler. Can I help?' he asked.

'There's another doctor gone to see him already, if you want to join her,' the guide said. 'You'll see her on the deck below. She's wearing a yellow raincoat.'

'OK. Thanks. Has anyone come up with an inhaler?'

'Not yet, but I'm going to put another call out,' she said.

Asthma attacks could be tricky. If nothing else, Sam thought, he could help calm down whoever was with the patient, so the other doctor could get on with treating the patient. He headed down to the next deck, and saw a woman wearing a yellow raincoat. She was talking to a man who was clearly panicking and wheezing, and the woman with them was wringing her hands and looking equally panicky.

'Hello. I'm Sam Price, and I'm an emergency doctor,' he said as he joined them. 'Can I help?'

'Hayley Clark—also an emergency doctor, from London,' the woman in the yellow raincoat said.

He noticed how blue her eyes were—like an Icelandic summer sky—and her sun-streaked blonde hair was caught back at the nape of her neck, with soft tendrils framing a perfect oval face.

What the hell was he doing, noticing the colour of her eyes when there was a sick patient who needed their attention? Besides, even if he was looking for a relationship—which he wasn't, after Lynda—she was probably already spoken for. Cross with himself for getting distracted, he paid attention to what she was saying.

'This is Milton Adams and his wife Lulu,' Hayley continued. 'He doesn't have his reliever or preventer inhaler with him, and we think the cold air probably brought on his asthma attack. He doesn't have any other medical conditions.'

'The guide's putting out a second call to see if anyone on board has an inhaler with them,' Sam said. 'But even if there isn't anyone, we can help you, Mr Adams.'

The man continued to wheeze, fighting for air, clearly panicked by the tightness in his chest.

Really, they needed to get him away from the cold air that had triggered the attack and into a warm place. But, given the state of his breathing right now and the fact that he was quite overweight, no way would Mr Adams be able to cope with the steep stairs to go back inside the ship. First, Sam thought, they needed to get Mr Adams stabilised so he was calm, and breathing more slowly. Anxiety released cortisol in the body, constricting the bronchial tubes even further, and panicking that you couldn't breathe caused a vicious circle: it tightened the chest muscles, which made it harder to breathe, which in turn made the patient panic more and then the chest muscles tightened even further.

'Mr Adams, can you sit up straight for us?' Sam asked. 'It'll help you breathe more easily, because bending over constricts your breathing.'

Milton Adams continued gasping, but to Sam's relief, he did as he was told.

'I'm going to loosen your tie and undo the button of your collar,' Hayley said, 'because that's also going to help you breathe more easily. Is that all right?'

The man nodded.

'I told him he ought to bring his inhaler. I *told* him,' Mrs Adams said, almost in tears.

Hayley reached over and squeezed her hand. 'Mrs Adams—can we call you Lulu?' At the woman's nod, she continued, 'I know how worried you are about your husband, but right now I really need you to do an important job for me and count. Can you do that for me?'

'Yes,' Mrs Adams said, her voice slightly quavery.

Brilliant management, Sam thought—she'd acknowledged the woman's fears and distracted her by making her feel useful. What Hayley had just said about counting told him that she'd intended to use the same method he would've used.

'Mr Adams—can we call you Milton?' At the man's nod, Sam continued, 'We want you to try to take some really long, deep breaths for us. I know right now it's scary, but I promise we can make you feel better. I want you to breathe in through your nose for a count of four and out through your mouth for a count of six. Can you do that for us?'

Mr Adams nodded, still fighting for breath.

'Can you count for us now, Lulu?' Hayley asked. 'Four in, then six out. Count with me for the first set so we can get the rhythm right together. One, two, three, four...'

Mrs Adams joined in with counting.

Sam took the older man's hand to reassure him. 'OK. Breathe in—now out.' Breathing to the counts would slow Milton's breathing down, making it easier for him.

'Purse your lips as you breathe out, Milton,' Hayley said. 'That helps to slow your breathing and keeps your airways open. That's it. Keep going. You're both doing really great.'

Mr Adams was still wheezing, but his colour was improving. 'Can you place one hand on your stomach, Milton, just below your ribcage?' Sam asked. 'Then, when you breathe in, focus on pulling down into your stomach. Use your stomach muscles to help you push out,' he said. 'It's called diaphragmatic breathing and it will really help you take deep, slow breaths.'

Eventually, Mr Adams's breathing pattern settled and he seemed noticeably calmer.

Sam caught Hayley's eye. 'Shall we all go downstairs, so we're away from the cold air?'

She nodded. 'And we can ask the crew if they'll sort out a bowl of hot water and lend us a towel.'

'Good call,' he said. They could make a tent with the towel and the bowl of hot water, and then Milton Adams could breathe in the moist air to help him recover.

Everyone else on board was on the upper decks by the railings, watching what sounded like a couple of whales playing in the water, so it made their passage down the stairs a bit easier—even if they were missing out on all the fun. They supported Milton Adams down the steep staircase to the inner deck, but he was wheezing badly again by the time they'd got him sitting down by a table.

'Could you get your husband a cup of coffee from the bar, please?' Hayley asked Mrs Adams.

'He doesn't like coffee,' Mrs Adams said. 'Or tea. Only hot chocolate.'

'Maybe make the coffee milky and sweet?' Hayley suggested. 'The chemical structure of coffee is similar to theophylline, which is in most asthma medications, so a hot cup of coffee can help with wheezing, shortness of breath and chest tightness. Plus the warmth of the liquid will help break up the phlegm and mucus, making breathing easier.'

'I'll drink the coffee,' Mr Adams wheezed.

'Great. Are you OK to sit with Milton while I sort out a towel and hot water?' Hayley asked Sam.

'Sure,' he said. 'What I'd like you to do, Milton, is to sit up straight for me again, and count the number of blue things in the room.'

'Blue things?' Mr Adams looked nonplussed.

'Blue things,' Sam confirmed. 'Count them, and

keep breathing like we did upstairs. I'll count while you breathe. In for four, out for six.'

As he'd hoped, the small task of looking round the room for blue things distracted the older man enough to help calm him further, and by the time Mr Adams had drunk the coffee and Sam and Hayley had arranged the bowl of hot water and towel as a temporary recovery tent so he could breathe in warm, moist air, he was looking in a much better condition.

When the boat arrived back at the dock, they were met by an ambulance. The guide came to join them as Sam and Hayley explained the situation to the paramedics.

'Thank you both so much for all your help.' Mrs Adams bit her lip. 'And you missed most of the trip and the whales because of us. I feel so bad.'

'We can arrange a replacement trip at no charge,' the guide said. 'And I'd like to thank you both, too. We have trained first aiders among the crew, of course, but we really needed a doctor to help us in this case.'

'No problem,' Hayley said.

'Call into the office whenever suits you best,' the guide said, 'and we'll rearrange your trip.'

'I ought to give you something for helping us,' Mrs Adams said.

'There's really no need,' Sam said. 'It's what doctors are supposed to do—help people who need it.'

'Agreed. Though if you really want to give us something,' Hayley added, 'then I'd like you to promise you'll talk to your asthma specialist about what happened today, Milton, and that you'll take your preventer inhaler regularly—even if you don't think you need it, because taking it regularly is what helps to keep you well.'

Milton looked slightly shame-faced. 'I will.'

'Good.' Hayley patted his shoulder. 'Best of luck, and enjoy the rest of your holiday.'

'You, too.'

When the ambulance doors closed and the Adamses were taken to hospital, Sam looked at Hayley. 'Would you like to go for a coffee? Or do you need to get back to whoever you're travelling with?'

'I'm on my own,' she said. 'So a coffee would be lovely—unless you need to get back to your travelling companions?'

'I'm on my own, too,' he said. 'Do you want to re-book your whale-watching trip first?'

She wrinkled her nose. 'I saw one come up out of the water and dive back in. Expecting anything more's probably greedy. Though if you want to re-book yours…?'

He smiled. 'I'm greedy enough as it is. I go every week.'

'Every week?' She looked surprised. 'Do you work at a hospital here, then?'

'No. I'm kind of on sabbatical,' he said. 'My brother has a tour company out here, specialising in extreme trips—taking people walking on a glacier and that sort of thing. I've been helping him. But I go whale-watching every Monday afternoon. It's the most amazing experience.'

She nodded. 'It's something Dani and I always wanted to see.'

'Danny?' Well, of course someone as pretty as Hayley Clark would be spoken for.

'Danielle. My best friend,' she explained.

How ridiculous that he should feel pleased that Dani was her best friend, not a partner. He was in no position to even think about starting a relationship, not with his new job starting in a fortnight.

Yet something about Hayley Clark tempted him.

Which was weird, because he'd had tourists throwing themselves at him all summer and not one of them had interested him.

What was it about her?

'She fractured her second and third metatarsal last week, so the orthopods said she couldn't come,' Hayley continued.

He'd come across those kinds of fractures before. 'Your friend's a runner, then?'

Hayley nodded. 'She was training for a charity run. Obviously she can't do that now, so we talked the organisers into letting me run in her place.'

'You're a runner, too?'

She grimaced. 'No. Actually, I loathe running. But the only way to keep her sponsorship money is if I run for her.'

'That's good of you.'

'She's my best friend, and she's been through a lot. And doing that for her helps me feel less guilty about coming here while she's missing out.' Hayley wrinkled her nose. 'Though I'm pretty sure she could've done the whale-watching—and if we'd asked at the tourist place, they could've found us some wheelchair-accessible trips.'

'But you would both have missed out on a lot. Not all the paths around the waterfalls and the geysers are wheelchair-friendly,' he said, 'and some of the slopes would make it seriously tricky going downhill.'

'That's what Dani said.'

He should shut up right now. What he ought to do was to suggest a couple of reliable tour operators and let her find her own way round the island. But the pull he felt towards her was too strong, and he found himself asking, 'How long are you staying?'

'Until Friday.'

Shut up, shut up, shut up.

But his mouth wasn't listening to his common sense. 'Then why don't you rebook your whale trip for tomorrow morning?' he suggested. 'And if you like, I'll take you on a personalised tour.'

She blinked. 'But aren't you helping your brother?'

It was the perfect get-out. He knew he ought to take it. But his mouth was on a roll. 'He's had a couple of cancellations,' Sam said, 'so I wasn't doing much this week. I'm free if you'd like to come with me.'

Hayley could practically hear Dani yelling in her ear, 'Say yes! It's the Year of Saying Yes.'

But Sam Price was a total stranger.

Even if he was a doctor and they'd just worked together to help a patient.

And, with that dark hair brushed back from his face and soulful hazel eyes, he was also the most attractive man she'd met since Evan, the first who'd even made her look at him, which made her feel guilty. It was only just over a year since Evan had died. Was she rushing into this?

She ought to be cautious. She was in a country where she didn't speak the language; even though everyone in Iceland spoke perfect English, this still wasn't England. She was a three-and-a-half-hour flight away from home. The sensible thing to do would be to say no.

But this was the Year of Saying Yes.

And maybe putting caution aside was something she needed to do for once. To help her move on.

'Yes,' she said.

CHAPTER TWO

THEY REBOOKED THE whale-watching tour for the following morning, then headed to a café in the centre of the city.

'I love the ambience here,' Hayley said when they were settled at a table.

'Reykjavik lives up to your expectations, then?' Sam asked.

'Very much,' she said. 'I had a walk round yesterday evening when I got here. I really want to explore that amazing-looking church—I've never seen a spire like that, kind of spreading out like wings.'

'The Hallgrímskirkja,' he said. 'It's meant to resemble the volcanic basalt flows—and actually there are a couple of caves by one of the beaches that have columns looking very much like that.'

'That's amazing.'

'The inside of the church is actually very plain,' he said, 'as it's a Lutheran church—the simplicity is lovely, though. And the views from the tower are amazing.' He paused. 'We could go and take a look after we've had coffee, if you like.'

'I'd like that very much,' she said, 'if you have time.'

She looked him straight in the eye. 'And if your partner won't mind.'

'No partner,' he said. Lynda had broken their engagement the week after he'd been suspended, and he hadn't been tempted to date anyone since. It was going to take him a while to trust again. And he wasn't actually dating Hayley, even if he did feel a strong pull of attraction towards her.

Though he needed to be clear that she wasn't involved with anyone, either. The lack of a ring on her left hand meant absolutely nothing, nowadays. 'I take it that it's the same for you?'

She nodded. 'No partner.'

This felt like another step towards dating. But it wasn't, he reminded himself. No commitments and no promises. They were just doing some sightseeing together, that was all.

She took a deep breath. 'I'm not looking for pity or anything like that, but I should probably tell you that he died just over a year ago.'

So she was still grieving?

If so, that made her safe, because it meant she wouldn't be looking for a proper relationship.

But to lose her partner... He judged her to be around his own age, early to mid thirties, so it must've been either an accident or a seriously aggressive form of cancer that had killed her partner; either way, she'd clearly been through a lot. 'I'm sorry,' he said. 'That must've been hard for you.'

She nodded. 'He was killed in an industrial accident. I'm just glad I'd kissed him goodbye that morning and my last words to him were "I love you"—I think if our last words had been something awful said in the middle of a row, it would've been harder to deal with.'

'Yes.' And Sam knew that one from experience. The morning when his career had imploded, he'd had a fight with his fiancée on the way to work. Lynda had wanted him to give up his mountain rescue work in favour of something that would boost his career at the hospital. Something on a dull committee. He'd refused.

But he should have taken notice of the way she'd been behaving towards him, that last year. Then he would've expected Lynda's reaction to his suspension, a few days later, instead of being shocked to the core by it.

'So how long have you been in Reykjavik?' she asked.

'Since the end of March,' he said.

She raised her eyebrows. 'That's quite a career change, from working in emergency medicine to being a tour guide.'

'Yeah.' Sam knew he was lucky. His family had believed in him. His older brother Martin had dragged him out to Iceland, saying that the job was only temporary, but he really needed the help—and someone who had mountain rescue team experience was the perfect person to come and help with glacier walking tours.

Sam knew that Martin hadn't needed the help at all—he just hadn't wanted Sam to sit at home alone and brood about the situation. And Sam would be grateful for ever to his brother for giving him something else to concentrate on, without expecting him to talk about the situation or his feelings.

Hayley winced at his flat tone. 'Sorry, that was re-

ally intrusive—you don't owe me any explanations.
Please forget I said anything.'

'It's OK. It was a mix of a rough patch at work and a
messy break-up.' Short and to the point. Hayley didn't
need to know his team had been suspended after a diabetic patient's death from a silent heart attack. He'd
been sure that they'd followed all the right procedures
during his admission and treatment, but the patient's
family had needed someone to blame for a death that
shouldn't have happened and they'd made a complaint.
The hospital trust had been duty-bound to take the
complaint seriously and launch an investigation.

A week later, Lynda had broken off their engagement, worried that the stain on his career would transfer to hers because she was his fiancée—according to
her, everyone would still think there was no smoke
without fire. How it had hurt to discover that the one
person he'd expected to bat his corner for him, the way
he would've done if their positions had been reversed,
didn't actually believe in him. All Lynda had wanted
was to buy him out of his share of their house and get
his name off the mortgage.

'I took a sabbatical because I needed a bit of space
to help me decide what to do next. Iceland's a good
place to think.' And he'd come to realise that Lynda
hadn't been right for him anyway. She'd wanted him
to be something he wasn't—the sort who'd serve on
committees and boards, moving away from medicine
to admin. Sam had wanted to make a difference where
it really mattered, saving lives and making his patients
better rather than talking budgets and politics. So her
breaking up with him had done him a favour, really.

'I think we all get rough patches at work,' Hayley said. 'Days when you lose people, or you know the system isn't going to get your patient the right help and you can't do anything about it.'

There was a hint of sadness in those blue, blue eyes, and he guessed she was thinking about her fiancé. But it was none of his business. He wasn't going to push her to talk.

'Though I'm sorry you had to deal with a break-up at the same time as a rough patch. That's a bit of a double whammy,' she said.

He lifted a shoulder in a half-shrug. 'If I'm being honest, we'd been heading for the rocks for a while. I'd been kind of deluding myself.' Knowing he was being a coward, but wanting to get back on safer ground and talk about something less emotionally daunting, he asked, 'So why did you come to Iceland?'

'I've always wanted to see the midnight sun,' Hayley said. 'And there were other things on my bucket list, like seeing the whales.'

'What else is on your list?'

'Seeing a geyser erupt,' she said promptly, 'and touching a glacier, and seeing the split between the continental plates. Oh, and I saw this video of people walking behind a waterfall—I'd really like to do that, too.'

'I can take you to do all that, as well as that beach with the cave that's a bit like the church columns.'

'Thank you. But it's your job, so obviously I'll pay you the going rate for a guide,' she said.

'No,' he said. 'Apart from my weekly self-indulgence of going to see the whales, I haven't really done anything just for fun. So if you don't mind me muscling in on your bucket list, and maybe making some suggestions of places I think you might enjoy, it'd be a holiday for me.'

She frowned. 'Surely you've already visited all those places with clients—I mean, aren't they on every tourist's wish list?'

'True, but seeing something through someone else's eyes keeps it fresh,' he said. 'Please don't offer to pay me.'

'At least let me pay for the petrol,' she protested. 'And buy you lunch.'

He really ought to shut up. But his mouth wasn't working to the same script as his head. 'As long as you'll let me buy you dinner tonight,' he found himself saying.

'I'd like that. Thank you.'

'It's a deal.' He reached across the table to shake her hand.

When Sam shook her hand, it sent goose-bumps over Hayley's skin.

This felt more like a date than agreeing to share some travel plans. Yet in a way it was a kind of blind date, because she knew hardly anything about him— just that he'd had some kind of career crisis and a bad break-up, so he was taking time out to decide what to do next with his life.

But, if she pushed him to talk about it, that would give him the right to ask her the same: and she didn't want to talk about Evan and how her life had sunk into a black hole after her fiancé's death.

She was just going to focus on the fun stuff. That was the reason she was in Iceland, after all. To help her move on. And if this was some kind of date—well, it wasn't serious, but maybe it was something that she needed. Something that perhaps they both needed.

After coffee, they went to see the church with its soaring ceilings and tall windows. Hayley loved the sheer simplicity of it, and the beauty of the simple crystal font. She enjoyed the tour of the city afterwards, with Sam pointing out the places of interest—the Town Hall, the Tjörnin lake behind it, which was a perfect mirror for the town hall and old buildings that lined it, the Parliament building and the striking black glass building of the Harpa concert hall. Sam knew lots of anecdotes and stories and entertained her thoroughly, though she wasn't entirely sure whether he was teasing her when he told her about the locals throwing yogurt at the Parliament building as part of a protest.

Before they stopped for dinner, he asked, 'Do you have any food allergies, or are you vegetarian?'

She smiled at him, liking the fact that he'd been thoughtful enough to ask. 'No and no. I'm very happy for you to recommend somewhere.'

He took her to a little bistro by the Old Harbour. 'They do some of the best fish in Iceland here,' he said. 'And I can guarantee it's freshly caught.'

The place was tiny and candle-lit; the interior walls were all of polished wood, and Hayley noticed that there were vintage photographs of the area hanging on the walls. 'Would I be right in thinking that this used to be a fishing shed?' she asked.

'A lot of the buildings in this area are,' Sam explained. 'They've been renovated and painted different colours. Some are shops, some are cafés and restaurants, and there's an ice cream shop here that does an amazing array of flavours.'

The ambience was lovely—but the food was even better. On Sam's recommendation, she chose 'catch of the day', which turned out to be a seafood risotto topped with fresh cod.

'The food is amazing,' she said.

And the dessert was spectacular: a chocolate dome that, when she poured hot caramel sauce onto it, melted into a rich chocolate pudding.

Even better than the food was the company. Hayley couldn't remember the last time she'd been out to dinner with a man, and Sam was *nice*. He had an innate kindness that appealed to her; and he was easy on the eye, too, with short dark hair brushed back from his face, hazel eyes and a sensual mouth.

Not that she ought to be thinking about his mouth. Or kissing. Or wondering what his hands would feel like against her skin. It made her feel disloyal to Evan—even though she knew that Evan wouldn't have wanted her to be alone for ever.

They lingered over coffee, took a last stroll round the Old Harbour area, and then Sam walked her back to her hotel.

'I can hardly believe it's half-past eleven at night and it's still so light,' she said, marvelling. 'Back at home it would be dark by now.'

'With your hotel being this side of the bay,' he said, 'you're going to get amazing views of the sunset across the sea.'

Just what she'd hoped for.

Ahead of them was a steel sculpture of what looked like a Viking boat; it glowed gold in the light of the setting sun. And when Hayley looked back over her shoulder, the sky was ablaze with orange and gold and hot pink.

'The midnight sun,' she said softly. 'I've always wanted to see it. And it's as incredible as I thought it would be.'

When they reached her hotel he asked, 'Shall I meet you on the dock outside the ship at nine?'

'That sounds good. See you there,' she said.

He didn't attempt to kiss her, and Hayley was shocked to realise that she was faintly disappointed. And then she felt ashamed. They weren't dating and they hadn't even agreed to have a holiday fling. Sam Price was simply a kind stranger she'd met by chance, and he'd offered to keep her company in her travels. She really shouldn't be throwing herself at him. And wasn't he still getting over a bad break-up? The last thing he needed was someone mooning about over him. Maybe she should have made a polite excuse and stayed on her own after all. Tomorrow, after the whale-watching trip, she'd feign a headache.

'Goodnight,' she said, and headed for her room.

Her window overlooked the sea, so she took some last shots of the sunset and emailed them to Dani, along with an account of her day and the fact she was acting in accordance with their agreement about saying yes to opportunities. She woke in the middle of the night and was surprised to see it was still quite light; back in London at this time it would be dark. She woke again in time for the sunrise and was stunned to see how the sea turned into a shimmering mass of gold and silver.

After breakfast, she walked down to the old harbour to meet Sam for the whale-watching trip. This time, nobody on board needed a doctor's help. They saw a school of porpoises, and then two minke whales together. When the whales leaped out of the water in a perfect arc and she gasped with pleasure, it felt natural for Sam to slide his arm around her shoulders—and for her to slide her own arm around his waist.

Though at the same time it felt wrong. This was exactly what she would've done with Evan. And Sam wasn't Evan. 'Sorry,' she said, sliding her arm away from his waist. 'I think I got a bit…well, carried away with the emotion of seeing the whales.'

'Me, too,' Sam agreed, removing his arm from her shoulders. He looked just as shocked as she felt.

They were careful not to even let their hands touch accidentally until they were back on land. She should make up some excuse, Hayley thought, say she had a headache or something—though it would be a shame to miss out on the trip they'd planned.

Sam looked slightly awkward. 'Would you still like to come and see the waterfall and the geyser?'

He was clearly offering her a chance to back out, recognising that the moment he'd held her on the ship had been difficult for her. But she could see something in his eyes. Something that struck a chord with her. Loneliness maybe, even if it wasn't something either of them would admit to. And it would be good to have some company. 'If you'd still like to go,' she said carefully. After all, it must've been awkward for him, too.

'Let's go, then.' Sam drove her out to see the Gull-foss waterfall.

'The water looks almost golden,' she said in amazement when they'd made their way down the path to the double drop.

'That's how it gets its name—*"gullfoss"* means "golden falls",' he said. 'Partly it's because of the sediment in the water.'

As they drew nearer to the edge, Hayley slipped on a smooth piece of stone and Sam caught her arm, steadying her. His touch felt almost electric. And she could see in his expression that it was the same for him—instant attraction that neither of them had been expecting or looking for, and it seemed that neither of them quite knew what to do with it or how to react.

'Sorry,' she said.

'Uh-huh.' But he didn't move his hand away. He just looked at her, as if he was as surprised by the feelings as she was. And then he cleared his throat. 'They say if you don't like the weather in Iceland, wait five minutes—and look, the sun's just come out.'

She looked to where he gestured, and hanging over the waterfalls was a bright rainbow.

It was a natural phenomenon, she knew, caused by the sunlight and the spray from the waterfall. But in a weird kind of way it felt as if it was Evan telling her was it OK, that she was ready to move on and he approved.

She shook herself. 'Photo opportunity,' she said brightly, moving away just the tiniest bit so his arm fell naturally away from hers.

And how stupid that she missed it being there.

What was she, a recycled teenager?

She was just going to have to ignore it and be sensible. She smiled, and took a snap of the rainbow on her phone.

When she'd had her fill of the waterfall and the rainbow, Sam drove them out to the Geysìr area. 'The old Geysìr is the one that all geysers are named after,' he said. 'Apparently it used to be even bigger than the one in Yellowstone, but it's been dormant for years.'

'So I won't actually get to see a geyser going up?' she asked.

'Oh, you will.' He smiled. 'Strokkur erupts pretty much about every ten minutes. And if you have a slow-mo setting on your phone, I'd recommend that because then you'll really see how it works. The water at the top of the pool is cooler and acts as a kind of lid to the hot water below, so the pressure builds up and then you can see it boil over and the geyser erupts. Then it leaves a sinkhole and the water drains back in, and the cycle starts all over again.'

She could see a circle of people standing round what she assumed was the geyser, and then suddenly a massive plume of water shot into the air. 'Oh! That's amazing.'

'Let's go and get a better view,' he said, and walked with her to where everyone was standing.

As he'd suggested, she filmed it on slow-mo. 'Dani would've loved this,' she said wistfully. So would Evan, though she didn't say it.

Then, as they moved deeper into the fields, his fingers accidentally brushed against hers. Again, she felt that swoop of butterflies in her stomach; and when she caught his eye, she was pretty sure it was the same for him.

What were they going to do about it? Ignore it? Or see where it led them?

There wasn't any future in it. Couldn't be. After the end of this week they'd be in different countries, thousands of miles apart, and he'd said nothing about returning to England.

The sky had turned the deepest summery blue, and the scenery was amazing. There were little puffs of steam rising from underground pools, and a tiny pot that produced a bubbling spout a few centimetres tall. Sam seemed to be careful to keep a little distance between them when he showed her the site of the old Geysìr, now just a pool with the occasional bubble to remind you that the water was extremely hot, and the twin pools of Blesi—one perfectly clear so you could see into the yawning cavern beneath it, and one that was the most amazing milky azure blue.

'The milky colour's from silicates in the water,' he said. 'That's the cool one—it's only about forty degrees Celsius.'

'Cool?' she asked.

'The other one's hotter,' he said.

'The milky blue pool: is that what the Blue Lagoon's like?' she asked.

'Pretty much. We can go there this evening, if you like—that's provided we can get a ticket, because evenings are pretty popular,' he added.

'I'd like that.' She smiled at him.

'Give me a second.' He made a quick phone call,

and she noticed that he spoke in fluent Icelandic. 'OK. We're in luck—I've booked us in.'

'Thank you.'

They had dinner at a little village outside the city— lamb stew and rye bread, followed by blueberries and thick Icelandic yoghurt—and then stopped off firstly at her hotel so she could pick up her swimming things and then at his seafront apartment so he could pick up his.

'I can't remember the last time I felt this relaxed,' she said as they sat in the warm water of the lagoon, her face covered in a mask of white silica and an ice-cold smoothie in her hand.

'That's what this is meant to be about,' he said with a smile.

'This must be amazing in the winter—sitting in a hot pool under the stars.'

'And with the rocks all covered in snow,' he agreed. 'It's pretty.'

Their gazes met, and for a second she thought he was going to kiss her.

He didn't, but she could feel the anticipation brewing between them as he drove them back to the city and parked outside his apartment building. Every time they'd accidentally touched that day, she'd been so aware of him. And she didn't think she was alone in that reaction.

'Shall we walk along the harbour again to catch the sunset?' he asked.

'That'd be nice.'

At her hotel, he turned to face her. 'Goodnight, Hayley.'

'Goodnight. Thank you for such a lovely day.'

'My pleasure. Would you like to see the glacier, waterfalls and beaches tomorrow, if it looks as if it'll be dry?'

Spending more time with him? Part of her thought it was a good idea; part of her didn't. But she found herself agreeing.

'You'll need sturdy shoes,' he said.

'And a waterproof, just in case the weather changes?'

He smiled. 'Yes. Wear layers. And hiking trousers are better than jeans, if you have them—we're going to get wet by the waterfalls, plus they're better protection than denim against the wind.' And then the look in his dark eyes grew more intense. He lifted one hand and placed it gently against her cheek. In answer, she tipped her head back very slightly. And then he brushed his lips against hers—more asking than demanding. She slid her arms round his waist, and he kissed her again, his lips teasing hers until she opened her mouth and let him deepen the kiss.

Desire flooded through her, mixed with a dose of guilt. But this wasn't being unfaithful to Evan. He wouldn't have wanted her to spend her life alone and mourning him. He would've wanted her to keep seeing the joy in life and focus on the good stuff. Sam Price was the first man she'd wanted to kiss since she'd lost Evan. And this was meant to be the Year of Saying Yes. So she leaned into Sam, kissing him back.

When he finally broke the kiss, there was a dark slash of colour along his cheekbones and his mouth was reddened; she was pretty sure that she looked in the same state.

'Goodnight. I'll see you tomorrow,' he said. 'I'll meet you here at nine—if that's not too early?'

'That's perfect,' she said.

And she couldn't wait.

CHAPTER THREE

ON WEDNESDAY MORNING, Hayley walked out of her hotel at nine on the dot to see Sam walking towards her from his car.

'Perfect timing,' she said with a smile.

'Absolutely,' he agreed.

Hayley tingled right down to her toes. Crazy how this man made her feel like a teenager. It had been a long, long time since she'd felt butterflies in her stomach just at the sight of someone.

'Before we go,' she said carefully, 'I think we ought to talk about last night.'

He nodded. 'I'm sorry. I shouldn't have kissed you.'

This was the crunch moment. 'I'm not sorry,' she said, and watched his eyes darken. 'We're both single.'

'So are you saying…?'

That maybe, just maybe, a holiday romance would be good for both of them. No strings, no consequences, no promises. And no depth, so saying goodbye would be easy. 'You're getting over a bad break-up. I'm getting over my partner's death. We're both…a bit stuck where we are, I guess. Neither of us wants anything permanent right now.'

He seemed to be following her thought processes exactly. 'But a holiday romance might help us both move on,' he said.

She nodded. 'With an end date. I'm only here for a couple more days.' Neither of them would get hurt in such a short space of time.

'Just so you know, I don't do this with every woman I meet,' he said. 'You're the first woman I've kissed since Lynda and I split up.'

'You're the first man I've even noticed since Evan died,' she said softly. 'And I think my years in emergency medicine have made me a reasonable judge of character. I'd already worked out that you're not one of these men who have notches carved on their bedposts. You're one of the good guys.'

He inclined his head. 'Thank you. Though I wasn't fishing for compliments.'

'I didn't think you were.' She smiled. 'So where are we going today?'

'I think,' he said, 'given what you've just said, I'd like to start by kissing you hello.'

'Sounds good to me.'

He took a step forward, rested his hands on her shoulders, and brushed his mouth lightly against hers. The butterflies in her stomach started doing a stampede; then he slid his hands down her arms, wrapped them round her waist, and kissed her more thoroughly.

Her knees were weak by the time he broke the kiss.

'Good morning,' he said.

She smiled. 'It is now.'

He stole another kiss. 'We're going to start at Reynisfjara, to see the beach with black sand and the basalt columns,' he said. 'And then we'll go to see a glacier and your waterfall.'

'That sounds perfect,' she said.

Once he'd parked at Reynisfjara and they were out of the car, he looked at her and held out his hand. She took it with a smile, and they walked hand in hand onto the beach. The sand was black and slightly pebbly, in sharp contrast to the turquoise blue of the Atlantic, and Hayley stood watching the waves crash onto the shore.

'The sea's pretty calm right now,' Sam said, 'but in the winter the Atlantic rollers can get absolutely huge.'

She could just imagine the massive waves thundering in.

'And right at this point there's nothing but ocean between you and the Antarctic.'

She blinked. Was he teasing her? 'Seriously?'

'Seriously.' He led her over to the cave with the hexagonal basalt columns.

'It reminds of me of Giant's Causeway in Ireland,' she said. 'And it's definitely like the church in Reykjavik.'

Tourists were standing on the shorter columns, posing for photographs. 'When in Rome—or, rather, Reynisfjara,' he quipped, and helped her climb onto the columns so he could take a photo with her camera. The touch of his hands, even through the material of her T-shirt, sent a thrill right through her.

Once she'd climbed down again, he pointed out the colony of puffins above; the tiny birds with their distinctive orange beaks moved incredibly fast, and Hayley had to admit defeat when she'd tried to take ten photographs of them and all had failed.

They walked hand in hand back to the car, then he drove them up a steep, winding track to the Dyrhólaey promontory, where they had a clear view of the rock with a 'door' in it that gave its name to the area. Sam stood with his arms wrapped round her waist. Up here where the wind was keen and the air was clear, she felt almost as if she were on top of the world.

'So what are those rocks jutting up over there?'

'Basalt stacks,' he said. 'The Reynisdrangar. Local legend says they were trolls who were trying to drag a ship from the sea onto land—but then the sun rose and the light turned them to stone.'

A land of legends, ice and fire.

A land that was going to start to heal her heart.

'Bucket list time,' he said. 'We're going to Solhei-majökull—you can actually get up close to the glacier and touch it.'

When they parked, she could see a lake, and immediately behind it was the glacier.

'But it's dark grey,' she said. 'Aren't glaciers white or blue?'

'The grey's from sediment,' he said, 'and the white bits are snow and fresh ice.'

She peered up at the glacier. 'And are they people over there, walking on top of the glacier?'

He nodded. 'That's the kind of thing my brother Martin's company offers—though it's not safe to walk on a glacier without a guide who knows the area and can tell if there are sinkholes.'

'And you're qualified to do the guided walks?'

'Yes. I was part of the mountain rescue team when I worked in Manchester—we're not far from the Peak

District or the Lakes. Actually, I was part of the team well before I qualified as a doctor, because I grew up in the Peak District. I'm also a qualified diver,' he said.

Mountain rescue and diving. Both of which were really dangerous. Both of which meant putting your life on the line. A chill went down Hayley's spine. It was just as well they'd agreed this would be only a holiday romance. She didn't want to be in another situation where she fell in love with someone who put himself in danger on a regular basis. She really couldn't bear to lose someone else the same way she'd lost Evan.

'Do you want to walk on the glacier?' he asked. 'I brought some kit with me, just in case.'

Under the rules of her agreement with Danielle, Hayley knew she ought to say yes. Instead, still thinking of the danger of his work on the mountain rescue team, she asked, 'Are you sure it's safe?'

He smiled. 'I know the area so, yes, it's safe. I wasn't sure of your shoe size, so I brought a few different pairs in case your hiking shoes weren't sturdy enough.' He glanced at her feet. 'Actually, if we do it, I'd really prefer you to wear the boots I brought with me. Not that there's anything wrong with your hiking boots,' he hastened to add, 'but ice walking needs a little bit extra.'

'If you're sure it's safe,' she said, 'then OK.' Walking on a glacier would be even better than touching one.

She put the shoes on and he fitted the crampons for her. 'These are to make it safer for you to walk on the ice,' he explained. He also gave her a helmet, ice axe and a walking pole. 'This will help to stabilise you and help you get a grip when you need to,' he said, 'as well as help you test the ice to make sure it's solid before you set foot on it.'

After a safety briefing, he showed her how to walk on the ice. 'You need to stamp down to get a good grip,' he said.

'I'm glad now that I didn't go for a run this morning before breakfast,' she said.

'As part of your training for the charity race, you mean?' He smiled. 'You'll definitely get a good workout here. It won't do much for your speed, but it'll be good for stamina.'

They went along the path that led to the glacier, and then they were walking across the ice. Hayley could hear crunching sounds with every step. Part of her was terrified, part of her was thrilled and part of her was awed at the sheer beauty of the ice landscape. 'The way the snow lies on the dark ice, all rippled—it's a bit like the way a sandy beach looks when the tide goes out,' she said. 'I thought glaciers would be just white or blue, nothing like this. With all that dark veining going through it, in places it looks like marble.'

'The veining is caused by ash from previous eruptions,' he said. 'I love the sheer wildness of the landscape out here.'

It showed in his voice and his eyes. And he really looked in his element out here, strong and confident, knowing exactly what he was doing. He wouldn't have looked out of place in an ad in a glossy magazine, tall and muscular and utterly gorgeous.

Hayley gained in confidence as she walked beside him, until she felt one foot start to give way. 'Sam!'

He grabbed her immediately, and drew her over to a safer part of the ice. 'OK?' he asked.

'A bit shaky,' she admitted, 'but I'm not going to stop.'

'You're doing fine,' he said, and took her hand.

It took a while for her heart to slow down again after the near miss, but having him holding her hand gave her more confidence, to the point where she was happy to stop and take photographs again.

When they'd gone back over the ice sheet to the start of their walk, she returned the ice pick and walking pole, took off the crampons and changed back into her own hiking shoes.

'That,' she said, 'was amazing. Thank you.'

'My pleasure.'

They took a swift lunch break at a small café, and then he drove them to the waterfall she'd so wanted to see, Seljalandsfoss.

'It's a bit slippery in places,' Sam warned, 'and the path is actually a collection of boulders, so watch your step.'

'Hey. I just walked on ice. I can do this.'

Walking behind the curtain of water was magical. As she'd expected, there was a lot of spray; and the noise as the water shot down into the pool was almost deafening. Watching the world from behind a waterfall was like nothing she'd experienced before, and she loved it.

'This is incredible,' she said, squeezing Sam's hand.

He smiled, and kissed her lightly; she tingled all over. It was the most romantic place she'd ever been kissed, behind a wall of water.

Then he helped her up the steep boulders to the other side of the waterfall.

'Today's been amazing,' she said when they got back to the car. 'I mean, how many times do you walk on a black-sand beach, on a glacier, and behind a waterfall all in the same day?' Then she grimaced. 'Sorry. I sound like a tourist.'

'No, it's nice that you recognise how special this place is,' Sam said.

'Can I buy you dinner tonight?' she asked.

'I was thinking, maybe I could cook for you,' he suggested.

'That'd be nice, but can I at least contribute wine and a pudding?'

'No need,' he said. 'And actually it'll be nice to cook for someone else, as well.'

Hayley could understand that; sometimes it just didn't feel worth the effort, cooking for one. Nowadays she relied on supermarket ready meals or a bowl of cereal.

Back at his apartment, Sam said, 'I rented this place for the summer. There's not exactly a lot to show you round—the kitchen's here, the bathroom, the living room, and through there's my bedroom.'

'Small but perfect for city living,' she said. She wondered why he wasn't staying with his brother, but it felt too intrusive to ask. The flat was very neat and tidy, and looked more like a show flat than a home, though there were a couple of photographs held onto the fridge with magnets. When she took a closer look, the photographs were of Sam and another man who looked enough like him to be his older brother, both standing on the top of an ice ridge.

'That's Martin. My brother,' Sam confirmed when he saw her looking at the photographs.

'Is there anything I can do to help?' she asked.

'Nope.' He made coffee and handed her a mug. 'Go sit down and chill out. The best bit about this place is the view—you don't need TV or anything when you have that,' he said.

As he'd promised, the view from his living room across the bay to the mountains was stunning, and Hayley found herself absorbed in it until he came to tell her that dinner was ready.

She joined him in the kitchen, where he'd set the small pine table for two.

He'd made a simple prawn salad for starters. 'I'm afraid it's bottled sauce rather than home-made,' he said.

She smiled. 'That's fine. It still tastes good.'

'So are you a cook?' he asked.

Once. 'When I get time. I'm often guilty of buying ready meals at the supermarket,' she admitted, 'but I guess it goes with the territory of working in emergency medicine.'

The main course was simple grilled fish, with new potatoes and asparagus—plus Hollandaise sauce, which he also admitted was ready-made.

'No need to apologise. I wouldn't have a clue how to start making it,' she said.

After dinner, he suggested going for a walk along the harbour to one of the coffee shops. Hayley thoroughly enjoyed walking there hand in hand with him, and watching the sun setting. When they walked back to his apartment, he slid his arm round her shoulders and hers fitted naturally round his waist. She felt closer to him than she'd ever been; and when he stopped to kiss her in the soft light that wasn't quite twilight, desire thrummed through her.

Outside his apartment building, he stopped and looked at her. 'I can drive you back to your hotel now— or maybe you'd like to stay tonight?'

Stay tonight.

Sam only had one bedroom, so Hayley knew what he was asking. Stay the night—and make love with him.

Part of her wanted to say yes. She'd enjoyed her day so much, everything from the sheer exhilaration of the ice walk through to the romantic stroll across the black sand beach. Yet he would be the first since Evan; part of her wondered, was she really ready for this or did she need more time?

'No strings,' he said, 'and if you say no, it's absolutely OK. We'll still go out exploring tomorrow.'

But it was the Year of Saying Yes.

And every time today they'd held hands or he'd put his arm round her or kissed her, she'd wanted more.

It was time to move on.

And Sam Price was the man who'd help her to do that. No strings. No commitments. Just these few days. A holiday fling with no complications for either of them.

'Yes,' she said.

'Is there anyone you need to call, to let them know where you are?' he asked.

'Maybe the hotel, as they're expecting me?'

'Sure,' he said.

She made the call quickly to explain she was staying with a friend for the night; and then she took his hand and drew it up to her lips. 'Ready,' she said.

Without comment, Sam took her hand and led her up to his flat.

Once inside, he kissed her, this time with more urgency than he'd kissed her by the waterfall. She slid her fingers under the edge of his long-sleeved top, and gently tugged upwards.

He took a step back and lifted his arms, letting her take it off completely.

She sucked in a breath as she took in the view: he was bare-chested, slightly dishevelled from where she'd just removed his top and utterly sexy. It made her want to touch him, especially because he had perfect musculature: well-toned arms, a broad chest and a six-pack leading down to a narrow waist. Sam had told her he'd worked with the mountain rescue team as well as in emergency medicine, and she could see he'd kept himself fit since he'd been in Iceland.

'So do I pass muster?' he asked lightly.

'Just about,' she teased.

'Good.'

'Not a gorilla,' she said with a smile, brushing the light sprinkling of hair across his chest, 'but also not looking as if you're so vain that you wax.'

'I had my back waxed, once.'

She waited, knowing there was more to this story: from what she'd learned about Sam so far this week, she knew he wasn't vain.

'It was to raise money for equipment for the mountain rescue team,' he admitted. 'I got people to sponsor me per strip. They paid me double if they wanted to take the strip off themselves.'

'Sounds painful. Having my eyebrows done is bad enough,' she said.

'It was for a good cause. Like you doing the running for your friend Dani.' He traced the curve of her eyebrows with the tip of his finger. 'You're beautiful.'

'So are you,' she said, and splayed her fingers across his chest.

'And you're wearing too much.'

'Do something about it,' she invited.

He peeled off her top, then traced the curve of her collarbones, making a shiver of pure desire run through her. Then he drew one finger slowly down her sternum until he reached the V between her breasts. 'Your turn,' he said, his voice husky.

Her hands shook slightly as she undid the button at the waistband of his hiking trousers, then took the tab of his zip and drew it down. She could feel the heat and hardness of his erection as she pulled the zip downwards, and it made her catch her breath. She pushed the material downwards, and let it pool around his ankles. He pulled off his hiking boots so he could step out of his trousers and she was amused to note that he removed his socks at the same time.

'My turn.' He did the same with her hiking trousers, teasing her by sliding his fingertips underneath the waistband and stroking her skin, and then finally undoing the zip and sliding them down. She copied what he'd done with his own hiking boots, and he smiled when he saw her socks. 'Pink and fluffy.'

'They're warm, and they stop my boots rubbing.'

He dropped to his knees before her and removed her socks. 'You have beautiful feet. Pretty toes.'

Her toenails were painted an in-your-face scarlet.

'I don't wear nail polish at work. This is my indulgence,' she said.

'And it's a nice one.' He rocked back on his haunches and looked at her. 'You're beautiful, Hayley. And I want you. More than I've wanted anyone in a while.'

'It's the same for me.' She dragged in a breath. 'But I'm not on the pill.'

'I have condoms,' he said. 'Not because I habitually seduce a girl in every group I take out—more like my big brother's idea of a flat warming present.' His mouth twitched. 'But he also got me a coffee machine, so I'm good.'

'Coffee and condoms.' She couldn't help smiling back. 'It's an interesting combination.'

'I can think of a more interesting combination.' He stood up, and brushed his mouth against hers. 'And a more comfortable place.' He took her hand, and led her to his bedroom.

It had the same clean lines as the other rooms in his flat, all pale wood and cream walls and slate-coloured linen.

And then she stopped thinking as he kissed her again, cupping her face and catching her lower lip between his. When he deepened the kiss, she tangled her fingers in his hair. He drew her closer, and unhooked her bra, then let her breasts spill into his hands.

'So beautiful,' he whispered.

She wasn't sure which of the two of them finished undressing the other, but at last they were naked. He pushed the duvet aside, then lifted her and laid her gently against the pillows. She tipped her head back, and he traced a necklace of kisses across her throat. She caught her breath, wanting more and pushing up towards him. He slid one hand between her thighs, teasing her with clever fingers as he stroked upwards; by the time he reached her sex, she was quivering.

But he hadn't finished. By any means. He shifted on the bed so he could stroke her skin with his hands and his mouth, until she was simmering like the volcanoes the island was built upon.

'Now?' he whispered.

'Now.'

He reached into the drawer of his bedside cabinet and retrieved a condom, then ripped open the foil packet.

'My turn,' she said, and rolled the condom on, taking it slowly. By the time she'd finished, his breathing had quickened.

And then at last he knelt between her thighs and eased his body into hers.

It felt good. Strange—his weight and the feel of his muscles weren't what she'd been used to, what she'd been missing—but good.

And when her climax hit unexpectedly, spilling through her, she held on to him very tightly, feeling the answering surge in his own body.

Once he'd dealt with the condom, he turned to her. 'Help yourself to anything you need in the bathroom— the towels are all fresh.'

'Thanks.' She enjoyed the shower; she was getting

used to the slightly sulphurous smell of the hot water, and she still found it amazing that the water was heated purely by geothermal energy. Iceland really was the land of ice and fire.

When she came back to the bedroom, wrapped in a towel, he'd pulled on a pair of jeans, though he hadn't bothered putting on a shirt.

'I know your hotel's only just down the road,' he said, 'but would you like me to put your clothes through the washing machine?'

She hadn't thought that far ahead—about having to leave here tomorrow in the same clothes she'd been wearing all day, even if she was only going between here and her hotel to change. 'Actually, thanks, that'd be good. Then I won't have to stop in at the hotel in the morning to get clean clothes.'

'Here—put this on, or if you'd prefer to wear one of my shirts then help yourself to whatever you want in the wardrobe.' He handed her a soft, fluffy towelling robe, then gathered up her laundry and headed out to his kitchen.

Sam was strangely domesticated for someone who seemed so at home in the wild landscape. And she rather liked that.

She borrowed a T-shirt from his wardrobe so she had something to sleep in, and wrapped the robe round herself before following him to the kitchen. He poured her another glass of wine, and they curled up on his sofa and watched the final rays of the sunset. Then he gently led her back to bed and made love to her again.

And it was so, so good to feel another body curved around hers as she finally fell asleep.

* * *

The next morning, Sam woke Hayley with a kiss. 'What would you like for breakfast?' he asked. 'I have to admit to developing a waffle habit out here—Martin bought me a waffle iron and some maple syrup to go with the coffee machine.'

'I'd love waffles. Thank you.' She smiled. 'Can I do anything?'

'There's very little that needs doing so, no, it's fine. I've put your dry clothes in the bathroom, by the way.'

She appreciated his thoughtfulness. 'Thank you.'

By the time she'd showered and changed, she could smell waffles cooking. She thoroughly enjoyed them, and was amused that he'd also provided a dish of blueberries and a dish of Icelandic yogurt in a nod to healthy eating.

'So would you like to see the geological stuff today?' he asked.

'Yes, please. And I'd also like to take you out to dinner,' she said, 'as it's my last day.'

'Thank you—I accept.'

She insisted on doing the washing up while he had a shower; then he drove her to Thingvellir National Park.

'The name means "Parliament Meadows" and it's where the original parliament was located,' he explained.

They walked down through a path in a canyon whose walls were dark brown and it felt to Hayley like some kind of lunar landscape.

'So is this rock basalt?' she asked.

'Lava lobes,' he said. 'We're walking between two

tectonic plates—this is where you can actually see the drift between the North American and Eurasian plates.'

'The place where the earth actually splits.' And where new land sprang up. 'Maybe this is a lesson for us,' she said. 'Even when something breaks and changes utterly, life still goes on—the land here grows and changes.' Just as they would grow and change from the wreckage of their old lives.

He looked at her. 'Maybe.'

Maybe, she thought, they were both starting to heal. And last night with Sam had shown her that she was ready to move on. To learn to love someone else. And she'd always be grateful to him for helping her get past the place where she'd been stuck.

After a day's exploring, they ate a final dinner in the city centre, then stopped for an ice cream in the Old Harbour area and walked back along the sea wall to her hotel, where they sat with their arms round each other and watched the final gold, orange and red of the setting sun.

'Thank you for making this week so good for me,' she said. There was a lump in her throat; right at that moment, she didn't want to leave. 'I have a ridiculously early flight tomorrow.' And she had a feeling that what she would miss most about Iceland was Sam. 'So I guess…' She swallowed hard. 'I guess this is goodbye.'

'I'm not very good at goodbyes,' he said.

'Me, neither.'

'So let's do it in Icelandic. *Bless*,' he said.

'*Bless*,' she repeated.

He kissed her lightly. 'Safe travels.'

'You, too.' She wasn't going to get clingy with him now. 'And thank you for everything.'

'Pleasure. Be happy, Hayley.'

'You, too.' She stroked his face.

He kissed her a last time, then turned and walked away.

Their paths would probably never cross again. Though she had a feeling that their holiday fling had done both of them some good.

And now it was time to get on with the rest of her life.

CHAPTER FOUR

'HE'S UTTERLY GORGEOUS—he reminds me of that American actor I like,' Danielle said, looking through the photographs on Hayley's laptop. 'I'm not surprised you fell for the guy.'

'I didn't fall for him,' Hayley protested.

Danielle scoffed. 'Of course not. That's why he's in half your photographs.'

'That's simply because he was there, showing me round the island. He was kind.'

'In those pictures, he doesn't look at you as if he was just being kind,' Danielle pointed out. 'And you don't look at him that way, either.'

Hayley felt the colour burst into her face.

Danielle laughed. 'Don't be embarrassed. I'm glad you kept up the spirit of the Year of Saying Yes. That trip did you a lot of good.'

'It was just one night,' Hayley muttered. 'Anyway, have *you* done anything on that front?' she asked, trying to deflect her best friend's attention.

'We're not talking about me. We're talking about you. Besides, I haven't met anyone who's really caught my eye, whereas you have.'

'It was a holiday romance. A fling,' Hayley said. 'I enjoyed it while it lasted, but now it's over and I'm fine with that, too.'

'But it did you good. Now you can really start to move on. You know Evan wouldn't have wanted you to lock yourself away.'

'I know.'

'And it's the Year of Saying Yes.'

'Right now I've only got time for work and training,' Hayley pointed out.

'We'll see,' Danielle said.

On Monday morning, Sam cycled to Muswell Hill Hospital and walked into the emergency department, ready for his first shift in his new job. As he'd expected, there was some admin to sort out first, including getting his hospital identity badge; and then Michael Harcourt, the head of the department, took him round to introduce him to the other staff.

'Ah, Dr Clark—just the woman I wanted to see,' Michael boomed as a woman in a white coat came out of a cubicle. 'Hayley, meet your replacement, Samuel Price. Sam, Hayley's just been promoted to senior registrar and you've taken over from her. You'll be working together.'

Of all the places…

Sam hadn't told Hayley that he was about to start a new job in London, and she hadn't told him where she worked. London was a massive city with quite a few hospitals. What were the chances that they'd end up working together? The way her pupils expanded momentarily told him that she was just as shocked and surprised as he was.

This was going to make things awkward. They'd had a fling in Iceland, agreeing that it would be nothing more than that, and they'd said goodbye. What now? Would she want to see if their fling could be something more, something deeper? Or had he just been her transition person, the one who'd helped her to move on after her partner's death, so she wouldn't want to pick up where they'd left off?

The problem was, he didn't know what he wanted, either. He'd really liked the woman he'd started to get to know in Iceland. But then again he'd liked Lynda, too—and his ex-fiancée had let him down so badly. Could he even trust his judgement any more? Would he be making a huge mistake if he started seeing Hayley?

She recovered first, holding her hand out. 'Welcome to Muswell Hill Hospital, Dr Price.'

So she was going to pretend that they'd never met before? OK. That was probably the safest way and saved any awkward explanations. 'Thank you, Dr Clark,' he said, giving her a polite nod and shaking her hand.

'We usually work on first-name terms here,' she said. 'Everyone calls me Hayley.'

'And I'm Sam,' he said.

'I've got a patient coming in any second now with a suspected broken hip. Want to come in at the deep end?' she asked.

'The deep end suits me fine,' he said.

'Good, good. Just as it should be. I'll leave you in Hayley's more than capable hands,' Michael said, and clapped him on the shoulder. 'Look after the lad for me, Hayley, there's a good girl.'

'You know we always look after our own in the Emergency department, Mike,' Hayley said with a smile. 'Let's go and find our patient, Sam.'

When the head of department had gone, Hayley looked straight at Sam. 'We probably need to talk and clear the air—but now isn't the time.'

Yes, they definitely needed to clear the air and establish a few boundaries—the more so because he still felt that physical pull towards her. 'Right now the patients have to come first—but I agree, we need to talk.'

'Lunch?' she suggested.

'Works for me.'

They went to the ambulance bay to meet the paramedics for the handover.

'This is Mrs Ethel Baker,' Dev Kapoor, the lead paramedic, said.

'Hello, Mrs Baker—can we call you Ethel?' Hayley asked.

At the elderly woman's nod, she said, 'I'm Hayley Clark and this is Sam Price, and we're going to look after you—we just need to talk to Dev first, if you don't mind, so he can tell us all about what's happened to you and save you having to go all through it over again.'

'All right, love,' Ethel said, her voice sounding very soft and very weary.

Sam noticed that Hayley took the older woman's hand and held it while she listened to Dev giving them the handover information; he liked the fact that she clearly had compassion and realised that the elderly woman must be in some pain and feeling very scared about what had happened to her.

'Mrs Baker's seventy-eight and she lives on her own. She had a fall last night and couldn't get up again, and she didn't have a call aid button round her neck. Her carer found her this morning and called us.'

No doubt she was cold, stiff and dehydrated, as well as suffering from whatever had caused the fall, Sam thought.

'She can't stand or walk,' Dev said, 'and we suspect a broken hip.'

Which could cause problems with future mobility and independence, Sam knew. 'Is there any medication we need to know about?' he asked.

'We've brought it all with us,' Dev said, handing him a labelled bag. 'The main thing is her Parkinson's medication.'

'Thank you,' Sam said.

'We gave her gas and air for the pain in the ambulance, and when the carer rang the emergency services we advised her not to give Mrs Baker anything to eat or drink, just in case she needs to go into Theatre. So she hasn't eaten or drunk anything since last night,' Dev confirmed.

'And I'm really gasping for a cup of tea,' Ethel said. 'Can I have a cup of tea now?'

No, she couldn't—not when she might be going into Theatre within the hour.

'We'll make you comfortable as soon as we can,' Hayley promised, 'though we will need to sort out some tests first.'

Between them, Hayley and Sam wheeled her to one

of the cubicles so they could assess her, and all the while Hayley held Edith's hand. Sam remembered the feel of her skin against his, and had to shake himself. Until they'd talked and worked out how to deal with the situation, he needed to keep a lid on his feelings.

'Can I ask you, is this the first time you've had a fall, Ethel?' Hayley asked.

'No—sometimes I freeze or I trip over my own feet. It's just how the Parkinson's is. Sometimes I'm on and sometimes I'm off,' Ethel said. 'I know I should have had my call aid button with me, but I just forgot to put it on yesterday.'

'It's easily done,' Sam said. 'Did you hit your head at all when you fell, or can you remember if you blacked out?'

'No. I was just cross with myself at being such an old fool as to fall over.'

There was definitely nothing wrong with her mental state, Sam thought; it was pretty clear to him that she hadn't hit her head. 'Are you in pain now?' he asked.

She nodded. 'It really hurts here.' She pointed to her upper right thigh.

Dev's assessment of a broken hip was probably right, Sam thought, because Ethel's right leg looked slightly shorter and was turned outwards; together with her inability to stand or walk and the position of her pain, the symptoms pointed towards a fracture.

'We can give you some more pain relief,' he said. Though the fact she'd broken her hip from a single fall worried him. Ethel was very slender, and it made him wonder. 'Has your doctor said anything to you about osteoporosis or brittle bones?'

She pulled a face and shook her head. 'Nothing like that,' she said.

'When you get older, especially if you're a woman,' Hayley said, 'your bones get less dense and develop a kind of honeycomb structure, which means they break more easily—it's called osteoporosis. Once we've got your hip sorted out, I'm going to ask the ward to refer you for a scan so we can see if your bones are thinner.'

'If the scan shows we're right,' Sam said, 'we can give you some tablets to help strengthen your bones, so then if you do fall again you're less likely to end up with a fracture. And we can give you some calcium and vitamin D supplements to help, too.' He paused. 'Can I ask, do you smoke or drink?'

Ethel looked slightly guilty. 'I don't drink much, just a port and lemon at the Legion on a Friday night with my mates. I've been trying to give up the ciggies—I just have the odd one or two. But don't tell my daughter. She thinks I stopped smoking five years ago. Though my old gran lived to a hundred and she smoked like a chimney,' she added, a spark of defiance in her voice.

Hayley smiled. 'So did my great-gran. But here's your reason to give up—smoking makes your bones thinner and that puts you at greater risk of breaking a bone the next time you fall.'

Sam liked the way that Hayley was sympathetic and realistic at the same time. She was kind, but she didn't try to pretend that problems didn't exist.

'You won't tell my daughter about the ciggies?' Ethel asked.

'No, but do you know if anyone's contacted her to

tell her you've been brought here?' Sam asked. 'If not, we can call her.'

'She's down in Brighton,' Ethel said. 'She works and she's got kids. I don't want to bother her.'

'If you were my mum,' Hayley said, 'I'd want to know straight away if you were taken to hospital.'

'I don't want to worry her,' Ethel again.

'We can tell her not to rush because you're going to be here for a while, if that makes you feel any better,' Sam said. 'But I agree with Hayley. I'd want to know if my mum was in hospital—and I'd be really upset if they didn't tell me.'

Ethel sighed. 'All right, then.'

Sam took her temperature and recorded it on the chart, then wrote her up for painkillers and a drip for the dehydration.

'We're pretty sure you've broken your hip,' Hayley said, 'but we need to send you for an X-ray to confirm the diagnosis.'

'If it's broken,' Ethel said, 'what happens then?'

'You'll need surgery,' Sam said. 'The surgeon might be able to use screws, rods and plates to fix it—or you might need a hip replacement.'

'So I won't be able to walk for ages?' she asked, looking worried.

'They'll have you on your feet again, the day after the operation,' Hayley reassured her. 'But let's make you more comfortable and get that X-ray done first.'

'All right, love.'

While Ethel was being seen by the radiologists, Sam removed a bead from a toddler's nose and Hayley phoned Ethel's daughter, who promised to drive straight up to the hospital. The X-ray confirmed everything they'd feared, and Hayley rang the orthopaedic team to ask for a surgeon to come down to the emergency department.

'Let's go and break the news to Ethel,' Hayley said, and they went to sit by her bed in the cubicle.

'I'm afraid you've definitely broken your hip, Ethel,' Sam said. 'You've broken it inside the socket of your hip.' He took a pad from his pocket and drew a picture of the fracture to show her. 'Unfortunately this kind of break won't heal well, so you'll need a hip replacement.'

'But luckily everything's still where it should be, so it's not complicated enough to worry us,' Hayley added. 'One of the surgeons is coming down to see you.'

'So what happens now?' Ethel asked.

'You'll have the operation later today,' Sam said.

'It'll take a couple of hours,' Hayley added.

'Will they put me out first?' Ethel asked.

'Not necessarily. The surgeon will talk through the anaesthetic options with you,' Sam said.

'After the operation, you'll stay on the orthopaedic ward,' Hayley continued. 'They'll give you painkillers and a drip, pretty much as you have right now, and they'll start to get you back on your feet tomorrow. A physiotherapist will come and see you and teach you some exercises to help with your strength and mobility.'

Ethel frowned. 'So how long will I have to stay in hospital?'

'Until you're back on your feet and mobile again,' Sam said, 'though you might not be quite as mobile as you were before and you might need more help at home.'

Ethel shook her head. 'I don't want to go into one of them nursing homes.'

'Do you live in sheltered accommodation now?' Hayley asked.

'No, I live in the same house I went to the day I married my Brian,' Ethel said. 'Fifty-eight years, I've lived there. But I do have a carer come in every morning to get me up and every evening to help me get to bed. That's the bit I have trouble with.'

'You're going to need a little more support than just twice a day,' Sam said gently. 'I know you're not keen on the idea, but you might need to go to a nursing home for a few weeks after you leave hospital—just for respite care, until you're totally on your feet again and ready to go home.'

Ethel pursed her lips. 'I'm not going into one of those places. They just stick you in a room in front of a telly and talk to you like you're a toddler. I might be old, but I haven't lost my marbles yet.'

Hayley squeezed her hand. 'Nursing homes aren't all like that. Is there anyone in the family you could stay with? Your daughter, maybe?'

'I can't live with my daughter,' Ethel said. 'I love her dearly, but we'd fight like cat and dog. Anyway, she doesn't have the room.'

'Maybe you could move closer to her, in sheltered accommodation,' Sam suggested, 'so you'd still have a lot of your independence but your daughter wouldn't be so worried about you because she'd know there was someone nearby if you needed help.'

Ethel didn't look convinced. 'I don't want to move.'

'We'll talk about it again after the surgeon's seen you,' Hayley said.

'I'm still not going in one of them nursing homes,' Ethel warned. 'They stink of boiled cabbage and pee.'

Hayley smiled. 'We can try and find you one that doesn't.'

'Hmm. Can I have that cup of tea now, please? I'm gasping.'

'Sorry, but you can't have a cup of tea until the surgeon's seen you,' Hayley said. 'You're going to have some form of anaesthetic, so it's not safe to have anything except water before the operation—and even water's banned for two hours before the operation. It's to make sure you're not sick during the operation and end up with something in your lungs.'

'Well, worse things happen at sea, as my old mum used to say,' Ethel said.

'I'll make you that tea myself after your op,' Sam said. 'And toast. I'm really good at toast.' He looked Hayley in the eye. 'And waffles.'

And he was gratified that she went very slightly pink. So she remembered, then? The question was whether she wanted to repeat it.

'We'll come and see you again as soon as the surgeon's available,' Hayley promised.

Between them, they saw an eight-year-old who'd been tripped over in the playground and ended up with a Colles' fracture of his wrist, a woman with what turned out to be an allergic reaction to her new eyelash extensions, and a man complaining of back pain after he'd overdone the gardening the previous day; and then it was time to see Ethel's daughter and the surgeon.

The surgeon sent Ethel for a DEXA scan, and meanwhile, Sam talked to Ethel's daughter about rehab options and how to get her mum the right support. The DEXA scan confirmed that Ethel had osteoporosis; and Sam accompanied Ethel and her daughter up to the orthopaedic ward to help settle them in.

When he got back down to the emergency department, Hayley tapped her watch. 'Quick lunch?'

And an overdue talk. 'Fine.'

She led him to the canteen, and they both selected a sandwich and coffee before finding a quiet table.

'Ethel's settled,' Sam said. 'I promised I'd go and see her at the end of my shift and make her that cup of tea.'

'Above and beyond, hmm?' Hayley asked.

'No. Just putting myself in the shoes of our patients and using a bit of empathy,' Sam said.

'I wasn't being snippy.'

'No.' The woman he'd met in Iceland had been warm and sweet. He'd liked her a lot. But that was when he'd thought she was only going to be a temporary part of her life. What now?

'I had no idea you were going to be our new registrar,' she said. 'You never said you were coming to London.'

Because he'd thought he'd never see her again. 'I had no idea I was taking your old job,' he countered.

She gave him a wry smile. 'Is this where we both do the bit from *Casablanca*, except it's hospitals rather than gin joints?'

'Pretty much,' he said.

'OK. Well, I'm not going to pussyfoot around it.'

She lifted her chin. 'You and me—I hope we can be friends.'

'Friends,' he said. Which wasn't quite how either of them had seen things in Iceland. And the attraction was still there between them; a couple of times during their shift this morning, they'd accidentally brushed against each other, and he'd seen her pupils dilate slightly. Just as his own probably had, and his skin had tingled where it had touched hers. Had it been the same for her, too?

'Anything else would be too complicated,' she said. 'I've seen too many departmental relationships end in tears. And especially now, as you and I are working closely together.'

'And I've taken over your old role, so you're effectively my boss. Fair enough.' Hayley had made it very clear she wanted to shut down the connection they'd shared. Which was a shame, because the more Sam saw of her, the more he liked her. They'd slipped into an easy working relationship, as if they'd known each other for years and knew how each other thought. The kind of relationship he'd thought he had with Lynda—and he'd been very wrong indeed about that. So maybe Hayley was right and they'd be better to keep this strictly platonic, rather than try to build on what they'd shared in Iceland. Trying to find a safer subject, he asked, 'How's the running training going?'

She looked surprised and then pleased that he'd asked. 'OK, though obviously Dani's not able to go alongside me and pace me when we do the outdoor runs. She sends me off and sits on a bench in the park with a stopwatch going and listens to music while she waits for me to get back to her. But at the end of the day my finish time doesn't really matter. What matters is that I actually finish.'

Maybe this would be a way of getting some of the easiness back between them. 'I've only just moved here and don't know any good running routes,' he said, 'so if you want me to join you when you're training outside and act as your pacemaker, you'd be doing me a favour as well. It'd be a win for both of us.'

'I guess.' She looked thoughtful. 'Do you mind if I talk to Dani about it, first?'

'Sure. Make it clear I'm not thinking of muscling in on her training sessions. It's simply a way of helping us both out.'

'So you and me, we're good?' she checked.

'We're good.' And he was just going to have to ignore that attraction he felt towards her, because they weren't going to be anything other than friends.

'Great. So have you settled in London OK?'

'I'm getting there,' he said. 'My flat's near enough for me to cycle in to work, and the department seems nice.'

'They're a good bunch on our team,' she said. 'Everyone pulls their weight, and everyone gets on well together. Actually, there's a team night out on Friday—it's the monthly quiz night at the pub across the road. We always have a team and there's usually one from Paediatrics and another from Maternity. And the pub does the best chips in London. Why don't you come along, if you're not busy?'

'I might just do that.'

'Oh, and while I remember—the departmental Christmas meal is the first week of December,' she added.

'Christmas?' He raised an eyebrow. 'It's only August. Isn't it too early to be thinking about Christmas?'

'If you don't book a venue well in advance, nowhere's got any spaces left,' she said. 'Surely it's like that in Manchester, too?'

So she remembered where he used to work. 'I guess.'

'We also do a Secret Santa, where you draw someone's name and buy them a present—Jennie, the senior receptionist, is in charge of that and she takes the deposit and choices for the meal, so have a word with her.'

'Right. Thanks.'

'Great. That's that organised, then.' She glanced at her watch. 'I guess we'd better get back to the department.'

CHAPTER FIVE

ON TUESDAY, HAYLEY and Sam were both rostered onto Minors and didn't see much of each other all day. But Hayley caught him at the end of their shift. 'I've spoken to Dani. She says if you'd like to join us tomorrow, we're doing the training straight after work and then grabbing something for dinner from the café in the park—obviously sitting at one of the tables outside, because we'll be a bit sweaty and disgusting after our run.'

'Sounds good. Thank you,' Sam said.

Wednesday was just as busy, but again Hayley caught up with Sam at the end of their shift. She'd already changed into her running gear, and waited for him to change, too.

'So where are we running?' he asked.

'Alexandra Park,' she said. 'It's by Alexandra Palace, the old BBC television studios—part of it used to be a theatre, in Victorian times. And there are amazing views from the park across the whole of London.'

'Are we walking there?' he asked.

'No. We're getting a taxi,' she said, 'because of Dani's foot.' She waved to a shorter, dark-haired woman who was sitting on one of the benches in the hospital's main reception area, and whose foot was encased in a walking cast. Next to her, propped against the bench, were crutches.

'Danielle Owens, meet Sam Price,' Hayley said when they'd gone over to meet her.

Danielle and Sam shook hands. 'Nice to meet you,' Danielle said.

Sam wondered how much Hayley had told her. Then again, they were best friends, and he knew from his sister that women talked about that sort of thing.

'So you're going to help us with the running training?' Danielle asked.

'If you don't mind,' he said politely.

'I'm glad of the help. I can't exactly get a megaphone and shout at Haze from the middle of the park to pick up her pace,' Danielle said, glaring at her cast. 'I wish I hadn't had to ask her to do this in the first place.'

'You didn't ask. I offered. And even *you* can't run with a fractured second and third metatarsal,' Hayley said firmly.

'Oh, I could do it, all right,' Danielle said with a grin. 'It just wouldn't be sensible. And I want this thing off my foot as soon as possible, so I'm doing what I'm told.'

'For once,' Hayley teased.

They took a taxi to the park, and Danielle went through the training programme briefly with Sam.

'So we have about six weeks between now and race day,' Sam said. 'You're doing interval training indoors on a treadmill, and then the longer runs outside.'

'Because the interval training will help with the

pace, but running indoors is very different from running outdoors—and, as the actual race is outside, then Haze needs experience in running outdoors,' Danielle explained.

'Agreed. This looks like a really workable plan.'

'Great. I'll let you set the pace for the four-miler, then,' Danielle said with a smile. 'I'm going to get some coffee from the café and do the dreaded four-letter-word thing with my foot. See you both when you're done.'

Sam discovered that Hayley had been telling the truth: the park was pretty, full of people walking dogs and parents with small children. The Alexandra Palace sprawled behind the trees, a huge yellow-brick Victorian building with red-brick detailing and arched windows, a glass roof and a tall transmitter mast. When they ran past the palace itself, the views over London were stunning. He settled into a slower pace than he would normally have taken, bearing in mind that Hayley was still a relative novice to running.

A couple of times, his hand accidentally brushed against hers, and it sent a tingle through him. Did she feel it, too? But she'd made it clear that as far as she was concerned they were colleagues only, so it was pointless wondering. Besides, even though he liked her professionally, that was a whole different thing than trusting her with his heart. There was a huge difference between a no-strings fling and a real relationship.

They rejoined Danielle around forty-five minutes later.

'So how was it?' Danielle asked.

'Wonderful,' Hayley said without batting an eyelid.

'You hated it,' Danielle said with a sigh.

'I'd much rather do dance aerobics than running,' Hayley admitted. 'But this is for a really good cause—the MRI scanner for the newborns in your department.' She looked at Sam. 'And it was better running with someone else. Even though you obviously had to slow down for me and I feel a bit guilty about that.'

'Don't. Running's still running,' he said. 'I enjoyed it too.'

Danielle pushed a menu towards him. 'My shout,' she said.

'There's no nee—' he began, and she rolled her eyes.

'Yes, there is. I'm saying thank you for helping us out. Be gracious,' she said.

'I told you she was bossy,' Hayley said with a grin. 'Take advice from someone who's known her since the first day at university. It's quickest to just agree with her, because she always gets her way in the end.'

'Then thank you, Danielle.' Sam chose pasta, salad and a glass of mineral water; Danielle and Hayley chose the same.

'So how are you finding Muswell Hill, did you do a lot of running where you were before, and where exactly were you before?' Danielle asked after she'd ordered and paid.

He laughed. 'In order: OK, yes, Manchester.'

She looked pained. 'A man of few words? How very disappointing.'

'If you meant the hospital, you work there yourself so you know what it's like. If you meant the area, I haven't been here for long enough to really explore it,' he said. 'But what I've seen is pretty, and I like the park. It's about a twenty-minute walk from the hospital, isn't it?'

'Uphill all the way, so it's a good warm-up for a run,' Danielle said. 'What made you move to London from Manchester?'

That wasn't something he was ready to open up about, at least not yet. He'd given Hayley the very bare bones; given that she was effectively his senior, he probably ought to fill in some of the gaps reasonably soon. 'It was time for a change,' he said lightly.

'Fair comment,' Danielle said. 'Haze said you spent the whole summer in Iceland, working with your brother.'

'It was kind of a sabbatical,' he said.

'Doing stuff like glacier walking? And I've seen all the photographs, by the way.'

'Yes, glacier walking's part of it. I did tours for very small groups in a four-wheel drive car, so our clients got to see some of the sights off the beaten track as well as the tourist hotspots—all of which are actually worth seeing,' he added, 'as you'll know since you've seen the pictures.'

'Don't you need training to do glacier walking?' Danielle asked.

He nodded. 'I was part of the mountain rescue team when I was back in Manchester, so it was an extension of the training I'd done in climbing.'

'Rock and ice,' she said thoughtfully. 'Does that mean you're into extreme sports?'

He looked at her, intrigued. 'Does that mean you are, too?'

'Please don't encourage her,' Hayley said. 'Remember, she's in a walking cast.'

'I don't do extreme stuff,' Danielle said, looking wistful, 'but I really did want to touch a glacier—I'd hoped to persuade Haze into doing the walking tour on it while we were there. That and the whales were the two things I was really looking forward to most.'

'Go to Iceland next summer, when your foot's healed properly and it will cope with the demands of ice walking, which in my professional opinion won't be for at least two months after that cast comes off,' Sam said. 'I'll get Martin, my brother, to take you out on the glacier.'

'Thank you. I accept. I have to admit, I was hideously jealous with every picture Haze texted me.' She reached over to squeeze Hayley's hand. 'And that proves I was right to make her go. She needed a break.'

'Before I started my new job,' Hayley said swiftly.

Sam intercepted the glance between them and could guess what Dani had really meant: space to move on from her partner's death.

'Iceland's a good place for thinking,' he said. 'It's something to do with the quality of the light out there.'

'You're hardly going to do glacier walking in London,' Danielle said, 'so what do you plan to do here?'

'Actually, you can do ice climbing in London, which is the next best thing.' He'd looked it up and planned to book a slot on the ice wall for his next day off. 'And, as there isn't exactly a need for a mountain rescue team in London, I've signed up for the MERIT roster.'

MERIT—the Medical Emergency Response Incident Team—was a small team of doctors and nurses who could be called out to the site of an accident to see casualties who had life-threatening injuries but might be trapped for another hour or more, or to do triage at the scene of major incidents such as a bus crash or an industrial fire.

There was a shared glance between Hayley and Danielle that he didn't quite understand. Now didn't feel like the right time to ask for an explanation, so he added, 'But what I really want to try is rap jumping.'

Hayley blinked. 'I've never heard of it. What is it?'

'Like abseiling,' he said. 'Except you go forwards instead of backwards.'

'Hang on. You're telling me you stand at the top of a building and then you just jump off?' Danielle asked.

'A very tall building or a cliff,' he agreed. 'But you're belayed the whole time, and you have a brake-man who slows you down—so you don't just hit the ground from a hundred and eighty feet up and break most of your bones. It's a gentle landing. Let me show you.' He found a video on the internet and handed his phone to her. 'Here.'

Hayley and Danielle watched the video together, both looking more and more shocked as the seconds ticked by.

'That's *horrific*,' Hayley said. 'Why would anyone want to take such a risk of something going wrong and put themselves in danger like that?'

'The adrenaline rush,' he said. 'And there are plenty of safeguards. It's probably less of a risk than cycling to work in London, and I do that every day.'

'You obviously didn't deal with many cyclist casualties in Manchester,' Hayley said feelingly. 'My first week's placement in the emergency department put me off cycling in London for good.'

'Everything carries a risk,' he said.

'But some things are riskier than others. Some things are…' She grimaced and looked away. 'Oh, just ignore me. I'm ranting.'

Why would she be so antsy about people taking risks? She'd said her fiancé had been killed in an industrial accident. But those were so rare. Was there more to this than she'd told him? Had her fiancé taken some extra kind of risk? What kind of accident had it been? Not that he could ask any of this without being intrusive. He could hardly ask her best friend either. So he'd just have to wait until Hayley was prepared to confide in him.

He switched the conversation to a safer topic, and discovered during dinner that he really liked Hayley's best friend: there was absolutely no sexual chemistry between them, but he liked Danielle's energy and sense of humour a great deal.

And he didn't let himself think about the chemistry between himself and Hayley. The way his skin felt super-sensitive when it accidentally brushed against hers. The way his pulse rate speeded up when he caught her eye. The way he really, really wanted to kiss her again.

'Can we give you a lift home in our taxi?' Danielle asked. 'I say "our"—Haze and I live in neighbouring streets.'

'It's fine,' he said. 'It's a downhill walk from here to the hospital, and anyway I need to collect my bike for tomorrow morning.'

'OK.' Danielle reached out to shake his hand, and

then said, 'Oh, come here,' and gave him a hug. 'It was nice to meet you, Sam. And we'll see you for training on Friday.'

'We can't train on Friday night. We've got the pub quiz,' Hayley said.

'Sorry—I was so focused on the race that I forgot it was this Friday. And our department is so going to beat you this time. I've had the team mugging up on literature and art. We know our stuff.' Danielle turned to Sam. 'How about Saturday for training?'

'It'd have to be the morning,' he said. 'I'm working a late shift on Saturday.'

'That's fine by me. Shall we meet here at nine?' Danielle suggested.

'One condition,' he said, 'you let me buy pastries and coffee afterwards.'

'I love pastries and coffee,' she said, her face full of enthusiasm. 'You're on. See you Saturday.'

'See you Saturday.' He looked at Hayley. 'See you in the department tomorrow.'

And he tried not to mind that she didn't hug him, the way Danielle had.

'Right, madam. So when exactly were you going to tell me that your new registrar was the gorgeous guy from Iceland?' Danielle asked, once they were in the taxi and out of Sam's hearing. 'Come on. You must've known that I'd recognise him from the photographs.'

'Um… Sorry.'

'So what happens now? Do you carry on where you left off in Iceland?'

Hayley shook her head. 'We're colleagues.'

Danielle raised an eyebrow. 'And why is that a problem? Half the couples I know first met at work. And he's *lovely*. I don't just mean the way he looks. He's a really nice guy. Not my type, but absolutely yours.'

'He cycles to work. He likes extreme sports.' Hayley sucked in a breath. 'And now I know he's signed up for MERIT. You and I both know how dangerous it can be out there. No, there are way too many risks in his life for me.'

'You need a little risk in life to keep you moving,' Danielle said gently. 'Don't throw the baby out with the bath water.'

'I can't do it, Dani,' Hayley said. 'I can't take that risk. What if something goes wrong?'

'What if it doesn't?' Danielle countered. 'And you know as well as I do, between the Medical Incident Officer and whoever's in charge of the inner zone at an incident, the MERIT team is only allowed in if it's safe for them to be there. I think you should give him a chance.'

'I can't. Losing Evan was like having a black hole punched into the middle of my life. I can't go through that again.' She dragged in a breath. 'Yes, I like Sam. I more than like him. He's good to work with, he's great with the patients and whoever comes in with them, and he's… Well, you've met him.' Physically, he was just her type and she was finding it hard to resist him. Every time his hand had accidentally brushed against hers in the park, she'd been tempted to let her fingers catch his and hold on. She'd really had to hold herself back.

'I think he more than likes you, too,' Danielle said. 'The way he looks at you is pretty obvious.'

'We agreed to be just friends. It's too complicated for anything else. We work together.'

'There's nothing wrong with working with your partner.'

Hayley looked at her and narrowed her eyes. 'Danielle Owens, is there something you'd like to tell me?'

'No.' Danielle flapped a dismissive hand. 'I'm not seeing anyone—and anyway, we're not talking about me. This is about you and Sam. Just give the man a chance.'

'I can't,' Hayley said. 'I just can't take the risk.'

Though she thought about it all the next day. And the next.

She was definitely aware of Sam. Every time their hands accidentally touched at work, it made her tingle all over. And she kept catching herself looking at his mouth and remembering exactly how good that mouth had made her feel. Remembering what it had felt like to make love with him. Remembering what it had felt like to wake up in his arms.

But how could she let anything happen between them again, knowing that he would voluntarily put himself at risk? That he was more than prepared to step into a disaster zone to help, regardless of the risk to his own life? She'd been there before and she'd lost. Badly. How could she put herself back in that position?

'Hey,' Sam said, when they broke for lunch. 'The pub quiz this evening doesn't start until seven, right?'

'Right.'

'Do you want to go for a coffee first?'

She ought to say no. But somehow she found herself agreeing. And so they sat in a café a couple of doors down from the pub, drinking lattes and eating pastries.

'There's something I wanted to talk to you about,' he said. 'The reason why I spent the summer in Iceland. Why I nearly left medicine.'

'You don't need to explain anything. Apart from the fact that I have nothing to do with the decision on employing staff in the department, I already know you're perfectly competent,' she said. 'We worked together on that boat to help Milton Adams with his asthma attack, and I've worked with you for a week here. I've seen more than enough to know you're good at what you do.'

He inclined his head. 'Thank you. I appreciate that. But things tend to leak out, so I'd rather you heard this from me. I took a sabbatical because I was suspended.'

It was the last thing she'd expected. She stared at him. 'You were suspended? But... Why?' She didn't understand.

'We lost a patient. He came in saying he'd been feeling fluey for about a week—his GP had told him to rest, but he wasn't feeling any better and his wife had nagged him to get another appointment. He couldn't get an appointment with his GP, so he decided to come in to us to stop his wife having a go at him. He said he'd had a bit of indigestion, but nothing serious.' He frowned. 'Something didn't seem right to me, but I couldn't quite put my finger on it. Not until I asked him about his medical history and he told me he was diabetic.'

'He'd had a silent heart attack?' she asked. Diabetes

could cause nerve damage, which made it less likely that the patient would feel any pains in the chest during a heart attack.

He nodded. 'I said I wanted to give him an ECG because that was the only way of checking if he'd had a silent heart attack, and if the ECG showed that was the case we'd start him on treatment immediately. We checked his sugar levels and they were off the scale. Halfway through the ECG he arrested again. Except we didn't manage to get him back.' He sighed. 'His family were distraught. I guess they couldn't accept that it had happened, and they were looking for someone to blame because that was the only way they could make sense of it. They made a negligence claim. Obviously the hospital had to investigate the case properly, so my team was suspended, pending enquiries.'

'Obviously they cleared you.' Or he wouldn't be working as a doctor now.

'Yes. I was the one who'd made the correct diagnosis and we'd followed protocol exactly. And all our paperwork was in good order, because that's how I was taught and what I expected from my juniors, too.' He grimaced. 'We did everything right. But it still didn't save our patient.'

'He'd already had at least one silent heart attack, from the sound of it,' she said. 'He could've had another one at any time—at home, on the way to the hospital or even in the waiting room. And, because he didn't get the usual pain signals, he didn't seek treatment in time and there was existing damage to his blood vessels and heart muscle, which meant his next heart attack was fatal. It wasn't your fault.'

* * *

Her reaction stunned him. It was what he'd expected from Lynda—real belief in him, instead of asking if he might have missed one little thing.

Hayley believed in him.

And she'd known him only for a few days—he and Lynda had been together for three years. If anyone should have doubts about him, surely it should be Hayley?

Something felt as if it had cracked inside him.

'I know you can't save everyone who comes into the emergency department,' he said. 'But this one really hit home. We all felt as if we'd failed. I resigned from the mountain rescue team. How could I go out to rescue people if I wasn't fit to practise medicine?'

'It was a formality,' she pointed out.

And if his own fiancée hadn't doubted him, maybe Sam would've felt that way, too. But the combination of the suspension and Lynda's lack of belief in him had knocked his belief in himself as a doctor.

'I wasn't the only one with doubts,' he said. 'One of my team has left medicine completely.'

'That's a shame.' She paused. 'And the timing was hard, too, being just after you broke up with your ex.'

This was his cue to tell her about Lynda. But the words stuck in his throat. In the end, he said, 'Martin realised that I was sitting at home brooding, going over and over what had happened and trying to work out what I could've done differently so I could've actually saved my patient. He dragged me out to Iceland on the grounds that he needed help with his business. He didn't actually need my help at all,' Sam admitted, 'but it was good to be kept too busy to think. And, as I said earlier, there's something about the light out there that makes it a good place to let things marinate in the back of your head. And it made me realise I didn't want to throw away thirteen years of training.' Five years of studying for his degree, two years of post-graduate foundation training, three years of core training and three years of higher specialty training, as well as the expertise he'd gained since then.

'I think,' she said, 'if medicine hadn't been your calling, then you would've ignored the tour guide on the boat when she asked if there was a doctor on board. Especially as she must've told you I was already helping.'

'An uncontrolled asthma attack can be pretty scary to witness,' he said. 'I thought I might be able to help you deal with whoever was accompanying the patient. And I guess it was a kind of test, to see if I'd done the right thing in accepting the job here.'

'You did,' she said. 'I don't know how good you're going to be where our quiz team is concerned, but you're definitely the right person for our team at the hospital.'

'Thank you. I wasn't fishing for compliments.'

'I know. I was just telling you straight, like Dani would.' She paused. 'This won't go any further than me, though I assume Mike knows.'

'It was in my application form—and I told him about it at the interview,' Sam said.

'If he'd had any doubts about you, he wouldn't have hired you,' she pointed out. 'And he did the right thing.'

'Thanks. I have to admit, I had my doubts when I applied.'

'That's understandable. I've never been suspended or investigated, but it must really knock your belief in yourself.'

'It did.' But what had really destroyed him was Lynda's lack of faith. The way she hadn't stood by him. The fact she'd broken their engagement because she'd thought he'd hold her back in her career.

'But from what I've seen you don't cut corners,' Hayley said. 'Your boss in Manchester must have told you that.'

He smiled. 'She did. I learnt a lot of Hindi swear words from her, the day she told me I was suspended.'

'I'm glad you didn't leave medicine,' she said. She lifted her coffee cup and clinked it against his. 'Here's to teamwork. Welcome to Muswell Hill. And also you'd better be good at general knowledge questions, because Dani will be unbearable if the Maternity team actually beats us in the quiz.'

He smiled then. 'Teamwork,' he echoed.

The emergency department team was victorious in the quiz, and Sam teased Danielle mercilessly about it the next morning when he met her and Hayley in the park for training. By the end of the next week, he felt completely part of the team and as if he'd worked at Muswell Hill Hospital for years instead of a fortnight.

But then he called in his next patient. 'Pauline Jacobs?'

She was middle-aged, overweight, and her face looked almost grey. 'I haven't been feeling well for the last few days,' she said. 'I know I shouldn't be bothering the emergency department, but I couldn't get an appointment with my doctor for another couple of weeks, and the pharmacist told me to come here.'

'You've done the right thing,' he reassured her. 'I'm Sam Price. May I call you Pauline?'

'Of course.'

'Tell me about your symptoms, Pauline,' he invited.

'I'm just so tired,' she said. 'I'd say I had the flu, but you don't get flu at the end of September, do you?'

He went cold.

No.

Not again.

'It's not common,' he said. 'So you're suffering from extreme tiredness and feeling fluey.'

'And I've been getting dizzy,' she said. 'Plus I'm out of breath just going up one set of stairs—by the time I've got to my desk on the second floor at work, I need a sit-down. I know I need to lose weight and I ought to go to the gym and get fit, but between teenagers and my job I don't get a second to myself. I haven't got time to do exercise.'

He was pretty sure he knew where this was going. 'Are you taking any medication?' he asked.

'Statins for my cholesterol, blood pressure tablets, and my diabetic tablets.'

'Have you been diagnosed diabetic for long?' he asked.

'Three years. I do watch what I eat, I really do, and I even turn down cake when people in my department bring them in for birthdays—but it's so difficult to lose weight.'

Especially when she was heading towards the menopause and had a battery of hormones to contend with as well. 'I think,' he said gently, 'you've had a heart attack.'

'But wouldn't I get chest pain?' Pauline asked, looking puzzled. 'When you see someone on the telly have a heart attack, they clutch their chest and everything. I've had a bit of indigestion, but that's my fault because I know garlic does that to me.'

'What I think's happened is something called a silent heart attack,' he said. 'And they're quite common—about a quarter of all heart attacks in the UK are silent. You're diabetic, so I take it your doctor talked to you about being careful about foot care?'

She nodded.

'That's because diabetes can cause nerve damage and the usual pain warning signals aren't transmitted,' he said. 'So the same reason you might not feel any problem with your feet is the same reason why you didn't feel any chest pain. I'm going to check your blood sugar levels and then give you an electrocardiogram—an ECG—which measures the electrical activity of your heart. It doesn't hurt,' he reassured her. 'I'll just stick some flat metal discs to your arms, legs and chest, and the wires will send all the information I need to the machine. Is that OK with you, Pauline?'

'Yes,' she said.

Pauline's blood sugar level was sky-high. He showed her the reading. 'You'd normally be after a reading of four to six.'

'But that's over twenty!' She bit her lip. 'I haven't

been stuffing my face with cakes and sugar, honestly I haven't.'

'Stress and illness can make your blood sugar level rise,' he said. 'I'm going to give you some insulin to bring your blood sugar level down, and then we'll look at the ECG.'

The printout from the ECG showed him exactly what had happened. 'OK, Pauline. There's some good news, and some not so good news,' he said.

'Tell me the bad stuff first,' Pauline said with a grimace.

'You've had a silent heart attack,' he said. 'But the good news is that it's what we call an NSTEMI.'

'Which is?'

'A non-ST segment elevation myocardial infarction,' he said. 'What that means is that it's less serious than the other type. The supply of blood to your heart is only partially blocked, and that means a smaller section of your heart will be damaged. I'm going to admit you to the cardiac ward,' he said, 'and they'll give you some blood-thinning medication to make sure no clots develop and cause a more serious heart attack. They'll also do some blood tests to measure if a special protein called troponin shows in your blood—which I'm pretty sure it will, because those proteins go into your blood if there's any damage to your heart. They'll give you a special scan called an echocardiogram, which shows a picture of the inside of your heart so they can see which areas have been damaged and how it's affected the way your heart functions. And they'll also want to check if your arteries have narrowed slightly.'

'What happens if they have?' Pauline asked.

'They can give you something called an angioplasty. It's where they put a little tube called a balloon catheter into an artery in your groin or arm, which goes through your blood vessels and up to your heart, guided by X-ray. The tube goes into the narrowed section of the coronary artery, then they inflate a little balloon at the end of the tube to open the artery, and put a bit of flexible metal mesh called a stent into the artery to help keep it open.'

'And that fixes every—' She stopped mid-word.

One look told Sam what had just happened.

History was *not* going to repeat itself. He wasn't going to lose Pauline Jacobs to a silent heart attack. He wasn't going to lose another patient to a silent heart attack ever again.

'Crash team!' he yelled, and hit the button.

He moved the back of the bed so Pauline was lying flat, gave two rescue breaths, and started chest compressions. When he'd counted to thirty, he checked Pauline's airway and gave two rescue breaths, then went back to chest compressions.

By the time he'd done the second set of thirty chest compressions, the team was in place, the defibrillator and pads were attached to Pauline's chest and Hayley pronounced, 'She's in VT.'

'We need to shock her,' he said. 'I'll keep doing the compressions until you're ready to defibrillate her.'

'Charging,' Hayley said.

He continued with the compressions.

'And clear,' Hayley said.

He moved his hands so she could give the shock,

then went straight back into the rhythm of thirty compressions and two breaths.

'Still VT,' Hayley said. 'Charging again. And clear.'

The second shock made no difference. Neither did the third.

'We are *not* losing her. Keep going,' he said. 'Adrenaline and amiodarone.'

'Drawing them up now,' Darryl, one of the nurses, said.

Sam continued with the compressions while Hayley administered the medication.

'Darryl, can you take over compressions?' Hayley asked.

'No,' Sam said. 'I can keep going.'

'Sam,' she said, her tone gentle yet firm.

'No,' he said. 'I'm not losing her.'

'Which is why you're going to let Darryl take over the compressions and you can do the next shock. Your arms are tired. Darryl will be more effective.'

He knew she wasn't playing power games, just being sensible—and because he'd told her what had happened in Manchester, he also knew that she was well aware of how this was affecting him. She was right to make him back off a bit. If their positions had been reversed, he would've said exactly the same.

'OK. Sorry.'

'No problem.'

'Charging,' he said. 'And clear.'

This time, to his relief, the defibrillation worked and Pauline's heart went back into a normal rhythm. She was still unconscious, but at least her heart was beating again.

'All righty. Well done, team,' Hayley said. 'You know the drill—Sam, let's get her on oxygen and a twelve-lead ECG. Darryl, call the cardiac unit and get her admitted. And then, Sam, if you can go with her to the CCU and do the handover?'

'On it,' Sam said.

'Me, too,' Darryl added.

'Are you OK?' she asked Sam gently when Darryl had left the cubicle.

'I'm fine.' He wasn't, but he had no intention of admitting how much this had shaken him and brought all his doubts back.

She squeezed his shoulder. 'Come and find me if you need me, OK?'

'Thanks.'

Once he'd done the handover at the cardiac unit, Sam was back in the thick of things—a teenager with abdominal pain that turned out to be a navel piercing that had become infected, a runner who'd been caught in the eye by a branch and had a scratch across his cornea, and a toddler with febrile convulsions.

At the end of his shift, he went to check on Pauline, who was lying in bed but was conscious.

'Thank you,' she said when she saw him. 'I believe you saved my life.'

'Not just me—the rest of the team saved you, too,' he said. 'How are you feeling?'

'As if a tank rolled over me,' she admitted.

He grimaced. 'Sorry. I'm probably responsible for the bruises on your chest. I did the compressions and I might've been a bit too enthusiastic.'

'If you hadn't done them, I wouldn't be here now.'

Her eyes filled with tears. 'And I thought it was just something stupid wrong with me and I should've just put up with it instead of coming to hospital.'

'I'm glad you came in and didn't leave it,' he said. 'You're in the right place.'

'They're going to do that thing with the balloon you were telling me about.'

He smiled. 'I'm impressed you remembered, considering you conked out in the middle of it. I know I can drone on a bit, but I don't normally make people unconscious.'

She laughed, then winced. 'That hurts.'

'Give it a little time,' he said. 'But I just wanted to see how you were doing.'

'I'm still here, thanks to you.'

'Good.' He hadn't been able to save his patient in Manchester from that silent heart attack, but he'd saved Pauline Jacobs. And that went some way to making things better. 'I'll let you get some rest.'

When he got back to the staffroom of the emergency department, Hayley was leaning against his locker. 'Well, hey there. How are you doing?'

'I'm fine,' he lied. It felt as if someone had pulled a plug and he was almost drained right out. But he'd promised to help her with the running training. He and Dani had agreed that she'd do the indoor sessions with Hayley, and he'd take the outdoor ones; tonight, they were planning to run a full 10K round the park.

'Given the caseload you had today, I don't think you are,' she said. 'I know how I'd feel if I had to deal with a case that reminded me of my worst day ever, so I'm pulling rank. No running training tonight. I'm cooking you dinner. It's nothing fancy—just stir-fried chicken, vegetables and noodles—but it's fast and it's healthy.'

'I'm not hungry.'

'I don't care. I'm cooking and you're eating. And you can wheel your bike back to mine.'

'That's a bit bossy,' he said, narrowing his eyes at her. Lynda had been bossy like that, too.

'Yes, it is,' she admitted, surprising him. Lynda wouldn't have admitted to being bossy.

'But sometimes, when you've had a rough day, you need someone just to push you to put one foot after the other,' Hayley said softly.

'But you're meant to be training for the race.'

'I'll switch my training days round. It's fine. Come on.'

Sam didn't have enough left in him to protest. He just let her follow him out to the bicycle shed, unlocked his bicycle, and put one foot in front of the other to go back to her flat.

CHAPTER SIX

'LUCKILY I'M ON the ground floor so you won't have to haul your bike up two flights of stairs,' Hayley said, and ushered him inside.

Sam left his bike propped against the wall, blocking her narrow entrance hall, and followed her into the main part of her flat. It turned out to be about the same size as his apartment in Reykjavik, with a bathroom, a bedroom, a living room and a kitchen that had an area to eat in. All the walls were painted cream and the furniture was light-coloured, making the place seem bigger and airier than it actually was. There were framed photographs on the mantelpiece in the living room, a big bookcase stuffed with an eclectic mixture of medical texts and novels, and a mix of photographs and postcards attached with magnets to her fridge. Everything was neat and tidy—pretty much as she was at work, he thought.

'Can I do anything to help?' he asked.

'Yes, you can lay the table and sort out something for us to drink—there's wine in the fridge if you want some, or there's a jug of filtered water.' She smiled at him. 'London water isn't exactly nice, and filtering makes it taste a little bit better. Or there's a bottle of sparkling water in the cupboard, though obviously it won't be chilled.'

'Plain water's fine, thanks.'

'The cutlery's in the drawer next to the sink, and the crockery and glasses are in the cupboard above it,' she said.

'OK.' Strange how just the mechanical act of setting out cutlery and plates made him feel more normal. And he was pretty sure that Hayley knew that, which was why she'd given him the task in the first place.

She busied herself with the wok, and five minutes later they were both sitting at her kitchen table with a plate of food in front of them. He wasn't hungry, but it would be rude to just leave it, so he forced himself to eat.

Only when they'd finished and she'd made them both a mug of coffee did he look at her and ask the question that had been bugging him since he'd accompanied her home. 'You're not making me talk about it?'

'Nope.'

The question must've been written over his face, because she said gently, 'There's a time for pushing someone to talk, and there's a time for giving someone space until they're ready.'

That sounded like personal experience. No doubt to do with her fiancé's accident. And hadn't she said she knew how she'd feel if she had a case that was similar to the one in her worst day ever? But it would be way too intrusive to ask her what sort of case that'd be. Instead, he said, 'Thank you.'

'No problem. Now, your choice: would you like to

listen to some music, or watch something really un-demanding and fun on TV? Of course, if you really want to watch an in-depth documentary on the finer points of quantum physics,' she added with a smile, 'I'm sure we can find one.'

'I think I'll give the quantum physics a miss,' he said. 'But thank you. I really don't mind.' He probably ought to make his excuses and leave. But he really appreciated that she'd worked out what he really needed—what he hadn't quite worked out for himself: space to let things settle in his head, and a bit of company so he couldn't brood about it.

'In that case,' she said, 'it's my choice and you get to watch my favourite episode of *Friends*—the one where Monica puts a turkey on her head. And we're having my posh chocolate biscuits with this, but don't tell Dani because she'll nag me about proper nutrition during race training and she'll force me to eat one of those protein bar things that are full of dates and taste *weird*.'

'I promise,' he said. And he couldn't help smiling when she sang along with the theme tune to the show and did the little claps. 'You really love this, don't you?'

'It's my favourite show ever,' she said with a smile. 'Which is why I've got it in a box set, in case it ever goes off my streaming service. Dani says I'm like Joey—I think a sandwich makes everything better.'

He laughed. 'She might have a point.'

'But it *does*. Or posh chocolate biscuits.'

'I guess.' And it was surprising how much better he did feel, sitting next to her on her sofa with a mug of coffee and Viennese chocolate fingers.

They somehow ended up moving closer during the TV show, and it seemed natural to put his arm round her. She leaned into him, and he turned his head so he could kiss her hair. She turned his head to look at him, and her pupils were huge; it seemed that the attraction between them in Iceland hadn't gone away at all, for either of them.

When he looked at her mouth, he couldn't resist dipping his head and brushing his mouth against hers. His lips tingled at the contact, and he wanted more. This time, when he kissed her, she kissed him back, and a shaft of pure need lanced through him.

Except he wasn't being fair to her. When he finally broke the kiss, he whispered, 'I'm sorry. I shouldn't have done that. It's been a hell of a day.'

She rested one hand against his cheek. 'I know—but remember that you saved Pauline Jacobs, and it wasn't your fault that you lost your patient in Manchester. If you have a silent heart attack, you don't have a clue about the damage that's been done to your heart, and if someone else had treated that patient in Manchester they would've ended up with exactly the same result that you did. It wasn't your fault. As you said, the relatives were grieving and they needed someone to blame. You were exonerated.'

But at the end of the day his patient had died. He sighed. 'Pauline's going to be covered in bruises from the chest compressions.'

'But she's here to tell the tale. Thanks to you.'

'And to the rest of the team.'

'But mainly to you,' she said. 'Because you're the one who spotted it was a silent heart attack. You were partway through doing the assessments and sorting out her blood sugar when she crashed.'

'I guess.' He dragged in a breath. 'I ought to go.'

'You don't have to.'

He gave her a rueful smile. 'Oh, but I do. Because I'm having inappropriate thoughts—seriously inappropriate thoughts—about you. And I'm not going to use you to make me feel better, Hayley. You deserve more than that.'

In answer, she reached up to kiss him again.

The next thing he knew, they were lying full-length on her sofa. His hands were under her top and his own top was somewhere on the floor.

'Um,' he said. 'Sorry. This wasn't meant to happen.'

'I know.' She stroked his face. 'We're supposed to be just colleagues. Friends, maybe.' She took a deep breath. 'Except I remember Iceland.'

'So do I,' he said softly. 'So what are we going to do about it?'

'The sensible thing would be for you to leave right now and go home,' she said.

But the way she said it sounded as if she thought there was an alternative. 'Or?' he asked.

'Or,' she said, 'I have a washing machine. I could run your things through it.'

Just he'd done for her, the night she'd stayed at his flat in Iceland.

'Which would your preferred option be?' he asked carefully.

'Both options are complicated.'

He frowned. 'How?' Surely him going home would put an end to things?

'We have work tomorrow. If you stay and we arrive at the hospital together—especially with you walking next to me, pushing your bike—the hospital rumour mill will go into overdrive.'

'Fair point.' He paused. 'And if I don't stay?'

'Then, if I'm honest, I think we're going to be delaying the moment rather than avoiding it altogether.'

'So if it doesn't happen now, it's going to happen sometime?' he asked.

She nodded.

He knew she was right. He was finding it harder and harder to resist her. The more he got to know her, the more he wanted her. 'So,' he said, 'it might be less complicated if I stay.'

'Except I don't want gossip. And you know how I feel about relationships within a department—it's a bad idea.' She drew in a breath. 'So this has to stay just between you and me.'

Keeping their relationship secret. As if she had no faith in him. He felt sick. He'd been here before. Lynda hadn't had enough faith in him to stick by him when he'd been suspended. What was the point in starting another relationship that wasn't going to last the distance? One where Hayley didn't even want people to know they were seeing each other in the first place?

'And I don't mean this to be like some dirty little secret,' she said, as if picking up on his thoughts. 'I just don't like being the centre of everyone's conversation, with people suddenly shutting up and looking guilty when you walk into the room.'

The penny dropped. After her partner had been

killed, people would have talked about her, worried about her—and she'd obviously hated it.

And then something else hit him. She'd said she didn't approve of relationships within a department. 'Did your partner work in the emergency department?' he asked.

'No. I think it would have been worse if he had. People meant well. But I hated everyone talking about me.' She blew out a breath. 'It just takes time, until you're ready to move on.'

Had their fling in Iceland helped her to move to the place where she was ready to start a new relationship? Or was she still stuck?

Sam only realised he'd spoken aloud when she said, 'Both. I want to move on. I know Evan wouldn't have wanted me to grieve for ever—just as, if it had been the other way round, I would have wanted him to find someone who loved him as much as I had.'

That, Sam thought, was the difference between Lynda and Hayley. Hayley had loved her partner for who he was. Lynda had loved the idea of what Sam could be: a mover, a shaker, CEO of a different hospital. Her career plan for both of them meant that, once he'd reached the top, he would've worked in partnership with her to develop a kind of super-hospital. Except that wasn't what Sam had wanted. He'd wanted to follow in his grandfather's footsteps and be a doctor— to spend his days with patients and feel that he'd been able to make a real difference to their lives.

He hadn't talked to Hayley about what she wanted from her career, but from working with her he was pretty sure that she didn't want to work in the admin side. Like him, she seemed to prefer treating her patients.

'So if we weren't working together, would you consider dating me?' he asked, wanting it out in the open.

'Yes. No. I don't know.' She raked a hand through her hair. 'Do you want me to be honest?'

'Yes.'

'This is complicated,' she warned.

'Tell me anyway.'

'OK.' She took a deep breath. 'There's something between us. There has been right from when I first met you. I want to do something about it, but then I feel guilty because of Evan. And then I feel stupid for feeling guilty, because he wouldn't want that. And then I feel ashamed of being such an idiot. And then I feel scared about starting all over again.'

'I think,' he said, 'you're warm and kind and caring—and it's natural to feel guilty and awkward and scared. How long were you and Evan together?'

'Two and a half years. You?'

'Three, so I know what you mean. It's starting all over again, finding someone you're attracted to and someone that you've got a lot in common with. And you're always going to compare the new relationship to the old, and wonder if you're doing the right thing.' Or making the same mistake. Not that he was going to tell her that right now.

'And wondering if everyone's going to judge you and think it's too soon…'

'Does it matter what other people think?' he asked.

'I guess not.' She wrinkled her nose. 'As I said before, it's complicated.'

'That pretty much sums up life,' he said. 'You brought me here tonight to feed me and give me a hug. To offer me comfort after a rough day.' He paused. 'But I think you need comfort, too, right now. And maybe we can both help each other towards a better place.

'You mean, having sex to take our minds off things?'

'Yes and no.' He stroked her face. 'As you say, it's complicated.' He *liked* her: she was straightforward with their colleagues, compassionate and kind with their patients and their relatives, and outside work she was funny and clever and sweet. 'We want to see each other—and at the same time we're scared of starting something that might go wrong. A no-strings fling doesn't feel quite right, but are either of us really ready for a new relationship?'

'I don't have any answers,' she said. 'But can we keep it simple for now, until we work out what we want and where this is going? Keep it just between you and me?'

'Yes,' he said, and kissed her.

She stood up, taking his hand, and led him to her bedroom. Like the rest of the flat, it had light-coloured furniture and cream walls, and everything was neat and orderly. And he liked the framed print of a blue-bell wood that hung over the bed. The whole place just radiated calmness, much like Hayley herself.

He was about to kiss her when he remembered something important. 'We can't do this. At least, not right now.'

She blinked. 'Why not?'

'I don't have any condoms.'

'I do.'

Which was odd, because he was pretty sure that Hayley Clark didn't take men to bed on a casual basis. Their fling in Iceland had been based on strong pull of attraction, something that was still bubbling below the surface.

But he let it go. Right now he really wanted to kiss her again. Make love with her. Lose himself in her and let her lose herself in him. And he had the strongest feeling that it was just the same for her.

She pulled the curtains and turned on the bedside light. He switched off the overhead light, leaving the room bathed in the warm light of the lamp, then pulled her into his arms and kissed her.

This felt so good, so right.

And when they'd made love and he'd dealt with the condom and she'd dealt with the laundry, it felt good to curve his body round hers, drawing her back against him. Back in his own flat, he would've been brooding over the events of the day. Here, with her, he felt as if he was starting to heal.

The next morning, Hayley woke just before her alarm, warm and comfortable.

Apart from that one night they'd spent together in Iceland, this was the first time she'd woken in someone's arms for more than a year. Part of her still felt a bit disloyal to Evan, but part of her felt that it was so good not to be alone and to wake sharing the day with someone else.

She twisted round in his arms, and woke him with a kiss. 'Hey, sleepy. We're on early shift.'

He was wide awake almost instantly. 'How long does it take to get to the hospital from here?'

'We've both got time for a shower and breakfast,' she said. 'You have the first shower while I get your stuff out of the washer-dryer. There are clean towels in the airing cupboard.'

'Thank you. If you have an iron,' he said, 'I'd appreciate borrowing it to get the creases out of my shirt.'

She liked the fact that he hadn't immediately assumed that she'd iron his shirt for him, even though she wouldn't have minded doing it. 'No problem.'

'And I'll make breakfast while you shower,' he said.

'Thanks—that'd be good.'

By the time she'd finished sorting out the laundry, set up the ironing board and made some coffee, he'd appeared with a towel wrapped round his waist and his hair still damp from the shower. 'What would you like for breakfast?' he asked.

'There's bacon and ketchup in the fridge and bread in the cupboard,' she said. 'If that works for you?'

'It does. Leave it to me,' he said.

When she'd had her shower and dressed, she headed back to the kitchen.

'Perfect timing,' he said, and assembled a sandwich for her.

'Thanks.' Evan hadn't been able to cook at all; they'd joked that he could burn water and keep his whole crew busy if he actually tried to make breakfast.

But Evan had never seen the inside of this flat. Hayley had negotiated an early termination of the lease on the flat they'd shared together, unable to bear walking in the door and not seeing him there. This flat was much smaller, but it was handy for work and it suited her just fine.

This was her life now.

And she'd promised Dani that she'd live it to the full.

'Thank you for last night,' Sam said. 'You're right—I was reliving that case in Manchester, and I needed someone to push me out of it. To make me put one foot in front of the other, as you said.'

'No problem,' she said. She'd had people to do that for her after Evan had been killed—people who'd made her eat and get out of the flat and *function*. Though she had a feeling that there was something Sam hadn't told her. The man she'd been working with was bright and capable. Although anyone would have their confidence knocked by being suspended during an investigation, he'd known that he'd done all the right things for his patient and he'd been exonerated. Why hadn't his partner supported him through the investigation? Had she been related to the patient he'd lost, maybe, and blamed him for it? Or had they broken up just before the investigation and he'd maybe thought that he'd been distracted by the break-up and not asked the right questions of his patient, so he felt as if it was all his fault?

It wasn't something she could ask straight out: the questions were harsh and obtrusive. And she couldn't quite work out how to frame them in a kinder or more tactful way.

Thankfully, he changed the subject. 'We need to re-schedule your race training. Dani's right, running outside isn't the same as running inside. Are you free after work tonight, or are you training indoors with Dani?'

'It's meant to be a day off,' she said, 'so we'll swap it for yesterday. If you don't mind, that is.'

'No. We'll do a run in the park tonight.' He paused. 'Are you, um, free at the weekend? We could maybe do something.'

'I'd like that,' she said. It was going to be strange, dating again. But if she didn't let herself think about the dangerous things Sam liked to do in his free time—or the fact that he'd signed up to the MERIT roster—maybe she could do this. Maybe she could move on from the sadness of the past and find a new future with Sam.

When they'd finished their sandwiches, he insisted on washing up.

And then he paused. 'So I guess I'll see you at work? And then for the running training after.'

'OK. Be careful on the roads.'

'I will.' He kissed her lightly. 'See you on the ward.'

She bit her lip. 'And as far as work's concerned—'

'We're colleagues and starting to be just good friends,' he said. 'Got it.'

Which was what she wanted. But the hint of hurt in his eyes, quickly masked, made her feel guilty. It wasn't so much relationships in the department that bothered her—it was the gossip. Even when it was meant well.

Over the next couple of weeks, Sam and Hayley grew closer. He was careful to be strictly professional with her at work, and although he did the outdoor training runs with her when it was just the two of them, everyone knew it was under Dani's instructions and he was just helping out as a friend. When they went out on a date, it always seemed to be somewhere a little out-of-the-way, so they'd be less likely to bump into someone from work.

Though she refused flatly to go on the team night out he'd organised for the middle of October. 'You've got to be insane, Sam. Go-karting's risky enough by itself, but go-karting on *ice*?'

'They have special tyres,' he said. 'It's safe. I don't understand why you're worrying.'

'You're a thrill-seeker,' she said.

He frowned. 'I like extreme sports that make my heart beat a bit faster, yes. It makes me feel alive.'

'You're crazy,' she said.

He didn't understand why she was so antsy about it. She'd been fine about glacier walking; she'd enjoyed it, even.

And then a nasty thought hit him. He wanted things to work out between him and Hayley, but she was so critical about the things that he found fun—just as Lynda had been. Although Hayley wasn't Lynda, was he making a similar mistake? Was he subconsciously ignoring signs of trouble if he ignored her criticisms?

He pushed the thought away. He was being unfair. Hayley was one of the good guys.

'Come with us,' he said. 'Even if you don't want to do any of the actual driving, you can still have a drink and something to eat with us.'

'It's really, really not my thing,' she said. 'Have fun. But I'll be on duty so someone else on the team who actually wants to do it can go and join in.'

He couldn't argue with that. But it did make him

wonder if there was something she wasn't telling him. Was it to do with her late fiancé? He needed to find a tactful way to ask.

The day of Sam's team outing, Hayley was working. Have fun, she texted him, even though she wished he'd picked something less dangerous to do. Then again, he could've suggested abseiling or the rap jumping he'd shown her on his phone, which would've been even worse.

Why, why, why did he have to be an adrenaline junkie?

And how was she ever going to silence her fears?

He hadn't been called out on the MERIT roster yet, but she knew it was only a matter of time. And if that call-out involved a fire…

'Stop it,' she told herself. 'Don't trouble trouble.' And she forced herself to concentrate on her patients.

Halfway through the afternoon, Sam walked into the department, looking slightly shamefaced, accompanied by Josh Willoughby, one of their newest junior doctors.

'Josh? What's happened?' she asked.

'I had a little bit of an accident,' Josh said, hanging his head. 'I, um, might have cracked a rib.'

'While you were go-karting *on ice*.' She gave Sam a pointed look.

'It was great fun, Hayley,' Josh said. 'Don't blame Sam. It's my own fault. I was showing off, going too fast, and I missed a corner.'

'Did you hit your head or anything?' She looked at Sam. 'Has he shown any signs of concussion?'

'I didn't hit my head; I just banged my ribs. I heard a crack and it hurts, which is why I think I broke it. But I definitely don't have flail chest,' Josh said. 'I can breathe just fine. A broken rib will heal itself within a month and all I need to do now is to take painkillers— if I don't get the pain under control properly I'll breathe too shallowly and I might end up with a chest infection.'

She couldn't help smiling at his earnestness. 'Did you learn that at uni or from us?'

'A bit of both,' Josh said with a smile. 'Sam's already checked me out and I know I'm fine.'

'But the fact Sam's brought you in makes me think there might be more to it than that,' Hayley said. She looked at Sam. 'Anything you'd like to tell me?'

'I didn't have a stethoscope handy and I want to be sure there isn't a pneumothorax,' Sam said. 'There's bruising already around the area where he hit the side of the go-kart, and it's tender. It hurts when he moves or breathes deeply. I know that's standard for a cracked rib, but I just want to be sure.'

After Manchester, she thought, it wasn't surprising that Sam was totally meticulous.

'Do you think you have any shortness of breath,' she asked Josh, 'or have you had any pain near the shoulder?'

'No,' Josh said.

'OK. I want to have a listen to your chest. Would you mind taking off your top?' she asked.

'Is that what it takes to get women to ask me to take my clothes off?' Josh asked. 'I have to break a rib?'

'I'm asking,' she said sweetly, 'exactly the same question a *male* doctor would ask you.'

'Spoilsport.' He took off his top, and she winced as she saw the bruising.

'That's nasty,' she said.

'And it'll get worse over the next few days,' Josh said cheerfully. 'I'm fine, Hayley. Really.'

'Hmm.' She examined him and Sam's diagnosis was spot on, though she wasn't entirely happy with Josh's breathing. 'X-ray for you,' she said.

'I really don't nee—' Josh began.

'Yes, you do,' she cut in gently. 'Humour me on this one.'

'But you've got all the clinical signs.'

'Sometimes,' she said, 'your intuition tells you that there's a problem—and at the advanced age of thirty-two I've learned to listen to my intuition.'

'She's right,' Sam said. 'Textbooks can't teach you about hunches; that comes with experience.'

'OK. X-ray it is,' Josh said.

Hayley could see immediately from the X-ray result on her computer screen that Josh had a slight tear in his lung, caused by his broken rib; air escaping from his lung was trapped between his lung and the wall of his chest. By the time he came back to the emergency department, Josh was slightly breathless.

'I was just running too fast to get you to sign me off,' he said.

'Nice try.' She showed him the X-ray on her screen. 'OK, Josh. Forget about my hunch. This is all textbook. If this X-ray belonged to one of your patients, what would you say?'

He sighed. 'There's a pneumothorax.'

'And what are we going to do about it?'

'Unless you have underlying lung disease,' Josh said, 'the tear in your lung will mend and the problem will resolve itself over a few days.'

'And if you're breathless?' Sam prompted. 'Which you are, right now?'

'Then you need to remove the air.' Josh wrinkled his nose. 'I know this is going to sound stupid, considering how many times I'm on the other end of a syringe, but I hate needles.'

Hayley smiled and patted his shoulder. 'You'll be fine, sweetie. You know the procedure, which is probably putting scary pictures in your head because today you're on the receiving end, but you also know I'll give you a local anaesthetic so it's not going to hurt. I can't let you walk out of here struggling to breathe when you've broken a rib and got a pneumothorax from go-karting on ice.' She gave Sam a sidelong look. 'Perfectly safe, indeed,' she mouthed.

'Sorry,' he mouthed back, looking guilty.

'OK, Josh. Sharp scratch,' she said, and administered the anaesthetic. She inserted a thin tube through Josh's chest wall with the aid of a needle, then attached it to a large syringe with a three-way tap. 'That's the hard bit done,' she said.

Josh grimaced. 'I hate needles. But I guess you're not so bad at this.'

'Glad to hear it—though I'd also like to know if I need to brush up on anything, because I never want to hurt my patients unnecessarily. Not that I really want to use my team as test cases,' Hayley said with a smile. 'OK. I'm going to suck out some air into the syringe, release it through the three-way tap, and repeat until I'm sure that most of the air has gone. Happy?'

'Happy,' Josh said.

'And while you're there,' Sam added, 'we might as well test you on your knowledge of painkillers.'

Which was a brilliant way to distract the younger man, Hayley thought.

'What would you prescribe to someone with a broken rib?' Sam asked.

'Paracetamol or anti-inflammatories, and if it's moderate pain then you can alternate them two hours apart,' Josh said, 'or in really bad cases you need something stronger like codeine. And before I can prescribe anything at all I need to know if my patient's a smoker, or taking any anti-clotting medication, has high blood pressure or asthma, or any history of heart or kidney disease or stomach ulcers,' he said, ticking them off on his fingers.

'Or if they're pregnant, have a history of stroke, or they're already taking aspirin,' Hayley added. 'That's all absolutely right, Josh. Does any of it apply to you?'

'No. Though I'd be really famous if I was pregnant,' Josh said thoughtfully.

Hayley laughed. 'You certainly would. OK. We're done. Is the pain mild or moderate?'

'Moderate,' Josh said.

'Take normal doses of paracetamol and ibuprofen. Alternate them two hours apart, just as you suggested,' she said. 'If the pain's worse tomorrow, come and talk to me about codeine. Are you on shift tomorrow?'

'Not until Tuesday,' Josh said.

'OK. Go home, take painkillers and rest,' she said.

'No heavy lifting. And I want to see you straight back here in which circumstances?'

'If I get a high temperature, chest pain, I'm coughing up loads of gunge or I'm really short of breath,' Josh said.

'Good. Make sure you do. Off you go,' she said. 'And next time you want to do something exciting, please don't listen to any suggestions from Dr I-Love-Taking-Stupid-Risks Price here.'

'I won't,' Josh said.

'I'll give you a lift home,' Sam said, 'once I've grovelled a bit to Dr I-Told-You-So Clark, here.'

'I'll be in the waiting room,' Josh said with a wary look, and disappeared out of the cubicle.

'Go on, then. Say it,' Sam said with a resigned expression on his face.

'I don't need to, because you already said it for me,' Hayley said. 'Poor Josh.'

'If it makes you feel any better, I feel really guilty,' Sam said.

'All this putting yourself at risk… It doesn't make sense, Sam. Why do you do it?'

'Why are you so anti anything with the slightest bit of risk?' he asked.

This was her cue to tell him the rest of it. The thing that held her back and scared her every day.

Because my fiancé used to risk his life every single day, and he died.

But here wasn't the right place to tell him. 'Can we have this discussion later?' she asked. 'I'm on duty and the waiting room's full.'

'All right. How about I cook us fresh pasta after your shift and we'll talk then?'

'That'd be good.' And by then hopefully the hard lump currently sitting just above her breastbone would dissolve into the right words.

'Your place or mine?' he asked.

'Yours,' she said.

'OK. I'll see you at half-past six.'

At half-past six on the dot, Hayley rang Sam's doorbell.

'Can I get you a glass of wine?' he asked.

She shook her head. 'But I'd kill for a mug of tea.'

'Go and put your feet up.' He made them both a mug of tea, and carried them through into the living room. She was sitting on the sofa, and she looked bone-deep weary. Miserable. As if something had been eating away at her.

And he had a pretty fair idea was it was, given that she'd promised to talk to him about why she was so antsy about risk. 'I'm sorry about what happened to Josh, Hayley. The last thing I wanted was for anyone to get hurt.'

'It's the last thing anyone wants,' she said, 'but it still happens.' She left her mug of tea where he'd placed it on the coffee table. 'And it leaves your life utterly crumpled in its wake.'

'What happened to make you so scared of risk, Hayley?' he asked softly.

'Evan. My fiancé.' She dragged in a breath. 'He was a firefighter.'

And he'd been killed in an industrial accident.

Things started to become horribly clear. Sam had a

nasty feeling that he knew exactly what she was about to tell him—that Evan had been trying to save someone from the industrial accident and had lost his life the process.

'Evan risked his life every single day,' Hayley said. 'He'd done all the training. He was good at his job. He'd never, ever do anything reckless or put any of his crew members at risk. But, that particular day, there was a fire at a local garage and workshop. Obviously with it being a workshop, there was flammable stuff everywhere— oil, chemicals, all sorts of things that could make the fire so much worse. A propane cylinder exploded, and the fire crew managed to get two more of the propane cylinders out before they went up. But then someone said the boss had had gone back in five minutes before to rescue his cat and her kittens from the office on the mezzanine floor, and nobody had seen him since. Evan thought the guy had probably keeled over from smoke inhalation, so he went in after him.' She shuddered. 'And the building collapsed when Evan was halfway up the stairs to the mezzanine floor.'

No wonder Evan hadn't survived, Sam thought.

'The last propane cylinder was right beneath where he was when the building collapsed, and it exploded. Evan was killed instantly.' She choked on a sob. 'At least, I hope it was instant. I hope he never knew what happened, that he never felt even the slightest bit of pain or knew what was happening to him.'

'I'm sure it was instant.' Sam held her close.

And now a lot of things were clearer to him. Why she was so panicky about risk. Evan had taken a risk, going into a dangerous situation to save someone from smoke inhalation, and it had gone tragically wrong.

'He was one of the good guys. Everyone loved him. Evan was the sort who'd do anything to help anyone.' She looked Sam straight in the eye. 'He was a lot like you. He put himself in danger to help others, just like you do. Except you do all the dangerous sports stuff as well. And I can't cope with that, Sam. You love it and I feel like the world's most miserable cow, holding you back from doing something you enjoy. It isn't fair of me. But it scares the hell out of me, Sam, and I'm so tired of being scared. Of worrying that I'm going to lose you, the way I lost Evan. And I just can't understand *why* you do it. Why you put yourself in danger all the time.'

He stroked her face. How could he make her understand that it didn't have to be that way? That not all risks meant there would be a tragedy?

'I've always liked extreme sports,' he said. 'I suppose it's the adrenaline rush—it makes me feel alive.' And he'd really needed that feeling after he'd been suspended, because it meant that he was feeling something other than as if he'd been sucked into the middle of a black hole. 'I used to go climbing with my dad and Martin right from when I was small, because we lived near the Peak District and Dad loved climbing. So did my granddad. I think it's in my blood. So when I was old enough, it just made sense for me to join the mountain rescue team. And I never once had a problem on the team when I was on a rescue, not even something little like a twisted ankle or a scratch or a bruise.'

'Don't you think of the risks when you go out?'

she asked. Her voice was calm, but he could see the anguish in her eyes. 'That you could fall? That a cliff could crumble beneath you without any warning and you'd end up breaking your neck at the bottom?'

He wanted her to understand that he wasn't just being a thrill-seeker. 'I do,' he said, 'and that's why I'm careful to use the right safety procedures on a rescue, and why I only use companies that have good safety records for the leisure stuff. And, yes, I know Josh cracked a rib today at the go-karting, but...' He stopped.

'But?'

He winced. 'Now you've told me what happened to Evan, I don't know if I can say it to you.'

Her eyes widened. 'Try me.'

'I don't want to make you feel bad.'

'Say it anyway.'

'OK. But remember you asked me to tell you what was in my head.' He took a deep breath. 'Sometimes, no matter how well you plan something, accidents just happen and you can't second-guess them. That's why our department exists in the first place. Accidents happen.'

She just looked at him as if her heart was breaking.

He stroked her face. 'I'm sorry Evan died. But there are always risks in everything you do, Hayley. You might be crossing the road or walking in the middle of a park. You can't guarantee that you won't be hit by lightning, or that a branch from a tree won't give way unexpectedly and fall onto your head, or that someone's foot won't slip and hit the accelerator instead of the brakes and a car will crash into you.'

'But the chances of those kinds of things happening are so small. Whereas putting your life on the line over and over and over again,' she said, sounding anguished, 'whether it's at work or what you do for fun—it's not a matter of *if* something happens but *when*.'

'But if nobody goes to rescue people in an emergency,' he said, 'then people will die when they might have been saved.'

'I know.' She looked miserable. 'And I feel guilty about that too. I'm being selfish. But when I lost Evan it was as if I'd been sucked into a black hole. I don't want to be in that position again.'

'Would I be right in saying that Evan loved his job?' Sam asked softly.

She nodded. 'He'd always wanted to be a firefighter, right from when he was small. He loved what he did. He was good at it—whether it was putting out a fire, or rescuing someone from a broken lift, or cutting a car open so the emergency services could get the casualty to safety, or talking to kids at school... He absolutely loved it.' A single tear leaked down her cheek. 'And he *died*, Sam. He was killed on duty.'

He wiped the tear away with the pad of his thumb. 'I'm so sorry that you went through this. And I wish there was something I could do or say to make it better. But I can't bring Evan back.'

'I know. And I just...' She swallowed hard. 'I'm sorry.'

'Don't be. I'm glad you're talking to me.' And what a hypocrite he was—he'd told her next to nothing about Lynda. 'At least now I understand why you're so wary about risk.'

'And you've signed up for the MERIT team.'

'Yes, though I'm sure you already know that the MERIT team are only allowed into an area if it's safe for them to treat patients. All the risks are monitored and kept under control as much as possible,' he said gently. But he also knew that it wouldn't be enough for her. Not now she'd lost Evan to his job. 'If you want me to withdraw my name from the team, then I will.'

She shook her head. 'I can't ask you to do that.'

'You're not asking. I'm offering,' he said.

'And you'll regret it. You'll start to feel that I'm holding you back and you'll resent it. In the end, it'll come between us,' she said.

Maybe she had a point. His mountain rescue work had certainly come between him and Lynda. Then again, Lynda hadn't given him a decent reason to give it up. Only that she'd wanted him to join some tedious committee or other instead because it'd be more high-profile and look better on his CV. In Sam's view, that wasn't enough.

'Did you ever tell Evan how much his job worried you?' Sam asked.

'No. Because, actually, it didn't worry me. I used to be able to accept the risk. I suppose I thought the worst would never actually happen because I knew he was always careful.' She dragged in a breath. 'But the worst *did* happen. And now the fear gets in the way.'

'What would he say,' Sam asked carefully, 'if he was here now and you told him that his job scared you too much?'

'Pretty much what you did,' she admitted. 'And I'm not seeing you as a replacement for Evan, or anything like that, Sam. You just happen to have some similar views on life. Only he didn't do all the risky stuff for fun.'

'I can tone that down, too,' he said. 'I admit, I did quite a bit more extreme stuff after I was suspended, simply so I had something else to focus on. Something that made me feel alive instead of just dragging through every day and waiting for someone to come up with a verdict. But I can tone it down now.'

She dragged a hand through her hair. 'I shouldn't expect you to change who you are for me. It's *wrong*.'

'But you lost Evan when he was doing his job in the emergency services. Of course you're going to worry yourself sick whenever there's a major incident, especially if I'm in the MERIT team that's called out—and even more so if that incident happens to be a fire. I don't want to put you through that.'

'So either you stop doing it and you'll start to resent me for holding you back, or you keep doing it and I'm frantic with worry every time you go out. There isn't a middle way,' she said miserably.

'There could be a kind of compromise. Maybe if you come with me to some of the leisure stuff—well, possibly not to go-karting on ice,' he amended, 'but to do something with just a tiny bit of risk. Then you'll see for yourself how safe everything is and it'll stop you worrying.'

'Kind of like immunotherapy? Building it up in little doses?'

'Kind of,' he agreed. 'So it's a compromise. We can work on this together.'

She grimaced. 'I feel horrible.'

'You're not horrible.' He kissed her lightly. 'It's because you care.' She wanted him to stop doing the dangerous stuff because she cared about him and she was worried he'd be hurt or killed—not because she cared more about her long-term goals and wanted him to spend the time sucking up to 'important' people instead, the way Lynda had.

Maybe he should tell her about that.

But he rather thought Hayley had had enough for today. He wasn't going to dump his own insecurities on her right now. 'Thank you for telling me about Evan,' he said. 'I know this must've been so hard for you. And I'm sorry if I made you relive some of the nightmare.'

'I... I should've told you before. Explained more.'

'I figured you'd tell me more when you were ready,' he said.

She swallowed hard. 'I'm sorry.'

'Don't apologise.' He kissed her lightly. 'You've had a rough day and you need food. Give me five minutes—it's fresh pasta and sauce, though I'm afraid none of it's home-made—it's from the posh deli counter at the supermarket.'

She gave him a wry smile. 'A tin of spaghetti hoops on toast would've done me.'

He looked at her. 'If you'd gone home on your own, you would have just made yourself a bowl of cereal, if that.'

'Busted,' she said.

'I can't promise you that things will always be safe,' he said, 'because even in the department something could happen. A drunk could swing a punch that accidentally connects with you and knocks you out, or you could get a needle stick injury while you're treating someone with HIV, or...' He held her close. 'But if you think about all the things that *might* happen, you'll drive yourself crazy. Think about how small the chances are of something bad happening—and how big the chances are that the worst *won't* happen.'

She swallowed hard. 'The bereavement counsellor I saw last year said something like that. But I can't seem to get the risks and the worries out of my head.'

'It's going to be OK, Hayley. We'll work this through. We'll find some kind of compromise that suits both of us.' It would just take time.

And for her, Sam realised, he was more than prepared to wait. Because Hayley was special. And they had the chance of making their relationship into something really good.

CHAPTER SEVEN

FINALLY IT WAS the end of October, and Hayley finished her last bit of training with Sam on the Friday night, running the full 10K outdoors. They met up with Dani afterwards to have dinner and discuss strategies for the race itself on the Sunday. Saturday was a rest day, and then on Sunday morning at nine o'clock the three of them headed to Alexandra Park for the start of the race, getting Hayley set up with her numbered bib and the electronic tag for her shoe that would record her time.

Dani seemed a bit distracted, but Hayley put it down to the fact that her best friend was watching the race instead of running it. It was nearly three months since Dani had been diagnosed with the fractured metatarsals, and although the cast was off now she still wasn't quite back to her full mobility. Hayley knew that taking it slowly was driving Dani crackers, though at least she was watching the race with Sam—who would make her be careful, but without making her feel as if she was wrapped in cotton wool.

Which was ironic, because Hayley didn't feel as if she could make Sam be careful without wrapping him in cotton wool.

Hayley was glad the weather was dry, cool and calm; the worst thing would've been running on wet roads with a bitter wind whipping through the runners. She would be happy if she could run the course in under an hour and a quarter. The route was lined with marshals, and some of the roads had been closed off for a couple of hours for the run. The course had two laps, partly along the streets and partly in the park; she'd also been told that there were two water stations, so she wouldn't need to take a water bottle with her.

It was the first time Hayley had done a race like this in a crowd, and after the first ten minutes she was surprised to discover that she was enjoying it. Plus running in a crowd meant that she didn't miss having either Dani by her side when she'd done the interval training on the treadmill at the local gym, or Sam by her side on the outdoor training.

She was flagging a bit on the second lap, but then she saw Dani and Sam near the finish line. They were cheering her on, and it spurred her to run harder for those last few metres. And then she was over the finish line, and a few moments afterwards she was swept into a hug by both Dani and Sam. Hayley found herself unexpectedly in tears with the emotion of it all.

'You're wonderful,' Dani said. 'Because of you, we've raised a ton of money for the new equipment for the ward.'

'People donated for you,' Hayley reminded her.

'But you're the one who actually ran it.' Dani hugged her hard. 'Thank you so much.'

Hayley hugged her back and then hugged Sam.

'Thank you both. I couldn't have done it without you training with me.'

He picked her up, swung her round and kissed her. 'You did brilliantly. I'm so proud of you.' Then he set her back on her feet and rested his forehead against hers as he realised what he'd just given away. 'Sorry. I know we were keeping this between us, but I kind of assumed Dani would know as she's your best friend.'

'She'd kept it sort of quiet, but I'd already guessed from the way you two look at each other,' Dani said with a smile, 'and it's a good thing.'

'Come on, let's go get your time,' Sam said to Hayley, 'and then I'm taking you both out for refuelling.'

Hayley was thrilled to discover she'd run the 10K in one hour, ten minutes and thirteen seconds.

'That's a personal best,' Dani said, 'and that's a really respectable time, especially for your first official run.'

'Seconded,' Sam said. 'As I said before, I'm so proud of you.'

'It doesn't mean I'm going to be a runner,' Hayley warned, 'because I'd much rather do dance aerobics. But I have to admit, I enjoyed it and I'm glad I did it.'

'Good.' Sam held her hand all the way into town, then found a table in one of the cafés on the high street and went to order pastries and coffees for all of them.

While he was at the counter, Dani said gently, 'You look happier than I've seen you since Evan died. You've fallen for him, haven't you? And Sam's lovely. I'm really pleased for you.'

'Yes, I've fallen for him,' Hayley admitted. 'It's not

just the physical stuff. It's who he is and how he makes me feel.'

'But?' Dani asked.

Hayley bit her lip. 'I still can't quite get past the way he's not bothered about putting himself in danger.'

'Which is understandable, because of the way you lost Evan,' Dani said. 'But that was an accident, Haze. A horrible, tragic accident. It isn't necessarily going to repeat itself.'

'I know. I have to deal with the panic. I have no idea how I'm going to cope when Sam gets called out on a MERIT case—I'll fret the whole time he's away until I know he's safe,' Hayley admitted.

'Talk to him,' Dani advised.

'I already have. I told him what happened to Evan and he understands how I feel.' She grimaced. 'But I still need time to get my head round it.'

Later in the week, Hayley and Sam had a couple of days off duty.

'We could go to London Zoo,' Sam said. 'I'd love to see the lions and tigers. And I read somewhere you can walk alongside the canal from Regent's Park to Camden Lock—it looks as if it's going to be dry, so how about it?'

'Great idea,' Hayley said.

And she thoroughly enjoyed wandering hand in hand with him around the zoo, seeing the lions and tigers up close, along with the gorillas and the giraffes, although her favourites were the penguins.

Because it was half-term, there were plenty of children walking around with their parents, and at that moment Hayley could just imagine herself and Sam in the same position—taking a few days off together in the school holidays, and going to see the sights. The Zoo, the Aquarium, the dinosaurs at the Natural History Museum…

'Penny for them?' Sam asked.

She smiled. 'Just wool-gathering.' They were still in the relatively early stages of their relationship, and they hadn't even had a casual discussion about how they saw their futures. She had no idea how he felt about long-term relationships or children. 'So have you got any idea what to get for your Secret Santa present?' she asked instead.

'Ah, now—that's supposed to be confidential,' he said with a smile. 'I might cheat and talk to my mum.'

'So you've got someone older and female.'

'Not necessarily. It might be someone younger and male.'

'In which case you wouldn't need to ask your mum.'

'Enough with the detective stuff,' he said, laughing. 'So when does all the Christmas stuff start here?'

'Not until the first of December,' she said. 'Mike's strict about that. And obviously for health and safety reasons we can only decorate the reception area. But basically on the first of December the tree goes up and everyone takes a decoration from the box when they come on shift and puts it on a branch. That way we all kind of decorate the tree together.'

'That's a nice idea,' he said. 'I like that. And there's the Christmas meal.'

'Don't forget the dancing afterwards. Mike's dad dancing is not to be missed,' she said with a grin. 'I guess we're not quite as Christmassy as some of the departments—the children's ward always has Santa coming round and the Friends of the Hospital always buy a little present for every child who's in, as well as something for their siblings.'

'Whereas we're more likely to be patching up Santa when he's off duty and either ended up being hit in the pub when he's trying to stop a fight, or when he's put his back out from lifting a present that's too heavy for him,' he said wryly.

'Exactly. Christmas Day can be a bit grim in the department if family tensions have gone too far,' she agreed.

'Well, we've got six weeks to prepare for it. Though I think I'm getting a bit sick of the Christmas music and Christmas goodies in the shops already.'

'Bah, humbug,' she said. 'Are you telling me you don't like Christmas?'

'Oh, I like Christmas,' he said. 'I hate present-shopping, so the internet's been brilliant for that, but I love spending time with my family and playing silly games and eating too much rich food and watching all the old classic Christmas films. My mum always cries her eyes out over *It's a Wonderful Life*.'

'So does mine. And Dani and I always watch *Love Actually*.' She bit her lip. 'Last Christmas was horrible. Dani's marriage was just about to collapse, I had to face my first Christmas without Evan, and even though we were busy at work I just…' She lifted one shoulder in a half-shrug. 'Well. This year will be better. I'm over that year of firsts—the hardest bit.'

'I think this Christmas will be better for me, too,'

Sam said thoughtfully. 'I mean, it wasn't super-horrible, but Lynda's family is very different from mine and we spent Christmas with them last year. They don't like bad cracker jokes or silly games. And they wouldn't dream of making sandwiches from the left-over turkey and going climbing on Boxing Day morning.'

'To be fair, mine wouldn't either,' she said. 'Go climbing, I mean.'

'What about the silly games and the cracker jokes?'

'Oh, they do all of them. Board games are the best.' She grinned. 'Though the rules change halfway through. And there are forfeits. And you get made to sing Christmas songs really loudly, whether you can sing or not. No singing, no supper.'

'That,' he said, 'works for me.' He paused. 'So we might get to spend Christmas together this year?'

'We might.' And Hayley was shocked by how much she liked the idea. 'I guess it depends on the duty roster,' she said lightly.

'We need to promise mince pies and chocolate Yule Log to the duty roster fairy,' he said.

She laughed. 'We can try.'

'Ready to go and grab some lunch?' he asked. 'According to the website I looked up, it's about a fifteen-minute walk from here to Camden.'

'Sounds good,' she said, and walked down path by the canal with him, enjoying the views.

They'd been walking for about ten minutes when they heard a scream.

'My little boy's fallen in! Help! I can't swim!'

Sam ran off in the direction of the scream, with Hayley behind him.

There was a woman with a pram at the side of the canal, clearly frantic; when Hayley looked into the water, she could see a child floating face-down.

'It's too far to reach him from the side of the canal. Even if there was a pole nearby, it'd be useless because he's probably unconscious and couldn't grab it. I'm going in,' Sam said, stripping off his coat and shoes.

Before she could say another word, he'd jumped straight into the water, without a second thought of what might be beneath the surface. Part of Hayley was horrified, but then her professional training kicked in and she grabbed her phone and called the emergency services. Although the handler answered on the second ring, it felt as if time had slowed down massively. 'A child's fallen into the Regent Canal.' She gave their location. 'Someone with me is getting him out, but when we saw him he was face-down and I think we'll need an ambulance.'

'We're dispatching one now,' the handler said. 'Can you stay on the line and keep us informed?'

'Yes,' she said. 'Actually, I'll get his mum to speak to you, because she can answer any questions you have about him for the paramedics.' She placed her hand on the woman's arm. 'I've got the emergency services on the phone. An ambulance is on its way, but they want us to keep them informed with what's happening.'

'My boy. Oh, my God. My boy,' the woman said, her voice raw with anguish.

At that moment, the baby woke up and started to scream.

'I'm a doctor—so's my partner,' Hayley said. She rocked the pram in a desperate attempt to calm the baby. 'We'll do our best for your boy, but I need you to talk to the emergency services. They need to know about your son. Can you do that for me?'

'Oh, my God.'

She really needed the woman to get past her panic and help them. 'I need to help Sam to get your boy out. I'm Hayley. What's your name?'

'Alice.'

'And your little boy?'

'Jack.'

'All right, Alice. Keep rocking the baby for me.' She handed her phone to the woman. 'The emergency services are on the line. They'll ask you questions about Jack, things they need to know that I wouldn't be able to tell them but you'll know the answers because you're his mum. And I'll also tell you things to say to them. Is that OK?'

'OK.' Alice was shaking, her face white with terror, but to Hayley's relief she put the phone to her ear and used her other hand to rock the pram.

Hayley went to the side of the canal and knelt down. Sam had just reached the side with the little boy, and Hayley leaned over and took the child from him.

It was very clear that the child wasn't breathing.

'ABC and CPR,' she said quietly to Sam.

He nodded, and while he was hauling himself out of the canal, she laid the child on the pavement and checked his airway. She fished water weed out of his mouth, then tilted his head back with one hand and lifted his chin with the other. She couldn't see any signs of breathing, and when she put her ear to the little boy's mouth and nose she couldn't hear or feel any signs of breathing, either. And there was no pulse.

She pinched the child's nose and put her lips over his mouth, and counted to two seconds in her head while she gave a slow full breath. She could see his chest rise and fall, and did a second breath.

'I'll do the compressions while you breathe,' Sam said; he put the heel of his hand on the middle of the little boy's breastbone and started counting as he gave the chest compressions.

She called to Alice, 'Tell them we've got Jack out and we started CPR ten seconds ago.'

She gave two more rescue breaths and checked for a pulse.

'Nothing,' she said quietly to Sam, and he continued with the compressions.

'Alice—do you have any clothes or spare blankets, anything dry?' she called.

'I've only got a change of clothes for the baby,' Alice said.

Thankfully the rocking had soothed the baby enough for the screams to die down to little whimpers.

'Is Jack breathing yet?' Alice asked, looking frantic.

'We're working on it—try not to worry, because this often happens when small children fall into very cold water,' Hayley said. Her own coat was dry; that would do to help cover Jack and keep him warm once they'd got the little boy breathing again.

Between her and Sam, they continued to do rescue breathing, checking for a pulse, and chest compressions. It felt as if they'd been working for ever, but neither of them intended to stop; given the temperature of the water and the little boy's age, there was still a good chance that Jack could recover.

And then finally he gasped and spluttered.

Hayley called, 'Alice, tell them Jack's taken his first spontaneous breath now.' She checked his pulse. 'And tell them there's spontaneous cardiac output now.'

Alice duly repeated what Hayley had said, but it was obvious to her that Alice hadn't taken it in. 'He's breathing on his own and he's got a pulse—tell them we're putting him in the recovery position.'

She stripped off her coat and covered Jack with it to help avoid hypothermia setting in. Alice was still shaking and tears were running down her face, so Hayley gently took the phone from her and spoke to the handlers. 'The ambulance is going to be here any second now,' she said to Sam.

Within a few moments, they could hear the siren of the ambulance, and the paramedics rushed up.

Between them Hayley and Sam gave the handover to the paramedics.

'The call centre told us the exact times you started CPR, his first spontaneous breath and his first spontaneous cardiac output,' the lead paramedic said. 'Thank God you were able to get the poor little scrap out.' They carefully removed the wet clothes from the little boy and wrapped him in a warm dry blanket.

'This is Alice, Jack's mum,' Hayley said.

'Alice, we're going to take Jack to hospital,' the paramedic said. She glanced at the pram. 'We can take you and the baby with us, the pram as well. You'll see us hook Jack up to various machines in the back of the ambulance but don't worry, it's all standard procedure because we need to monitor his heart rate and oxygen levels on the way. At the hospital they'll continue monitoring him for a while and do tests to check that he doesn't have any injury to his neck or spine.'

Alice nodded. 'Thank you.' She turned to Sam and Hayley. 'And thank you both so much—without you, he would be dead.' She was clearly fighting to hold back the tears. 'He would have drowned. I don't know what I can do to thank you.'

'No need.' Sam waved away her thanks with a smile. 'We're both emergency doctors so this is our job—it's just we were on the side of the canal today instead of at the hospital.'

'Let us know how he is, later today,' Hayley said, and gave Alice her phone number.

Once the paramedics had taken Jack, Alice and the baby to the ambulance, Hayley turned to Sam. 'We need to get you into dry clothes,' she said.

'We're hardly going to persuade a taxi driver to take us back to my place in this state,' he said ruefully, looking down at his soaked clothes. 'Do you know if we're near any shops?'

'There's Camden market,' she said.

He stripped off his top and his socks, then put his coat and shoes on. 'Hopefully they'll let me just buy the stuff and change in their changing rooms.'

'Let's get you some dry clothes, and then a hot drink,' she said.

It didn't take him long to buy a pair of jeans, a sweater and underwear; once he'd changed into dry clothes, Sam turned to her. 'Do you mind if we go back to my place for the hot drink?' he asked. 'I stink of canal water and I could really do with a shower.'

'Yes, of course.'

Hayley didn't say anything on the way back to Sam's, using the noise of the train on the tube tracks as an excuse not to talk. But inside she was a mass of seething emotions.

He'd jumped straight into the water. Not a single glance first to check if it was safe. And there was no way you could see to the bottom of the canal. He could have been caught in water weed and been unable to get back to the surface; or he could have been caught on rusty, twisted metal that someone had dumped at the bottom of the canal. If there were rats around—and there probably were—then he might have been infected by Weil's disease.

Worse still, Sam *knew* her fears. He would've known that she would worry even before he'd jumped into the canal. He'd said about trying to compromise, taking him with her to the adrenaline junkie stuff he liked so she could see it was safe, gradually overcoming her fears. Yet today he'd gone straight in without trying to find a safer way to rescue the little boy...

Then she was angry at herself. Of *course* he'd reacted by jumping in and rescuing the little boy. That was who Sam was. He saw a problem and he fixed it. He didn't hold back or wait for someone to take the lead. He just did it.

And she was holding him back with her fears.

He'd done a brave thing today. A wonderful thing. He'd saved a child's life. Instead of celebrating that and praising him, she was being selfish and thinking of the possible loss to herself. Fearing that she'd end up being lost and bereft again, the way she'd been when Evan had been killed.

Back at Sam's flat, she made two mugs of tea on autopilot while he showered. When he walked back into the kitchen, still damp from the shower, he looked at her. 'Do you need sugar in yours?'

'I don't take sugar.'

'Sweet tea's meant to be good for shock.'

'That's a myth,' she said. 'And I'm in not in shock.'

'You haven't said a word since we got on the tube. What's wrong?'

'I…' She blew out a breath. 'You saved that little boy's life.'

He shrugged. 'Anyone else would have done the same.'

No, they wouldn't. Not the way Sam had done it. The scary way. 'You went straight in without thinking of the danger to yourself.'

The critical tone in Hayley's voice touched a raw nerve. Right now, she sounded like Lynda. Sam hadn't lived up to Lynda's expectations; Hayley's tone made him wonder if he was making the same mistake all over again. 'This isn't about the little boy, is it?'

'No. Because now I've seen you in action in an emergency, Sam, and you lied to me. You don't even think of your own safety before you act.'

'What was I supposed to do—let him drown?'

'No, of course not.'

'There wasn't an alternative to going in there myself. Surely you could see that, too? Even if there had been a life-saving pole, he wouldn't have been able to grab it and hold on until I could pull him in. It was the only way to rescue him.'

'I know, and don't you realise how much I hate myself for this? I can't get past the fear, Sam, I just can't, and I hate the idea of losing you, and you *know* why I feel this way.' Her voice had risen almost to a wail. 'I've been here before.'

'So you're angry with me?' She was blaming him for making her remember Evan's death?

'Yes. And I'm even more angry with myself, because I know this is who you are and I shouldn't want to change you.'

Her words took some of the fight out of him. This wasn't another Lynda situation and he was over-reacting. Hayley was as upset with herself as she was with him. He wrapped his arms around her. 'I'm sorry.'

'I'm sorry, too. It's wrong of me to feel this way.'

That was true. 'It's also understandable.' He stroked her hair.

'I worry that it'll be the same on a MERIT call-out. That you'll put yourself in danger—if they tell you it's not safe to go in but you think you can rescue someone, you're doing it anyway.'

'I wouldn't take stupid risks.'

'You just did,' she pointed out. 'So that doesn't re-assure me at all.'

He sighed. 'Lynda hated my mountain rescue work.'

'Your ex? She worried about you like I do?'

'Not quite. You worry that I'll be hurt or worse. She worried that mountain rescue work wasn't high-profile enough and I could have spent my time on some finance committee instead.'

She pulled back, frowning. 'Why on earth would you be on a finance committee?'

'To give my career a boost.'

'But you're a doer, not a talker.'

'It wasn't how Lynda saw things. She wanted to change me, too—to make me into someone I wasn't.'

Hayley bit her lip. 'I'm sorry.' Then her frown deepened. 'What did she want you to be?'

'The CEO of a hospital, eventually.'

'But then you'd spend your days in an office and dealing with admin and politics, not patients. And I don't think that would make you happy.'

Sam realised that Hayley understood him, and the rest of his anger dissolved.

'Is that why you broke up with her?' she asked.

'Yes. Though Lynda was the one who ended it. I guess I was a bit self-deluded. I thought she'd eventually realise this is who I am and I can't change.'

'I'm not asking you to change. Just to…maybe see the risks and think them through.' She looked at him. 'Do you want to be a CEO?'

'No. I'm not interested in managing staff and premises. If I'd wanted to be a CEO, I would have studied economics or law and gone into finance,' he said. 'I just want to work with patients. Though I'm not an unambitious wimp,' he added.

Hayley looked surprised. 'Of course you're not. Is that what she thought?'

'She thought I should have gone for promotion much more quickly than I did.'

'She obviously wasn't a medic, then,' Hayley said dryly, 'or she'd know that you can't cut corners on your training.'

'Actually, she's a paediatrician. And she's already a consultant.'

'Oh. Is she older than us?'

'No. But she's on several committees. She's a mover and a shaker. And very, very ambitious.' Sam blew out a breath. 'I guess she thought I held her back.'

'That's a shame. For both of you.'

'Maybe it's why we both dragged our feet about setting a date for the wedding,' he said. 'Maybe neither of us was prepared to admit we'd made a mistake. I wasn't what she really wanted, because I don't care about politics and power.'

'Was she what you wanted?' Hayley asked softly.

'I thought so, when I met her. But I know now that I want someone who'll support me instead of criticising me all the time.'

And Hayley had been critical of him—not just now, but ever since he'd been in London. She'd gone on and on about the adrenaline junkie stuff. And she hadn't been fair to him. 'I'm sorry. I wasn't trying to undermine you.'

'I know. You worried about me getting hurt. There's a difference,' he said.

'I was still criticising you.' She rested her head against his shoulder. 'I don't care whether you're a CEO or you're right at the bottom of the ladder, as long as you enjoy what you do. Life's too short to do a job you hate.' She swallowed hard. 'Though I can't help the way I feel about the risky stuff.'

'I'll try to think before I leap, in future. Literally as well as metaphorically.' He paused. 'Today made me realise how much I've missed diving. I was going to volunteer for the local search and rescue team—but I'm guessing that would be too much for you.'

'I'd spend the whole time worrying that you'd be caught on something at the bottom of the river and the air in your tank would run out, or a derelict building would crash down around you,' she admitted.

'The chances of that happening are about as small as being hit by lightning,' he pointed out. 'Especially when I've got a team keeping an eye on me. There are people monitoring a diver's air and depth and they'll spot the signs if something's wrong and get someone down there to rescue a stuck diver.'

'I know all that, in my head—but there's huge a difference between knowing something logically and knowing it emotionally,' she told him.

'I guess.' He held her close. 'I don't have any answers right now, but at least we're talking about the problem. We'll find a compromise. It'll just take time. And patience.'

And he definitely had patience—because he was falling for Hayley. Apart from his physical attraction to her, he liked her. She was sweet and funny and kind. And she was completely terrified of the stuff he loved doing... But they'd work something out. He was sure of it. It would just take a little time.

CHAPTER EIGHT

Michael Harcourt, the head of the department, waited for all the emergency staff on duty to gather in the department, his expression serious. 'Everyone, we've got a major incident situation,' he said. 'There's been a big industrial fire at the other side of Muswell Hill in a clothing factory—at the moment the fire crew think it's likely to be an electrical fault that caused it. Obviously with cotton and other flammable material in the stockroom, the flames took hold very quickly. We need to triage all walk-ins, the same as we triage people coming in from the fire—obviously we need to treat the majors and the resus cases here, but refer all the walk-ins with minor injuries to local pharmacists, their family doctors or the next nearest emergency department. All our ambulances are on the way to the factory right now, and there's a MERIT coming in from Islington.'

Adrenaline surged through Hayley, mingled with relief. MERIT doctors were never used from the hospital that was receiving the casualties from a major incident because they were needed in their own department. So at least Sam would be out of the way of the fire. The very last thing she wanted was for Sam to be anywhere near a fire.

She pushed back the memories of the last big industrial fire they'd had to deal with in the department. The fire that had claimed Evan's life. *Not now.* She had to focus on saving the lives of the patients who were brought in by ambulance.

'We know we have casualties with burns and with smoke inhalation, but what we don't know is how many or how serious their conditions are. The burns unit is on standby, and I've called all the staff in. You all know the drill, so we're on code red,' Michael said. 'Any questions?'

When none were forthcoming, he read out the roster; Sam and Hayley were both rostered to Resus, dealing with the most serious casualties.

Michael took Hayley to one side before she headed to Resus. 'Are you all right, Hayley?'

'Yes.' As long as she focused on their patients and didn't think about the reason why they were being admitted, she'd be OK.

'Good. But I have a fair idea of how difficult this is going to be for you. If it gets too much, then you step out,' he said. 'And that's an order.'

'Got it.' She squeezed his hand. 'Thank you.'

'We always look after our own in this department,' he said.

The walking wounded were the first to come in—some with burns, and some still coughing after inhaling smoke. The Casualty Clearing Station had triaged them already; anyone who could walk was coded as a Priority Three, meaning they needed treatment but it could be delayed until the more urgent cases had been seen, and they had green tags for easy identification. Priority Two were intermediate cases, more serious than P3s, and the patients had yellow tags; and Priority One cases were the most urgent and the patients would die without immediate intervention; they had red tags and were most likely to go straight into Resus.

But triage was always an ongoing situation, Hayley knew; someone who had a chest injury might be classed as a P3, but if they developed a pneumothorax they'd become a P2 until that was dealt with. So there would be a second layer of triage before they saw their patients, to see if anyone's condition had changed and become more serious.

Sam was waiting for her to join him in Resus. 'Are you OK?' he asked.

'I'm fine,' she said. 'As long as I'm too busy to think.'

'Do you want me to have a word with Michael and see if he can swap you to a different area, given that the cases we get in Resus—?'

'Thank you,' she cut in, pretty sure that he meant that the Resus cases were the serious ones, the ones where they were most likely to lose someone—and, given that it was a fire, this was way too close to the day she'd lost Evan. 'I appreciate your support, but Michael's already told me to step out if it gets too much. And I'd rather be in Resus, where I know I'm going to be too busy to think. Where I really need to concentrate on my patients.'

'OK. But promise you'll tell me if you need anything at all,' he said, squeezing her hand briefly.

'Thanks. But I'll cope.'

She and Sam helped to treat the minor injuries while they were waiting for the more serious cases to come in, cleaning burns and applying dressings and giving information sheets on how to care for the burns at home and when to seek further medical help.

Their first case was a man who'd been working in the stock room when the materials had suddenly blazed up, trapping him. The fire crew had managed to get him out, but not before he'd suffered severe burns.

'Peter Freeman, aged fifty,' Dev, the senior paramedic, told them. 'We've intubated him and he's been on high-flow oxygen.' He handed them a bag. 'We removed what's left of his clothing and his jewellery, and it's all safely in here. We've used a cling film dressing on his burns and put a cold wet towel on top of that to cool him down—he's been cooling for about fifteen minutes now.'

It was important to cool the burned area as quickly as possible, but at the same time they needed to be careful of the risk of hypothermia, Hayley knew.

'We've cannulated him and we started him on a litre of warmed fluid on the way in,' Dev said. 'And we've given him some initial pain relief.'

'Great—thanks, Dev,' Sam said. 'And I see you've got him sitting up.'

'Most of the burns are to his chest, arms and face,' Dev said. Sitting the patient upright lessened the risk of swelling—and it was particularly important to avoid swelling of the throat when burns to the head and neck were involved.

'Mr Freeman, my name's Hayley and this is Sam,

and we're going to look after you here in the emergency department at Muswell Hill Hospital,' Hayley said. 'You've got a tube in to help you breathe, so you won't be able to talk, but if we do anything that makes you uncomfortable, please just lift your hand and we'll stop, OK? And we'll talk you through everything we're doing so you know what's going on. We're going to start with taking a tiny bit of blood from you so we can run some tests, OK?'

Mr Freeman managed a tiny nod.

She took a sample of blood and sent it for urgent haemoglobin, cross-matching and coagulation screen.

'And now we're going to take the wet towels and the dressings off so we can assess your burns, clean them and put new dressings on,' Hayley said. 'I know it's going to be uncomfortable, but we'll be as gentle as we can.'

Between them, Hayley and Sam gently unwrapped the towel and the dressings. The skin on his upper torso and the back of Mr Freeman's hands and forearms, which had clearly taken the brunt of the injury where he'd tried to shield his face from the flames, was dry and white, with no blisters; there was no capillary refill.

Working to the rule of nines—where you could estimate the body surface area affected by using multiples of nine—they assessed the extent of Peter Freeman's injuries.

'Over twenty per cent, full-thickness burns,' Sam said quietly. 'He's going to need surgery.' Removing the burned skin and tissues would help to prevent infection and allow the wounds to heal.

'And we need to watch out for shock,' she said. The cling film dressing would have helped to stop leakage of plasma and blood—but the bigger the burn area, the bigger the likelihood of the patient sustaining hypovolaemic shock. This was where the circulatory system couldn't provide enough oxygenated blood to the body, so the vital organs were deprived of oxygen. The problem was that the most common signs of shock—pallor, clammy skin, and shallow breathing—were masked by Mr Freeman's condition and the fact that he was intubated. 'We need to put CVP line in so we can keep an eye on his blood pressure, I think.'

Sam nodded.

'Mr Freeman, we need to be able to measure your blood pressure, so I'm going to put a special catheter in your arm to let us do that. Is that OK?' Hayley asked.

He gave a tiny nod.

She explained the procedure to him and why they needed to do it, and then between them she and Sam inserted a central venous catheter. At least now they'd have an indication of his blood pressure and it would also help them to manage fluid replacement.

'We might need to do an escharotomy, too,' Sam said quietly. The burned skin could act like a tourniquet if there was swelling and oedema in the tissues underneath the burn, and cause problems with the circulation; where the chest was concerned, it could also cause problems breathing because the lungs couldn't expand properly. Putting an incision through the burned skin relieved the pressure and stopped the circulatory problems.

They cleaned the burns, then covered them with a

pad and gauze bandage; covering the exposed nerve endings helped to reduce the pain.

'We're going to send you through to the burns unit, Mr Freeman,' Sam said. 'They'll be able to keep monitoring you and they'll be able to check your dressing and make sure there isn't any infection. You're going to need to have surgery and skin grafts on your chest and arms, but the surgeon upstairs will talk that through with you.'

Once Mr Freeman had been transferred to the burns unit, they had another patient in with burns, this time to her legs.

Sam introduced them both quickly. 'Mrs Marchant, we're going to assess your burns,' he said, 'and then we'll clean them and put dressings on. We'll talk you through everything we're doing, but let us know if you're worried about anything.'

'I... I've never been so scared in my life,' she said.

Hayley noted the hoarseness of the woman's voice. Was it because she'd been crying or maybe straining to make her voice heard at the factory, or was it an early sign of problems with smoke inhalation?

'Mrs Marchant, can I ask you to cough and spit for me?' she asked, handing their patient a tissue.

Mrs Marchant looked confused, but nodded, and coughed and spat into the tissue that Hayley gave her.

Hayley took a brief look at the sputum and relaxed. There were no signs of soot, which would've signalled potentially serious problems, and there was no sign of cyanosis around Mrs Marchant's mouth. All the same, she said, 'Just before we look at your burns, I want to double-check your breathing, because if you've inhaled smoke it can give you carbon monoxide poisoning.'

'Like the thing people get if they sleep in a house with a dodgy boiler, or in a tent with one of those disposable barbecue things?'

'Exactly,' Hayley said.

Her level of consciousness was fine; although her pulse rate and blood pressure were both raised, that was most probably a reaction to the terrifying event she'd been caught up in. Hayley listened to Mrs Marchant's chest; everything sounded normal, and her breathing looked normal, too. Mrs Marchant had clearly been crying, so the hoarseness was probably due to that. But, with smoke inhalation and carbon monoxide poisoning, things could change rapidly. She needed a blood sample analysed for carboxyhaemoglobin, to see how serious the carbon monoxide poisoning was. 'I'm just going to take a small sample of blood for testing,' she said.

'I used to hate needles. But they're like nothing after you've been in a fire and don't think you're going to get out in time,' Mrs Marchant said, sounding shaky.

Was that how it had been for Evan? Those last few moments, knowing that he wasn't going to get out?

She pushed the thought aside.

Not now.

Focus.

'We'll assess your burns now,' she said.

These were deep dermal burns: the skin was dry, cherry red and blotchy, and there were blisters. There was no capillary refill, she noticed.

'We'd like to check where you can feel things,' Sam said, 'so I'd like you to close your eyes for me, Mrs Marchant. I'm going to touch the skin on your legs with a piece of cotton wool, and I'd like you to tell me when you can feel it. Is that OK?'

'Yes,' she said, and closed her eyes.

He dabbed the cotton wool lightly against their patient's skin; Hayley knew that he needed to touch rather than stroke, because a moving sensation was conducted along pain pathways and wouldn't tell them where she actually felt sensation.

By the time Sam had finished and said that Mrs Marchant could open her eyes again, she looked terrified. 'I couldn't feel anything. Does that mean I'm not going to walk again or something?'

'No,' Sam reassured her. 'It means that you have deep dermal burning.'

'What's that? Second degree? Third degree?'

'In between,' he said. 'It's not as serious as full-thickness burns—what we used to call third degree—so you'll recover without needing surgery. With this sort of burn, it's common not to be able to feel anything on your skin. It will heal within the next three to eight weeks, but you will be left with some scarring.'

She put a hand to her mouth, and a tear trickled down her cheek. 'My husband always said my legs were my best feature.'

'Your husband,' Hayley said softly, 'will just be glad you're alive. He won't care about the scarring. It's *you* that matters.' And she knew that from bitter, bitter experience. She wouldn't have cared if Evan had come home with scars. She'd just wanted him *home*.

* * *

Hayley's face had no colour in it at all, Sam noticed.

'Do you need five minutes?' he asked her quietly.

'No. I'll manage. The patients always come first.'

This must be so hard for her, he thought, remembering his own nightmare case. But it was typical of Hayley to put the patients before her own feelings. And maybe keeping busy and keeping her focus on her patients would stop her remembering the worst of the day that Evan had been killed.

They were in the middle of cleaning and dressing Mrs Marchant's burns, careful not to burst the blisters, when a middle-aged man came into the room. 'Brenda? Brenda Marchant?' he asked. 'The nurse said she was in here. She said I could come and find her.'

'Over here,' Sam called.

The man rushed over to them.

'Oh—Timmy.' Mrs Marchant burst into tears, and her husband hugged her fiercely.

'Oh, God—when I heard it on the news, I thought I'd lost you. I went to the factory and they told me they'd sent you here.'

'My legs,' she said. 'They're burned. They're going to be scarred. I'm going to be ugly.'

'No, you're not. And I don't care if you've got scars, as long as you're all right.'

Sam glanced at Hayley and saw a film of tears in her eyes. She'd been in precisely that position last year. And he was pretty sure that she wouldn't have minded a few scars if her fiancé had at least made it out of the building alive.

'Sorry, am I getting in the way?' Mr Marchant asked.

'You thought you'd lost her. Of course you want to be with her. Give her another hug, and then if you wouldn't mind sitting to the side, that's fine,' Hayley said.

But Sam heard the crack in her voice. *You thought you'd lost her.*

She'd been there. The difference was, in her case, her worst fears had been confirmed.

Once they'd finished dressing Mrs Marchant's wounds, explained everything to her husband and sent her out into the department for continued monitoring from the inhalation risk, Sam turned to Hayley. 'Coffee break. Now.'

'We haven't got time,' she protested.

'Hydration's important,' he said, 'because this is going to be a long day. We're taking five minutes to grab a coffee, stick enough cold water in it so we can gulp it straight down, and maybe grab a sandwich.' He wrinkled his nose. 'Technically, you're my superior so I can't pull rank. But I can still nag. And I'm nagging now.'

'I'm fine.'

'You don't look it,' he said.

She lifted her chin. 'I'm fine.'

She was far from fine, he was sure, but maybe now wasn't the time or place to push it. 'OK, coffee and food.'

As he'd suggested, they grabbed half a cup of coffee each, poured enough cold water in it so was cool enough to drink straight down, and shared the first pack of sandwiches they could grab from the vending machine.

Their next patient was a man who'd inhaled smoke and fallen unconscious.

'He was identified by one of his colleagues as Keith Cooper. We're not sure of his age—mid-forties, perhaps,' the paramedic said. 'His chest wall moved normally and symmetrically,' the paramedic continued, 'but the cyanosis was obvious so we intubated him and put him on high-flow oxygen. He hasn't regained consciousness yet.'

'OK. I'm glad you intubated him before the oedema caused by the inhalation made it impossible. Thanks,' Sam said.

He took a blood sample for analysis; if it turned out that more than ten per cent of the total haemoglobin was carboxyhaemoglobin, they'd give Keith some protein thromboprophylaxis as well as keeping him on high flow oxygen. If he'd inhaled carbon particles or toxic fumes, there was a risk of tracheobronchitis and pneumonia.

Between them, they checked Keith's pulse rate, blood pressure and circulation.

'There's some singeing of his eyebrows and around his nose,' Hayley said.

'We've got him on oxygen and a drip, and there's not much more we can do until he's conscious again and the blood results are back,' Sam said. 'I think we should send him up to the burns unit because he's going to need mechanical ventilation for a while.'

'Agreed,' she said.

They alternated between seeing burns victims and smoke inhalation victims for the rest of the day. Sam kept an eye on Hayley, ready to support her if she had the slightest wobble; but she was completely professional and focused on their patients' needs. Then again, he hadn't expected anything else from her. He'd liked her strength and calmness right from the outset, when he'd first seen her helping a middle-aged man with an asthma attack and no inhaler.

While they were between patients, one of the firefighters came in to see them.

'Haze! I heard you were in here so I've sneaked in for thirty seconds to say hello. You doing OK?' He gave her a one-armed hug, which she returned.

'Joe! It's good to see you.' She frowned. 'What happened to you?'

'The building collapsed on us,' he said. 'I got caught by a bit of falling debris. Bust my shoulder.'

Sam noticed that she went white again at the firefighter's words.

Wasn't that how Evan had been killed—the building had collapsed on him?

'I'm fine,' Joe said. 'Just cross that I didn't get out of the way in time.'

'Uh-huh,' she said.

'I know you're busy, and I'll let you get on, but I had to come in to say a quick hello. Don't be a stranger, Haze. We've missed you.'

'Give my love to the crew,' she said.

'I will. Take care,' Joe said, and walked out of Resus.

When they'd finally processed all the casualties from the fire and the waiting room had returned to just the normal kind of evening cases, it was time to go home. And Sam made sure he was waiting by Hayley's locker when she walked into the staffroom.

'Someone very wise once cornered me when I'd had a really bad day and she made me put one foot in front of the other,' he said softly.

She just looked at him and said nothing.

Yeah. He knew how that felt. 'I think,' he said, 'that's the sort of day you've had. So I'm taking you back to my place and cooking you dinner. Nothing fancy. Whatever I've got in the fridge, which could be anything from cheese on toast to pasta and pesto.'

She shook her head. 'I'm not hungry.'

And he knew that tone, too. Where you'd reached the bottom and you had nothing left to give. When you needed someone to take the burden of thinking from you.

'I don't care if you're not hungry. You need to eat. Get your stuff.'

Dully, she took her things from her locker. She let him put his arm round her and shepherd her out of the hospital.

'What about your bike?' she said when they went out of the hospital gates.

'It can stay here overnight and I'll walk in tomorrow,' Sam said. 'It's not a problem. Come on. We're going home.'

CHAPTER NINE

SAM TOOK HAYLEY back to his flat. Just as she'd done for him on the day when Pauline Jacobs had had a silent heart attack in the department, he simply got her to do a simple task to take her mind off things; he asked her to lay the table in his kitchen while he made them both an omelette.

'There's water in the fridge,' he said, 'and there's a bag of salad, a box of baby plum tomatoes and some dressing. You know where the crockery and cutlery are.'

She busied herself putting the salad in a bowl and pouring them both some water; by the time she was done, he was ready to serve up.

She picked at her omelette, and ate about half of it.

'I'm sorry,' she said. 'You've gone to all this trouble, and I...'

A single tear spilled down her cheek and she lapsed into silence, as if all the pain inside had grown so much that it blocked her words from coming out.

Sam knew what that felt like. When everything seemed hopeless and you were choking with misery. So he pushed his chair back, went round to her side of the table, scooped her out of her chair then sat down in her place and settled her on his lap. He held her close, stroking her hair. 'It's OK, Hayley. It was only an omelette—nothing fancy. It doesn't matter that you didn't finish it. You ate something, that's the main thing.'

'I just…'

Her shoulders heaved, and finally she began to sob.

He held her until she was all cried out, then reached across the table for a glass of water. She sipped it gratefully.

'Talk to me,' he said. 'Don't let it all stay in your head and your heart, where it'll destroy you. Let it out. Tell me.'

'The clothing factory fire.' She dragged in a breath. 'It just brought the day of the workshop fire straight back. Especially as it was Evan's crew dealing with it.' She gulped. 'His friends—*my* friends—I've been avoiding them because it's too hard seeing them without him. Today was the first time I'd seen any of them since the funeral. Joe was so nice about it. And I hate myself for being so selfish and pathetic. For being such a coward.'

'You're not selfish, pathetic or a coward,' he reassured her. 'It's completely understandable. It's hard to face people when you've lost someone.'

'If it had been the other way round, if I'd been the one who was killed, Evan wouldn't have avoided the social stuff, the way I have. He would've still come to the ward's Christmas party and the summer barbecue. I just…' She shook her head. 'Today brought back all the bad memories and I hate that I had to push myself through it. This is my *job*. I ought to be able to deal with major incidents—just as you have to face treating patients with heart attacks. I know we can't save everyone; but the next time you get a case similar to someone you lost, you're supposed to try and put it out of your head and just get on with it and help people—because that's what doctors *do*.'

'That's exactly what you did today. You got on with it and helped people.' He stroked her hair. 'I'm guessing this is the first big fire the department has dealt with since Evan died?'

'Yes.'

'It's really hard, having to repeat the worst day of your life.'

'And then you have to pull yourself together afterwards. You've got people asking you all the time if you're all right, and you know you're supposed to say yes even when the real answer's no, because it's the polite thing to do. Plus, if you admit how bad things are, people will start going silent when you walk into the room, because they simply don't know what to say to you. The next thing you know, you're the subject of the hospital grapevine, with everyone talking about you and suddenly changing the conversation and looking guilty when you walk over.'

He understood her aversion to hospital gossip. Even though he was pretty sure that the people in their department were all nice people and had only talked about her because they were worried about her and wanted to help, he could understand that it wasn't much fun being the subject of everyone's scrutiny.

'So did you live at your flat with Evan?' he asked.

She shook her head. 'We lived three roads away, in

a slightly bigger flat. We were saving up for a place of our own. But I couldn't handle living there when he died, Sam. I hated walking into the flat and expecting to see him there, and for a second thinking that I *could* see him or hear him—and remembering all over again that he wouldn't be coming home any more. So I talked my landlord into letting me terminate my lease early and I moved here about a year ago.'

'Do you still see Evan's family?'

'No. They weren't close. Anyway, they lived miles away.'

Distance in all senses of the word, he thought. His own family would've made sure that his partner still felt included. They would've made the effort. But not all families were like that.

'I noticed there weren't any photographs of him with you on your mantelpiece or your fridge—they're all of your family, Dani or the department,' he said.

'I haven't put his photographs up in my new flat. It hurt too much to see them,' she admitted.

'Maybe,' he said, 'looking at some pictures of him are what you need to do right now. So you've got some good memories to get you through today.'

She looked at him as if surprised that he'd make the suggestion. 'I guess. There are a few on my phone.'

'You get your phone,' he said, 'and I'm going to make us some hot chocolate, and then maybe we can look through the photos together.' If he could make her feel better, if he could make the good memories outweigh the bad for her, then he'd be happier. He hated seeing her in so much pain.

By the time he'd finished making the hot chocolate and ushered her through to the living room, she'd pulled up the photographs on her phone.

'This is the summer he died,' she said. 'We'd decided not to have a holiday that year, because we'd got the wedding coming up in September, so we just had days out. We went to Brighton so we could paddle in the sea.' There were pictures of them together on the rides on the pier, with the sea in the background, and with Brighton's iconic Pavilion.

What Sam noticed was that they looked really happy together.

They'd thought it was their last summer before getting married; yet it had been their last summer, full stop.

How horribly, horribly sad.

'He looks a nice guy,' Sam said.

'He was. He got on well with everyone. And he put his life on the line to help people—just as you will with the MERIT team.' She swallowed hard. 'And it scares me, Sam, to the point where I can hardly function. I hate the idea of having to go through all that again.'

'Then it's simple. I'll give up MERIT,' Sam said. 'I can still make a difference to people's lives in our department.'

She shook her head. 'I don't think it will be enough for you. I know you miss the mountain rescue work. And I don't want to stop you doing something you love.'

'So what are you suggesting?' he asked, not sure where she was going with this. 'Because if you don't want me to stop doing the MERIT team but you also don't want to have to cope with me doing it… That sounds like you want us to go back to being strictly colleagues. That it's over between us.'

'No,' she said. 'I don't want that either. I just don't want to lose you. But I'm pushing you away and this is supposed to be the Year of Saying Yes.'

'And now you've really lost me. What do you mean, the Year of Saying Yes?' he asked.

'Dani and I made a pact in the summer, when her divorce from Leo came through. She said she didn't want to waste her life being miserable over someone who didn't love her, and she said Evan wouldn't have wanted me to be miserable and lonely. So we agreed we'd say yes to every opportunity to make our life better and happier.' She swallowed hard. 'Which was why I ended up going to Iceland on my own, after she broke her foot.'

'And why you and I had a holiday fling?'

She nodded. 'And then you turned up in our department. I honestly intended to be just colleagues, perhaps friends, but I just couldn't resist you.'

'Only you can't get past the rescue stuff.'

'I don't want to lose you,' she repeated.

'I don't want to lose you either. And if being with you means I have to give up MERIT, then I'm prepared to do that.' He gave her a wry smile. 'Which I think tells you how I feel about you, because I would never have given up the mountain rescue stuff for Lynda.'

'But you loved her, didn't you?'

'I did. Until I realised that she didn't love me for who I was—she loved me for who she thought I could be,' he admitted. 'Then I was suspended and she worked out that I never would be the man she thought I could be.'

Hayley frowned. 'Hang on. She dumped you after you were suspended? But I thought you broke up before then?'

Even though he didn't want to make Lynda the scapegoat here, there wasn't any other way of putting it. He looked away. 'Yes. It was the week after my team was hauled in to see the head of department. When I was suspended, she thought that my career was over.'

'But why on earth would she think that?' Hayley's frown deepened. 'You're meticulous at work. You never cut corners. There's no way the investigation would've had any other outcome—of course you and your team were always going to be exonerated.'

Hayley's faith in him warmed him from the inside out. It was so very far away from Lynda's attitude. 'I have to be honest and say that she had a point. There was always the chance I might've done something wrong, or there was something I missed recording that could've made the difference. Nobody's perfect,' he pointed out.

'But you were exonerated.'

'That doesn't really matter. You know what they say about mud tending to stick? When it came to getting promoted, Lynda's view was that people would remember what had happened with me and then look a bit more closely at the other candidates, finding one of them more suitable than me.'

'That would be unfair discrimination,' Hayley said. 'And anyone who'd ever worked with you would *know* you're good at your job.'

'Even so. She had a point about people remembering and having doubts, even if they got past them. And if mud stuck to me, it would also stick to her by association. She was engaged to someone who was suspended— so, whatever the outcome, the investigation would harm her career.'

Hayley's eyes glittered with what looked like outrage. 'That's—that's…' She shook her head. 'I can't believe someone would be that selfish and shallow. She was your fiancée, for pity's sake! The one person you'd expect to believe in you and have your back.'

His thoughts exactly. Lynda's lack of faith in him had cut him to the quick. 'It didn't quite work out that way.'

'She didn't believe in you. I can't get over that. That's so horrible.' She blew out a breath. 'So when I went all quiet on you, I was worrying that you were going to end up the same way as Evan—but I'm guessing you've got similar worries about things repeating themselves, and you started thinking that I didn't believe in you, too?'

'I was probably being paranoid,' he said, 'and letting what happened with Lynda act as a kind of filter to the way I saw things. But you also said you didn't want anyone to know we were seeing each other,' he reminded her. 'I thought maybe you were ashamed of me.'

'No. I told you it was complicated. I knew it was time to move on, but I still felt guilty Plus you were the first person I'd dated since Evan, and…' She rubbed a hand over her face. 'I don't know how to put this. You would've been grilled to an inch of your life by half the hospital if they found out I was seeing you. And then everyone would be talking about us, and saying how pleased they were that I'd finally decided to move on—as if I was replacing Evan and scrubbing him out of my life. I just couldn't face that.'

'You can't replace a person,' he said, 'and you'll always love Evan. Of course you will. You were engaged to him for how long?'

'A year and a half,' she said, 'and we dated for a year before we got engaged.'

'Anyone who asks you to share their life will understand that you'll always love Evan,' Sam said, 'and that's fine—because love doesn't have limits like that. He was an important part of your life. Loving him and cherishing your memories doesn't mean that you can't share your future with someone else—that you can't love someone else and live a rich, happy life together.'

Love didn't have limits.

Yet she was limiting him.

'I can't make you give up MERIT,' she said. 'It's part of who you are. You're an emergency doctor. You save lives. And I can understand that it's important to you to use your skills to do that on the front line. To make a difference where you're really needed.'

He nodded. 'But you're important to me, too. I don't want you to worry yourself sick and remember how you felt when Evan was killed, every time I'm called out on a job.'

'Let me go through this logically,' she said. 'The Medical Incident Officer won't let anyone on the team take unnecessary risks. A doctor at the site will have to wear personal protective equipment, and will only be allowed in the area right next to the incident if the service responsible for safety at the scene says it's safe to be there.'

'Exactly,' he said. 'The rule is not to risk your own safety, ever—because as a rescue worker you're meant to be helping, not adding to the problem.'

But Evan risked his own safety. And then he was killed.

Though she didn't say it, he clearly guessed what she was thinking, because he squeezed her hand. 'I'm a doctor, not a firefighter,' he said. 'I know my limits and I won't take unnecessary risks.'

She'd worry whenever he was on a MERIT incident. Of course she would. But over time she'd become more confident that she wasn't going to lose him.

'I love you and I want to be with you,' Sam said softly. 'But I also want our relationship to be public. I don't want to feel as if I'm the shameful secret you don't want anyone to know about.'

'I'm not ashamed of you,' she said. 'You're a good doctor. A good man. I'm proud of you. You've been through an experience that would make a lot of people walk away from medicine altogether—but you're still here, doing your best to make the world a better place.' She took a deep breath. 'You make my world a better place, Sam. With you, I've been happy for the first time since I lost Evan. And you're right. I'm never going to forget him and a part of me will always love him. But there's room in my life for another relationship—and I want that relationship to be with you.'

'I love you,' Sam said. 'I'll compromise and tone down the dangerous stuff.'

'You're never going to be able to talk me into doing mountain-climbing or even skiing, and I'm not even sure I can bear to watch you do it,' Hayley said, 'but I won't stop you from doing what you need to do. I'll trust that you won't take unnecessary risks. I'll worry about you—of course I will—but it's part of who you are. Part of why I love you. I won't stop you doing any of the stuff you need to do.'

He kissed her. 'Today's been a rough day. But it's going to get better, because from now on we're going to be right by each other's side.' He paused. 'It's probably the wrong time to ask you this, but I think we've already wasted enough time. And today's taught me that life is really precious, and you should seize it and make the most of it.'

'Seize the day,' she said. 'That's a good plan.'

He slid off his sofa and knelt before her on one knee. 'Hayley Clark, I love you and I want to spend the rest of my life with you. Will you marry me—and preferably as soon as possible?'

Given that it was the Year of Saying Yes, there was only one answer she could make. 'Sam Price, I love you, too. Yes.'

CHAPTER TEN

December 1st

IT WAS THE night of the departmental Christmas party, with a sit-down meal in the function room of the local pub and everyone pulling crackers and wearing the paper hats and groaning over the terrible jokes.

Michael Harcourt, the head of the department, presided over the Secret Santa, and everyone laughed when Josh's present turned out to be a miniature model of a go-kart and a home-made rib protector crafted from bubble-wrap.

'There is one more thing,' Sam said when Michael had finished, 'except I need to be the one to give this, not Michael.' He walked round the table to Hayley's chair, and held out a cracker to her.

She smiled, knowing what was inside; they'd agreed to go public on their relationship, and Sam was making it very public indeed. She pulled the other end of the cracker, revealing a velvet-covered box, and everyone gasped.

Sam adopted the traditional pose of going down on one knee, and held out the box to her. 'Hayley

Clark, would you please do me the honour of becoming my wife?'

'Yes,' she said, and he took the simple diamond engagement ring from the box and slid it onto her left hand.

'I think this calls for bubbles,' Michael said. 'Congratulations, both of you.' He shook their hands warmly.

'So have you set a date?' Dev asked.

'Christmas Eve,' Sam said.

'So we have a whole year to wait for wedding cake?' Melissa, one of the nurses, asked.

'Um, no. More like a shade over three weeks,' Hayley said.

'What—you're getting married *this* Christmas Eve?' Josh asked, sounding shocked.

'Yes. We'll be giving out the invitations to our wedding tomorrow,' Sam said. 'And we hope to see as many of you there as possible.'

'How on earth are you going to organise a wedding in three weeks?' Melissa asked. 'I mean, I know you two are efficient machines, but weddings…'

'We gave notice to the register office ten days ago and we have a venue booked nearby—and the venue's organising the bar and the catering for us,' Sam said. 'I'm hiring a suit and Dani's already taken Hayley shopping for a dress. Plus we've been making lists of people we need to call for everything else.'

'My aunt makes cakes,' Josh said. 'So if you can't get a baker, I can ask her to make the cake for you.'

'My sister does flowers,' Melissa said. 'I can ask her to do yours for you.'

'And my brother's a photographer,' Darryl said. 'I know he's not doing anything on Christmas Eve. I can book him for you.'

'What about a band?' Dev asked.

'Dani's asking Maybe Baby,' Hayley said. The maternity unit and paediatric ward had a house band between them, which often played at hospital functions. She smiled. 'I think you've all answered Melissa's question between you. It looks as if we're organising it by teamwork. And thank you, all of you, for being so supportive.'

'It's really good to see you happy again, Hayley,' Melissa said, and hugged her. 'I can't think of a nicer couple for this to happen to. And it's so romantic, getting married on Christmas Eve. This is going to be one of the best Christmases ever.'

Michael started handing out glasses of bubbly. 'Agreed. And I propose a toast: to Hayley and Sam.'

'Hayley and Sam,' everyone chorused, lifting their glasses.

Christmas Eve

'Turn round so I can check it's all perfect,' Danielle said when she'd done up the zip at the back of Hayley's dress.

Hayley dutifully performed a pirouette. 'Do I look OK?'

'More than OK,' Danielle said, and gave her a swift hug. 'That dress is perfect for you.' The cream dress had a sleeveless V-necked lace bodice and a full skirt with layers of tulle and organza that floated down to just below Hayley's knees.

Hayley stepped into her dark red high-heeled court shoes, which matched the spray of roses she was using for her bouquet, and also matched Danielle's empire-line knee-length bridesmaid's dress.

'Don't we look fabulous in our tiaras?' Danielle asked, standing next to her in front of the mirror and pouting.

But there was an over-brightness to her best friend's smile that worried Hayley. 'We do. Dani, are you sure everything's OK?'

'Of course it is. Why wouldn't it be? It's your wedding day.'

Which was precisely the reason Hayley knew Danielle wouldn't talk to her today about what was really wrong. She made a mental note to pin her best friend down the day after Boxing Day, when she and Sam were back from their brief honeymoon in Iceland, and find out exactly what Danielle was hiding. 'I love you,' she said. 'If it wasn't for you insisting on the Year of Saying Yes, I wouldn't have met Sam in Iceland, I wouldn't have given him a chance when he started at the hospital, and I wouldn't be here right now, getting ready to marry him.'

'Don't make me cry,' Danielle warned. 'I haven't got time to redo my make-up—or yours.'

And it was hard to make Danielle cry. Something was definitely up, Hayley thought. But she'd get to the bottom of it in a couple of days.

Hayley's mother called up to say the cars were there: a vintage black Thunderbird for Danielle, herself and

Hayley's sister Joanna, and a vintage cream Rolls-Royce for Hayley and her father.

'You both look amazing,' Hayley's father said, blinking back the tears when Danielle and Hayley walked downstairs. 'Ready?'

'Ready,' Hayley confirmed.

All she needed was the deep red velvet cape that Danielle had borrowed from a friend to wrap round her shoulders, to keep her warm until they were back indoors again—and then she was sitting in the back of the Rolls-Royce with her father, being driven to the register office where Sam was waiting for her.

Sam waited at the register office, feeling sick.

'She'll be here. Dead on time, too,' Martin, his brother, reassured him. 'We're early.'

'I suppose so.' Sam blew out a breath. 'Why do I never get nervous like this at work or on the mountain rescue team?'

'Because you know what you're doing in the emergency department or doing rescue, and you're prepared for anything,' Martin said, clapping him on the shoulder, 'whereas this… You just have to be patient. She'll be here.'

'I guess I'm not very good at waiting,' Sam said ruefully.

At that moment, Hayley's mother and sister walked in, and took their places on the left-hand side of the room. Hayley's mother gave him a reassuring smile.

'See?' Martin whispered.

Anton Powell, the obstetrician who played lead guitar in the Maybe Baby band, had brought an acoustic guitar to the register office. At a nod from Hayley's mother, he began playing Bach's 'Air on a G String'. Sam heard the door open, then looked behind him to see Hayley walking towards him on her father's arm, with Danielle walking behind them. His heart skipped a beat: she looked so beautiful. And today she was joining her life to his. For ever.

When Hayley got to the front and sat down between her father and her bridesmaid, the registrar introduced herself as Camilla Fletcher, explained that the register office had been sanctioned by law, and added, 'If any person present knows of any legal reason why these two people should not be joined in matrimony they should declare it now.'

As Sam expected, there was complete silence.

'I now ask the bride and groom to come and stand before me,' Camilla said. 'Before you are joined in matrimony it is my duty to remind you of the solemn and binding character of the vows you are about to make. Marriage in this country is the union of two people voluntarily entered into for life to the exclusion of all others. I am now going to ask you each in turn to declare that you know of no legal reason why you may not be joined together in marriage.'

Sam repeated the words after her. 'I do solemnly declare that I know not of any lawful impediment why I, Samuel Price, should not be joined in lawful matrimony to Hayley Clark.'

Hayley smiled at him and repeated the declaration.

'I ask you now, Samuel Price—do you take Hayley Clark to be your lawful wedded wife, to be loving, faithful and loyal to her for the rest of your life together?' Camilla asked.

'I do,' Sam said, and smiled at Hayley—who made exactly the same answer to her own question.

Then came the contracting words. Sam took a deep breath and echoed Camilla's prompting. 'I call upon these persons here present to witness that I, Samuel Price, do take thee, Hayley Clark, to be my lawful wedded wife, to love and to cherish from this day forward.'

Once Hayley had made the same declaration, Camilla said, 'The exchanging of rings is the traditional way of sealing the contract that you have just made. It is an unbroken circle, symbolising unending and everlasting love and is the outward sign of the lifelong promise that you have just made to each other.'

Martin stepped forward with the rings.

'I give you this ring as a symbol of our love,' Sam said. 'All that I am I give to you. All that I have I share with you. I promise to love you, to be faithful and loyal, in good times and bad. May this ring remind you always of the words we have spoken today.'

Hayley mouthed, 'I love you,' as he slid the ring onto her finger. And then she made the same declaration, and slid the wedding ring onto his finger.'

'Today is a new beginning. May you have many happy years together and in those years may all your hopes and dreams be fulfilled,' Camilla said. 'Above all, may you always believe in each other and may the warmth of your love enrich not only your lives but the lives of all those around you.'

And Sam knew without a doubt that Hayley believed in him—just as he believed in her. The glance they shared told him that she knew exactly what he was thinking.

'It now gives me great pleasure to tell you both that you are now legally husband and wife. You may now seal the contract with a kiss.'

Sam didn't need a second invitation. He bent Hayley back over his arm and kissed her thoroughly, to the cheers of their family and closest friends.

'Now, ladies and gentlemen, please be seated while the register is completed,' Camilla said. 'As you have witnessed, a civil marriage is a brief, simple ceremony—but, Hayley and Sam, you are legally and solemnly joined together in matrimony and I would like to be the first to congratulate you both—and to wish you a very happy Christmas.'

'Thank you,' Hayley said, almost shyly.

Both their fathers signed the register while Anton played a love song on the guitar. Dani joined in with the singing, then Hayley's sister Joanna, then Sam's sister-in-law Robyn, and by the end they were all joining in with the chorus of the well-known classic hit.

'And it's right,' Hayley whispered to Sam. 'Love *is* all we really need.'

Once Darryl's brother had taken photographs of the wedding party outside on the steps of the register office, they headed across the road to their reception venue: a Victorian gothic church, which had been turned into a community arts centre.

'Excuse me a minute,' Martin said.

A few seconds later, snow began to fall very softly. Martin reappeared with a huge grin on his face.

'Well, hey—it's Christmas Eve. And you need to have snow at Christmas, don't you?'

'How on earth did you manage that?' Hayley asked.

'Snow machine,' he said, smiling. 'Don't worry—it's biodegradable and non-toxic, and I cleared it with the venue last week.'

Everyone in the wedding party burst into an impromptu chorus of a Christmas song about snow.

Hayley and Sam laughed, and thoroughly enjoyed having their wedding photographs taken in real snow on Christmas Eve.

Then they headed up to the top floor of the building. There was a canopy of fairy lights in the vaulted ceiling, and there were floor-to-ceiling lancet windows set within tall Gothic arches. At one end of the room, a large table was set up for the sit-down meal, covered in a white damask tablecloth. The arrangements in the centre of the table were holly and ivy, in keeping with the theme of Christmas; there was a large real Christmas tree next to the stage at the other end of the room, with a large silver star on the top; and there were sprigs of mistletoe strategically dotted round the room.

Sam's face actually ached from smiling, but he didn't care. He couldn't remember ever being this happy—and, best of all, that happiness shone from Hayley's eyes, too.

After the meal, Martin switched back into best man mode, and introduced all the speeches.

The first was from Hayley's dad. 'I'm going to keep it short and sweet,' he said. 'I want to welcome Sam to the family. And I'm so glad to see my little girl happy.

Everyone, please raise your glasses and toast the bride and groom.'

'The bride and groom,' everyone echoed.

Sam stood up next. 'When I was whale-watching in the middle of the North Atlantic Ocean, I never expected to meet the love of my life. So I'd like to make a very special toast to our bridesmaid, Danielle. If it wasn't for her breaking her foot, I'd never have met a woman with eyes like an Icelandic summer sky and a smile that makes my heart beat faster.' He raised his glass. 'Thank you, Dani—for being an excellent bridesmaid and for being your wonderful whirlwind self.'

'Dani,' everyone chorused.

'I'd also like to thank everyone who's helped with the organisation of our wedding,' Sam continued. 'We've really appreciated it. Everyone in Muswell Hill has made me feel really welcome and I'm proud to be part of such a team—and I'm even prouder to be Hayley's husband.'

Everyone cheered.

And then it was Martin's turn. 'As the best man, I'm supposed to tell you scurrilous stories about my little brother. If I did that I'd be here all night and there wouldn't be time for cake or dancing, so I'll keep it brief. Given that my brother met Hayley while they were whale-watching and he talked the emergency department into doing go-karting on ice, I'm half surprised that he didn't talk Hayley into doing something insane for their wedding—like getting married at the top of an indoor snow ski-slope or in an aquarium among the sharks.'

Everyone laughed, especially when Sam said mournfully, 'Now, why didn't I think of that?'

'But seriously, Hayley's utterly lovely,' Martin said, 'and she makes my brother happy—which makes our whole family happy. I'd like to welcome Hayley to our family, and may I ask you all to raise your glasses in a toast to the bride and groom—the new Dr and Dr Price.'

'Dr and Dr Price,' everyone chorused.

After the meal, the venue staff cleared the tables and set everything up for the evening buffet. Hayley and Sam wandered hand in hand around the hall, chatting to everyone while Maybe Baby were playing Christmas songs that had people up on the dance floor.

When the hall was mostly full, Martin stepped over to the PA system. 'The bride and groom are going to cut the cake.'

Thanks to Josh's aunt, they had an amazing cake with four layers—lemon, chocolate, vanilla and fruit cake. There was a deep red ribbon around the bottom of each layer, the same colour as Hayley's bouquet and Danielle's dress, and around the sides were deep red and white poinsettias.

Hayley put her hand on the knife, and Sam put his hand over hers. Together, they posed for photographs and then cut the very first slice. 'And we'd like to say a special thank you to Josh for asking his aunt to make this wonderful cake,' Sam said. 'Especially after the go-kart incident.'

'You're just lucky she didn't ice that cake with go-karts,' Josh said with a grin.

And finally it was time for the first dance. Maybe

Baby struck up their chosen song and Sam took Hayley into his arms, swaying with her in time to the music.

'I love you just as you are,' he said.

Hayley smiled up at him. 'I wouldn't change anything about you, even the dangerous stuff—because I love you and I trust you.'

He kissed her. 'Merry Christmas, Dr Price—and happy wedding day.'

'Merry Christmas, Dr Price—and happy first day of the rest of our lives,' she said.

'The rest of our lives,' he echoed. And it was the best feeling in the world.

* * * * *

Look out for the next great story in the
MIRACLES AT MUSWELL HILL HOSPITAL *duet:*
THEIR PREGNANCY GIFT

And if you enjoyed this story,
check out these other great reads
from Kate Hardy

MUMMY, NURSE…DUCHESS?
THE MIDWIFE'S PREGNANCY MIRACLE
CAPTURING THE SINGLE DAD'S HEART
HER PLAYBOY'S PROPOSAL

All available now!

THEIR
PREGNANCY
GIFT

BY
KATE HARDY

Published in Great Britain 2017
By Mills & Boon, an imprint of HarperCollins*Publishers*
1 London Bridge Street, London, SE1 9GF

© 2017 Pamela Brooks

ISBN: 978-0-263-92675-0

Our policy is to use papers that are natural, renewable and recyclable
products and made from wood grown in sustainable forests. The logging
and manufacturing processes conform to the legal environmental
regulations of the country of origin.

Printed and bound in Spain
by CPI, Barcelona

To Tony and Debbie, with much love.

Books by Kate Hardy

Mills & Boon Medical Romance

Paddington Children's Hospital

Mummy, Nurse…Duchess?

Christmas Miracles in Maternity

The Midwife's Pregnancy Miracle

Her Playboy's Proposal
Capturing the Single Dad's Heart

Mills & Boon Cherish

Holiday with the Best Man
Falling for the Secret Millionaire
Her Festive Doorstep Baby

Visit the Author Profile page
at millsandboon.co.uk for more titles.

**Praise for
Kate Hardy**

'With great story build-up and engaging dialogue,
A Baby to Heal Their Hearts by Kate Hardy is a
sure winner!'

—*Harlequin Junkie*

CHAPTER ONE

'I CAN'T WAIT to get rid of you,' Danielle said. 'You've made me miserable, you've stopped me doing everything I love doing, and I do actually *hate* you.'

She looked up to see Alex, the new consultant on the maternity ward, standing in the open doorway of her office.

He raised an eyebrow. 'Practising your break-up speech?'

Dani felt the colour flood into her face. 'I hope I'd be a little kinder than that.' Certainly kinder than Leo had been to her, last Christmas Eve, when he'd told her that their marriage was over and he was leaving her for someone else. Someone else who was expecting his baby—when he'd told Dani only a few months before that he wasn't ready to start a family.

She pushed the thought away. 'If you must know, I was talking to my walking cast.'

'Right.'

There wasn't even the glimmer of a smile, and she sighed inwardly. From what she'd seen of him over the last couple of months, Alex Morgan was good with their patients, but all his social skills seemed to switch off as soon as he had to deal with his colleagues on anything other than a work basis. He hadn't been to a single team night out, always ate lunch on his own, and if he was in the staff kitchen he never joined in with the conversation.

She didn't think he was being snooty; but she didn't think he was shy, either. There was obviously a reason why he kept his distance from everyone else, but Dani—who'd always got on well with everyone—had no idea how to reach him. He was possibly the most difficult person in the department to have as the co-organiser of the ward's Christmas party, but she'd just have to make the best of it.

'You wanted to see me?' he asked.

'We need to talk about organising the ward's Christmas meal. Are you busy at lunchtime today, or can we discuss it over a sandwich?'

'Sorry. I have meetings,' he said.

Dani didn't believe a word of it, but the ward's Christmas meal still needed to be sorted out. If she gave Alex a longer timeframe, he'd be forced to pick a day. And if he picked one of the two evenings this week when she was busy, then she'd move her other arrangements because she really wanted to get this done and dusted. She gave him the sweetest, sweetest smile. 'OK. Do you have time for a coffee after work some time in the next two weeks to discuss it?'

He masked his expression quickly, but not before Dani had seen it. He'd obviously realised what her game plan was, and he couldn't think of a decent excuse that would work for two whole weeks.

Gotcha, she thought in satisfaction.

He took his phone out of his pocket and made a show of checking his diary, though she was pretty sure it wasn't that full.

'How about tomorrow?' he suggested.

'That'll be fine, as Hayley's training with Sam tomorrow night.' She glared at her cast. 'Thanks to this.'

'Uh-huh.'

OK. So he wasn't going to bite. Anyone else would've been polite enough to ask what she'd done to her foot, or at least make a comment. But Alex clearly didn't want to get into conversation with her. Fair enough. She couldn't force him to make friends with her. If he wanted to keep himself to himself, that was his decision and it wasn't her place to try and change it.

'Thank you. I'll meet you outside the staffroom tomorrow after our shift,' she said.

'Fine,' he said.

And still he didn't give her a single smile.

She sighed inwardly, and got on with writing up the case notes from her clinic that morning.

God, what was wrong with him? Alex wondered as he headed to his own office. Danielle Owens was *nice*. She'd been friendly right from his first day on the ward, trying to make him feel part of the team, and in response he'd been completely standoffish. Meeting her for a drink tomorrow night to discuss the team's Christmas meal was the only social invitation he'd accepted in the two months he'd been working at Muswell Hill Memorial Hospital, and that was solely because the head of the department had blithely informed him that his predecessor had been scheduled to organise it with

Dani and he was sure that Alex would be happy to step into those shoes, too.

Actually, Alex wasn't happy about it. At all. But he didn't have much choice.

Maybe he should've taken a longer break. But six months was surely long enough to get your head round the fact that you weren't who you thought you were, and everything you'd always believed wasn't true. He needed to stop sulking about it and just get on with things. And he'd really missed his job. At least he knew who he was at work. Alexander Morgan, obstetric consultant.

He shook himself. Now wasn't the time to start brooding. Or to wonder whether his shortness of temper and foul mood was an early sign of the incurable neurodegenerative disease that the man he now had to think of as his father was suffering from. He had notes to write up, a sandwich to eat, and a clinic to sort out.

'OK, Mrs Hamilton—may I call you Judy?' Dani asked.

The other woman nodded, looking wretched.

'According to our notes, you're sixteen weeks pregnant at the moment, and your midwife asked if I could fit you into my clinic today.'

Judy dragged in a breath. 'Thank you so much for seeing me, Dr Owens.'

'Call me Dani. And it's no problem. So tell me how things are going,' Dani said.

'It's awful,' Judy said. 'I've never felt so ill in my entire life. I can't keep anything down, even water. I've tried everything—sniffing lemons, drinking ginger tea and eating a dry biscuit before I get up in the morning. I'm not doing any cooking, and when I do try to eat it's things that don't smell and are high in carbs and not fatty, but I still can't keep anything down.'

Judy was doing all the right things to help with morning sickness, Dani knew; but what she was suffering from sounded rather more serious than everyday morning sickness.

'Nothing works, and all I seem to do is throw up all day.' Judy grimaced. 'My boss sent me home from work today, saying I had to take a few days off, and there was blood in the vomit last time I threw up. That's why I called my midwife, because I was so worried.'

'I'm glad you did. Did the blood look like little streaks?' Dani asked.

Judy nodded.

'OK. I know it looks scary but it's actually quite normal in pregnancy,' Dani reassured her. 'When you've been sick a lot, the lining of your oesophagus gets irritated and it's more likely to get a tiny little tear in it, which is why you saw blood. But we really need to get to the bottom of why you're being sick all the time. Are you OK for me to take a blood sample from you?'

Judy looked slightly nervous. 'I hate needles, but yes.'

Dani took a sample of blood to check Judy's electrolytes, renal function and liver function.

'And can I ask you to get on the scales for me?' She checked the display. 'You've lost four kilograms since your last check-up.'

'Is that bad?'

'It's completely what I expected, with what you've

told me about being so sick,' Dani said, and handed Judy a sample bottle. 'Can you do me a midstream urine sample, please?'

While Judy was in the toilet, Dani sent the blood tests off. When Judy came back, the urine sample was quite dark, indicating that Judy was dehydrated, and a dipstick test showed signs of ketones, where the body broke down fat instead of glucose for energy.

'Is it all OK?' Judy asked.

'All your symptoms added together are giving me a better picture,' Dani said. She checked Judy's notes. 'When you had your twelve-week scan, the radiographer confirmed there was only one baby.' And, to Dani's relief, there was also no indication of a molar pregnancy.

'And then I was sick on the bed,' Judy said miserably. 'Everyone I know says morning sickness goes by twelve weeks, but that was a month ago for me. I feel worse every day, instead of better.'

'Morning sickness can last for up to twenty weeks,' Dani said, 'but in your case I agree with your midwife. I think you have hyperemesis gravidarum—which is a very severe form of morning sickness.'

'Did I do something wrong to get it?' Judy asked.

'No. We don't actually know what causes it, though it does seem to run in families. Do you know if your mum had it, or do you have a sister who had it?'

Judy shook her head. 'Mum never said, and I'm an only child.'

'The most likely cause is hormonal activity, which I know doesn't help you much,' Dani said.

'I feel rotten, but I can live with that as long as the

baby's all right.' Judy bit her lip. 'Though I can't eat anything, so I'm scared the baby's not getting proper nutrition.'

'Try not to worry,' Dani said, and squeezed her hand. 'It's very possible that the baby will be smaller than average because of your situation, but we'll keep a close eye on you. I hope it reassures you to know that being sick isn't going to hurt your baby—though obviously it's very miserable for you.'

'I can't believe how bad all kinds of things smell, even tins. I can't stand being on the Tube because of the smell of people's armpits—and it must be so much worse in summer.' Judy shuddered at the thought, and retched again.

Dani handed her a tissue. 'I'm going to admit you to the ward and put you on a drip so we can get some fluids into you,' she said. 'We can also give you some medicine that will help to stop the sickness.'

Judy frowned. 'But won't that harm my baby?'

'No. We'll give you some tablets that are safe for the baby,' Dani reassured her. 'You'll be able to take them at home as well.'

Judy closed her eyes for a moment. 'I'm so tired. I don't think I can cope with this for much longer.'

'Hyperemesis can last for a long time, and I have to tell you that in some cases it doesn't actually get better until the baby arrives,' Dani warned.

'So I might be sick like this for the rest of my pregnancy?'

'Hopefully not. Let's see how you're feeling after a day or so in here,' Dani said. 'Once you're no longer dehydrated, you've had some proper rest and maybe managed to keep something down, you'll feel a bit better.'

'So I have to stay in?'

Dani nodded. 'For a day or two, so we can keep an eye on you. And, because we want you on bed rest, we'll get you to wear compression stockings and give you some heparin injections, to make sure you don't develop any blood clots. I'll have a word with your consultant at the end of my clinic, and he might come and have a chat with you. But in the meantime I'll get one of the midwives to help settle you onto the ward. Is there someone we can call for you?'

'My husband,' Judy said.

Dani checked his mobile number with Judy. 'I'll call him while you're getting settled on the ward, and maybe he can bring you some things from home.'

'Thank you.' Judy's eyes filled with tears. 'I feel so stupid, making such a fuss.'

'You're not making a fuss,' Dani said. 'You have a medical condition that's making you feel awful, and my job's to help you feel better. You did exactly the right thing, calling your midwife—and your midwife did the right thing, telling you to come here.' She opened the door of the consulting room and went over to the first midwife she could see. 'Jas, I've got a mum with hyperemesis and I want her admitted to the ward and put on a drip. Would you be able to settle her in for me, please?'

'Sure,' Jas said with a smile.

'Thanks.'

Back in the consulting room, Dani introduced Jas to Judy. 'Judy, this is Jasminder Lund, one of our midwives. Jas, this is Judy Hamilton. Judy, Jas is going to look after you, and I'll pop in and see you after my clinic.'

'Thank you so much,' Judy said, and let Jas lead her out to the ward.

Dani called Judy's husband and explained what was happening, and then checked Judy's file to see who her consultant was. Hopefully it would be Anton Powell; he was always really good with worried mums.

The file said otherwise and she sighed inwardly. Oh, great. It *would* have to be Alex Morgan. But Dani would just have to sideline her impatience with him, because Judy and the baby's welfare came first.

She saw the rest of the mums on her list, then went to find Alex in his office.

'Do you have a moment, please?' she asked. 'I need to talk to you about one of your patients.'

'Sure.' His voice was carefully neutral, and so was his expression.

'Judy Hamilton. She's dehydrated, losing weight, her urine showed ketones, and I'm waiting for her bloods to come back.' Dani swiftly ran through the case with him. 'I've admitted her with hyperemesis, and asked Jas to settle her in and put her on a drip.'

'Good call,' he said.

'I told her I'd talk to you at the end of my clinic, then go and see her.'

'I'll come with you,' he said.

On the way to Judy's room, he collected a cup of ice chips.

When they walked in, Judy was retching miserably into a bowl. Without a word—and before Dani could do it herself—Alex found a cloth and moistened it. When Judy had finished being sick, he wiped her face gently, and handed her the cup of ice chips. 'I know right now you can't keep anything down, but you might find that sucking on an ice chip will make your mouth feel a little better,' he said. 'Hello, Mrs Hamilton. I'm Alex Morgan, your consultant, and Dani here's told me how terrible you're feeling.'

'I'm sor—' she began.

'There's nothing to apologise for,' he cut in, 'so please don't worry. Hyperemesis is a medical condition that unfortunately affects some women, and right now I'm guessing you're really tired, really unhappy and feeling absolutely terrible.'

She nodded, and brushed away a tear.

He smiled at her. 'The good news is that we can help you. I know Dani's already explained that we've put you on a drip to rehydrate you, and we can give you some medication to help with the sickness. It won't hurt the baby and we'll keep a very close eye on you so we can make you more comfortable.'

Dani was stunned by that smile. It lit up his face, and Alex's blue-green eyes were amazing. When he smiled, he was probably the most gorgeous man in the entire hospital. But she damped down the attraction as soon as it flared. This was so inappropriate, it was untrue. Apart from the fact that he was her senior on the ward, she was pretty sure he didn't like her, and she wasn't wasting any more of her emotions on men who couldn't or wouldn't love her back.

But if Alex could be as charming as this with their mums, why couldn't he be like this with the rest of the staff? He'd have everyone eating out of his hand instead of feeling as if they were treading on eggshells around him. Though he had at least agreed to meet her tomorrow and discuss the ward's Christmas meal. Maybe she could turn that planned coffee after work into dinner, and get him to be a little more receptive to changing his attitude at work.

'If you're worried about anything at all, we're all here to help,' Alex continued. 'The midwives here are a great bunch and really know their stuff, and the doctors are all really approachable.'

Dani stored that one away to tell them, because she was pretty sure Alex hadn't told them that himself.

'And remember, no question is ever silly. You won't be the first to ask it and you won't be the last. We'd all much rather you asked than sat there worrying,' Dani said, and squeezed Judy's hand briefly in reassurance. 'I called your husband, and he's going to bring in some clothes and toiletries for you straight after work.'

'Thank you,' Judy said, a tear leaking down her face.

It wasn't the first time Alex had worked with Dani, but he'd forgotten how lovely she was with their mums—patient, kind and reassuring.

Though it wasn't just her manner at work that attracted him. It was her energy, the brightness of her dark eyes and her smile. In another life, he would have asked her out on the first day he'd met her.

But he wasn't in a position where he could consider starting a relationship, or even having a simple friendship with someone. Not until he'd sorted his head out.

He was going to have to be very careful. Because he had a nasty feeling that Danielle Owens could be very dangerous to his peace of mind.

CHAPTER TWO

'DARLING? SAD NEWS, I'm afraid. Stephen died last night.'

Alex replayed his mother's message on his voicemail for the tenth time. It still hadn't quite sunk in. Stephen was dead. *His father was dead.* At the rather less than ripe old age of fifty-seven.

So if Alex had inherited the faulty gene and he followed Stephen's pattern, that meant he had twenty-two years of life left—the last five years of which really wouldn't be worth living.

He swallowed hard. It was an 'if', admittedly, but there was still a fifty per cent chance that he had the gene. Scary odds. The simple toss of a coin.

He picked up the phone to call his parents, but then put it down again. What could he say? How could you really be sorry for the death of someone you barely knew, had met twice and who had never really acknowledged you as his child? It'd be just a platitude. Meaningless. And his relationship with his parents had been seriously strained since his mother had dropped the bombshell eight months ago that his father wasn't actually his father, and his biological father had advanced Huntington's disease. Right now Alex wasn't in the mood for polite awkwardness, and he didn't want to make the situation worse by accidentally saying something wrong.

And there was nobody—absolutely nobody—he could talk to about this. He was an only child; and he'd distanced himself from everyone in his life since learning the news. He'd broken his engagement to Lara, and avoided all his friends, even his best friend Tom, until they'd got the message and stopped calling him. So being alone now was completely his own fault: but, on the other hand, how could he have been unfair enough to dump his worries on any of them?

My dad isn't actually my dad, and my 'real' dad— who I've never met—might have passed on a genetic disease that'll leave me a drooling, shambling wreck when I'm only in my fifties.

How could he possibly have married Lara, knowing that she would end up having to be his carer rather than his partner? How could he have denied her the chance to have children, too—because, if he had the faulty gene, there was a fifty per cent chance of passing that same gene on to his children and condemning them to an illness that still had no cure?

Lara had clearly thought the same, because Alex had seen a very different side of her when he'd told her the news. Of course she'd been sympathetic when the bombshell had first dropped—but he'd noticed her backing away a little more each day, once they'd looked up the symptoms of Huntington's and seen what the end stage was like.

She hadn't wanted to come to America with him,

either, saying she was too busy at work—but he'd seen the real reason in her eyes. She was afraid of facing what might be ahead for them. Alex hadn't wanted her to stay with him out of duty, especially once he'd seen the burden that Stephen's partner Catriona carried. But he knew that if Lara broke their engagement, people would judge her harshly and see her as the woman who hadn't been prepared to stand by her man. That wasn't fair, because Huntington's was a horrible disease and it would be a massive burden. So he'd done the right thing by both of them and ended it. And it had under-lined for him that he'd be spending the rest of his life on his own. It wasn't fair to ask someone to share a future that could be so, so difficult.

He'd heard through the grapevine that Lara had met someone else. He hoped her new partner would give her the shiny, hopeful future he hadn't been able to promise her. Though right now his own hopes of a shiny, hopeful future had just taken another battering.

The only thing he could do was head for the gym and push himself in the weights room until he was too physically exhausted to think. And please let tomor-row be a better day.

Danielle was half tempted to throw her glass of water over Alex Morgan. For pity's sake. He'd agreed to meet her to sort out the ward's Christmas meal. It shouldn't take too long. Surely he could manage his dislike of her for that short a time and actually pay attention to what she needed to discuss with him?

But just for a moment there was something in his

expression. As if he'd been sucked into a black hole and there was no way out.

Maybe this wasn't about him not wanting to deal with her.

Her fixer instincts kicked in. 'Are you all right?' she asked.

Sheer panic flashed over his face and was swiftly hidden before he drawled, 'Why do you ask?'

'Because,' she said, 'I've asked you the same question three times now and you still haven't replied.'

'It's been a busy day,' he said.

'About the same as mine.' Maybe it really was that simple, after all, and she was just making excuses for him. The guy didn't like her and wasn't even bothering to hide it. And she'd had enough. It was time to face this head on and sort it out. 'Look, do you have a problem working with me? Have I done something to upset you?'

He looked surprised. 'No, nothing like that.'

Seriously? Did he not know he behaved as if she was the horrible child who'd had a screaming tantrum and popped all the balloons at his birthday party before stamping on his presents and tipping his cake onto the floor?

Or maybe he was one of those bright but emotionally clueless men and he didn't mean anything by his behaviour after all. OK. This was her cue to change the subject and talk about the Christmas meal again. Except she remembered that look of utter devastation in his eyes and it made her decide to take a risk. She chose her words carefully. 'Alex, I know you don't really socialise with the team, and it's absolutely none of my business why you choose not to, but right now you seem really unhappy and as if you could do with a friend.'

That was an understatement.

Except Alex had chosen to push his friends away. Just as he'd chosen to make sure he kept all interactions with his colleagues strictly professional since he'd started at Muswell Hill Hospital.

'Just so you know,' Dani said, 'I'm not a gossip. Anything you decide to tell me will stay with me.'

It was tempting to confide in her. So very, very tempting. Her warmth and kindness drew him.

In other circumstances, Alex would've already asked Dani out. He liked the way she was at work, friendly and kind with everyone, reassuring their patients and giving the junior staff a chance to boost their experience and shine. Not to mention that she was gorgeous. A pocket Venus, with that glorious dark hair she kept tied back at work, dark eyes that seemed to understand everything, and a perfect rosebud mouth that made him want to kiss her.

But he couldn't get involved with anyone. Not now. Not with that ticking time bomb hanging over him. It wouldn't be fair.

'I…' He searched for an excuse, but the words just wouldn't come.

'OK. This is what we're going to do. We're going to eat carbs,' she said softly, 'in a quiet place where nobody can overhear us.'

He couldn't quite process what she meant, because his head was all over the place.

As if she'd guessed, she said, 'We'll get a pizza delivered to my place. Which isn't a come-on.'

Pizza. Her place. He blinked. 'Won't your partner mind?'

'I've been divorced officially since the summer. Which doesn't mean that I'm desperate to replace my ex and get married again, if that's a concern for you.' She paused. 'I should ask you the same. Will your partner mind?'

'No partner.' He'd broken off his engagement to Lara the day after he'd come back to England from America.

'That's settled, then.' She gathered up the papers she'd spread in front of her and put them back into the cardboard wallet file. 'Let's go.'

Enough of his brain cells still worked to make him ask, 'Is it far? Should you be walking anywhere with that thing on your foot?'

She smiled, as if pleased that he'd remembered about her foot. 'It's not that far and yes—that's why it's called a walking cast. Trust me, I'm not doing anything that will set back the date when I can get rid of this thing. I'm counting down the days.'

He was aware he'd never actually asked her about it—which was pretty rude of him. Being polite to his colleagues didn't mean getting close to them. 'What did you do?'

'Stress fracture. Second and third metatarsal.' She rolled her eyes. 'Probably caused by my new running shoes. Which are *so* being replaced when I can run again. Unfortunately, that'll be after physio and well after the charity run is held, but my best friend is the most wonderful woman in the world and she talked the event organisers into letting her run in my place. We're raising money for the new baby-sized MRI scanner for the ward,' she explained.

'Put me down for sponsorship.'

She smiled. 'There's no need. That wasn't a hint. And I talk too much. Right. Pizza. What do you like?'

He couldn't think straight. 'Anything.'

'Is there anything you hate? Olives? Anchovies?'

He grimaced. 'Not anchovies, please.'

'Let's keep it simple, then. Margherita pizza and dough balls,' she said. 'And I have salad in the fridge. So we're sorted.'

Before Alex could even offer to pay, she'd already called the order through and was shepherding him out of the door of the café.

As they walked back to her place, he was relieved that she didn't push him to talk. She didn't chatter on about nothing, either; she was surprisingly easy to be with. And oh, God, it was good not to feel quite so alone. That phone message last night had felt as if the axe hanging over him had taken a practice swipe a little too close to the top of his head.

She unlocked the door to her flat and ushered him inside. 'OK. I can offer you three types of tea, very strong coffee, a glass of water or a glass of wine.'

When Alex couldn't gather his thoughts enough to respond, she said, 'I'll be bossy and choose. Wine it is. Hope you don't mind white.'

'It's fine, thank you.'

This was what he'd admired about her on the ward. The way she saw what needed to be done and got on with it, sorting things out without a fuss. She was a bit on the bossy side, perhaps, but her smile took the sting out of that. She had a good heart. Enormous. Look at the way she was being so kind to him right now, when he'd been surly and was an utter mess.

She took a bottle from the fridge and poured him a glass of wine. Then she set the table and put a salad together.

When the pizza and dough balls arrived, he stared at her in dismay. 'Sorry. I've been so rude.' The least he could've done was offer to help lay the table. Instead, he'd just sat there and stared into his glass.

'Don't apologise and don't worry about it. Eat your pizza and drink your wine,' she said.

So she wasn't going to make him talk?

Relief flooded through him. Part of him wanted to talk, to let all the poison out; but part of him still wanted to lock everything away, the way he had for the last few months.

They ate their meal in silence, but it wasn't awkward. Alex felt weirdly comfortable with her; and at the same time that feeling of comfortableness unsettled him. He knew Dani on a professional level, but they weren't friends. Shouldn't this feel strained or, at the very least, slightly awkward? But right now he felt as if he'd known Danielle Owens for ever.

What was a little more worrying was the way every nerve end tingled with awareness when his hand accidentally brushed against hers as they reached for the dough balls at the same time. In another world, another life, this meal would've been so different. The start of something, full of anticipation and possibilities.

But he was a mess and she was being far kinder to him than he deserved, after being so standoffish and difficult at work.

She topped up his glass without comment, and he had just about enough presence of mind to grab a tea towel when she washed up their plates.

And then she shepherded him through to the living room.

'All righty,' she said. 'You look as if you were in pretty much the same place as I was, last Christmas. I was lucky because my best friend dragged me out and made me talk. So I'm paying it forward and being the person who makes you talk. Spill.'

Talk. How on earth could he put the mess of his life into words? Alex looked at her. 'I don't even know where to start.'

She shrugged. 'Anywhere. Just talk. I'm not going to judge and I'm not going to tell anyone else what you tell me.'

This was his cue to refuse politely and leave. But, to his horror, instead the words started spilling out and they just wouldn't stop.

'It started eight months ago. My mum asked me to meet her for lunch. And then she told me my dad wasn't my dad. I'd grown up believing I was one person, and then suddenly I wasn't who I thought I was.'

She said nothing, but reached over to squeeze his hand briefly. Not with pity, he thought, but with fellow feeling—and that gave him the confidence to open up to her.

'Apparently she and dad were going through a rocky patch. He had a two-month secondment up in Edinburgh and my mum had an affair with an actor who came into the coffee shop where she worked while my dad—well, the man I grew up thinking was my dad—was away. I'm the result.'

He shook his head to clear it. 'I always thought my parents had the perfect marriage, something real. They've been together for thirty-seven years. I thought they were happy.' How wrong he'd been.

'I guess you never know what's really going on someone else's marriage,' Dani said.

And it had made him wonder how happy his parents were now. Had his mother had other affairs to stop her being bored and lonely while his father worked long hours? Had his father looked elsewhere, too?

The news had totally shaken his belief in love and marriage. Especially when Lara had then started to back off from him. He'd thought she loved him. Obviously not as much as he'd believed, because it had been so easy for her to walk away.

'Did the other man know about you?' Dani asked.

He nodded. 'Mum told him when she realised she was pregnant. He said he had the chance of starring in a TV series in America and having a kid would hold him back. So he dumped my mum and went to Hollywood. Then Dad came back from Edinburgh, and she made things up with him. She told him a couple of weeks later that she was pregnant, and I guess she must've fudged her dates because I always believed I was a couple of weeks early.'

'There's no chance she might've been wrong about her dates and you could be your dad's child?' she asked.

He shook his head. 'I always wondered why I never

looked anything like him. Now I know—it's because we don't actually share any genes.'

'Why did your mum tell you about it now?'

'More than thirty years later?' He grimaced. 'Because Stephen—the actor she had an affair with—contacted her. It took him a while to find her. We'd moved a couple of times, and he didn't know if she'd stayed with my dad or not, or if she'd changed her name.'

She waited, and finally he let the words that had been choking him spill out.

'Stephen was diagnosed with Huntington's and his doctor told him he needed to tell his children.'

'Did he have any other children?' she asked.

He shook his head. 'Just me. And, before you ask, no. I haven't taken a test to find out if I have the faulty gene.'

'I wasn't going to ask,' she said mildly. 'It's none of my business.'

He sighed. 'Sorry. Mum keeps nagging me. I'm over-touchy about it.'

'I think anyone would be, in your shoes. There's a fifty-fifty chance you've inherited Huntington's. Taking the test could set your mind at rest—or it could blow your world apart completely. It takes time to get your head round that and decide whether you really want to know.'

She actually understood?

He wasn't just being stubborn and unreasonable and difficult about things?

'Have you talked to your dad about it?' she asked.

'Which one?'

'Either. Both.'

But he knew which one she meant. 'The one I grew up with. No. It's been a bit strained between all of us ever since Mum told him. He moved out for a few weeks afterwards. They're back together again now, but it's very fragile. I think seeing me kind of rubs his nose in it—I'm a physical reminder of the fact that Mum had an affair. So I'm keeping my distance and letting them patch things up without me getting in the way and making things worse.'

'Were you close growing up?' she asked.

'Yes.' That was the bit that hurt most. Because of this mess, Alex had lost his real dad, the man he'd looked up to right from childhood. Why couldn't Stephen have just continued being selfish and kept the news to himself, instead of making the effort to find his son? How ironic that maybe Stephen had tried to be unselfish for once in his life but instead had performed the ultimate selfish act and broken up a family. 'I idolised my dad. One of the reasons I became a doctor is because I wanted to follow in his footsteps—it's a different specialty, because he was an orthopod and I fell in love with obstetrics during my placement year, but I always looked up to him and he always had time for me.' And now all that was ruined. It was very clear to Alex that Will Morgan didn't see him as his son any more.

'Maybe you need to talk to him on your own, without your mum,' Dani suggested. 'The news must've been a huge shock to him. And maybe he's not looking at you as a reminder of her affair, Alex. Maybe he's worried that you're going to reject him as some kind of interloper, and now you know he isn't your biological dad maybe you don't think of him as your dad any more, so he's trying to take a step back and not put any pressure on you.'

It was the first time Alex had considered that. He'd been so sure that his father had seen him as a horrible reminder of his wife's affair. But was the real reason that Will had backed away that he was scared Alex was going to reject him?

'Thank you,' he said. Truly grateful to her for making him see things differently, he reached over and squeezed her hand.

Mistake.

Because touching her again, this time not accidentally, made his skin tingle.

And this really wasn't the most appropriate time for his libido to wake up.

Clearly his touch didn't have quite the same effect on Dani, because, totally businesslike, she asked, 'Have you met your biological father?'

'Yes. I went over to America a week or so after Mum told me about him. It wasn't the easiest of meetings and Stephen didn't really acknowledge me—though he wasn't that well. I did go to see him again a few days later and we managed to talk a bit.' He shrugged. 'I didn't feel any real connection to him.' Nothing like the connection he'd once had with Will Morgan, the man he'd grown up believing was his father. 'Stephen's my biological father, but it doesn't feel as if that means anything at all.'

'It takes more than sperm to make someone a dad. We see that every day at work,' she said.

He liked how clear-sighted she was. 'But meeting him, seeing how much his health had deteriorated, made me think,' he said. 'Stephen's partner Catriona had become his carer, and I didn't want to put that kind of potential burden on my partner. So when I came back from America I ended my engagement.'

She raised an eyebrow. 'Did you give her the choice, or did you make the decision for her?'

The question caught him on the raw—she'd said she wasn't judging him, but the tone of her voice said otherwise. That he was at fault for setting Lara free. 'It was more a case of jumping before I was pushed.'

'I'm sorry. Just the way you said it...'

He sighed. 'Yes, I ended it. But she'd backed away from me ever since I told her about the Huntington's. I don't blame her. Would you want to get married to someone, knowing that in twenty years' time or even less you'll have to be their carer?'

'Maybe. Maybe not. Though that's what marriage is meant to be—in sickness and in health. Whether you know about it beforehand or not.' She looked him straight in the eye. 'But I'd want the choice to be mine, not made for me.'

'I saw the relief in her eyes,' he said softly. 'Because if she'd been the one to end it, people would've thought she was heartless.'

'Wasn't she?'

'Not everyone can cope with that kind of burden. Stephen was lucky, because Catriona really loved him and was prepared to look after him. But it's a massive task—one I wouldn't want to dump on someone.' He blew out a breath. 'Lara wasn't heartless. She just couldn't cope. And I didn't want her to stay with me out of duty or feel bad for ending it.'

'So you ended it. Making you look like the heartless one.'

'Or the one whose life went into meltdown.' He sighed. 'I pushed everyone else away after that, too. My best friend. Friends at work. I didn't want to be a burden to anyone. And the very last thing I wanted was pity.'

'Noted,' she said. 'Do you miss her?'

'I did at first, but not any more.' Not since he'd stopped believing in love. 'Everything's different now. I took a sabbatical to try and get my head round the situation. I went travelling.'

'Did it help?' she asked.

'Not that much,' he admitted. 'I really missed work. At least there I know who I am. I thought maybe a new start in a new place would help, and that's why I accepted the job at Muswell Hill.'

And that explained a lot, Dani thought. She understood now why Alex kept people at a distance, not even making friendships at work: because he knew he had a fifty per cent chance of inheriting Huntington's and didn't want to be a potential burden to anyone. But at the same time he was missing out on so much. It would be years and years before he started showing symptoms, if he had them at all. Years and years of being isolated and alone. What kind of life was that?

'I know you don't want pity and I'm not dispensing that—but this new start isn't helping, is it?' she asked softly.

'The job is. I love what I do.' He sighed. 'But the rest of it's still going round my head. Especially now.'

'Now?' she prompted softly.

'My mother left me a message on my answering machine last night. Stephen died the night before last.'

So any chance Alex might've had for closure with his father was gone for good. 'How old was he?'

'Fifty-seven. Twenty-two years older than I am right now. And, from what his partner told me, the last five years of his life were barely worth living. In the end he couldn't do anything for himself—he couldn't wash himself, he couldn't feed himself, he couldn't get out of a chair or walk without help. He needed total nursing care.' He dragged in a breath. 'That's not living, Dani, it's just *existence*.'

She reached over to squeeze his hand again. 'It's a tough thing to face. But it's not necessarily going to happen to you, Alex. Yes, there's a fifty per cent chance you've inherited Huntington's, but there's also a fifty per cent chance you haven't.'

'And the only way to know for sure is to take the test.' He looked at her, unsmiling. 'Which I don't want to do.'

She didn't think he was a coward. He had been brave enough to end his engagement and take the blame when he hadn't been the one at fault. If he tested positive, she was pretty sure he'd be able to face up to the implications. 'What's stopping you?' she asked, keeping her voice kind.

'There doesn't seem to be any point. If I'm positive, there's nothing anyone can do about it. I can't make any lifestyle changes or take any kind of treatment that would prevent me developing Huntington's or even stave it off for a while. And if the test is positive, it'd crucify my mother—she'd blame herself, even though she couldn't possibly have known that Stephen had Huntington's when they conceived me.' He sighed. 'And I think that the guilt, the sheer pressure on her, would finally crack my parents' marriage. I need to give them the chance to rebuild their relationship.'

'Or maybe not knowing one way or the other is like having a sentence hanging over them and putting just as much pressure on them,' she said. 'What if the test is negative?'

'I don't know. If I'm honest about it,' he said, his expression grim, 'I think my parents would still be struggling. For all I know, they've been unhappy for years.'

'You can't be responsible for someone else's relationship,' she said gently.

'I just feel so guilty,' he said. 'My father's dead— and I don't feel anything.'

'I'd be more surprised,' she said, 'if you were utterly devastated by the death of someone you'd only met twice, who'd spent most of your life denying that you had anything to do with him, and who from the sound of it treated your mother quite badly.'

He looked at her. 'You really tell it like it is, don't you?'

She shrugged. 'It's who I am. Bossy.'

'No, you're honest. And you've put things into perspective for me. Thank you.'

'You're welcome.' She squeezed his hand again. 'And I want to remind you that what you've told me tonight will stay completely confidential.'

'I appreciate that. You're nice,' he said. 'Kind.'

'Hmm. I've been told I'm too opinionated and I think I'm always right.'

He couldn't help smiling. 'Probably by someone who couldn't organise their way out of a paper bag or make a decision.'

'Oh, he made a decision, all right.' The words came out before she could stop them.

'Your ex?' he guessed.

'It's not a pretty story. I'll give you the short version.' And the short version didn't sting as much because she kept the emotion out of it. 'He had an affair, I had absolutely no idea, she fell pregnant—and he left me for her on Christmas Eve last year.'

He winced. 'That's horrible timing.'

Yeah. She knew. And it was unbelievable how many songs were about being abandoned at Christmas. She'd stopped listening to music on the radio or streamed through her phone, because the songs just made her feel worse.

And what a Christmas gift. Hello, darling, I want a divorce.

Only a few months before that, she'd suggested trying for a baby. Leo had shut her down, and she'd tried to stem the longing. It had hurt so much to find out he was having the baby he'd refused her with someone else, and to realise that after all it wasn't the baby he hadn't wanted—it was her.

Because he hadn't loved her any more.

Because she wasn't loveable.

'Though I guess he did the right thing, standing by the mother of his child.' She spread her hands. 'Someone always gets hurt in that kind of situation. It just happened to be me, this time round.'

'For what it's worth,' Alex said, 'I think your ex was utterly stupid. Why have an affair when you're already married to a woman who's bright, full of energy and totally lovely?'

She smiled. 'There are answers to that, but they're a little cynical. And thank you for the compliment. I wasn't fishing.'

'I know. I was just stating a fact.'

'Thank you.' She paused. 'I thought you didn't like me. Because of the way you are at work.'

He shook his head. 'It's not that. I didn't want to make friends with anyone.'

'Don't punish yourself,' she said gently. 'None of this Huntington's thing is your fault. And it doesn't mean you can't have friends.'

'I don't want to end up being a burden to anyone.'

'Firstly,' she said, 'you don't know for sure that you have it. Secondly, if you do have it, medicine might have advanced enough for there to be some sort of treatment by the time you start getting symptoms. Thirdly, Huntington's is really rare, but there are a lot of other medical conditions where people need a lot of support in the end stages. It's miserable enough suffering from a difficult medical condition, without cutting yourself off from people and making yourself lonely as well.' She paused.

'My grandfather had dementia. He didn't want to be a burden, so while he was still in the early stages he made my mum promise to put him in residential care rather than run herself ragged trying to care for him and look after me and do her job. She felt horribly guilty about it, but finding him a care home meant she could spend time with him as his daughter rather than his carer and that made things a lot easier for both of them. Yes, it was still hard for her, losing a little bit more of him every time she saw him, but he didn't feel he was a burden. And she's made me promise that if she gets dementia I'll do the same for her. There are ways round things.'

'Sometimes it's hard to see them.'

'Sometimes you're too close to things and it takes someone else to see it for you,' she pointed out.

'True.' He paused. 'I'd better let you get on. Thank you for the pizza and the pep talk.'

'Any time.' She stood up. 'Hey. Before you go.'

He turned to her, expecting her to say something; instead, to his shock, she put her arms round him, holding him close for a few moments.

When was the last time anyone had hugged him? The last time he'd actually let anyone hug him?

Months ago. What felt like a lifetime ago.

'What was that for?' he asked.

'Because,' she said softly, 'it seems to me you've had a rough few months, you've been a little bit too noble and self-sacrificing, and in the circumstances I think you've been needing someone to hold you for way too long.'

She was right. Except now it made him feel like a man who'd trudged through the desert for days and had finally found an oasis. Unable to stop himself, he put his arms round her and held her close, breathing in the soft vanilla scent of her shampoo.

And from holding her it was only one step to sliding his cheek against hers. Turning towards her. Letting his lips touch the corner of her mouth. And then finally kissing her properly, losing himself in the sweetness of her mouth.

It suddenly slammed into him what he was doing.

Kissing Danielle Owens.

He had no right to do this.

He pulled back and looked at her in anguish. 'I'm sorry. I shouldn't have done that.'

'No?' She traced his lower lip with her fingertip, and it made him ache.

'This is a bad idea,' he said. 'I'm not in a place where I could even consider asking you out, and offering you a fling would be—well, not very honourable.'

'When my divorce came through,' she said, 'I made a pact with Hayley, my best friend. We agreed that this is the Year of Saying Yes.'

'The Year of Saying Yes?' He didn't quite understand.

'It means you say yes to every opportunity that makes your life happier, even if it's only for a little while. I was supposed to be going to Iceland with Hayley—but I broke my foot so I couldn't go. Though I made her agree to go on her own, so she got to see all the things on her bucket list: the midnight sun, watching whales in the sea, walking on a glacier. I'm hideously jealous, because a lot of them were on my list, too—but no way was I going to hold her back. And she admitted I was right to make her go because she had a wonderful time.'

'So what are you saying?'

'I'm saying,' she said, 'that maybe you could do

the same. It doesn't have to be a year of saying yes. Six months, maybe, or even a week.' She paused. 'Or just tonight.'

His breath caught. 'Are you suggesting…?'

'I'm saying that you need to stop thinking and start doing. Live in the moment. No strings.'

Make love with Dani. Right at that moment, he wanted it more than he could ever remember wanting anything. But he had to be sensible and hold himself back. 'There's just one tiny, tiny thing. Given that I might be carrying a faulty chromosome,' he said, 'I don't want to take any risks of passing it on. And I don't have a condom.'

'Whereas I do,' she said. 'Which isn't to say that the Year of Saying Yes means I sleep with every man I meet.'

He didn't think that Dani was the type to sleep around. Far from it. 'Have you actually slept with anyone since Christmas Eve?' he asked.

'No, and if I'm honest I didn't sleep with Leo very much in the last six months of our marriage,' she admitted. 'But I'm prepared now, in case I do meet someone.'

Someone.

Him.

The possibilities made every nerve-ending tingle.

'So have you slept with anyone since you ended your engagement?' she asked.

'No,' he admitted.

'Which means this is going to be faintly awkward and embarrassing, and there's no guarantee that either of us will remember what we're supposed to do.'

He couldn't help smiling. Which meant he'd smiled twice in one evening. *Twice in eight months.* And it was all thanks to Dani. 'That's really terrible, considering what we both do for a living.'

'Maybe we should just stop overthinking it,' she said.

'The Year of Saying Yes?'

'Or six months. Or a week. Or just tonight,' she said. 'Maybe we should just consider this a rebound thing. No consequences, no worries, just a moment out of time for both of us.'

She was right. They were both overthinking it. And it sounded as if her world had been shattered, too, by her ex. Maybe tonight they could salvage something for both of them.

He kissed her. 'Yes.'

CHAPTER THREE

IT WAS THE first time Dani could ever remember propositioning anyone. And in some ways she was taking advantage of Alex; he'd opened his heart to her and told her exactly why he was keeping a distance between himself and the rest of the human race. He was vulnerable. Hurting.

Then again, so was she. She'd spent months trying to convince herself that she was over Leo. She didn't love her ex any more; but she was finding it hard to get past the knowledge that she hadn't been enough for him. That something in her was lacking. That maybe she was too bossy and unloveable—and that was why he hadn't wanted to have a baby with her.

She hadn't even told her best friend about that bit, feeling too ashamed of herself. Other people had it much worse—Hayley had had to bury the love of her life when she was only thirty years old—and Dani knew she was just being a whiny, selfish brat about her own situation.

But just maybe she and Alex could help each other feel better. If only for a little while.

She stroked his face. 'I'm glad it's a yes.'

He turned his head to press a kiss into her palm. 'Me, too.'

His blue-green eyes had darkened. Gratifyingly so. And Dani felt desire kick deep inside her.

'Then let's go somewhere more comfortable.'

She'd half expected him to hold her hand, but she wasn't prepared for him to scoop her up in his arms—as if he wanted her so much that he couldn't wait. It shocked her and thrilled her at the same time.

'Which door?' he asked when he carried her into the hallway.

'On your right,' she said.

He finessed the door handle, switched on the overhead light and closed the curtains, all without dropping her.

And then he let her slide down his body so she was left in no doubt about how much he wanted her.

She reached up to him and kissed him.

He untucked her shirt from her skirt, and unbuttoned it really, really slowly, keeping his gaze fixed on hers the whole time. Whenever his fingers brushed against her, it made her skin tingle.

'My turn,' she said, and undid his shirt. She blew out a breath. 'Nice musculature, Dr Morgan.'

He inclined his head to acknowledge the compliment. 'Thank you.'

She pushed the soft cotton off his shoulders. 'Nice arms.'

In return, he pushed her shirt off her shoulders. 'Turn round.'

Not sure where he was going with this, she did so.

'Nice back, Dr Owens.' And then he kissed the

nape of her neck before loosening her hair from the scrunchie she kept it in at work.

Her knees went weak. Alex's touch was doing things to her that she'd forgotten could even happen.

'May I?' he asked, his fingers at the clasp of her bra.

'It's the Year of Saying Yes,' she reminded him, though she liked the fact that he'd asked.

'I know. But if you change your mind about this...'

'I'm not going to change my mind,' she said.

He unsnapped her bra and let the lacy garment fall to the floor, then slid his arms round her and cupped her breasts. 'Beautiful,' he said, and kissed his way along her shoulder.

Desire shivered through her. 'Alex.'

'I know. Me, too.' He turned her to face him and kissed her lightly. 'You're gorgeous.'

She hadn't felt it. Not for months and months and months. She'd felt ugly and rejected and unloveable, and hated herself even more for being so self-indulgent when so many worse things were happening in the world. But Alex's touch was helping to salve the bruise that went right through her.

'So are you,' she said.

She paused with her fingers on the waistband of his trousers. 'May I?'

'Yes,' he whispered, and the huskiness of his voice sent a thrill down her spine.

She undid the button, lowered the zip and eased the material over his hips. The trousers pooled at his feet and he stepped out of them. She picked them up and hung them neatly over the back of her chair, and Alex laughed softly.

'What?'

'Very organised.'

'If you'd been wearing jeans, I would've left them on the floor. But these are your work—'

He stopped her by kissing her. 'I was teasing. Actually, I really like the way you just sort everything out without comment or fuss. It's adorable.'

That hadn't been what Leo had said. Her ex had seen her as a control freak. An emasculating bitch. And Dani wasn't entirely sure that her best friend was right when Hayley had said it was simply Leo trying to make excuses for his behaviour and pin the blame on her.

'Dani,' Alex said, his voice gentle. 'The deal was we're not thinking. We're just feeling. Tonight is to-night.'

'Yeah. Sorry.'

He drew her into his arms and stroked her hair. 'Your ex was incredibly selfish and incredibly stupid. Don't blame yourself.'

Much, much easier said than done.

'No,' she fibbed.

'Dani.' He tilted her chin upwards, making her meet his eyes. 'You're lovely. Don't let anyone make you think otherwise.'

His kindness almost brought tears to her eyes.

He slid his hands down her sides. 'Right now, you're wearing too much. And I'm not happy about your standing around in that walking cast.' He groaned. 'And that makes me feel horrible. I'm pushing myself onto an injured woman.'

She wasn't sure how much was theatrical teasing and how much he meant it, but the teasing note in his voice made her feel better. 'It's removable. And if you carry me to bed it'll take the pressure off my foot.' Pressure that wasn't really there in the first place, but she was going along with his line of whimsy.

He slid the zip of her skirt downwards, got her to step out of it, and then folded it neatly and hung it on the chair with his trousers. 'I'm a neat freak, too,' he said.

Dani was grateful for that.

'And you're beautiful, but this overhead light is a little too harsh.'

'I'll switch the bedside light on if you deal with the main light,' she said.

'Deal.'

And funny how the softer light made the room feel so much more intimate.

She'd never shared this bed with anyone, and part of her felt apprehensive about sharing it now. Was she doing the right thing? Was she just setting herself up for heartbreak?

But then she stopped thinking as Alex dropped to his knees in front of her and peeled her tights downwards. He nuzzled her abdomen, and she couldn't help the sharp intake of breath.

He undid her cast and removed it gently, then finished taking off her tights, letting her lean on him for support. 'You mentioned something about carrying you to bed.'

'Uh-huh.' She stole a kiss. 'Strictly speaking, I should've been wearing a Regency dress and you should be in a frock coat and a flowing shirt with a waistcoat, cravat and silk breeches.'

He raised an eyebrow. 'Just call me Darcy, hmm?'

'Something like that.'

'It's too late for the outfit,' he said. 'But I can still do the carrying. Though, before I forget myself completely, where do you keep your condoms?'

'Top drawer of my bedside cabinet,' she said.

'Would you mind if I…?'

'Sure,' she said. Whatever she'd previously thought about Alex being rude and difficult, she'd changed her mind. He had perfect manners.

And then she stopped thinking as he scooped her up and carried her over to her bed. He pulled the duvet back and laid her back against the pillows. And she felt weirdly shy all of a sudden; he must've sensed it, because he climbed into bed next to her, pulled the duvet over both of them and drew her into his arms.

'You can still change your mind,' he said. 'The Year of Saying Yes is about seizing opportunities, not making yourself do something you don't want to do.'

'I want to do this,' she said. 'But it's been a while.'

'Same here. And we agreed, no pressure. This is just for tonight. A moment out of time.'

'Never to be spoken of again.'

'Exactly. And now we stop speaking,' he said, and kissed her.

And after that it was easy to stop thinking, stop speaking, and just lose herself in pleasure—to let herself enjoy touching him, exploring the hardness of his muscles and the softness of his skin.

Alex dipped his head and nuzzled the hollows of Dani's collar bones. He loved the way her skin felt against his mouth, and the soft fruity scent of her shower gel. She arched back against the bed and he moved lower, taking one nipple into his mouth and sucking hard. She slid her hands into his hair, urging him on.

And he forgot all the nightmares that had plagued him over the last few months. All he could think of was Dani, and how much he wanted to be inside her. How much he wanted to give as much pleasure as he took.

He kissed his way down over her abdomen, then shifted to kneel between her legs.

'Alex, yes,' she whispered as his tongue stroked along her sex.

He teased her, flicking the tip of her clitoris with the tip of his tongue, until her hands clenched in his hair and her body tightened beneath his mouth. And then he ripped open the foil packet he'd taken from her bedside cabinet, slid the condom over his erection and pushed into her.

'Alex,' she whispered, and he held still, letting her body adjust to the feel of him inside her.

Her dark eyes were wide with pleasure, and he loved the knowledge that he'd been able to do that for her.

'I wanted the first time to be for you,' he said softly.

Her eyes filled with tears, as if she wasn't used to her feelings being considered like that. Then again, given the little she'd told him about her past, consideration hadn't been high on her ex's agenda.

'Hey. It's the Year of Saying Yes,' he said.

She smiled. 'Yes.'

And then she took it to another level, wrapping her legs round him to draw him deeper and tensing her muscles round him.

'Oh. Yes.' The breath hissed out of him.

And then he stopped thinking, instead responding to the physicality between them and revelling in the way she made him feel.

By the time he climaxed, his head was spinning; and then he felt her body rippling round his as her own climax hit. He wrapped his arms round her and held her tightly until it had all ebbed away.

'I'd better deal with the condom,' he said finally.

'There are fresh towels in the bathroom. Help yourself to anything you need.' She paused. 'Stay tonight.'

He ought to say no. Put distance between them. Go back to being sensible and isolated.

But every bit of him yearned to say yes. To spend the night with her wrapped in his arms, to let her take the loneliness away—and to make her feel less alone, too.

As if his dilemma showed on his face, she said softly, 'It's the Year of Saying Yes.'

So what else could he do?

'Yes.'

The next morning, Alex woke, feeling slightly disorientated: this wasn't his bed, and he was spooned against a warm female body, with his arm wrapped round her waist.

Dani.

Thanks to her, his heart felt lighter than it had for months. But it still didn't change the stark reality of his situation. Even though he wished things could be different, last night had to be just that: last night. A one-off. Something that had healed some of the pain for both of them, but still a temporary solution.

He was about to try and disentangle himself from her when there was a sharp shrill, a groan, and then she reached out to hit the top of the alarm clock and the noise stopped.

And then she turned to face him. 'Good morning.'

'Good morning,' he said warily.

She pressed her palm briefly against his cheek. 'Don't look so worried. I usually hit the gym before work, so you've got plenty of time to have breakfast and then get back to your own place for clean clothes.'

Of course. Dani was organisation personified. 'Thank you,' he said.

'There are clean towels in the airing cabinet, if you'd like the first shower. And there's a new spare tooth-brush on the middle shelf of the bathroom cabinet.'

She thought of everything.

'I'll go and make some coffee and sort out some breakfast.'

He frowned. 'Isn't that going to make you late for the gym?'

'No. I'm going to skip it today,' she said. 'And before you start feeling guilty about it, it's nothing to do with you and everything to do with pacing myself with my foot.'

'Thank you.' He paused. 'Dani, we need to talk about this. If things were different...' He grimaced and shook his head. 'But they're not. I'm sorry. I feel bad about this, but I can't even consider having a relationship. Not with the Huntington's thing hanging over me.'

'I know. And it's the same for me. I'm not looking for a relationship right now either. We agreed last night that it was just going to be last night. Between you and me. Never to be spoken of again.'

The problem was, he wanted to repeat it. Waking up with her in his arms had felt so good. But he couldn't be selfish enough to ask her. 'Uh-huh.'

'Which means we can be professional with each other at work,' she said.

'Agreed.' He paused. 'Though we still need to sort out the departmental Christmas meal.'

'Maybe we can have a second try at it tomorrow evening,' she said. 'Maybe, strictly as colleagues, we can try the different meal options between us—actually, there are four, so either we can drag some colleagues along or we can do it on two evenings. Or just one evening and be super-greedy.'

Strictly as colleagues: so this wasn't a date masquerading under another name. 'Do you have anyone in mind?'

'We could…' She paused and shook her head. 'Actually, no. We'll keep it to just us.'

'All right.' And funny how the guilt he'd felt had just drained away.

'Go have your shower,' she said, and climbed out of the bed.

Alex's pulse spiked. Just as he'd thought, the first time he'd met her, she was a pocket Venus, all curves— but her curves were toned from a mixture of running and her programme in the gym. She was utterly gorgeous.

And his thoughts were completely inappropriate. They were supposed to be just colleagues from now on.

He closed his eyes, and then he heard her laugh. 'It's a bit late to be shy, Alex.'

'I guess.' And when he opened his eyes again he saw that she was wearing a fluffy towelling bath robe.

'Sorry, I don't have a spare bath robe to offer to lend you—and if I did, it wouldn't fit you anyway. But I'll leave you to sort yourself out while I sort out breakfast.'

'Thanks.'

When he'd showered and dressed, he joined her in the kitchen.

She was drinking coffee and finishing a piece of wholemeal toast spread generously with peanut butter. 'What would you like?' she asked. 'Toast, oatmeal, yoghurt?'

'Toast would be lovely—but I'll make it,' he said. 'You're not wearing your walking cast, so you're absolutely not waiting on me.'

'Anyone would think you were in cahoots with my best friend,' she said, rolling her eyes. 'She nags me about my cast, too. And I hate the thing.'

'The more you wear it, the more quickly you'll heal and can get rid of it.'

'The word "rest" wasn't in my vocabulary until August this year, and I hate feeling so constrained,' she said, rolling her eyes. 'OK. Help yourself to breakfast. Milk's in the fridge and coffee's in the pot. I'll go and get showered and dressed.'

Funny how easy she was to be with, Alex thought. And he was in a much better place than he'd been in last night. Enough to let him be nosy and look at the photographs held on her fridge with magnets while he ate his toast.

He recognised the woman with her in several of the photographs—Hayley from the emergency department—and guessed that this was Dani's best friend. There were others from what he assumed were team nights out; there was one where she was holding a biscuit tin above her head as if it were a trophy, and there were half a dozen midwives with her.

'That,' Dani said, coming to stand beside him and peering at the photograph, 'is the only time in the last year that we've beaten the emergency department in the monthly pub quiz. How's your general knowledge?'

'I…' Oh, help. He didn't like where this was going.

'I'm guessing it's good,' she said. 'The Emergency lot are getting very cheeky about their winning streak. We need a secret weapon to take them down a peg or two. I think you'd fit the bill rather nicely.'

'I'm not sure I can handle a crowd,' he said.

'Then you can work up to it,' she said. 'Maybe start by having lunch with a couple of us from the ward today, instead of a sandwich on your own and hiding behind a journal.'

'Maybe.' Though he had a feeling he wasn't going to have a choice in the matter. Dani was clearly in fixer mode.

She glanced at her watch. 'And I guess you need to get going.'

'I'll do the washing up first.'

'If you do, you'll be late,' she said with a smile. 'And there's not that much to do. Go. I'll see you at work.'

'OK. And thank you.'

'Pleasure.' She rested her hand briefly on his forearm, and it was all he could do to stop himself lifting her hand to his mouth and pressing a kiss into her palm. 'Alex, I meant what I said. Nothing you told me last night will go any further than me, but any time you need a friend to talk something over, you know where I am.'

A friend.

If only she could've been more than that.

'I appreciate it.'

'And remember, the only person who decides when to do that test is you. Which is when you're ready, and not a second before then.'

How good it felt to have her batting his corner. To have someone who understood and wasn't judging him.

'I'll see you at work,' she said. 'And I'll book us a table for tomorrow night so we can agree the menu.'

'Sounds good,' he said.

Dani texted him later to say their table was booked for seven, tomorrow evening. And, just as he'd suspected, that day she made him join her and Jas, one of the midwives, for lunch. Although he'd been antsy at the idea, given that he'd kept himself at such a distance from everyone in the previous two months, he was surprised to find himself relaxing with them.

Though at the same time he was so aware of Dani. How she'd felt in his arms. The warmth of her skin against his. He shook himself. Now was really not an appropriate time to remember that.

'I'm glad I'm getting to know you a bit better,' Jas said. 'You're good with our mums, but I was beginning to worry that you were one of those consultants who prefers to keep a distance between himself and the midwives.'

He knew the type she meant, and it was an attitude he hated. 'I'm not. And I'm sorry I've come across as a snob with a superiority complex.'

'When really you're just a little bit shy,' Dani said.

'And sweet,' Jas added.

He couldn't help laughing. 'I wouldn't describe myself as sweet either.'

'You'll do,' Jas said with a grin.

Alex had missed this kind of teasing camaraderie. Even though part of him felt that he needed to keep his distance so he wouldn't become a burden to anyone, maybe Dani had a point about the potential of a horrible disease being enough to deal with without isolating himself into the bargain.

He didn't get to see anything of Dani the next day, between Theatre and two busy clinics. But she'd left him a text reminding him to eat sparsely because they were having three courses and they might have to double up on the pudding.

They'd arranged to meet at the pub; he'd just bought a drink and was leaning against the bar when she walked in, wearing smart trousers to hide her walking cast teamed with a pretty top. He realised that she was wearing lipstick—something she didn't do at work. So was she wearing it for his benefit? His pulse rate spiked and he really had to resist the urge to kiss it off her.

He raised his hand to get her attention; she smiled and walked over to him.

And funny how her smile made his heart felt as if it had done a somersault.

Colleagues and friends *only*, he reminded himself. It wasn't fair to either of them to act on this attraction. 'Can I get you a drink?' he asked.

'Thanks. Sparkling water, please.'

Once they'd got their drinks, they made their way to the restaurant. After the waiter had shown them to their table and brought menus, Dani took out a file with the details of the Christmas meal.

'OK. Because our departmental Christmas meal is on a weeknight, we can get away with organising it this late,' she said. 'There are a couple of other places that can fit us in, but I've eaten here with Hayley a few times so I know the food's good. We get the function room to ourselves, and once we've eaten they're going to move the tables so we've got a dance floor. Maybe Baby are doing the music.'

'Maybe Baby?' Alex asked, mystified.

'They're kind of our house band,' Dani explained. 'Half of the band's from our department and half's from Paediatrics. From our department, Anton plays lead guitar and Gilly plays the bass, then from Paediatrics, Keely's the singer and Marty's the drummer. They play at most of the hospital functions and they're really good—they play everything from the latest chart stuff through to oldies.'

'Sounds good. So really we need to focus on the menu, crackers…maybe a Secret Santa?'

'Jas is organising the Secret Santa—she's doing the names next week,' Dani said. 'But yes, we need to agree on the menu and crackers. There's an option to donate money to cancer research instead of having novelties in the crackers.'

'We should do that,' he said. 'Novelties always get left on the table; all we really need are the paper hats and terrible jokes.'

'Agreed. So. Food. They sent me a list of options, and I checked the normal evening menu on the website and some of our options are available tonight,' she said. 'Carrot and coriander soup—well, soup's a soup. Then there's the salmon mousse with pickled cucumber and rye bread, which covers fish; ham hock terrine with apple chutney, which covers meat; and what do you think about arancini with a Parmesan crisp for the veggie option?'

'Sounds good,' he said. 'What about the main course? I'm assuming there's the traditional turkey with all the trimmings.'

'There is,' she said. 'And roast sirloin, so that gives us two traditional options.'

'So we need a veggie option and a fish option.' Funny, he'd thought this was going to be dull. But it was actually fun. Or maybe it was just because it meant he could spend time with Dani.

He was really going to have to be careful.

'There's a leek, chestnut and cranberry tart that sounds nice,' she said. 'Or a butternut squash risotto.'

'Chestnuts are maybe more Christmassy,' he said. 'What about the fish?'

'Sea bass or salmon.'

'We've got salmon in the first course,' he said. 'So maybe sea bass would be better.'

'Perfect. And then for pudding there's traditional

Christmas pudding with brandy sauce; passionfruit cheesecake; dark chocolate torte; and cheese and crackers.'

'Coffee after?' he checked.

She nodded. 'With Christmas petit fours.'

'Perfect. OK. So what are we trying?'

'This is why I told you to eat sparsely,' she said. 'I can already vouch for the Sunday roast dinner here, so maybe if we order the fish and the tart. And Christmas pudding and cheese and crackers are standard everywhere, so we can get away with ordering the cheesecake and the chocolate. But that leaves us four starters.'

'Bring it on,' he said with a grin.

Alex Morgan, now he'd thawed out a bit, was *nice*, Dani thought. More than nice. She really liked him.

It would be all too easy to lose her heart to him.

But his situation meant that he wasn't in the market for a relationship; and Dani had promised herself that never again would she fall for someone who couldn't love her all the way back. Leo's double betrayal had hurt her deeply. And although she'd agreed the Year of Saying Yes with Hayley, she'd done it purely to help her best friend move on from the tragedy of Evan's death. She wasn't sure she was ready to risk her own heart again. Leo had made her feel unloveable, and she wasn't going to put herself in another situation where she'd fallen for someone who didn't feel the same way.

She and Alex were strictly colleagues, she reminded herself. Friendship was as far as they could go. And that would have to be enough. Because the night they'd spent together couldn't be repeated.

CHAPTER FOUR

'DANIELLE OWENS SPEAKING,' Dani said, answering the phone.

'Dani? It's Hayley—we've got a patient coming in who's been in a car accident. She's thirty-two weeks. The paramedics have talked to me on the way in and it sounds as if we're looking at an abruption. She's in shock, she's in pain, her uterus is woody and they can't feel the foetal parts easily.'

An abruption—where the placenta was torn away from the uterus—was a life-threatening emergency and there was a strong chance that the baby could die.

'She'll be here in about ten minutes. Can you come down?' Hayley asked.

'I'm on my way,' Dani said. She put the phone down and grabbed the first midwife she could find. 'Gilly, I've just had a call from the emergency department. We've got a mum coming in at thirty-two weeks with a suspected abruption, so I need an anaesthetist and a theatre, please.'

'I'm on it,' Gilly said. 'And I'll get the neonatal special care unit on standby.'

'Thanks, Gilly.' Dani knocked on Alex's door and

filled him in on the situation. 'Given that we might have to operate, can I grab you now?'

'Of course. I'm not due in clinic for another hour, but I'll make sure everyone knows where I am if I'm going to be late.' He closed the file he was working on and logged off the computer. 'What do you know about the mum?'

'The paramedics were called out to a car accident. She's in shock, has a woody uterus and it's hard to feel the baby.'

'That definitely sounds like a potential abruption,' he said. 'Let's keep our fingers crossed that the baby makes it as far as the hospital.'

They headed out of the ward, and her fingers brushed against his as they walked into the lift. How ridiculous that her skin should tingle when he touched her. He really needed to stop this. She was off limits. Colleagues only.

And oh, how he wished it could be otherwise.

Hayley met them at the emergency department.

'Do I need to introduce you to each other?' Dani asked.

'No, we've worked together a couple of times,' Alex said.

'That makes things easy, then,' Dani said. 'Haze, I've filled Alex in on the situation.'

'Good. I'll sort out blood tests and a cross-match of four units of blood, with fresh frozen plasma on standby as soon as she comes in, but in the meantime I have Hartmann's solution available,' Hayley said. 'The paramedics are giving her oxygen and putting an IV in. She's due here any minute now.'

'Thank you. We'll examine her and do an ultrasound,' Alex said. 'Do you have a portable machine here?'

'Yes. I'll make sure it's in Resus,' Hayley said.

'If the baby's still alive and mature enough to be delivered, we'll take her up to Theatre and do a section,' he said.

'And if the baby's not OK?' Dani asked.

'Then we know the mum will deliver the baby not that long afterwards, so we'll focus on the mum,' Alex said. 'We'll need to treat her for shock and try to avoid DIC.'

Disseminated intravascular coagulation was where the normal blood clotting process was disrupted. The blood formed small clots and couldn't flow properly through the tissues, leading to organ damage; at the same time, the patient could bleed heavily. And it was a life-threatening condition: between ten and fifty per cent of patients with DIC didn't make it.

He blew out a breath. 'Poor woman. I hope we can get her the right result.'

The paramedics came in and did the handover, and helped move Mrs Kirby from the trolley to the bed in Resus.

'Mrs Kirby, I'm Alex Morgan and I'm a consultant from the maternity department,' Alex said. 'This my colleague Dani from Maternity, and Hayley from the emergency department. I know you've been in a car accident and right now things seem very scary, but I'm going to examine you to see what's going on with the baby, if that's all right.'

'Is my baby OK?' Mrs Kirby took the oxygen mask

off; her voice was high-pitched with panic. 'The paramedics couldn't feel the baby or get a heartbeat.'

It's sometimes difficult to feel what's happening
because you're in a lot of pain and your uterus tends
to feel hard in this sort of situation,' Dani explained.
'I know it's hard but try not to worry. Alex and I are
going to do an ultrasound to see what's going on.'

'Can we call anyone for you?' Hayley asked.

'The paramedics already called my husband. He's
on his way.'

'I'm going to examine you now,' Alex said. 'I'd like
you to put the mask back on, and lift your hand or tap
me if anything hurts.'

'I don't care about me,' Mrs Kirby said. 'I just want
my baby to be OK.'

Dani held her hand and helped her put the oxygen
mask back on. 'We'll do our best,' she said. When Alex
examined Mrs Kirby, Dani could see from his expression that he wasn't happy: clearly her uterus felt woody.

'I can see there's no sign of a vaginal bleed,' he
said. 'So I'm not going to do an internal examination.'

If blood from the detached placenta wasn't coming through the cervix, that meant the abruption was
concealed—so it was more serious and they couldn't
tell how much blood she'd lost.

'I need to take some blood from you so we can
check it's clotting properly,' Hayley said, and quickly
took the samples.

Dani had the portable ultrasound ready. 'I'm going
to squeeze some gel onto your tummy now. It's exactly the same sort of scan you had for your dating

scan and the twenty-week scan, so try not to worry,' she said gently.

She glanced over at Alex. He was holding Mrs Kirby's hand and looked white-faced and grim; clearly he didn't think this was going to be good news.

She swept the head of the scanner over Mrs Kirby's stomach. She couldn't see the abruption clearly, but on the screen she could just about see the baby moving. The heartbeat didn't look brilliant but, most importantly, it was *there*. She nodded at Alex.

'It's good news,' Alex said to Mrs Kirby. 'We can see the baby's heartbeat, so we're going to take you into Theatre for an emergency section and deliver the baby now.'

Mrs Kirby pulled off her mask again. 'Isn't thirty-two weeks too soon?

'The baby will be small and will need to be in Special Care for a while, but thirty-two weeks is still OK for delivery. The team here is really good,' Alex reassured her.

By time they went up to Theatre, the units of blood for transfusion were ready and the blood test results were back. To Dani's relief, the coagulation screen was reasonable and it looked as if they might be lucky and avoid a situation where their patient developed DIC. The transfusion was set up and, while Dani and Alex scrubbed up ready for the operation, the anaesthetist talked Mrs Kirby through the fact that was going to need a general anaesthetic for the birth, so her husband would have to wait outside rather than being there for the birth, but could see the baby straight away afterwards. Karin, the specialist from the neonatal special care team, was ready with the crib.

'Ready?' Alex asked.

Alex performed the section with Dani assisting; and although part of her admired how skilfully he worked, part of her was waiting desperately to hear that first cry. Had they done the section in time, or was it too late for the baby?

She only realised she'd been holding her breath when there was a thin wail. The sound she'd been waiting to hear.

'Well done, team,' Alex said.

'Not a brilliant first Apgar score, but he's starting to pink up now,' Karin said, sounding relieved.

'Nice work,' Dani said to Alex.

'Thanks.' He looked relieved. 'I'm just glad we were on time for the baby, though we're not out of the woods yet with the mum or the baby.' They hadn't had time to give her a steroid injection to help mature the baby's lungs, plus Dani knew that Mrs Kirby was more at risk of a post-partum haemorrhage because of the abruption.

'We'll keep a very close eye on her on the ward, and Special Care will have the baby under close monitoring,' she said.

'Do we have a camera here?' he asked. 'Or at least can someone take a photograph of the baby for Mrs Kirby before you take him off to Special Care? She's had a horrible experience and I don't want to make her wait until she's out of the recovery room before she sees him.'

'I'm on it,' Karin said.

Between them, Alex and Dani finished closing the incision and sewing all the layers together while Karin took a photograph and then the baby was taken off to the neonatal special care unit. And then finally the anaesthetist brought Mrs Kirby round.

'Wonderful news, Mrs Kirby. You've got a beautiful little boy,' Alex told her with a smile.

'Is he all right? Can I see him?'

'I'm afraid Karin's taken him to the neonatal special care unit, and we need to wait until you're fully round from the anaesthetic before we can take you to see him, but she did take a photograph for you first.' He handed her the photograph.

A tear trickled down her cheek. 'He's beautiful.'

'He's holding his own,' Alex told her. 'He's about three and a half pounds, which is a nice weight for a thirty-two-weeker.'

'He's got all his fingers and toes—including nails,' Dani said. 'Though you'll notice he's a bit wrinkly. He'll fill out and double his weight over the next two months.'

Mrs Kirby bit her lip. 'Is my husband here? Can he see the baby?'

'I think he might be in Special Care with your baby right now,' Dani said. 'I'll get hold of the team and ask him to come in to you.'

'Thank you,' Mrs Kirby said, the tears really flowing now. 'Thank you for saving my baby. You're both heroes.'

'We just did what we're trained to do,' Alex said, and squeezed her hand. 'We're going to take you to our recovery suite now, and then when we're happy you can go up to the ward. Once you're able to sit in a wheelchair, your husband will be able to take you to Special Care so you can see the baby.'

'It won't be too long,' Dani said, 'though I know any waiting's hard, especially in circumstances like yours. Try not to worry.'

'Just as long as the baby's all right.'

'He's in great hands,' Alex said.

Hands. Dani remembered just how good Alex was with his hands. How he'd made her feel. It would be oh, so easy to fall for him.

But that wasn't the agreement. And Alex had huge issues. He wasn't in a place where he could let himself fall for someone—and Dani didn't want to repeat her mistake of loving someone who didn't love her back.

They were strictly colleagues and friends, she reminded herself.

It was all they could be.

Alex dropped in to see the Kirbys at the end of his shift. 'How are you feeling?' he asked Mrs Kirby.

'I've had better days,' she said wryly. 'But I know I'm lucky to be here. And even luckier that our son's still alive.'

'Karin tells me he's a fighter and he's doing well,' Alex said.

'We'd like to name our baby Alex, after you,' Mrs Kirby said. 'If it wasn't for you, he wouldn't be here now.'

'It was teamwork, so it wasn't just me—it was the anaesthetist, Dani, Hayley and Karin as well,' Alex said.

But the words put a lump in his throat. A baby

named after him. He wouldn't have a child of his own—a child who would maybe have had his name as a middle name, and maybe give that name to his own son. As an only child, Alex wouldn't be an uncle. There wouldn't be future generations to remember him with a smile. But his name, his work, would live on in this baby.

'Thank you. It's a real honour.'

She looked at him. 'Are you all right, Dr Morgan?'

'Yes.' He smiled at her. 'After all these years, I still get misty-eyed when I deliver a baby.' He checked her temperature and pulse, and wrote it up on her notes. 'I'll see you tomorrow,' he said. 'But if you need anything, just call one of the team. They're all really approachable on the ward.'

And it made him think on his way home. Life was short. And his own might turn out to be very messy indeed, so he couldn't waste time. He needed to repair the rift between himself and his family, and the sooner the better.

He took his phone from his pocket and texted his father to ask if he was free to meet up for a pint on Saturday evening—just the two of them. Maybe neutral territory would help them deal with the situation better. Though he really, really hoped that Dani was right about this—that Will feared he was going to be rejected, rather than being the one doing the rejecting.

He was beginning to think that either his text hadn't gone through or his father's phone was switched off when his phone beeped.

OK. Tell me where and when.

It was only then that Alex realised how tense he'd been, waiting and half expecting Will to refuse. In the end he named a pub roughly halfway between them that specialised in the kind of real ale he knew his father liked, and Will texted back a terse 'OK'. Then again, Alex knew better to read anything into the length of his father's reply. Will was a man of few words.

On Saturday evening, Will was already there at a table when Alex walked in, five minutes early.

'I've already bought you a pint,' he said. 'The Championship ale looked good on the board, and it's not bad.'

'Thanks.' Alex paused. 'So how are things?'

Will shrugged. 'Getting there, I suppose. Why did you want to see me without your mother?'

'I wanted to talk to you on your own about something.'

Will frowned. 'Are you in trouble?'

Yes, but not in the way his father was obviously fearing. Alex took a deep breath. 'I know we've always done all this English stiff upper lip business and never talked about our feelings, but I've been talking to a friend about the situation. She made me face up to a few things.'

'She?'

'We're just colleagues,' Alex said, before his father could make any more assumptions.

'Oh.' Will looked faintly disappointed.

'And I don't think I can make things any worse than they are right now,' Alex said, 'so I wanted to apologise.'

'Apologise?' Will looked surprised. 'For what?'

This felt as if he was ripping the top off his father's scars, but Alex knew it had to be done or the poison would continue to fester. 'For reminding you of Mum and Stephen every time you see me.'

Will looked shocked. 'Is that what you think?'

'Ever since Mum told us about what happened, you've pretty much avoided me, so that's what it feels like,' Alex said. 'But if it's not that seeing me brings up painful memories, then my friend might be right.'

'About what?'

Alex squirmed. This definitely ranked as one of the most uncomfortable conversations he'd ever had. But if they were to have a chance of moving forward, he had to go through with this. 'That now I know you're not my biological father, you think I don't see you as my father any more.'

'Uh-huh.'

Alex sighed. 'Dad, has anyone ever told you how bloody difficult you can be?'

Will stared at him. 'You just called me "Dad".'

'What else am I going to call you? That's who you've been for the last thirty-five years,' Alex pointed out.

'So you still think of me like that?'

'Of course I do,' Alex said. 'The only thing that's changed is a bit of genetic coding that I didn't know about before, and that doesn't make any diff...' He broke off and grimaced. 'Well, I guess it does make a difference if I've inherited *that* gene, but otherwise it doesn't change the fact that you're the one who taught me to kick a football, swim, and ride a bike, and yelled at me so I knuckled down to study properly for my exams. You're my dad. Always have been, always will be.'

Will looked hugely relieved. 'I'm glad.'

'So you really thought I'd put a total stranger above you in my life? Why didn't you say something before?' Alex asked.

'You had enough to deal with, without fussing about my feelings. Anyway, *you* could've said something,' Will pointed out.

'I am now.'

Will raised an eyebrow. 'I thought they were supposed to teach you personal skills as part of your doctor training nowadays?'

Alex laughed. 'If you were a mum with a complicated pregnancy, you'd think my bedside manner was perfect.'

'Whereas I'm a sixty-three-year-old retired orthopod. And, from what I can see, your bedside manner is no better than mine.'

'Like father, like son,' Alex said quietly. 'I'm not so good with words outside work, but I'm learning to talk things over.'

Will looked thoughtful. 'Then I should make the effort and join you.'

'What about Mum?' Alex asked.

Will sighed. 'I'm trying, Alex. The stupid thing is, if she'd told me the truth when she was pregnant, it wouldn't have mattered. It's the fact that she kept it from me for all those years that upset me most. It made me wonder what else she hadn't told me. And, even though she says there isn't anything, it's so easy to misread things.'

Alex was truly shocked. 'You think she had other affairs?'

Will blew out a breath. 'I'll be honest with you. It did cross my mind. I'm not proud of myself—I actually asked her, and I could see how much I hurt her by doubting her. There wasn't anyone else. Stephen just caught her at a bad time, when she was very unhappy. We weren't getting on well and I'd just gone off to Edinburgh on secondment. I didn't talk it over properly with her first and just expected her to get on with it. So it's not all her fault.'

Before his mother's shock news, Alex had always looked up to his parents as an example of the perfect marriage—two people who'd loved each other for decades. When so many marriages seemed to collapse after five minutes, his parents' marriage had made Alex believe that love could really last. Learning that he was the product of an affair had really floored him. And now it looked as if his parents' marriage was going to crumble.

'Are you thinking about a divorce?' he asked.

Will grimaced. 'I love your mother. Always have. And I think she loves me. But we're both treading on eggshells all the time, and I don't really know how to stop it.'

'Go to counselling?' Alex suggested. 'Talk to someone who isn't involved and won't judge or take sides?'

Will pulled a face. 'I hate the idea of it, having someone prying in my head. But if that's what it takes to sort things out between your mother and me, I guess I'm going to have to man up and do it. Because I don't want to throw away thirty-seven years like that.' He looked at Alex. 'As we're bringing everything into the open, you should know that your mother thinks you're punishing her.'

Alex frowned. 'Punishing her? How?'

'By not coming home very often and—more importantly—by refusing to take the test to find out if you've got the faulty gene.'

'I'm not punishing her.' Alex sighed. 'The reason I haven't come home is because I thought my being around would make things worse between you. And as for the test, what if it turns out to be positive? She'll blame herself and break her heart over it. At least this way, not knowing, she can't blame herself.'

'Actually, uncertainty,' Will said quietly, 'is what causes the most problems for patients.'

'I'm nobody's patient.'

'I know.' He sighed. 'And you're an adult. It's your choice.'

'Knowing one way or another isn't going to make any difference,' Alex said. 'You know as well as I do that there isn't a cure for Huntington's and there aren't any lifestyle changes that would stave it off or stop it progressing.'

'Have you talked it over with your fr—your colleague?' Will corrected himself.

'Sort of. She says the only person who can make the decision is me, and only when I'm ready to face the results.' He paused. 'Dad—if it was you, would you want to find out that in twenty years' time your quality of life will be next to nothing? That you won't be able to control all your movements, you'll become too clumsy and forgetful to be able to do the job you love, you'll have mood swings and be impossible to live with, and you'll have difficulty swallowing and even speaking? That you'll need help to do the simplest of tasks, you'll get to the point where you need full nursing care, and—worst of all—you'll just be a burden to everyone around you, to the point where they won't be able to remember the good times but just the sheer grinding drudgery of life as a carer?'

'I don't know,' Will said. 'I plan things. So I think that yes, I probably would want to know one way or the other. If the test was negative, then fine. If it was positive, then at least I'd be spared the uncertainty, the worry that every time I spill my coffee it might be the first sign of a neurodegenerative disease instead of being just a silly little thing that happens to everyone. I'd want to be able to plan my own care, to warn my family what to expect as the disease progresses and most of all to make sure they know I love them while I'm still capable of telling them so.' He paused. 'I don't say it often enough, Alex, but I love you. I've loved you since the moment I first held you in the delivery suite. And just because I'm not your real dad—'

'Oh, but you *are* my real dad,' Alex cut in. 'It takes more than a random sperm to make a father. You've always been there for me.' Unlike Stephen. 'And I'm sorry I've let you down this year.'

Will shook his head. 'You haven't let me down. It's been difficult for all of us.'

'I wish Mum had never met Stephen.'

'But then,' Will said, 'we wouldn't have had you. And that's the bit I'll never regret.'

Will's face was bright with sincerity, and it put a huge lump in Alex's throat. 'Thanks, Dad.'

'Come home soon,' Will said. 'Bring your colleague.'

'She's strictly my colleague, Dad. I'm not in the right place for it to be anything else.'

'Pity.'

Yes, it was. The more he got to know Dani, the more he liked her. It wasn't just the physical side of things either—he liked her for herself. But he wouldn't ask her to take on the enormity of his burden, just as he'd made sure that Lara was free to find someone who'd give her the love and happiness she deserved.

Will finished his pint, then gave Alex a hug. 'I mean it. Come home soon.'

'I will,' Alex promised.

Even though it was a Saturday evening and Alex was pretty sure that Dani's social diary was full to the brim, he called her on the way back from the pub.

'Hey. Are you at home?'

'Yes. Why?'

'Are you busy, or can I pop in and see you for a minute?'

'Of course you can,' she said. 'Is something wrong?'

'No. I just wanted to talk to you about something.'

'OK. I'm around all evening.'

'See you in a bit.'

Alex called in to the supermarket to get some nice flowers—even if one of the high-end florists had been open, he was pretty sure that Dani would prefer something a little less flashy and over-the-top—then headed for her flat.

She looked taken aback when she opened the door to him and he handed her the flowers. 'What are these for?'

'To say thanks,' he said.

She frowned. 'For what?' Then she shook herself. 'Come in and tell me. Coffee, tea, wine or water?'

'Coffee would be great, thanks.' He followed her into the kitchen and tried not to think about how it had felt to kiss her there.

Dani put the kettle on and shook grounds into her cafetière, then put the flowers in water. 'These are really lovely—thank you.'

'It's the least I could do. You know your pep talk? Well, I met my dad for a pint tonight. We talked. *Really* talked.'

'And?'

'You were right.' And he still couldn't believe how wrong he'd been. 'It wasn't that seeing me rubbed his nose in it. He thought I didn't see him as my dad any more.'

'So things are better between you now?' she asked.

'Yes. If it hadn't been for you then I would never even have talked to him about it.'

'Being bossy has its benefits,' she said with a grin.

He wanted to hug her.

But he could also remember what it felt like to hold her properly. To carry her to her bed. And, much as he wanted to repeat it, in the circumstances it really wasn't fair.

'Not joining me in coffee?' he asked instead when

she only made one mug of coffee and then filled a glass with cold water.

'I'm on a health kick, getting ready for the walking cast to be off and my foot to be officially in rehab,' she said. 'Plus it's a bit hypocritical of me to bang on to Haze about the importance of hydration if I don't bother doing it myself.'

'Haze—that's Hayley in the emergency department, right?' he checked.

'Yes. The one who's running for me. Actually, it was my evening to train with her tonight. I'd just got back when you called.'

'You're training with her?' He gave her foot a pointed look.

'As in bossing her about. Sitting on a gym ball next to her treadmill in the gym and directing her when to change the incline or the speed, and distracting her to keep her going through the tough bits. Sam's doing all the proper outdoor stuff with her.'

'Sam?'

'He's one of the registrars in the emergency department. He's saved me from sitting on a bench and freezing my backside off while Haze does a practice run round the park.'

'Got you. So if he's training, too, does that mean he's running the race as well?' Alex asked.

'No. Sam joined Muswell Hill after the closing date for the race. He's just helping out because he's a runner and—well, it's a way of him getting to know people when he's still new to the team.'

'Uh-huh. So do you have a sponsor form, or are you raising the money online?'

'Both.'

He grabbed his wallet, emptied out all the notes and handed them to her. 'Sponsor money.'

Her beautiful dark eyes widened. 'I can't accept that.'

'It's for equipment for our department so yes, you can,' he corrected. 'Plus you're the one who's having this Year of Saying Yes. So, under those rules, surely you have to say yes?'

'That,' she said, 'is very cheeky of you. But thank you.' She opened a drawer, took a form and a pen from a cardboard folder and handed them to him. 'Actually, I'll be cheeky now. Would you mind gift aiding it, so we can reclaim the tax?'

'No problem.' He filled in the relevant bits of the form and signed it.

'Thank you. I appreciate it.' She put the form back in the folder, along with the money.

'So how's the training going?' he asked.

'Good. Haze absolutely hates running, so she's doing an amazing job. Without her, I would've had to give the sponsorship money back.'

'She seems nice,' Alex said.

'She is. We met on our first day at university. Her room was next door to mine. I had hot chocolate, she had choc-chip cookies, we were both feeling incredibly homesick, and we cried all over each other,' Dani said. 'We've been best friends ever since.'

Pretty much like the way he'd met his own best friend. Except Alex had pushed Tom away. Maybe it was time to repair some bridges there, like the one he'd just repaired with his father. Maybe he should ring Tom.

Funny how Danielle Owens had made such a huge difference to his life.

And he damped down the regrets before they had a chance to strike hold.

CHAPTER FIVE

OVER THE NEXT couple of weeks, Dani managed to persuade Alex to join her for lunch almost every day with a couple of other people from the ward, and she was pleased to see that he started relaxing with the team enough to drop his aloofness. She was still aware of the slight distance he kept between himself and his colleagues, but his working relationship with the rest of the team was so much better than it had been.

She didn't manage to persuade him to take part in the pub quiz against the emergency department, but he had at least paid his deposit for his place at the ward's Christmas meal and was on the brink of agreeing to go to the team's pizza and bowling night later in the month.

On the last Sunday of October, Dani headed down to Alexandra Park with Hayley and Sam, getting Hayley set up with her numbered bib and the electronic tag for her shoe that would record her time. She noticed the glances between Hayley and Sam; it looked to her as if they were sorting out their differences and Hayley was starting to accept the fact that Sam's job meant he put himself in danger from time to time. So maybe, just maybe, they would move on together. Find happiness.

Although Dani was really pleased for her best friend, because Hayley really deserved to find love again, part of her was quietly envious. How long was it since she'd last felt loved and cherished?

She pushed the thought away. She was *not* going to let Leo spoil the rest of her life. She'd learned the hard way that it was pointless loving someone who wouldn't or couldn't love you back. And today was a good day. The hated walking cast was finally gone and she could start to rehab her foot properly. She'd focus on that.

'Are you OK, Dani?' Sam asked, looking concerned, when they were standing by the barrier next to the runners.

'I'm fine,' she lied with a smile. Actually, she wasn't feeling that great. Maybe she was coming down with something, and that was why her mood had dipped today.

She chatted to Sam as they waited for Hayley to come past them at the end of her first lap, and then they walked further down to the finish line. Dani could see Hayley starting to flag, but then Hayley looked up and saw Dani and Sam cheering her on, and it seemed to give her a last boost.

Once Hayley was over the finish line, Dani and Sam swept her into a joint hug. 'You're wonderful,' Dani said. 'Because of you, we've raised a ton of money for the new equipment for the ward.'

'People donated because of you,' Hayley reminded her.

'But you're the one who actually ran the race so we

could keep the sponsor money.' Dani hugged her hard. 'Thank you so much.'

Hayley hugged her back and then hugged Sam. 'Thank you both. I couldn't have done it without you training with me.'

Sam picked her up, swung her round and kissed her. 'You did brilliantly. I'm so proud of you.' Then he set Hayley back on her feet and rested his forehead against hers. 'Sorry. I know we were keeping this between us, but I kind of assumed Dani would know as she's your best friend.'

Yeah. Dani knew. It radiated out of the pair of them. 'She'd kept it sort of quiet, but I'd already guessed from the way you two look at each other,' Dani said with a smile, 'and it's a good thing.' It was. She was genuinely pleased for them.

But part of her couldn't help wishing that it had been different between her and Alex. That he would've been here with them today, hugging her and kissing her and looking at her as if she made his world feel full of sunshine, the way that Sam looked at Hayley.

And what kind of miserable cow was she, to envy her best friend's happiness?

She and Alex had agreed to be friends, so it was pointless wishing it could be otherwise. The best thing she could do now was to join a dating site or something and find someone she could have some fun with.

'Come on, let's go get your time,' Sam said to Hayley, 'and then I'm taking you both out for refuelling.'

Even though Dani really didn't fancy coffee and pastries—which had to be absolute proof that she was going down with a bug—she didn't want to spoil Hayley's joy at not only running the race but achieving a personal best time, too, so she joined them at the café.

But on the way back to her flat Dani realised what had been subconsciously nagging at her for the last day or so.

Her period was nearly two weeks late.

OK. Maybe it was stress—she'd been busy at work, and there was the whole thing about breaking her foot; although she'd tried to stay cheerful about it, she'd felt hampered and miserable about not being able to do the kind of exercise she loved. Yes, she'd actually had sex with someone in the last month, but given the circumstances Alex had been very careful indeed about contraception. They'd used protection.

On the other hand, she was an obstetrician and she knew from experience that the only contraception that was one hundred per cent reliable was abstinence. How many mums had she seen in her career who'd had a hard time adjusting to an unexpected pregnancy?

She pushed the thought away. She was just a bit under the weather, that was all. Maybe she was going down with a bug. It was completely ridiculous to think that the way she felt could be due to being pregnant.

But she still couldn't shift the idea. If another woman had described the symptoms to her, she would've asked about the possibility of pregnancy: going off coffee, feeling slightly sick, having tender breasts.

Or maybe she was panicking over nothing, blowing this whole thing out of proportion. Her breasts were probably a bit tender simply because her period was due any day now, and the rest of the symptoms were all just in her head.

In the end, instead of going straight home, she called in to a supermarket and bought a pregnancy test. She'd do the test, see for herself that the result was negative, and then she could put this crazy notion completely out of her head. Of course she wasn't pregnant.

Though, once she got home, she found herself sitting on the loo with the test stick in her hand and she just couldn't produce any urine at all.

Oh, for pity's sake. How stupid and pathetic was this?

After three big glasses of water and pacing up and down her flat for ten minutes, she tried again. This time, to her relief, she managed to get a urine sample; she replaced the cap and laid the test stick flat on the bathroom sink while she washed her hands. She'd bought one of the newest digital tests, so there would be no chance of misinterpreting the result. In three minutes' time, she'd know for sure. There was even a little line along the bottom of the screen, showing that the test was working; as each minute passed, another segment of the line disappeared. There would be no mistake here.

She swallowed hard as she watched the last segment. One minute to go. She'd never known the seconds tick by so slowly before. But everything was going to be all right. The screen would say say 'not pregnant' in big black letters and she could laugh the whole thing off as the product of an overactive imagination.

She looked away for a second.

And then she looked at the screen and it felt as if her heart had stopped.

Instead of the reassurance she'd expected, there was a single word.

Pregnant.

She blinked hard. She had to be seeing things. Panicking over nothing.

But when she looked again, the word was still there. On its own. No reassuring 'not' had appeared above it.

Pregnant.

What the hell was she going to do?

She splashed her face with water, and looked at the screen again. No change. Still defiantly *pregnant*.

Funny. A year ago, she would've been overjoyed. Amazed, given that she and Leo had hardly made love any more, but overjoyed. She'd got to the stage where delivering babies wasn't quite enough for her, and she'd wanted a child of her own. To make a family, with her husband. When she'd broached the subject to Leo, he'd told her that he wasn't ready—that he wanted to notch up another promotion before he felt comfortable trying for a family, and all his time was taken up working for the promotion. So she'd damped down the longing for a baby and just carried on as usual.

Except Leo had been carrying on, too. In a different sense of the phrase. With someone else. And he'd given his lover the baby that he'd refused to give his wife.

She dragged in a breath. Here she was, a year later, still damping down the fact that she wanted a baby— she hadn't even admitted that bit to Hayley.

And now she was unexpectedly pregnant, by a man she barely knew.

And she didn't have a clue what to do next.

She wasn't sure if she was pleased, terrified, or what. Everything suddenly seemed topsy-turvy. Weren't accidental pregnancies meant to happen to careless teenagers who didn't think of the consequences, not thirty-two-year-old obstetricians who'd been careful with contraception?

'Danielle Owen, stop being such a wimp,' she told herself sternly. 'You're Dr Organised, the one everyone comes to for advice, remember?'

Maybe that was the way forward: to pretend it was happening to someone else. What would she advise someone else to do, in her shoes?

She sat down at her kitchen table with a pad and a pen to make a list.

Talk to the father.

Given that they weren't a couple, and their night together had been a one-off, this conversation would've been awkward in any case. But what was going to make it so much worse was the Huntington's situation. If Alex hadn't inherited the faulty gene, he couldn't pass it on. But if he had inherited the faulty gene, there was a fifty per cent chance that he'd passed it to the baby. The only way of knowing for sure was to do a test—and she knew how strongly he felt about not doing the test.

Maybe that conversation shouldn't be the first one.

She wrote down the next item on her list.

Talk to your best friend.

Except right now Dani was pretty sure that Hayley was happy for the first time in well over a year, and she really didn't want to pile her worries onto her best friend and wreck that happiness. Hayley had had a horrible time, losing her fiancé in the most tragic circumstances—Evan, as a firefighter, had been killed trying to rescue someone from a fire. She deserved to enjoy every bit of happiness, now she had the chance, instead of worrying about Dani's situation.

Dani put a line through that option.

Talk to your GP.

Again, it was a conversation that she would need to have at some point in the next couple of weeks. But this was Sunday afternoon, well outside normal surgery appointment times. So that call wasn't going to be top of her list either.

Talk to your parents.

It was a possibility. Dani knew her parents would support her. But right now they were in Scotland, visiting her grandparents. They'd be left worrying about her, and that wasn't fair—not when they were hundreds of miles away and it would be hard for them to get to her. She struck a line through that option, too.

Which left her with option one.

Talk to the father.

Discussing the situation with Alex.

She'd have to think very, very carefully about how she broke the news to him. And she really didn't know enough about Huntington's to have that conversation.

Well, OK. Lack of knowledge. That was something she could fix. She grabbed her laptop and went looking for information.

An hour's research left her drained and miserable. Alex hadn't been exaggerating. There wasn't a cure, there was nothing you could do to stave off the disease, and there was no real way of predicting when you'd start to get symptoms. But while she'd been doing the research she'd also thought of someone else she could talk to about the situation. Emma, who'd trained with her as a student and had gone on to specialise in IVF and genetics. And, more importantly, Emma worked at a different hospital, so there was no chance of anyone seeing them together, jumping to conclusions and gossiping—which meant there was no chance of Alex hearing something through the hospital grapevine and leaping to his own conclusions before she'd had a chance to talk to him.

She grabbed her phone and called Emma.

Given the way her luck seemed to be running that day, she wasn't too surprised when her call went through to voicemail. She sighed inwardly and left a message on the answering service, trying hard to sound bright and cheerful. 'Hi, Em. It's Dani. I was wondering if I could pick your brains about something over a pizza some time in the next few days? Look forward to hearing from you.'

Which gave her the rest of the afternoon to brood, clean her flat, and try to work out how on earth she was going to break the news to Alex.

She was still no nearer to any kind of solution when her phone rang.

'Hey, Dani! It's Em. Sorry I missed your call earlier. I'd put my phone on silent because I was babysitting my niece this afternoon and she'd actually gone to sleep,' Emma said.

'No worries. Thanks for calling back,' Dani said.

'So what do you want to pick my brains about?'

'Some advice for a patient about a genetic matter.'

'*My* advice?' Emma sounded surprised. 'Wouldn't you be better off talking to the genetic team at Muswell Hill, given that she's your patient?'

'It's a bit of a sensitive situation,' Dani hedged.

'Ah—in that case I'm guessing she works with you and she doesn't want anyone else to know about the pregnancy yet.'

It was close enough not to feel like a complete lie. 'Yes.'

'OK. Let's talk. Are you free tonight?'

Dani felt the tears of relief well up and blinked them away. 'Yes—yes, I am.'

'Great. Let's go to Luigi's. Meet you there at half seven?'

'Brilliant. And it's my shout,' Dani said, 'as I'm making you work for your supper.'

Emma laughed. 'You're on. See you later.'

* * *

At the Italian restaurant, Emma looked pointedly at Dani's foot. 'So the evil boot is off at last?'

'It is indeed. And Haze ran in my place this morning and raised a ton of money towards the scanner,' Dani said with a smile. 'Thanks for your donation, by the way.'

'My pleasure, and good for Haze. You should've brought her along tonight. I haven't seen her for ages and it'd be good to catch up,' Emma said.

'I kind of need to keep this confidential,' Dani said.

'I can't imagine Haze gossiping, but I guess you made a promise to your colleague,' Emma said with a shrug. 'Let's order, then you can tell me all about it.'

Once they'd ordered—and Dani claimed to be drinking water only as part of a health kick, now she could rehab her no longer broken foot—Emma took a swig of her red wine. 'So tell me about your friend and the genetic stuff.'

'The mum's in the early stages of pregnancy—but she's worried because the dad might have Huntington's,' Dani said.

'Might? So he hasn't actually had the test yet?' Emma asked.

Dani shook her head. 'Though one of his parents died from it, so she knows there's a fifty per cent chance he's inherited the faulty gene.'

'Huntington's. That's a fault on chromosome four,' Emma said thoughtfully. 'So if he's clear, the baby's fine. If he's not, the baby has a fifty per cent chance of inheriting it.'

Dani already knew that, and it scared her spitless. What if the test showed that the baby was in the wrong side of that fifty per cent? Could she go ahead and have a child, knowing that the baby had inherited a neurodegenerative disorder that didn't have a cure? And, worse, that the child would probably die in early middle age, needing full nursing care and having no real quality of life for the last few years? On the other hand, she hated the idea of having a termination. Her job as a doctor was to protect life.

Whatever option she took, the baby would lose.

And she wasn't sure she could live with that kind of guilt.

She swallowed hard. 'So what are my friend's options?'

'She really needs to get her partner to have the test,' Emma said, 'and then if it's positive we can test the baby.'

There were two problems there, Dani thought. For a start, Alex wasn't her partner. She could handle that—some of her friends were single parents, and she knew she'd have support from her family and friends—but the second problem was the really tricky one. And that was where she really hoped Emma could give her some practical suggestions. 'The thing is, he doesn't actually want to have the test.'

'Ah.' Emma grimaced. 'That makes things a bit more difficult. You said she was in the early stages of pregnancy—how early?'

'Very early days. She did the test this week when she realised she was a couple of weeks late. So I guess that'd be roughly six weeks since her LMP.'

'OK. So right now she's in a place where she knows nothing. There's a fifty-fifty chance he has the faulty gene. If he does have it, there's a fifty-fifty chance the baby has inherited it. Which works out to a one in four chance for the baby having it. And if you're the one facing that risk, it's scary stuff indeed.' She blew out a breath. 'Your poor friend must be worried sick.'

'Uh-huh.' That was putting it mildly. This morning, Dani had thought she was going down with a bug. Right now, she knew for definite that she was pregnant and there were horrible odds that the baby had inherited the neurodegenerative disease that had killed Alex's father. 'Is it possible to test the baby without the dad needing to have the test?'

'In theory, yes. We can do CVS at some point between ten and fourteen weeks,' Emma said.

Chorionic villi sampling or CVS was where a small sample of the placenta was taken via a needle through the abdomen; as an obstetrician Dani knew that the placenta contained the same genetic material as the baby, so the lab could test the placental samples and be sure that the result would be the same as if they'd taken cells from the baby.

'But, apart from the one per cent risk of CVS causing a miscarriage,' Emma said, 'that kind of testing is a real ethical minefield. For a start, it breaches the father's rights, because if the baby's positive then it means he's positive—he'll know without having the test himself. Plus the baby can't give consent to testing.'

'So you can't actually do the test in practice?' Dani asked.

'We can do the test,' Emma said. 'But under the code of ethics we're bound by, the mum would have to sign

papers before we did the CVS, agreeing to a termination if the results show that the baby has Huntington's.'

'Seriously?' Dani looked at her friend, totally
shocked.

'Seriously, and it's a horrible decision to have to
make,' Emma said. 'It's a shame her GP had didn't
send her for genetic counselling before they started
trying for a baby, because she could've been given
a few more options to help avoid the baby inheriting
Huntington's. She could've had pre-implantation genetic diagnosis. That's the area I'm working in at the
moment. It means if a couple has a known genetic
problem between them—say one of them has sickle
cell disease—they can have IVF. We'll wait for two
or three days until the embryo has divided into eight
cells, then we'll take one of those cells from the embryo and check to see if it contains the gene that causes
the problem. If it doesn't, then we know the baby can't
inherit the condition and we can transfer the embryo
to the mother's womb; then the IVF process contin-
ues as normal.'

Meaning that if Alex had Huntington's, with PGD
his baby wouldn't inherit the condition.

She realised that Emma was waiting for her to say
something. OK. She'd respond as a fellow doctor, not
as a mum-to-be. 'It's pretty amazing that you can run
those kinds of tests from a single cell.'

'I know. That's why I'm specialising in it,' Emma
said. 'I love the idea of being able to help people avoid
their baby inheriting a condition that's made them lose
people too early in their family—people with a family history of Duchenne's muscular dystrophy, say, or

haemophilia. I know it's kind of like playing God, but it's so nice to be able to take away the worry and the heartache. To make a real difference to my patients. A parent with sickle cell who has PGD will know their child definitely won't have to suffer the same kind of pain they've gone through.'

'I get that,' Dani said. 'And that would definitely be an option for my friend in the future.' For Alex, maybe. Because their one night wasn't going to be repeated. 'Except I don't think this baby was actually planned.'

'You and I both know that, even if they were super-super careful, the only guaranteed method of contraception is abstinence,' Emma said. 'Tell her not to beat herself up about it. It's not her fault.'

Wasn't it? Dani had already been thinking about that. How she'd been the one to proposition Alex, even though she'd known his situation. Then again, he'd been the one to kiss her, so maybe they were equally to blame.

'If your friend wants a confidential chat with me, I'm more than happy to talk to her. Give her my number—I won't pass anything on to your team,' Emma said. 'But that poor woman's got some really difficult decisions ahead of her. I hope she's got a good support team.' She smiled. 'Actually, I already know she does. She's got *you*.'

Yeah. Dani had herself. And she knew she was resilient. She'd got through Leo's betrayal and the divorce. She'd get through this, too.

Dani forced herself to smile back. 'Thanks for letting me pick your brain, Em. It's been really helpful.'

'Any time.'

Dani switched the conversation to something much lighter and tried to enjoy the rest of the evening as much as she could; but she knew was going to have to talk to Alex about the situation. It would be easier if she had some idea how he was going to react, but she didn't know him well enough to have a single clue.

She'd need to be careful about this. Find the right words and the right time.

Somehow.

CHAPTER SIX

'CAN I HAVE a word?' Dani asked, leaning round the door of Alex's office.

'Sure. I assume it's about a patient so you need me to get the notes up?'

'No, actually,' she said. 'And I don't really want to talk here.'

Puzzled, he said, 'OK. Where and when?'

'Are you free this evening?' she asked.

'Yes.'

'OK. Say eight o'clock, my place?'

'Sure.'

It seemed a bit strange that she hadn't suggested dinner; for the last month Alex had been very aware of Dani's attempts to make him be more sociable. Maybe he was misinterpreting things, though he thought she'd looked worried about something. It was clear that she wasn't going to tell him what the problem was until later that evening, so he did what he'd learned to do ever since he'd found out the truth about Stephen—he compartmentalised it rather than brooding over it and just got on with the rest of his day.

And it turned out to be a good day, when he helped

to deliver a breech baby. The bit he loved most about his job were those first few magical seconds of a new life, hearing the baby cry and seeing him open his eyes.

At eight on the dot, Alex rang Dani's doorbell.

'Come in. Wine, coffee, something cold?' she asked.

'No, I'm fine, thanks.'

She led him through to her living room and gestured to him to sit down.

'So what did you want to talk to me about?' he asked.

She swallowed hard. 'Um, there really isn't an easy way to put this.'

And she wasn't one for beating around the bush. One of the things he liked most about her was her straightforwardness. Why was she suddenly being so awkward? 'Put what?'

She was silent for so long that he was about to repeat his question.

And then she said, her voice so soft that he could barely hear her, 'I'm pregnant.'

For a second, the world felt as if it had spun off its axis. No. He must have misheard. Dani couldn't be pregnant. She couldn't. They'd used a condom, and he'd been absolutely meticulous about putting it on and taking it off. There hadn't been a rip or tear. The condom hadn't burst. And, although he'd stayed overnight, they hadn't made love sleepily without a condom in the middle of the night. He'd just held her close and woken with her in his arms.

He stared at her. 'Can you repeat that?'

'I'm pregnant.'

So he hadn't misheard. 'How?'

She swallowed hard. 'We're both obstetricians. Surely we both know the mechanics of how a woman gets pregnant.' She dragged a hand through her hair. 'This wouldn't be an easy conversation in any situation, but with your family history it's a whole lot harder.'

She could say that again.

Dani was pregnant. And if Alex had inherited Huntington's from Stephen, that meant there was a fifty per cent chance that the baby could have inherited it from him—a situation he'd wanted to avoid so much that he'd broken his engagement to Lara over it.

'But we were careful,' he said, still trying to process the news.

'Yes. And we both know there's a tiny, tiny chance that any form of contraception will fail. A stupidly small chance if you're careful—which we were. But it happened.'

'You're absolutely sure you're pregnant?' he checked.

'Of course I'm sure!' Outrage flashed momentarily in her expression. 'I wouldn't have said anything to you without doing a test first. I did it yesterday afternoon. And it was one of the digital tests. There's no margin of error. The thing actually says the words on the screen so you don't have to work out whether that's a really faint blue line or your eyes are deceiving you. It was very definite. I'm pregnant.'

Pregnant. He couldn't quite get his head round this.

Though he knew without a doubt that the baby was his. Dani wasn't the sort to sleep around.

Of course he'd be there for her and the baby. Of course he'd accept his responsibilities. There was no question about that. And yet at the same time he was terrified that he'd passed the bad gene onto the baby. How could he possibly condemn his own child to the kind of death his biological father had had—to the one that he, too, might face?

It was all his fault. If he hadn't given in to that urge to kiss Dani, she wouldn't have suggested that he stay the night, and he wouldn't have carried her to her bed.

Instead, he'd followed Stephen's genes and been utterly selfish. He'd desperately wanted to take the warmth and comfort she'd offered, so he'd taken a risk. A calculated risk, one that meant she should've been protected from pregnancy—on average, two in a hundred women would become pregnant if they used condoms over the course of a year. Assuming that those hundred women had sex twice a week, that was two pregnancies out of ten thousand times of having sex. He and Dani had made love only once.

But once was all it took…

'Say something, will you?'

'What?' He blinked at her stupidly.

She glared at him. 'I've just told you I'm pregnant. And you've hardly said a word.'

'I don't know what to say.'

'So, what, you think it's all my fault?' Her glare hardened. 'Because I was the one who propositioned you, and I was the one with the condom that turned out to be faulty?'

Was that really what was going through her head? He thought she blamed her for it? 'No, of course I don't blame you. I could have said no and I didn't. It was both of us.'

She didn't look particularly mollified. 'So what happens now?'

He rubbed a hand across his face. 'Last time I was in this room with you, you said that it was up to me to do the test. That I didn't have to do it until I was ready.'

She narrowed her eyes at him. 'And?'

'And now, I admit, I feel as if my hand's been forced. Now it would be wrong of me not to do the test, because you need to know for the baby's sake.'

Her face looked pinched. 'There's a fifty per cent chance you have the gene, and if you do have it that means there's a fifty per cent chance you've passed it on. So that's a twenty five per cent chance the baby has it—one in four.'

He knew those odds only too well. He'd worked it out for himself months ago. 'That's why I broke off my engagement with Lara. Because she deserved the chance to have a family without having to worry about that.'

She rolled her eyes. 'There's more than one way to make a family, Alex, and you know it. Among other things there's IVF with donor sperm or PGD, plus there's fostering and adoption.'

He sighed. 'I know. I'm sorry. That's not what I meant.'

She folded her arms. 'This is why I'm talking to you about the situation. It's your baby, so you need to have a say in what happens now.'

'I don't really have a say,' he said. 'If I don't do the test for Huntington's, how else will you know if the baby's OK or not?'

'I can have the baby tested,' she said, 'but the baby

can't give consent to the procedure.' There was the tiniest wobble in her voice, telling him just how upset
she was about the situation. 'And that means I have to
sign papers before they do the test, agreeing to have
a termination if the test results come back positive.'

He looked at her, utterly shocked. 'Seriously?'

She nodded. 'I didn't know that until yesterday. I
talked to a friend I trained with, who specialises in genetics and IVF. She explained it all to me. She works in
a different hospital, so if anybody did see us by chance
or overheard what we said, nobody's going to connect
our conversation with you and me.'

He felt his eyes widen. 'Hang on. You told her about
us?'

'No. I told her about the situation, and she assumed
it was a friend who was affected. I didn't correct her.'
She dragged in a deep breath. 'But it's such a mess,
Alex. If I have the baby tested, then it also breaches
your rights. Because if the results mean I have to have
a termination, then you'll know you definitely have
Huntington's because there's no trace of it in my family history. And that isn't fair, because you haven't
agreed to take a test.'

He looked at her. 'But if the baby doesn't have Huntington's, that still doesn't mean I'm clear. It might be
that I have the faulty gene but on this occasion I didn't
pass it on.'

'Right now, the baby has a one in four chance of
having Huntington's,' she said. 'And I really don't like
those odds.'

He knew he had to do the right thing, even though
it tied him up in knots because he hadn't wanted to

know for definite whether he had Huntington's. He'd wanted to enjoy however much life he had left without feeling as if he had an axe hanging over his head. Now he had no choice. 'OK. I'll do the test,' he said.

'And what if you're positive?'

'Then we'll get the baby tested. It'll have to be through CVS.' He paused. Even though he could work it out for himself—they'd had sex four weeks ago—he needed to ask. 'Exactly how pregnant are you?'

'My LMP was six weeks ago,' she said.

'So I need to get the test results back within the next five to eight weeks, to hit the right window if the baby has to be tested.' And that could open up a whole new can of worms. 'If the baby tests positive, we have a decision to make. Do we go ahead and have the baby, knowing that a cure for Huntington's might not be available in my lifetime, let alone the child's? Or do we...?' He stopped, not wanting to voice it.

'Terminate the pregnancy,' she finished, 'because otherwise we're condemning a child to an incurable neurodegenerative condition?' Her face was anguished. 'I don't know. Either way, we lose.'

'It's a one in four chance we'll have to have that conversation.'

'They're huge odds, Alex. *Huge.*'

He could see the panic in her eyes. 'I know.'

'And we ended up the wrong side of the tiny odds that the condom wouldn't work. How do we know we won't end up the wrong side of such massive odds as these ones?'

He could see in her face that she was torn apart by this. He was feeling shell-shocked by the possibilities himself, and he'd only known for a few minutes; she'd had a day or so to think about the situation, run through the options and worry about them even more.

'How are you doing?' he asked carefully.

'I'm holding it together at work, but inside I'm a mess,' she admitted. 'I wasn't expecting this.'

Neither had he.

'And I can't see a way forward. Anything we do will be wrong.' She dragged in a breath. 'You don't want children.'

'I didn't.' Not since he'd discovered the truth about his parentage. Before then, he'd thought he was ready to start trying for a baby on his honeymoon. Afterwards, the situation had changed. Become much bleaker.

He and Dani hadn't discussed it, so he had no idea of her views on the subject. 'Do you want children?' he asked.

'I did. Which was why it hurt so much that Leo left me for the other woman—that she was carrying his baby.' She looked away. 'Last year, at the beginning of summer, I told him I wanted a baby. He said he wasn't ready to start a family. That he was working towards a promotion and he wanted to get that sorted out before we started trying for a baby. And all the time he was sleeping with the other woman. Which I guess was why he wasn't sleeping with me—though I thought he wasn't sleeping with me because he was stressed about work and maybe because he was scared that I'd do something stupid to force his hand, like forget to take the Pill.'

Alex wasn't sure what shocked him most—the sheer selfishness of her ex's behaviour, or the way he'd tried to make Dani feel that it was her fault. 'You wouldn't do anything I've that. You're not devious,' he said.

'Thank you.'

She looked relieved that he believed in her integrity. But what she'd just told him made things that much more complicated. She'd wanted a baby and her ex had denied her that opportunity. He'd rubbed salt in the wounds by having a baby with someone else. And now Dani was pregnant—albeit it was unplanned. Having to face the possibility of a termination, when she'd so wanted a child, must be torture.

Neither of them had signed up for this.

But no way was he going to start a relationship where he could end up being a burden to his partner. He wasn't selfish like his biological father. He'd been brought up by a kind, decent man, and he'd do the right thing by Dani and their baby.

He knew what he needed to do right now. She looked lonely and lost and defeated. He needed to reassure her. Hold her close, like she'd held him close when he'd felt lonely and lost and defeated. So he stood up, went over to her chair, scooped her up and sat down in her place, settling her on his lap with his arms wrapped round her. 'Neither of us bargained for this,' he said. 'Neither of us has a clue what's going to happen or what we do next. But I do know one thing: I'm not going to walk away from my responsibilities. I'll be there for you and the baby.'

Tears formed in her eyes. 'How? We're not even a couple.'

'And we can't be, if I have Huntington's. That's not negotiable.' He knew he was being stubborn and difficult, but he just couldn't budge on that point. It was too important.

'Alex, it could be years and years before you start to get symptoms. In that time, researchers could find a cure, or at least a way to manage the condition or slow it down.'

'They can manage some of the symptoms now,' he said dryly. 'But you have to be realistic. Most people get forty years of good health before they start getting symptoms. I'm thirty-five. That gives me five years before it starts, Dani. Supposing I have it but I didn't pass it on to the baby, and we go ahead with the pregnancy— the baby won't even have started school by the time I start getting symptoms.'

'*If* you have it,' she said. 'And that's a fifty-fifty chance.'

'You said it yourself: the risk of the baby having it is huge, and my risk is twice as high,' he said softly. 'And you need to be realistic about what could happen. I know this is all going to sound really bleak, but it needs facing.' And the best way for her to do that was to hear directly it from him. 'If Stephen passed the faulty gene to me, then I'll need medication for mood swings and depression. I'll need medication to manage involuntary movements, and occupational therapy to help me as my motor skills decline. I'll need help managing my food, from turning everything into soup to eventually needing a PEG feed. And then there's communication— speech difficulties are often one of the first things to occur, and the cognitive problems vary from moment to moment. I might be able to make an articulate request to you over breakfast, and then five minutes later

I won't be able to repeat it. I won't have the words or anything approaching them. It's going to be frustrating, both for me and anyone trying to communicate with me, and with the mood difficulties as well I might not be able to control an aggressive response,' he warned.

'Was that what it was like for Stephen?' she asked.

Alex nodded. 'His partner was really kind. He was at the stage where he couldn't communicate very well and Catriona really helped me to talk to him. But I could see the strain on her, Dani. She loved him enough to stay, but seeing him decline a little bit more every single day and not being able to do anything to stop it—it was killing her.' He blew out a breath. 'The first time I saw Stephen, he could only really communicate with me via a picture board. The second time, he was having a good day and could manage a few words. But by the time I met him he needed full nursing care, Dani. He needed someone to wash him and dress him and feed him. He needed someone to lift him into a chair and push him around. He couldn't do a single thing for himself. And I would really, *really* hate to be that helpless. To put that kind of burden on the woman I love.' He held her close. 'What I'm saying is that there's a very real chance I don't have a future. But in the meantime I'm going to do my best to be there for you and the baby. I'll support you every step of the way for as long as I can.'

'What if the baby has Huntington's?' she asked.

'Right now we have a three in four chance of that not being the case.'

She didn't say it, but he could see it in her eyes. That risk wasn't anywhere near low enough.

'I'll ring my family doctor for an appointment to-morrow and I'll ask him to refer me for testing,' he said. 'And we're going to have to take this thing day by day. In a few weeks we might have to make a really horrible decision—but it'll be an informed decision and we'll talk it through and we'll make that decision *together*.' He leaned his forehead against hers. 'In another life I wouldn't be Stephen's biological son, I'd be Will's, and you and I would've planned this baby and both been thrilled about that pregnancy test. Or even if the baby wasn't planned we would've been able to share the joy, once we'd got over the shock of the news. I'm so sorry I've taken that joy away from you.'

She stroked his face. 'It's not your fault.'

Oh, but it was. 'I can't promise you that the future's going to be OK. Until we get the test results back, we won't know anything for sure,' he said. 'But I promise you I'll be there for you. Have you made an appoint-ment yet with your GP?'

'No. I wanted to talk to you first.'

He nodded. 'If you want me to go with you, then I will.'

'No, it's fine.' She paused. 'If you want me to go with you to any of the genetics stuff, then I will. Be-cause this goes both ways, Alex. You need as much support as I do.'

'I can't ask that of you.'

'You're not asking me. I'm telling you it's how it is. We're in this together.'

'That's the whole point. If I have Huntington's, I don't want to be a burden.'

'And if you don't?'

'Then…' He blew out a breath. 'Then it's a different matter.'

'We might be parents next summer.'

Which told him that for her, if the baby didn't have Huntington's, a termination wasn't an option. Though that was the way he felt, too. And now he knew he might be a father… He'd had a happy childhood. Idyllic, even. He'd grown up feeling loved, and he wanted the same for his own child. Yet how could he burden his child with having to watch his condition deteriorate, feeling helpless because there was nothing anyone could do to cure him? Wouldn't the baby be better off not knowing him?

'We might,' he said guardedly.

'And yet we barely know each other.'

Because the baby was an unexpected result from one night of comfort. They weren't in love with each other. They were attracted to each other, and he knew he liked her. What he wasn't sure about was what she thought about him. If she liked him, too, was that enough to make a solid relationship? And was that even what she wanted, or did she think they could work something out about the baby without having to live together and try to make a family?

'I can't promise you a future. Not right now,' he said. 'But we can do something about not knowing each other very well. I'll start. I'm an only child, my dad's a retired orthopod and my mum's a part-time coffee shop manageress, and they live on the other side of London.'

'I'm an only child, too,' she said. 'My mum's a history teacher and my dad's an accountant. They live in Surrey.' She paused. 'What else do you want to know?'

'If you weren't a doctor, what would you be?'

'A forensic scientist,' she said promptly, 'and I'd be one of the ones who does facial reconstructions from skeletons.'

He raised an eyebrow. 'That's very specific.'

'Mum's a history teacher,' she reminded him. 'I guess I inherited her love of history. When I was really little, I wanted to be an archaeologist. I can remember going up to Northumbria on holiday and seeing Hadrian's Wall and all the shoes and the letters at Vindolanda, and wondering what the people who lived there and wore the shoes and wrote the letters looked like. Then we went to Bamburgh and I was allowed to help the archaeologists in a little tiny bit of the dig. I didn't actually find anything, but I loved being able to help, and the archaeologist made a bit of a pet of me and let me handle things they'd just found.' She smiled. 'There was this little bronze hippo that fitted into my palm. It was so amazing. And I spent the rest of the holiday digging holes in the beach, trying to find a hippo of my own.'

He could just imagine it, and it charmed him.

And he had to damp down the sudden surge of longing at the idea of having a daughter who looked like Dani and who dug holes in the beach, trying to find lost treasure. He couldn't let himself bond with this baby. Not until they all knew where they stood.

'We used to go to the beach on holiday, too, when I was small; but it was always Cornwall and always involved building sandcastles,' he said. 'My granddad—mum's dad—loved military history, so they were never just your four basic buckets as towers with a little bit of wall in between. Our castles were always proper motte-and-bailey ones, with massive ramparts.' He smiled back at her. 'So I guess if I hadn't been a doctor I might've ended up being a builder, the sort who restores ancient buildings.'

'So there's one thing we have in common, then. A love of history.'

'And beaches.' He paused. 'Here's another one for you. Dog or cat?'

'Dog,' she said promptly. 'That was what I missed most about home when I was a student. I could talk to Mum and Dad, and send texts and photographs to their phones, but I really missed curling up with the dog when I was reading, or taking the dog out for a walk in the middle of a revision session to clear my head. I think that's why I started running in the park; it meant if I went to a park that had a dog area I could stop and chat to the owners and make a fuss of their dogs.' She wrinkled her nose. 'Which is possibly a bit wet of me.'

'No, it's not.' He liked this softer side of her. And he could just imagine her walking through the park, pushing a baby in a pram with a dog trotting alongside her. He shook himself mentally; he couldn't let himself go too far along with that fantasy and imagine what their baby might be like, not when they still might have a hideous decision to make. He'd already had to pull himself back from the idea of having a daughter. 'What sort of dog?'

'A liver and white English springer spaniel, like the ones I grew up with,' she said promptly. 'What about you? Dog or cat?'

'Dog,' he said.

'What sort?'

'Golden retriever. Ours was big and soft and fluffy, and she thought she was a lapdog. So you'd have thirty kilos of dog sprawled on your lap, whether you wanted it or not.' He smiled at the memory.

'She sounds gorgeous,' Dani said. 'What was her name?'

'Sally.'

'Ours was Oscar,' she said. 'Mum and Dad decided not to replace him when he died. But I think they'll get another when they retire. Maybe something smaller and less busy than a springer, but I think Mum really misses having a dog.'

It sounded as if Dani really missed having a dog, too. Had she had a dog with her husband, and her ex had claimed the dog as part of the divorce settlement? Alex didn't want to rub salt in her wounds by asking. But it was another bit of common ground between them. The more he was finding out about her, the more he thought they might be compatible. That they might have a chance of a future together.

'OK. We have history and dogs in common. And you're a runner.'

'From the way you just said that, I assume you're not?' she asked.

'Not outdoors,' he said. 'I run on a treadmill as a warm-up at the gym, but I'd much rather do a weights session. It clears my head better.'

'Give me cardio any day. Dance aerobics, or a bit of plyo—I've really missed not being able to do burpees and jumping onto a box.' She smiled. 'So we're opposites on exercise. What else do you do for fun?'

He shrugged. 'Video games.'

She groaned. 'Don't tell me—the shoot-'em-up type?'

''Fraid so. You?'

'I'm not really a gamer. Though I do like sudoku puzzles. That's my usual vice before bed—three puzzles.'

'Mine's cryptic crosswords at the breakfast table,' he said. 'How about reading?'

'Crime novels. Preferably ones with a forensic scientist, though there's a series I really love with a forensic archaeologist,' she said. 'You?'

'Thrillers. I'm a big Lee Child fan,' he said.

'So we're sort of on the same page,' she said with a smile.

He groaned. 'I'm ignoring that terrible pun.'

'What, not even the glimmer of a smile, Dr Morgan?' She batted her eyelashes at him.

Alex couldn't help smiling. In other circumstances, he would've kissed her. But he needed to keep a little distance between them. Even though that probably counted as shutting the stable door when the horse had run to the other side of the country, given that right now she was pregnant with his baby.

'I've got another one. Foodie or not bothered?' she asked.

'Eating out, I'd probably go for the foodie option,' he said. 'Eating in... I tend to cook very simple things that don't take a lot of time.' He looked at her. 'Though I noticed there's a shelf of cookery books in your kitchen, so I'm guessing you're foodie all the way.'

'Yup. I buy pomegranate molasses and actually use

it,' she said. 'It's another thing that relaxed me when I was a student. Cooking something complicated, so I had to concentrate on that and let all the stuff I'd revised percolate into my brain, or else I'd burn dinner.' She grinned. 'It was great. I'd cook for everyone, we'd share the costs—and because I cooked it meant I could weasel out of doing the washing up. Wins all round.'

God, he really liked this woman.

Please let the test results be on their side. Because he was beginning to think that a life with Dani would be a very good life indeed.

'How about music?' he asked.

'Anything I can sing along to. You?'

'Indie rock,' he said. 'And blues guitar—Dad loves Peter Green, so I grew up with that and John Mayall playing in the car.'

'Sounds good. Another one for you: theatre or cinema?' she asked.

'Cinema, and I like suspense movies,' he said. 'You?'

'Both. Because I really, really like musicals, and they're awesome on stage.'

He looked at her, surprised. 'Seriously?'

'I'm word-perfect on *Mamma Mia* and *Grease*,' she said with a grin. 'Come with me next time one of them's on in the West End.'

'Can't. I'll be babysitting.' The words came out before he could stop them.

'Nice excuse,' she said. And then her smile faded as she clearly realised what he meant.

Babysitting their baby.

Except they didn't know whether their baby was going to have the bad gene. Or what they'd decide to do.

'How is this going to work out, Alex?' she asked.

He sighed. 'I haven't a clue. Once we've got the test results, we'll have a better idea of what our real options are. Until then, I guess we have to take it day by day and try not to think about it.' He stroked her face. 'All that stuff people say about a problem shared being a problem halved—that's not true. In our case it's a problem doubled.'

'I'm sorry.'

'It's not your fault. It's circumstances,' he said.

'It's not your fault either,' she said, as if guessing what was in his head.

He rather thought it was, but he wasn't in the mood to argue with her. Instead, he said, 'So are you getting any kind of early pregnancy symptoms?'

'Yes and no.' She wrinkled her nose. 'I was just feeling a bit under the weather. I thought maybe I was going down with a bug, because that was the only reason I could think of why I wouldn't fancy celebrating Hayley's run with coffee and pastries; but then on the way home it occurred to me that my period was two weeks late. With the build-up to the race, and being busy at work, and having that wretched walking cast, I'd completely lost track of the date. I did the pregnancy test to prove to myself that I was being totally unreasonable and ridiculous—that I was just late because I was busy and stressed.'

'Except you got the result you weren't expecting.'

'And I didn't know how you were going to react—especially in the circumstances.'

'I'm still getting used to the idea,' he said. And it was growing on him. Scarily so. He needed to keep the brakes on until he knew what the situation was with his own health. 'But you and the baby are my responsibility. That's not going to change.'

'I'm an adult. I'm responsible for myself,' she said.

'What I mean is I'll support you,' he said. 'Whatever decisions we have to make, we'll make them together.'

Dani liked the fact that Alex had immediately accepted his share of responsibility for the situation. The fact that he'd support her with the baby.

But what about them?

Did their relationship stand a chance? She knew he'd keep her stubbornly at a distance until he'd got the result back of his own genetic test—hadn't he broken his engagement for exactly that reason?—but, if the test was negative, did they have a chance to make a real go of things between them?

The more she got to know him, the more she liked him.

And she was definitely attracted to him.

But she'd made that mistake with Leo. She'd fallen in love with a man who'd fallen very quickly out of love with her. If she let herself fall for Alex, what if he ended up feeling the same way about her that Leo had? What if he thought she was bossy and impossible and couldn't stand to be with her? What if he tried to love her and couldn't—because the truth was that she was unloveable? She really didn't want to risk her heart again.

But everything was so mixed up.

As if he guessed at her thoughts, Alex stroked her face. 'Hey. We'll find a way through this. We just need to take it one day at a time.'

'One day at a time,' she echoed.

'I'm going to let you get some rest,' he said. 'And I'll see you tomorrow at work.'

'OK.' She wriggled off his lap. 'And thank you for being so—well, nice about it.'

'None of this is your fault,' he reminded her. 'It's circumstances. And we'll sort it out. Together.'

CHAPTER SEVEN

ALEX CALLED HIS family doctor first thing the next morning and was relieved to get an appointment for later that day, after his shift ended.

'So what can I do for you, Dr Morgan?' the doctor asked.

Alex explained the situation about his biological father having recently died from Huntington's. 'So I'd like you to refer me for testing, please.'

'Are you showing any symptoms of the disease?' the doctor asked.

'Not yet,' Alex said grimly. Though he'd been watching himself closely.

'Then we can offer you a pre-symptomatic predictive test. It'll show whether you've inherited the faulty gene, but we can't tell you when you'll start to show symptoms. You'll need to have genetic counselling before we do the test,' the doctor said.

'We can skip the counselling,' Alex said, 'because I already know I want to do the test.'

The doctor shook his head. 'When we do testing like this, it's always in conjunction with genetic counselling and it tends to be four appointments—one where they gather information, one with an in-depth discussion, one where they actually do the test, and one where you get the results. The whole process can take up to six months from start to finish.'

The problem was, he didn't have six months. 'I understand that,' Alex said carefully, 'but in this case I can't wait that long because there's a baby involved. We didn't plan the pregnancy; and, apart from it not being fair on any of us to have to wait that long for the results, we need to know as soon as possible in case we need to do a prenatal diagnosis test for the baby. I know it takes at least two weeks between the blood test and getting the result, because you need to check the CAG repeat in the DNA, but can we at least telescope the first three appointments together?'

The doctor looked thoughtful. 'I might be able to fast-track the counselling in this situation, but you will still need to see a counsellor.'

'I'll do whatever it takes,' Alex said, 'but I need an answer as fast as possible.'

'From what you've told me, you've known about the situation for a while and chose not to get tested before. The first thing the counsellor's going to ask is why.'

'Because knowing wouldn't make a difference,' Alex said. 'I can't change my lifestyle or take any kind of treatment to stave it off, so it felt a bit pointless having a test. But my circumstances have changed now, and so has my opinion—I need to know if I've inherited the faulty gene, for the baby's sake.'

'What support do you have?' the doctor asked.

A mother who was racked with guilt, a father who'd be there for him but Alex had a nasty feeling that it would put extra strain on his parents' relationship, and Dani: though it wasn't fair to burden her with his worries either. Plus he'd deliberately pushed all his friends away. Which left him isolated, by his own choice. 'Loads,' he lied.

'Sometimes it can be helpful to talk to a stranger who's been through a similar situation,' the doctor said, 'so I'm going to give you details of a support group.'

'Thanks,' Alex said, though he was pretty sure he wouldn't use it. He could support himself.

'In the circumstances, I'll try to fast-track the testing, so hopefully you'll hear from the team some time this week.'

'Thank you,' Alex said quietly. 'I really appreciate it.'

'I hope this all works out the way you want it,' the doctor said.

So did Alex.

When he'd left the doctor's surgery, he called Dani.

'Hello?' she said, her voice croaky.

'Dani, it's Alex. Sorry, did I just wake you?'

'It's OK. I just nodded off when I got in from work, that's all.'

He felt guilty for waking her, but he'd wanted her to know the news as soon as possible. 'I've just seen my family doctor. He's referring me for the pre-symptomatic diagnostic test and counselling. In the circumstances, he's going to try and fast-track it and I should hopefully hear something this week.'

'That's good,' she said, still sounding sleepy.

'Since you've been asleep, have you eaten yet?'

'No. I was too tired to cook anything when I got in,'

she admitted. 'I sat down, planning to have a power nap, but it went on for a bit longer than I expected. I'll probably just make myself some toast.'

Toast wasn't good enough nutrition for a pregnant woman, in Alex's view. 'I can bring something round,' he said.

'Are you offering to cook dinner for me?' She sounded surprised.

'As obstetricians,' he said gently, 'we both know that one of the symptoms of early pregnancy is tiredness—and as an obstetrician I'd be happier to know that you're resting rather than rushing around. I'll pick something up from the supermarket. Apart from the obvious things to avoid, is there anything you'd rather not eat?'

'No. I'll eat pretty much anything, as long as it's fairly bland,' she said. 'And thank you.'

When he'd been to the supermarket, he went to Dani's flat. 'I bought ravioli—and I checked that the ricotta in it was pasteurised—and I've got a plain tomato sauce to go with it, plus some Parmesan and ciabatta bread. And I thought you might like some fresh strawberries and pineapple for pudding.'

Tears welled in her eyes. 'That's so lovely.' And then she blinked back the tears. 'Sorry. I'm being wet.'

'It's hormones,' he said. 'You're the least wet person I know.'

'It's still really kind of you to do this for me.'

There was nothing kind about it; she was expecting his baby and he wanted to take care of her. And what he was about to suggest didn't necessarily mean getting close to her; it just meant he was stepping up to his responsibility to her and to the baby. 'Maybe I can do this for a while,' he said, 'so you don't have to cook until you're feeling less tired.'

She blinked. 'You'd seriously come here every night just to cook me dinner?'

'Or we could alternate dinner between your place and mine, but I'll do the cooking. If you come to me then you take a taxi, and I'll drive you home afterwards.'

She frowned. 'I can drive myself.'

He shook his head. 'I'd feel happier if you didn't.' As her frown deepened, he added, 'I'm not casting aspersions on your ability or anything like that. What I mean is that you're working full time and you're pregnant, tiredness is a symptom of early pregnancy and you need your rest, and driving in London isn't exactly restful.'

'There's the Tube. And walking. Walking's good for pregnant women. And I'll probably have to switch my dance aerobics class for an antenatal aqua aerobics class—given that I haven't quite rehabbed my foot yet,' she said with a grimace.

'Even so. I'd be happier if you let me drive you. Humour me?' he asked.

For a moment, he thought she was going to refuse; then she nodded. 'All right. And thanks. Actually, it'll be nice not to have to think about cooking. I'm not getting any morning sickness, but I'm just bone-deep tired. I really wasn't expecting to feel like this.'

'I wouldn't dare tell you to take it easy, especially as living with the walking cast drove you stir-crazy,' he said, 'but maybe you need to pace yourself a little bit until you get used to being pregnant. If I can take up the slack for you, I will. Whatever you need, just let me know.'

'OK. I appreciate it. Cooking dinner for me would be great,' she admitted. 'Just for a few days, until I get my energy back and stop falling asleep all the time.'

'It's going to be simple food,' he warned. 'You have no chance whatsoever of pomegranate molasses being one of the ingredients, but just tell me what you'd like or what you can't face eating, and I'll sort it out.'

She smiled. 'Probably not spicy food at the moment— I had the vegetable chilli yesterday for lunch at work and it gave me heartburn.'

'Noted.' He paused. 'Have you booked in to see your family doctor yet?'

'I've got an appointment at the end of the week, but you and I know the appointment's just routine and to get me logged into the system.'

'Are you going to book a dating scan?' he asked.

She winced. 'I kind of want to hold off until we know what's happening. I'll be ten weeks at the beginning of December, but we might not know your results by then—or, if we do and it's bad news, we'll need CVS to test the baby. So I'm going to try and stave it off for a couple of weeks more.'

The dating scan was the thing all his patients and their partners looked forward to most—actually seeing their baby on the screen. They all kept a copy of the scan photograph with them and showed it off proudly. Yet Dani couldn't relax and enjoy her pregnancy until she knew the truth about his DNA. This whole thing was a waiting game for both of them.

He wrapped his arms round her. 'Sorry. I feel as if I've taken all the joyful stuff out of pregnancy for you.'

'It's not your fault,' she said, though he knew she

was being kind. Of course it was his fault. He was the one who might have the faulty gene.

'Do you want me to go with you when you have the counselling appointment?' she asked.

'No.' He could see the hurt in her expression, but what choice did he have? Until he knew whether he'd inherited Huntington's from Stephen, he needed to keep her at a distance. 'This is something I need to do by myself,' he said gently, 'but you have my full support and I'll be there for you and the baby. Anything you need, I'll be there.'

'The same goes for you.'

No, it didn't, but he wasn't going to get into a fight with her about it. 'Sit down and put your feet up, and I'll sort out dinner.'

'Thank you.'

She was almost asleep again in the fifteen minutes it took him to heat the bread through, heat the sauce, boil the kettle and cook the ravioli. And how he would've liked to curl up with her on the sofa with a good book, letting her use him as a pillow while she slept and holding her close, enjoying her warmth against him. But he couldn't allow himself that kind of domestic pleasure just yet. Maybe not ever, if his results said the wrong thing.

If only his mum had never met Stephen...

'Hey, sleepyhead.' He stroked her cheek. 'Dinner's ready.'

She blinked at him. And how he wanted to scoop her up and carry her to bed. Just to hold her. Be close to her.

Which was dangerous. He needed to keep that little bit of distance, for his sanity's sake.

'I laid the table in the kitchen,' he said. 'I hope you don't mind me rummaging around.'

'No, it's fine,' she said. 'Thank you.'

She was quiet throughout dinner, but he put that down to tiredness.

'Do you want me to run you a bath before I go?' he asked.

'No, because I'd probably fall asleep in it,' she said.

Just for a second, he could see wistfulness in her face. As if she'd wanted to ask him to stay and hold her until she slept. Something that any normal man would do for his pregnant partner.

But their situation wasn't normal. And he dared not let himself get close to her, in case the test showed the worst-case scenario. He absolutely wouldn't burden her, the way Stephen had burdened his partner.

'I'll see you tomorrow, then,' he said. 'Sleep well.'

She nodded. 'And thanks, Alex.'

Alex was relieved to have a call from his family doctor's surgery the next day, saying they had managed to fast-track an appointment for him and the counsellor could see him on Friday afternoon. Dani was already in clinic, and he could hardly interrupt her for something personal. Plus his own clinic was due to start in a couple of minutes.

In the end he texted her.

Counselling appointment Friday afternoon.

She'd pick it up later when she had time.

Then he looked at his first set of notes.

How ironic that today his first parents had a genetic

problem in their family, though it was a haemoglobin problem rather than Huntington's. And they'd just had their CVS test results back.

This could so easily be Dani and himself, in a few weeks' time...

He pulled himself together and called the Giorgious in.

'Nice to meet you. I'm Alex Morgan,' he said. 'So how are you feeling, Mrs Giorgiou?'

'A lot better now we have the test results back,' she said feelingly. 'The last few weeks have been horrible, having to wait and not knowing whether our baby was going to be all right or whether he—well, or she—was going to have thalassaemia. I had no idea I was a haemoglobin Lepore carrier. Nobody in my family has ever had any symptoms and I only found out because of the routine antenatal testing.'

'That's when they called me in for screening,' Mr Giorgiou said. 'I was adopted, so I don't really have any medical history about my birth family. They did the tests and discovered I'm a carrier for beta thalassaemia.'

Alex knew that the beta thalassaemia and haemoglobin Lepore genes were more common in people with Southern European origins, like the Giorgious, but unless you had a family history you'd never suspect it. 'It must have been a bit of a shock to both of you,' he said.

'It was,' Mr Giorgiou agreed. 'I'd never even heard of thalassaemia or Lepore haemoglobin before, so I didn't have a clue how serious it was, or if it meant the baby would be ill or I'd be ill when I'm older.'

'The counsellor was really nice,' Mrs Giorgiou said. 'She explained that the baby would inherit one of two haemoglobin genes from each of us, either a normal one or a problem one. She drew us a diagram to show there was a one in two chance the baby was a carrier, a one in four chance the baby would be completely OK, and a one in four chance the baby would have inherited the problem gene from each of us and have full-blown thalassaemia.'

'She said if it was the worst-case scenario, the baby's blood cells would break down easily and he'd need a blood transfusion every three weeks, and medication for the rest of his life,' Mr Giorgiou said. 'I was horrified to think that we both feel so well, and yet we could've given our baby such a terrible disease. I looked it up on the Internet, and it looks as if the only cure is a bone marrow or stem cell transplant—and that's if you can find a suitable donor.'

'And there are risks from the transplant, too,' Mrs Giorgiou added. 'Waiting for the results was the worst two weeks of our lives.'

He could imagine it. Especially as he and Dani were just about to go through something similar. 'I'm very pleased to see from your notes that it wasn't the worst case,' Alex said.

'All the same,' Mrs Giorgiou said, 'I feel bad that the baby's a carrier. If his partner is as well, that means our grandchildren have a huge risk of getting thalassaemia.'

'Did the counsellor explain about PGD if you want to have another baby in the future?' Alex asked. 'She might have called it pre-implantation genetic diagnosis.'

Mr Giorgiou nodded. 'She said we could have IVF treatment and they could test the embryo to make sure the baby hadn't inherited the bad gene from either of us.'

'That's really good to know,' Mrs Giorgiou said. 'Because we do want more children, but we don't want to take the risk of the baby having full-blown thalassaemia. It's a one in four chance, and that's too high.'

The same risk that his and Dani's baby had of inheriting Huntington's. 'Of course.' Alex smiled at them. 'I've got the results through of the tests that the midwife did when you came in this morning, and I'm pleased to see that your urine sample's clear of any problems, your weight gain is average, and your blood pressure's fine. I'll just examine you now, if I may.'

The examination turned out to be perfectly routine. 'All's going well,' Alex said. 'Do you have any questions for me, or is there anything you're worrying about?'

'No—now we've got the results, it's all good,' Mrs Giorgiou said.

'The community midwife will see you for the triple test,' he said, 'and then it'll be your twenty-week scan here at Muswell Hill. If you're worried about anything in the meantime, talk to your midwife—she'll get in touch with us if she needs to.'

'Thank you.' The Giorgious shook his hand and left.

Alex wrote up his notes and stared thoughtfully at the screen. Would he and Dani be lucky enough to have good news? Or were they in for at least six weeks of waiting and worrying?

* * *

The rest of the week went quickly, and finally it was time for Alex's counselling appointment.

'Dr Morgan?' the counsellor said, coming into the waiting room.

He stood up. 'Call me Alex,' he said.

'And I'm Libby,' she said. 'Come through to my office. Can I get you a glass of water or a cup of tea?'

He shook his head. 'Thanks, but I'm fine.' He just wanted to get this over with.

'Your family doctor has told me the situation,' Libby said. 'We usually allow a month or so between appointments, so you've got time to think about things and process all the information.'

'I'm sorry, but I really don't have time for that,' Alex said. 'I asked my family doctor if we could fast-track it so we cover the first three appointments today.'

'In the circumstances, I completely understand why. You're a doctor, so I'm sure you already know most of the clinical stuff, but I still need to go through it with you,' she explained, 'because there's a huge difference between knowing something with your head and knowing it with your heart.'

He smiled wryly. 'That sounds like the kind of thing I say to my patients who have major complications— but nothing we say will change the result here. There's a baby involved, so for everyone's sake I need to know if I have the faulty gene or not. If I do, then we need prenatal testing, whereas if I don't my...' Dani wasn't his partner, but what else could he call her? 'My partner won't have to go through CVS.'

Chorionic villus sampling was where a tiny piece of the placenta was removed via a needle through the mother's abdomen; there was a small risk of miscarriage, and it also meant another three-week wait for the test results.

'I understand that the baby's your first concern,' Libby said, 'but you need to be prepared to face the implications for you, too—and your plans for the future might be affected by the test results.'

'I'm prepared to face it now,' Alex said. 'I admit I dragged my feet on this when it was just me affected by it, because I felt it was pointless knowing. If the test result is positive, there's nothing I can do to prevent getting Huntington's or even delay it. So it would just make my mum blame herself even more for the fact I have an incurable neurodegenerative disease.'

'Whereas right now it's an axe hanging over your head and you're going to wonder if every time you trip over or spill a cup of coffee or forget a word or get snappy with someone, it's the first sign of the disease,' Libby pointed out gently.

'There is that,' he said, 'but I'd rather have a good quality of life without knowing I'm definitely going to end up with it.' Even if it did mean keeping himself cut off from everyone.

'Most of people I see decide to take the test because they want to take out the uncertainty and plan for their future,' she said. 'The third most common reason is family planning.' She paused. 'Would it be useful for your partner to talk to me?'

'She's an obstetrician, too—she knows the procedures and the risks,' Alex said.

'So if your test is positive, you'll have prenatal testing?'

'That's why I need the test fast-tracked,' Alex said. 'Prenatal testing is usually done somewhere between eleven and fifteen weeks.'

'And your partner's how pregnant at the moment?'

'About seven weeks. It's still early days. But I know it takes time for you to get the test results, and if we need prenatal testing that'll be another three weeks, so I can't just wait until Dani's past the first trimester.'

'And you know that if you have prenatal testing, you'll have to agree to a termination if the baby's positive, because the baby can't give their consent?' Libby asked.

'Yes. And we'll deal with that when we come to it,' he said.

'If your result is positive,' she said, 'then you obviously know that for future family planning you can have pre-implantation—'

'—genetic diagnosis,' he finished with a smile. 'Yes. We can have IVF and the embryos will be tested, and we can use an embryo that hasn't inherited the mutated gene on chromosome four.'

She smiled back. 'I don't mean to sound patronising, Alex. Most of the people I see have done their research already, and you'll know more than average because of your job, but I still need to be sure that you know all your options and you've had a chance to think about what everything means.'

'I have,' he said, 'and I'm ready to sign a consent form saying that it's an informed decision.'

'Let's do the form first, then,' she said, and handed it to him. 'Read it through, and if you have any questions I'll do my best to answer them before you sign.'

He read it through. 'No questions,' he said, and signed it.

'Thank you. I'm going to take a blood sample for the test now. You already know that genes are made from DNA, and DNA is made from four chemicals—adenine, guanine, cytosine and thymine, all known by their initial letters. One section of the Huntington gene has three chemicals—CAG—repeated a number of times, and in the pre-symptomatic diagnosis test we look at the number of the CAG repeats on the gene.'

Alex already knew all this, but he wasn't going to push the issue; as Libby had told him, it was her job to be sure that he knew all the information and all the options.

'If there are about twenty-six repeats, that's normal; twenty-seven to thirty-five means it's an intermediate case and you probably won't develop the symptoms but you might still pass it on to your children; thirty-six to thirty-nine means it's an abnormal result and you might or might not get symptoms, most likely later in life; anything over forty means it's abnormal. I'm afraid that if you do have an abnormal result, we can't actually tell you when you'll start to develop symptoms, just that you will.'

'And a very large number of repeats makes the Huntingtin protein on the Huntington gene sticky and causes aggregates in the brain cells, which is what we think causes the cells to die off,' he said.

'You've clearly done your research,' she said. 'There are some studies going on looking at cell replacement therapies, and others looking at gene variants so we can look at biological pathways we should use to target new drug therapies, could be that we can repair damaged DNA.'

'But it's all in the early stages and there are no guarantees any of them will work,' he said.

'Everything has to start somewhere.' She took the blood sample and labelled it. 'I'll be in touch in two or three weeks, when we have the results back.'

'You can't just tell me over the phone?'

'No, I really can't,' she said gently. 'You've already bent the rules quite a bit—most of my patients have three appointments, with a gap in between them so they have a chance to get their heads round all the information.'

'Sorry.' He sucked in a breath. 'I know I'm being pushy. It's just…'

'Horrible having to wait,' Libby finished. 'All I can suggest is that you try to find some way of distracting yourself so you don't focus on the worst-case scenarios.'

'And try not to look things up on the Internet, because it's usually the extreme cases that come up first in a search engine,' he said. 'I say that to my patients all the time. I think I've got a lot more understanding about how they feel now.'

'I can't make you any promises,' Libby said. 'But when we do get the results back, I'll call you immediately.'

'Thank you.' He shook her hand. 'And I'm sorry that I'm a walking cliché.'

'You mean, medics always make the worst patients?' she asked with a smile. 'I'll let you off. Try to have a good weekend. And if you do want to talk to me before the results come back, you've got my contact details.'

'Thanks. I appreciate it.' He shook her hand, then left the office and texted Dani.

Appointment went fine. Waiting game now.

She called him straight back. 'Are you OK?' she asked.

'I'm fine.' He lied automatically, not wanting to burden her. Right at that moment he didn't have a clue how he felt. Just numb.

'Stop pushing me away,' she said. 'We're in this together.'

No, they weren't. He'd seen the burden that Stephen's partner had carried, and he'd promised himself that he would never, ever put anyone in that situation. 'I'm fine.'

'If this baby is a boy,' she said, 'I sincerely hope he hasn't inherited your stubbornness, or the terrible twos is going to be the worst time of both our lives put together and quadrupled.'

And then it really hit him.

There was a one in four chance the baby might have Huntington's; but there was also a three in four chance the baby didn't have Huntington's. Which meant that next summer he'd be a dad.

A baby of his own.

It was something he'd always assumed would happen eventually, that he'd settle down with someone and raise a child. He'd planned to do that with Lara, until his mother had dropped the bombshell that Will wasn't his father and he might have inherited an incurable neurodegenerative condition. And since then his life had been stuck on hold.

'Alex? Are you still there?'

'Yes. Sorry.'

'You mean, your head's all over the place and you're thinking about the worst-case scenarios. When are the results back?'

'Two or three weeks.'

'So we're going to keep ourselves too busy to think. Days are easy because work's always busy,' she said. 'But evenings… Start making a list, Dr Morgan, of everything you've ever wanted to do in London. Because we're going to do the lot.'

'You need to pace yourself,' he reminded her.

'There is that. I might fall asleep on you—so you can drive,' she said. 'That way you'll still have to concentrate on something else if I'm zonked out. But in between we're going to keep too busy to think.'

Right at that moment he loved her for her bossiness.

And then he felt as if all the air had been sucked out of his lungs.

Loved?

He couldn't let himself think like that about Dani. Not until he knew the truth about his genetic history. And even then only if the results were the right ones.

'Alex. We'll start tonight,' she said. 'Dinner out. My shout. Come over right now.'

And even though he knew he ought to keep her at

a distance, the warmth in her voice and the way she
understood what was going on his head just drew him.

　'I'm on my way.'

CHAPTER EIGHT

DANI LOOKED AT Alex narrowly when she opened the door to him, and he could practically feel the concern radiating from her.

'I'm fine,' he lied, before she could ask him.

'Like hell you are. You've just set a clock ticking. Nobody feels all right in those circumstances. Come here.' She hugged him.

He closed his eyes and rested his cheek against her hair. It would be so, so easy to kiss her, to lose himself in her. But that wouldn't be fair to either of them.

'Thank you for the hug,' he said, and pulled away.

There was a flash of hurt on her face, quickly masked, as if she realised that he was putting distance between them and hated it, but she understood his reasons.

'OK. Dinner. I managed to book us a table for seven o'clock,' she said, and I thought we'd take a stroll into the centre of Muswell Hill—because walking is good exercise for pregnant women and it's a good way to rehab my foot.'

It was overcast but not raining, so he didn't argue; he waited for her to put on her coat and then walked into the town centre with her. Every so often his hand accidentally brushed against hers, and he longed to catch her fingers between his and hold her hand properly. But how could he lead her on, with this axe hanging over their heads?

Her road was filled with beautiful Edwardian houses, some of which had clearly been turned into flats. Even though it was barely the second week of November, some people already had Christmas lights up outside their houses, varying from a simple string of fairy lights woven through the branches of a tree through to more elaborate displays, and most of the shops had displays of Christmas presents in their windows.

Dani had booked a quiet table in an Italian restaurant just off the Main Street. It was unlikely that anyone would see them together, but if they did no doubt Dani would claim it was a discussion about the ward's Christmas party. And Dani, he was beginning to realise, could be very persuasive. Left to his own devices, he would've sat on his own in his flat and brooded. She'd made him go out; even though some of the Christmassy music playing grated on him because it felt way too early—and this might turn out to be the worst Christmas of his life, so he really didn't want to think about it—at the same time the familiar music felt weirdly comforting.

Or maybe just being with Dani was comforting.

She chose chicken cacciatore with a side of mashed potatoes and buttered spinach; Alex ordered the same because he couldn't focus for long enough to concentrate on the menu, plus he didn't think he'd actually be able to taste anything.

She grabbed her phone. 'Right. Let's start making the Keeping Ourselves Too Busy To Think list.'

'Is this an extension of your Year of Saying Yes?' he asked. The Year of Saying Yes—which had got them into trouble in the first place.

'Sort of,' she said. 'We're going to make a list of things we'd like to do.'

'I can't actually think of anything,' he admitted. His head was full, but with the wrong stuff. All the what-ifs. Now he'd actually set the test process in motion, he couldn't stay in denial about his potential future.

Her eyes were filled with sympathy rather than pity, as if she knew exactly how he was feeling. 'OK, I'll start. We could go ice skating.'

'Apart from the fact that you're pregnant and it's not just you that might be hurt if someone knocks you over on the ice, you're still recovering from a fractured metatarsal,' he reminded her. 'Is ice skating really going to be the best thing for your foot?'

'Maybe not.' She gave him a grin. 'So I guess bungee jumping is out of the question, then?'

'Of course it—' He stopped as the penny dropped. 'Oh. You were teasing.'

'Not about the ice skating,' she said. 'I love the whole kit and caboodle, all the music and the lights and the skating and the hot chocolate, but the Christmas rinks won't be open for at least another week anyway. Though that means my foot will have another week's rehab before they open.'

'That's still a no to skating,' he said.

'Are you telling me that you can't skate, Dr Morgan? Tsk.' She pursed her lips. 'You know, I could teach you.'

'Not this year.'

'OK.' She sighed. 'So you're saying we can't do anything physical.'

Nothing that would put them up close and really personal. Dancing was completely out of the question. Not that he had the words to tell her that. 'We could do ten-pin bowling,' he said, seizing on what she'd organised for the ward's last team night out and which he'd managed to avoid.

'All right. I'll add that to the list. And we could go to some shows—comedy or music,' she suggested.

'I'm not a huge fan of opera,' he said, 'but I'd be up for anything else.'

'I'm not an opera fan either. We'll add a couple of shows. How about museums?'

'I've already visited the main ones a few times over the years,' he said, 'but I guess they're so big that you can always find something new at every visit.'

'Or we could go to some of the lesser-known museums,' she said. She tapped something into a search engine and scrolled down the list of results. 'Here's one I've definitely never been to. Apsley House—it was Wellington's home, so you get the military history you used to share with your granddad and I get the social history I shared with my mum.'

He was surprised that she'd remembered what he'd

told her about his grandfather; then again, at work he knew she paid attention to detail.

'Apparently the house has fabulous artwork,' she said. 'It's only open at weekends at this time of year, though.'

'We ought to make a note of opening times anyway,' he said.

'Agreed. And maybe we can do some of the touristy things we haven't got round to doing,' she said. 'How about the London Eye?'

'And the Cutty Sark,' he said.

'Madame Tussaud's?'

Between them they managed to come up with a list by the time the waiter brought their meal.

'So what we'll do when we get back to my place,' she said, 'is write each idea separately on a slip of paper, stick them in a jar and shake them up, and we take out a piece of paper every evening—that's what we'll do the next evening, or if it's something where we can't get tickets we'll book that for another time and take out a new bit of paper for something to plan the next night's distraction.'

'I can see why they get you to organise most of the ward's social stuff,' he said wryly.

She spread her hands and grinned. 'Because I'm horrendously bossy?'

'Because,' he said, 'you're full of great ideas. And I really appreciate you doing this for me, Dani. Waiting is… Well, I had patients earlier this week who'd had to wait for the results of genetic testing after CVS, after she found out at routine screening that she was a haemoglobin Lepore carrier; when they tested the dad, they discovered he was a beta thalassaemia carrier.'

Dani frowned. 'That's a tricky combination. Is the baby OK?'

'The baby's a carrier, but at least it's not going to have full-blown thalassaemia,' he said. 'They were lucky.'

'Hopefully we'll be lucky, too.'

But was hope enough?

Back at her flat, they went through the list of suggestions and wrote each one down on a piece of paper, then folded the piece of paper and dropped it into a jar.

'You pick tomorrow's,' Dani said.

He placed his hand over the top of the jar, gave it a shake, drew out a slip and read it out. '"The British Museum".'

'Which is one of my favourite places in the world,' she said with a smile. 'Meet you at the Tube station tomorrow at half-past eight and we'll head off to Holborn?'

'Are you sure that's not too early? You look a bit tired,' he said.

'I'm fine.'

He gave her a speaking look. 'Now who's fibbing?'

'I'll be fine.' She paused. 'Alex, do you want to stay here tonight?'

He stared at her, not sure what to say. Part of him wanted to be with her; part of him knew he needed to keep his distance. And he hated being torn apart like this.

She sighed. 'I'm not propositioning you, if that's

what you're thinking. And anyway, considering we've already... Well.' She rested her hand on her abdomen. 'What I meant was if you'd rather not be on your own, you're very welcome to stay. It's possible for us to share a bed without having sex.'

That was the real problem. The intimacy. Getting close to her, getting used to waking up with her in his arms—it would be oh, so easy. Dani's warmth and energy drew him like a magnet. But what if his test was positive? It would make things so much harder if he'd got close to her by then and had to back away. Better to keep his distance now.

'I'll be fine,' he lied.

'More like you'll be lying awake at stupid o'clock with all the worst-case scenarios running through your head,' she said.

How well she knew him. Or maybe it was what any normal person would do in his situation. He had no idea. But he definitely couldn't let himself give in to the longing to stay with her. Not tonight. Not until he knew where he stood, in genetic terms. 'I'm going to walk home,' he said, 'and by the time I get home I'll be physically tired and I'll sleep.'

'But if you can't, ring me,' she said.

Of course he wasn't going to be selfish enough to do that. He'd sit and flick through channels on the television and find something to distract him until his eyes closed. 'You need your sleep,' he reminded her.

'But I can still be there for you.' And her smile made his heart skip a bit. 'Just, if I fall asleep on your shoulder on the Tube tomorrow and start snoring, I'll need to you to sing or something to drown me out so people don't laugh at me.'

He couldn't help smiling. 'OK. See you tomorrow. And thank you.'

When Dani joined Hayley at the table in the canteen, she thought her best friend looked terrible, as if she wasn't sleeping. She'd seen Hayley this unhappy before, and reached over to squeeze her hand. 'Are you OK?'

'Yes—well, trying,' Hayley admitted.

'You're still worrying over your daredevil doctor?' Dani asked wryly.

'One who jumped into the canal the other day, to rescue a small child.'

'To be fair, that's a good thing to do,' Dani pointed out.

'I know. Which is why I hate myself for over-reacting. We had a huge row about it and I'm still feeling guilty. He's a good man, Dani.'

'And you love him.' Dani tried not to think about her own feelings for Alex. Or her growing conviction that he wouldn't be able to love her back.

'It's complicated,' Hayley said.

'But worth fighting for,' Dani said. 'I like him. A lot. He's good for you—and I think you're good for him.'

'Yeah.' Hayley wrinkled her nose. 'I just need to learn to stop worrying.'

'Something like that,' Dani agreed.

'At least we've got dance aerobics class tonight. That always makes me feel better,' Hayley said.

'Ah. I'm not going to be able to make it for a couple of weeks.'

'Oh, no—I hope you haven't fractured your foot

again.' Hayley looked concerned. 'Have you been running on it?'

'No and no,' Dani reassured her. 'I'm being sensible.
No, just a friend is having a bit of a rough time and I'm
trying to distract them.'

'Right. Well, if you need a co-distractee...'

Trust Hayley to offer. 'Thanks, Haze. I'll let you
know,' Dani said. 'Oh, and Alex from my department
is joining us for lunch when his clinic finishes.'

'Alex.' Hayley raised an eyebrow. 'Is there anything
you want to tell me?'

Tons. But she thought that Hayley had enough to
worry about. 'Just helping him settle into the department and get to know people better. You know what a
bossy, interfering cow I am.'

'What a lovely, organised woman with a huge heart
you are,' Hayley corrected. 'I could smack Leo. How
did he manage to convince you that it was all your
fault when he's such a cheating, lying slimeball?' She
reached over the table and hugged Dani. 'You deserve
so much better than him, Dani.'

'Uh-huh.' And even though Dani knew Leo had
lashed out to try and distract himself from his own
guilty feelings, she still wondered if there was a lot of
truth in what he'd said. That she'd never find someone
to love her because she was unloveable.

'You *do*.' Hayley stuck her hand up and waved.
'Alex,' she explained at Dani's mystified look. 'Let's
change the subject.'

'Good idea,' Dani agreed.

Having lunch with Dani and Hayley made Alex realise
what a hole there was in his own life. Seeing them to-

gether, the way they were so in tune, made him miss his own best friend. Especially as Tom had been the first friend he'd made at university.

Maybe he needed to start rebuilding some bridges.

He called Tom that evening on the way to Dani's from the supermarket—they'd agreed to chill out with a film in her living room rather than going out, as Dani had actually admitted to being tired. His heart was thumping madly; would Tom even speak to him, or would he just refuse to answer the call? Had he changed his number?

If the call went to voicemail, he'd hang up.

But then he heard Tom's voice, so familiar and yet sounding strange at the same time. 'Hey, Alex. How are you?'

So simple. So accepting. Why wasn't Tom giving him a hard time for spending the last ten months resolutely out of contact? 'I'm getting there,' he said carefully.

'Your head's in a better place now?' Tom asked.

Alex frowned. 'How much do you know?'

'When you did your big burning of bridges thing and sent me that text saying you'd gone travelling and you might not be back for a year, I rang your dad, because I thought you might be having some kind of breakdown and we needed to do an intervention,' Tom said. 'And he told me everything.'

'Oh.' Yet Will had said nothing to Alex. 'So you know about Stephen.'

'And the Huntington's. And the fact you don't want to take the test. Yes. You *idiot*. None of that was a valid reason for pushing all your friends away.' But it was said with affection. 'Did travelling help?'

'Not that much,' Alex admitted. 'And I'm sorry. You're right. I shouldn't have pushed anyone away, and you're the one person I probably should've talked to about it. But I had a hard job getting my head round it, and when I actually met Stephen...' He sighed. 'I guess it freaked me, seeing what the worst-case scenario looked like. And I just didn't want to be a burden to anyone, the way he was.'

'Idiot,' Tom said again. 'Of course you'd never be a burden. That's not how friendship works. You're there for each other in the good times and the bad. And if you do end up needing full nursing care, you're going to be bored out of your skull and need to see a few different faces during your week, aren't you?'

'Um.' Alex squirmed. 'So you kept in touch with Dad?'

'Yes. He said you were working in Muswell Hill. I thought about ringing you and suggesting we go out for a pint, but I wasn't sure you were ready to talk to me. I've been kind of hoping you'd call me.'

'A pint,' Alex said, 'sounds really good. And I'm sorry. I've behaved really badly.'

'Yup,' Tom agreed. 'But I don't think any of us knows how we'd really react in your situation until it happens.' He paused. 'So when are you free for that pint?'

'It's a bit complicated at the moment,' Alex said. 'A couple of weeks?' And then, if the results went his way, maybe he could ask Tom how he felt about being his best man. And godfather to the baby.

Which was when he realised just how much he wanted that. A life with Dani and their baby. No shadows of an incurable disease hanging over them.

'OK. Call me when you're ready.'

'Tom. Thanks. For not giving me the hard time I deserve.'

'Oh, I have years and years to make you suffer,' Tom said.

Alex could practically see the mischievous grin on his best friend's face. 'For what it's worth, I've missed you.'

'And I missed you, too, mate. Welcome back.'

'Thanks. I'd better go. Talk to you soon.'

'"Soon" had better be less than ten months this time,' Tom said.

'It will be. I promise.' His heart lighter, Alex ended the call.

Over the next couple of weeks, Alex and Dani were both busy at work. Christmas cards started to appear on all the noticeboards along with the thank-you cards from grateful new parents, and the reception area was decorated with a tree, tinsel and baubles. But Dani didn't think it felt quite like Christmas for either of them. She was remembering the run-up to Christmas last year, when Leo had made his shock announcement; and Alex was growing more and more tense with each day that passed, bringing his test results closer.

There was nothing either of them could do to influence the results of the test. Either he had the faulty gene or he didn't. But she kept him busy with their jar of distractions, and he was careful to make sure she didn't tire herself out.

But the hardest thing for Dani was the fact Alex was resolutely stubborn about keeping his distance. She knew he worried about being a burden, but couldn't he see that it didn't have to be that way? And if he did have the faulty gene, surely now—when he didn't have any symptoms—was the time to live life to the full?

Or was she just kidding herself, thinking that he was keeping his distance until he knew the results of the test, when in reality he just wasn't interested in a real relationship with her and she was expecting more than he was prepared to give?

The stupid thing was, the more time she spent with him, the more she grew to like him.

She more than liked him. Being with him made the world seem a brighter place, and she enjoyed sharing discoveries with him at museums on their dates-that-weren't-really-dates.

Which was really dangerous. Hadn't she learned her lesson from Leo—that it was pointless trying to love someone who didn't love you back?

Dani was still brooding about it when Hayley met her for lunch in the last week of November.

'I have some news,' Hayley announced.

'You've been promoted?' Dani guessed.

'Better than that.' She leaned forward. 'Sam asked me to marry him, last night. And I said yes.'

'That's fantastic!' Dani reached across the table and hugged her. 'I'm so pleased for you.'

'And I really want you to be my bridesmaid,' Hayley said. 'If you'd like to.'

'Like to? I'd be thrilled. That's just wonderful.' Dani grinned at her. 'It's the best news I've heard in ages.'

'And you'll help me choose a dress?'

'Of course I will. When do you want to go shopping?'

'As soon as possible,' Hayley said.

Dani blinked. 'When's the wedding?'

Hayley looked awkward. 'That's the thing—it's Christmas Eve.'

'*This* Christmas Eve? As in about a month away?' Dani asked.

'Um, yes.' Hayley bit her lip. 'Sam and I got a bit carried away with not wanting to wait any longer than we have to to get married, and a Christmas wedding would be so romantic—but I know what Christmas Eve means to you.'

The day Dani's husband had walked out on their marriage, saying there was someone else and they were expecting a baby. And Dani hadn't been looking forward to the first anniversary.

But no way was she going to rain on Hayley's parade. 'Actually,' Dani said, 'I'm really glad you're getting married on Christmas Eve. Because it means that this year I'm going to have a really, really good day on Christmas Eve. As your bridesmaid, I get to wear a gorgeous dress; I get to eat good food; and I get to have a good old dance with my mates—that is, I assume there's going to be dancing at your reception?'

'There certainly is—we're going to ask Maybe Baby to play, if they can make it.' Hayley looked anxious.

'But are you sure you don't mind the date? Because we can change it.'

'I'm really sure,' Dani said. 'Don't change it. I'm thrilled for both of you. This year, I'm going to have a happy Christmas Eve.' She pushed away the thought that Alex's test could be positive and if that happened then they'd be waiting for the results of their baby's screening test. 'And I'm going to be having too much fun to think about what it was like last year.' Her smile faded. 'There is one thing, though. Being Christmas, they're bound to play certain songs—is there any chance you can ask Maybe Baby not to play "Last Christmas"? Just I don't quite think I can handle the lyrics this year.'

'Of course I will.'

'It's going to be a while yet before I stop myself skipping it on the Christmas anthologies,' Dani said. 'We've got the ward's Christmas party next week, and I've asked Anton if he can keep it off the set list.'

Hayley gave her a hug. 'We're going to have only happy Christmas songs at the reception. Stuff like "All I Want For Christmas Is You".'

'Brilliant. Have you actually sorted out an "our song"?'

'Three of them,' Hayley said with a broad smile. 'Bach's "Air on a G String" while I walk down the aisle.'

'That's nice.'

Her smile broadened. 'Then "All You Need Is Love" when we sign the register.'

Dani laughed. 'I *so* know where you've pinched that from—and we are going to get the chance to watch our favourite Christmas movie together in December, aren't we?'

'We certainly are,' Hayley said. 'I'm not missing the Christmas Lobster for anything. And then we're having Bruno Mars' "Just The Way You Are" for the first dance.'

'I like that,' Dani said. 'Because it sounds as if you've come to terms with Sam being Sam.'

'Doing all his dangerous stuff,' Hayley said, but Dani could tell the grumpiness was feigned.

Dani smiled. 'It's the Year of Saying Yes, remember.'

'Not that you seem to have been doing too much of that yourself, Dani,' Hayley pointed out.

Oh, but she had. Which was why she was nine weeks pregnant right now. Part of her longed to confide in her best friend—but if she told Hayley that she was pregnant, then she'd have to tell her the rest of it. That Alex was taking responsibility for the baby and looking after her, and they were sort of dating each other to keep their minds off things—but they also weren't quite dating because he was keeping his distance, either because he was scared about being a burden to her or because he didn't love her but didn't want to let her down. And that she and Alex might have a really hideous decision to make, if his test results came back positive. The whole thing was such a mess, and she didn't want to drag Hayley into the middle of it. Especially now, when Hayley was planning to marry the man she loved and who loved her all the way back.

Instead, she smiled sweetly. 'Maybe I'll meet someone at your wedding reception.'

'You have to say yes to everyone who asks you to dance, you know,' Hayley warned.

Dani smiled. 'Of course. So is your engagement common knowledge, or is it still under wraps?'

'It's still under wraps. You're the only person we've told apart from our parents,' Hayley said, 'but Sam's going to propose to me at the ward's Christmas party—it'll be the last gift in the Secret Santa.'

'That's so romantic. So when do you want me to go dress shopping with you?'

'This weekend?'

'Sure.' Dani felt slightly guilty, as it meant Alex would have some time alone when he wouldn't be distracted and could brood about things, but she would still be able to see him in the evening.

Part of her was tempted to ask Hayley if she could bring a plus one to the wedding, but then again everything was still up in the air. The results of Alex's Huntington's test were due any time in the next week, and if they were positive then the last thing he'd want to do was to go to a wedding. Plus, if his results were positive then she would've had the CVS and be waiting for the results of that, too.

She pushed the thought aside. 'What else can I do to help?' she asked.

'I've done a Dani and made a list of things to tick off,' Hayley said with a grin, 'and I think we're pretty much sorted. Sam's arranging everything at the register office and the venue, so the major thing left is the dress.'

'Unless you know someone who can make it for you and actually has space in their schedule, we're going to have to look at dresses you can buy off the peg, be-cause there won't be time to have it made for you,' Dani said, remembering her own wedding and the time it had taken to have the dresses made to measure.

'Maybe we can sit down with my laptop tomor-row night and make a shortlist of dresses we like and which shops they're in,' Hayley said, 'and then I can check if the shop has the dresses in the right size for us to try on Saturday.'

'Perfect plan,' Dani said with a smile.

That evening, Dani went to the cinema with Alex, and was mortified to find that she'd nodded off in the mid-dle of the film.

'Was I snoring?' she asked, squirming.

'Yes, but fortunately it was an action film and the explosions on screen were louder than your snores. Just.'

'Very funny.' She paused. 'Alex, there's something I need to talk to you about. I'm so sorry to let you down, but I can't do our distraction thing tomorrow night. I know you'll keep this confidential—Hayley's getting married on Christmas Eve, and I need to help her with her wedding dress. She asked me to go over to her place tomorrow and help her with a shortlist, and then on Saturday we're going to try them on. I'll be as fast as I can.'

'Take as long as you need,' he said. 'In the circum-stances, Hayley's wedding should take precedence.'

'I want to support both of you. Maybe we can do something in the evening?' Dani suggested.

'Sure.' He paused. 'Does Hayley know?'

'About what?'

'The baby.' He dragged in a breath. 'My test.'

'No, to both.'

'So I'm your only support, too.' He paused. 'You really ought to tell her.'

'I don't want to be a burden to her.' Dani shook her head. 'Not now, when she's got a chance to be really happy again. I think I told you, her fiancé Evan was killed in an industrial fire a year and a half ago, trying to save someone, and it broke her heart. Although she and Sam got close, he's on the MERIT team, which means he's putting himself at risk in the same way that Evan did, and she found it pretty hard to deal with the idea.'

'But obviously they've sorted it out now.' He looked at her. 'You've been nagging me when I say I don't want to be a burden to anyone, but you're doing exactly the same thing.'

'No, I'm not. I fully intend to tell her everything. Just not until after the wedding. I want her to enjoy her special day without worrying about me.'

'I guess.' He sighed. 'I'm sorry. I wish things were different.'

That he didn't have the spectre of Huntington's in his genetic make-up? Or that he was in love with her and they would make a life with the baby together?

She didn't dare ask—because she wasn't sure she could cope with the answer.

'And are you OK about the wedding being on Christmas Eve?' he asked, surprising her.

'Yes.'

'Really?' he checked. 'Because that's obviously something else you wouldn't be able to tell her.'

'Actually, she's already asked me the same question,' Dani said. 'And it is fine. Because at least this year I have my best friend's wedding to enjoy. I'm going to have a great Christmas Eve, with good food and good music and a pretty dress, instead of having the person I thought loved me stomping all over my heart. I'm looking forward to the wedding. Sam's a nice guy and he's going to make my best friend really happy. Which makes me really happy.'

'That's good.' He saw her back to her front door. 'Well. I'll see you at work tomorrow.'

'You're welcome to come in for a coffee or whatever.'

He shook his head. 'You need your sleep.'

It felt like an excuse. What had made him so antsy? she wondered. Was it the discussion about weddings? Or was he using this as an excuse to distance himself from her even more?

CHAPTER NINE

ALEX WAS SHOCKED to discover how much he missed Dani's company the following evening. And he felt at a total loss on Saturday. He spent the morning at the gym, then did his Christmas shopping in the afternoon—and he found himself having no idea what to do about Dani. Should he buy her a present? They weren't exactly dating, but she was expecting his baby, so she counted as more than just a colleague. Their whole relationship was back to front and upside down.

Once he got the test results, they could move on. But he was still waiting to hear, and every day that passed seemed to drag on for longer and longer and longer. Several times now he'd had to stop himself ringing Libby and asking her if something had gone wrong or if he'd missed a message. Given the time of year, there was a strong chance that someone in the lab or Libby herself had gone down with a virus, and that was the reason for the delay. Maybe there was a backlog in the lab. There was nothing he could do to influence things, so he'd just have to wait until they were ready to give him the results. But patience, he thought, was seriously overrated as a virtue.

Finally, on the day of the ward's Christmas party, Libby left a message on his voicemail. 'Can you call the office to make an appointment, please?'

He went cold.

That had to mean the results were finally in.

Which meant that the axe was about to fall. Whether it was going to hit him or miss him, he had absolutely no idea. He had no control over this at all.

Oh, for pity's sake. Why couldn't Libby have told him in her message and put him out of his misery, instead of making it drag out like this?

His hand was actually shaking as he returned the call.

'It's Alex Morgan. Libby asked me to call to make an appointment,' he said when the receptionist answered.

'Of course,' the receptionist said. 'Would you like to come in today?'

Which meant even more waiting. Except now that there was a definite time limit to the wait, it was unbearable. 'Could you tell me the test result over the phone, please?'

'I'm sorry, I'm afraid I don't have access to the results.'

He dug his nails into his palm in sheer frustration. 'OK. Could Libby tell me?'

'She's with another patient right now, I'm afraid, so I can't put you through to her. We don't make appointments for Fridays, so shall I make you an appointment for next week if you can't make today?'

'I can make today,' Alex said quickly. If he had to

keep waiting, he'd be a basket case by tomorrow, let alone next week. 'When can you fit me in?'

'Half-past five?'

It would mean he'd have to leave early, but he'd have a quiet word with the head of department to explain and he was pretty sure it wouldn't be a problem. 'That's fine,' he said. 'Thank you. I'll be there.'

Should he ask Dani to go with him? he wondered as he ended the call. Then again, it would be too complicated to get her to leave early, too, especially on the day of the ward's Christmas party when everyone would be going to the pub straight from work and she was the main organiser of the event. She already had enough on her plate. Plus, if it was bad news, he'd rather that she heard it from him once he'd had a chance to come to terms with it.

If it was bad news, then he'd send her a text saying that he'd gone down with a virus and was sorry to dump all the Christmas party stuff on her. And then he'd work out just how he was going to break the real news to her first thing tomorrow.

Somehow he managed to deal with a ward round, a clinic and an emergency Caesarean section. Dani was in clinic all day and he didn't get a chance to see her, let alone leave her a message. And what could he say, in any case? After a quiet explanation to their head of department, he left the ward and headed to Libby's office.

Her previous appointment was running fifteen minutes late. By the time the counsellor finally called him in, Alex felt sick with anxiety.

'Come in and sit down, Alex,' she said with a smile. Was that a smile of relief, because it was good news;

or a smile of sympathy, because it was bad news? He didn't have a clue. This was worse than waiting for all his exam results rolled into one—far worse, because at least with exams he'd had a good idea how he'd performed, but with this there was no way of knowing and it was completely out of his control.

'Your results are back,' she said, 'and I'm pleased to say there are twenty-five CAG repeats.'

He stared at her, trying to process what she'd just said.

Twenty-five CAG repeats.

Finally it clicked. 'That's in the normal range. At the top end of the range, but still normal. So you're saying I don't have Huntington's?' he checked.

'You don't have Huntington's,' she confirmed.

He blew out a breath. 'You could've told me that in your message. Or your receptionist could have told me that over the phone.'

Libby shook her head. 'We've been through that, Alex. We always give the results face to face, never in a message or over the phone. And we never give results on a Friday because we don't want anyone being unsupported over a weekend. Having a negative result has just as much impact as a positive one.'

'Of course it doesn't—a positive result means the axe hanging over you actually falls on your neck, whereas a negative one means it misses,' he snapped. Then he grimaced. 'I'm sorry, Libby. That was unfair of me. I've been on tenterhooks waiting for the results, but that doesn't give me the right to take out my frustrations on you, and I apologise.'

'No problem. It's a perfectly normal reaction, and

I'm not going to take it personally. As I was saying,' she said gently, 'having a negative result can have a huge impact on you. You've had your life on hold for months, and now you can move on again. Of course you're going to be relieved, but there are going to be all sorts of other emotions in there as well—guilt that you might have hurt someone over the situation, or made them worry about you. And this has been a real emotional ordeal for you, because you're not the only one affected by the result.'

He rubbed a hand over his eyes. 'This means the baby's OK. I don't have the bad gene, so I can't have passed it on. Dani won't have to have CVS, and we won't have to worry about making a really hideous decision.' He looked at Libby. 'Actually, I can't quite take this in.' He'd tried to prepare himself for the worst-case scenario, because the odds were so high. And now that worry wasn't there any more, he felt disorientated.

'Can I get you a glass of water or a cup of tea?' she asked.

He shook his head. 'Thanks, but I need to go. I'm supposed to be at the ward's Christmas party. I'm co-organising it.' Not that he'd done a huge amount. Dani had shouldered the burden.

'Can you text your co-organiser with a white lie and say you've got a tummy bug or something?'

He smiled wryly. 'That was my plan if the test was positive. But it's not. And now I can move on.'

'It might be an idea to have some time to yourself, just to process the news and get used to the idea,' Libby warned. 'Because sometimes relief puts people in a bit of a whirl, and they end up saying the wrong things.'

'No. I need to tell Dani.' And, more than that, now he knew he didn't have to keep himself at a distance any more, he could finally act on the feelings he had towards her. This would be a new beginning for Dani, himself and the baby. 'Thank you, Libby,' he said. He shook her hand. 'Thank you for everything.'

Once he'd left the building, he called his parents.

His mother answered. 'Alex? Is everything all right?'

'Everything's fine, Mum. I'm in a bit of a rush right now as I'm on the way to the ward's Christmas party, but I wanted you to be the first to know. I took the test for Huntington's, and I'm fine. So you don't have to worry any more. It's all good.'

'Oh, Alex. Thank God you're all right. Thank God my stupidity…'

He could hear her crying, and guilt twisted into him. He should've done this when she'd first told him the news about Stephen, instead of leaving her to wait and worry and come to the worst conclusions. He'd thought he was being oh, so noble—but now he realised he'd actually been stubborn and unreasonable and selfish. And he felt thoroughly ashamed of himself. 'I'm sorry, Mum. For everything. But it's all going to be OK now.' He swallowed hard. 'I'll take you and Dad out to dinner next week to celebrate,' he said. 'We'll talk soon. I have to go. But I love you, Mum. And Dad. Tell him for me.'

'Love you, too,' she said through her tears.

At the pub, there simply wasn't time to tell Dani the news—there were last-minute things to sort out. Besides, he didn't want to tell her in front of a room full of people. He'd wait until the end of the evening, when he saw her home and it would be just the two of them.

He wasn't sitting anywhere near Dani during the meal; instead he was with Jas and Gilly, the midwives, but thanks to Dani making him go to lunch with them so he got to know them better, he was relaxed in their company and found himself enjoying the party and the banter. He felt slightly guilty that the box of posh chocolates he'd brought as a Secret Santa present was so boring, when so many of the others were inventive and clearly based on long-standing departmental jokes. But the food was good, the company was good, the jokes in the crackers were incredibly corny, and he liked the fact that even their head of department was wearing a paper hat and joining in with the raucousness.

And he didn't have to fake a single one of his smiles.

After the meal, Anton and Gilly left the table and joined the rest of the band on stage; once the tables had been cleared away, everyone started dancing and singing along to the Christmas favourites that the band were playing.

He didn't get a chance to see Dani until Maybe Baby started playing a slow dance. 'Dance with me?' he asked.

She smiled back at him. 'Sure.'

It felt so good to hold her close.

He desperately wanted to tell her the good news, but now really wasn't the right time—they needed to be on their own. But hopefully she'd let him see her home and he could tell her then.

* * *

At the end of the night, the staff who were on early shift the next morning had already gone home. The band packed up their gear, and everyone else said their goodbyes.

'Can I walk you home?' Alex asked.

'OK,' Dani said.

He smiled at her. 'It was a good night,' he said.

Yes, and it had been nice to see him come completely out of his shell and relax with everyone; she'd seen him laughing with Jas and Gilly at the far end of the table from her. She knew how tense he was about the results he was still waiting for, so she was glad that the party had been a kind of light relief for him.

But something was still bothering her. 'Where did you disappear to before the party? I thought you might've been in Theatre, but someone said they'd seen you leave the ward earlier.'

'I had an appointment. The counsellor rang me,' he said.

She blinked at him. 'You mean you've got the results?'

'Yes. And I'm clear. Twenty-five CAG repeats. I don't have Stephen's faulty gene.'

She stopped dead, flung her arms round him and hugged him. 'You're all right. You're not going to get Huntington's!' She held him tighter. 'And that means the baby's OK, too.'

Everything was going to be all right. Especially as his arms were wrapped round her. Relief and joy flooded through her. They wouldn't have to make a hideous decision. It was going to be fine.

But then, as they stood there together, the little bubbles of joy started to burst as she realised the implications of what he'd just said. She pulled away and stared at him. 'Wait. You've known all night that you don't have the gene and you didn't tell me until now?'

'The middle of the ward's Christmas party is hardly the easiest place for a conversation—especially for one like this.'

'You could have texted me,' she pointed out.

'I wanted to tell you myself, not send you an impersonal text message as if it was something that didn't really matter.' He looked at her. 'I don't want to fight, Dani.'

'Neither do I.' But she was hurt, all the same. Something as important as this, and he hadn't included her. Even though they were in this together. If it had been the other way round, she would have made the time to tell him. How stupid she'd been to think that they'd got closer over the last few weeks. How stupid she'd been to let herself fall for another man who didn't love her back. 'You didn't even tell me you had the appointment.'

'I didn't get a chance. They called this morning. And you and I haven't exactly been in the same place all day. I wasn't just going to leave you a text so you worried yourself sick with waiting. Believe me,' he said, his voice dry, 'waiting for news when you know you won't hear for weeks is nothing like knowing you're actually going to hear in a few short hours. It's like all your exam results days rolled into one, except this time you haven't got a clue what the result's going to be.'

'You still could've told me.' But instead he'd chosen to block her out, yet again.

'I'm sorry.' He sighed. 'But we don't have to worry about the baby any more, Dani. Everything's going to be fine.'

And she didn't have to hold off on the scan. She could finally let herself think about the child growing inside her and make plans for their future. Part of her was thrilled, but part of her was hurt at the way he'd excluded her yet again. 'Uh-huh.'

'And we can get married.'

Had she just heard him correctly? 'What?'

'We can get married,' he repeated.

Marriage wasn't something they'd ever discussed. Alex had made it clear that he'd step up to his responsibilities for the baby, but he hadn't said anything about his relationship with her. They'd tacitly left it that he wasn't in a good place until he knew the truth about his genetic heritage; and they wouldn't discuss it until then. She'd thought maybe they'd got closer on their dates-that-weren't-really-dates, but he'd said nothing about his feelings.

And now he was casually saying that they could get married?

He wasn't telling her that he loved her and wanted to be with her, or making any kind of declaration of his feelings towards her at all. Just the plain, bald statement that they could get married. Almost as if he was suggesting a trip out or having fish for dinner on Friday instead of sharing his life with her.

So he wasn't asking her to marry him because he loved her. This had to be a mixture of guilt and responsibility talking; he was suggesting that they should get married simply because he thought he ought to, for the baby's sake.

No way.

Dani been married before, but Leo had at least loved her when they'd got married, even if he'd fallen out of love with her afterwards. And she knew what it felt like being married to someone who'd fallen out of love with her. How much worse would it be if she married someone who didn't love her in the first place?

'No,' she said.

He stared at her. 'What do you mean, no?'

'I mean,' she said, 'my best friend is about to get married to someone she loves deeply—someone who loves her all the way back. I'm not prepared to settle for less than that. So, no, Alex, I won't marry you.'

Why was he looking so shocked? Did he really think she'd marry him just to give the baby his name? This was the twenty-first century. They could sort out the baby's name and he could see the baby without them having to be married.

Alex had spent the last few months being stubborn about not letting people close because he'd thought he'd be a burden to them in the future—wrongly, on all counts. Well, now it was her turn to be stubborn. Though she was pretty sure her reasons were a great deal sounder than his had been. She absolutely wasn't going to get married to someone who didn't love her.

'Right now,' she said, 'I think you have an awful lot of bridges to rebuild. I suggest you go home and make a start on that.'

He lifted his chin. 'I said I'd see you home safely.'

'I'm thirty-two years old, and I'm perfectly capable of seeing myself home safely,' she said wearily. 'Right now, I don't even want to talk to you.' She wanted to push him in a puddle, but fortunately for him the evening was dry. 'Please, just go home.'

'Dani—'

'Go home, Alex,' she said, and turned away from him.

Alex stared at Dani as she walked away.

It was late, and she was pregnant. The decent thing to do would be to see her home safely, make sure that she was all right.

But she'd made it very clear she didn't want him to do that.

OK. He'd compromise and walk behind her at a suitable distance. Far enough away that he wasn't going to crowd her or upset her, but near enough to be at her side in a few seconds if he was needed.

Doggedly, he walked behind her, keeping a good thirty metres between them and hanging back at the corner of her road. As soon as she closed her front door behind her and he knew she was safe, he walked back to his own flat.

Why had she refused his proposal?

He thought about it.

My best friend is about to get married to someone she loves deeply—someone who loves her all the way back. I'm not prepared to settle for less than that. So, no, Alex, I won't marry you.

Was she saying she didn't love him?

Or was she saying she didn't think that he loved her?

He could ask her for clarification, but right now she'd made it clear she didn't want to talk to him. And he could hardly ask Hayley, given that Dani hadn't told her a word about what was going on.

He thought about it some more. Leo had left her because he'd fallen for someone else. Dani wanted someone who loved her.

Alex loved her.

But he hadn't actually told her that. He'd been so busy trying to keep his distance that he'd kind of assumed she'd realise how he felt about her.

Telling her now would definitely seem like too little, too late. He needed to prove to her that he loved her, and that it wasn't just because of the baby.

He needed to woo her, properly.

And he'd really have to hope that she'd give him a chance.

CHAPTER TEN

ON FRIDAY, ALEX and Dani were both on a late shift. Mid-afternoon, when they were due a break, he went into the staff kitchen and to his relief found her there alone. 'Dani, can we go and talk in a quiet corner of the canteen?' he asked.

'Sorry, I'm busy,' she said.

'You're on a break,' he said, 'and it's your Year of Saying Yes, so technically you have to agree.'

'Maybe I've stopped doing that,' she said, narrowing her eyes at him.

'I wasn't trying to push you,' he said.

'No?'

'No.' He sighed. 'I was trying to make light of things and instead making a mess of it. You and I are at odds right now and we need to clear the air—if nothing else, to make things less awkward for the people who have to work with us. I'm sorry I've been such a clueless idiot, especially as you've been so brilliant with me over the last few months. Come and have a cup of tea or whatever with me, Dani. Please.'

She looked reluctant.

'Plus we need to discuss some practical things about the baby, and it ought to be sooner rather than later.'

'I guess.' She wrinkled her nose. 'All right. A cup of tea.'

'Thank you.' It was a start. And hopefully he could build on things from here and prove to her that he loved her—that he wanted to marry her for her own sake, and the words had all come out wrongly yesterday.

He found them a quiet table in the canteen.

'So what did you want to talk about?' she asked.

'We know I don't have the faulty gene, which means the baby doesn't either,' he said. 'So you don't need CVS now, and can go ahead with the dating scan as normal.'

She looked at him. 'Where exactly are you going with this?'

'I'd like to come to the scan with you,' he said.

'There's really no need. I can manage by myself.'

'I know you can manage, but it's my baby, too. And I want to be there,' he said. 'For selfish reasons. Because I'd like to see the baby's heartbeat on screen.' And to hold her hand while they looked at the screen together, though Alex judged it was probably better to keep that bit to himself for now.

'Have you told your parents the news yet?' she asked.

'About the baby?'

'About the test.'

He nodded. 'I told Mum about the results yesterday, when I came out of the counsellor's office. And I spoke to Dad this morning. I told him I'd kept the test quiet because I didn't want them having the stress of waiting for the news, but it's all good now. He said things are better between them, so I think it's finally going to be all right.'

'What about the friends you pushed away?' She paused. 'Or Lara?'

'No. But you were right yesterday. I do have a lot of bridges to rebuild.'

She lifted her chin. 'And now you know you don't have the gene, you can maybe repair your engagement.'

Was that what she really believed? That he was going to walk away from her, even though she was expecting his baby, and try to make things up with his ex? Then again, it had been almost a year since her husband had left her for someone else. Of course it would be the first thing she'd think of.

'Apart from the fact that I've heard on the grape-vine Lara's seeing someone else, I'm not in love with her any more,' he said. Because he was in love with Dani—not that he thought she was ready to hear that yet. 'That's one of the other things I wanted to talk to you about. You had a late night last night, and I'm guessing you're feeling it a bit today. I'd like to keep cooking dinner for you, so you get a chance to put your feet up and rest in the evening.'

'I'd rather you didn't,' she said.

OK. He'd try another way. 'And I think we should continue our distraction list.'

She frowned. 'Why? You don't have to wait for the news any more so you don't need your mind taken off things.'

And now was the time to be honest with her. 'That's

not why I want to do it,' he said. 'I enjoyed spending time with you, and I want to do more of that.'

She looked at him as if she didn't believe a single word.

'Plus, while we were doing the distraction stuff, I bought tickets for a couple of things, and it would be a pity to waste them.'

Her frown deepened. 'You didn't tell me you'd bought tickets for something.'

'I'm telling you now.'

She lifted a shoulder in a half-shrug. 'You could take someone else.'

'In theory, I could,' he said. 'But the tickets are for things I wanted to share with you.'

Her eyes filled with tears. 'Don't pretend feelings you don't have, Alex. I've been there before and I never want to be in that situation again.'

So he'd guessed right: it wasn't that she didn't have feelings for him, but that she didn't believe he had feelings for her. 'I know, and I'm not pretending anything,' he said. He looked her straight in the eye. 'I could tell you, but I don't think words are enough. You need to see it for yourself.'

She said nothing.

Then again, he didn't deserve to have this made easy for him. 'We synchronised our off duty, so I know you're not working tomorrow. I'll pick you up at one.'

'I…' She sighed. 'You're not going to give in, are you?'

'No.' Because this was way too important. He'd been an idiot and pushed her away, but he intended to fix it. He wasn't going to let her put barriers up and push him away, too.

'All right. I'll see you at one.'

'Thank you.'

Dani was ready before one o'clock the next day, knowing that Alex would be dead on time. Did he mean it about wanting to spend time with her? Or was he still thinking about things from a dutiful perspective, as the father of her baby?

For now, she'd reserve her judgement.

Alex rang her doorbell. 'OK to go?' he asked when she answered her door.

She pulled on her coat. 'Yes. Where are we going?'

'Somewhere I hope you'll like.'

Which told her nothing, but she wasn't going to argue with him. She was picking her battles carefully.

They caught the mainline train from Alexandra Palace and then the tube to Covent Garden. Alex shepherded her through the crowds and she hadn't a clue where they were going until they stopped outside the theatre and she saw the show's name all lit up: *Mamma Mia*.

'You bought tickets for this?' she asked, surprised.

He shrugged. 'It's one of your favourite musicals. Word perfect on the songs, I think you said.'

'But this isn't really your kind of music,' she said. She knew he preferred rock and blues.

'It's yours, and that's what matters,' he said.

So he really had been paying attention to some of what she'd said?

'Thank you.' But she felt really guilty when she discovered how good their seats were. Given that he could only have bought them in the last couple of weeks, he must've had to go through one of the ticket resellers to get them. She bit her lip. 'I hope you didn't pay an exorbitant price.'

'That's between me and the Internet,' he said with a smile. 'But, instead of feeling guilty, I'd rather you just bought me an ice cream in the interval. I want you to enjoy this.'

The music and dancing worked its usual magic on her, and Dani found herself holding Alex's hand in the second half of the show. She was surprised that he actually stood up with her and most of the rest of the audience for the finale and sang along to 'Mamma Mia', 'Dancing Queen' and 'Waterloo'—although he was far from word perfect, he was at least making the effort. For her? Or was she kidding herself?

'Do you have time for dinner?' he asked afterwards.

'OK, but as you bought the theatre tickets I insist on buying dinner,' she said. 'That's not negotiable.'

'All right. And thank you.'

And she didn't pull her hand away when he curled his fingers round hers and they walked back to Covent Garden.

This felt more like a real date than their 'distraction' dates ever had. So did Alex have feelings for her? Or was he still thinking mainly about the baby?

She pushed the thought away and concentrated on enjoying the Christmas lights at Covent Garden and finding somewhere to eat.

Afterwards, Alex saw her back to her flat. 'Can I see you tomorrow evening?' he asked.

She shook her head. 'Sorry. Hayley and I are watching our annual Christmas film.'

'Annual Christmas film?' he asked, looking mystified.

'Our favourite Christmas move—*Love Actually*. We watch it every year and argue over whether our favourite moment is Hugh Grant dancing or Colin Firth with his terrible Portuguese,' she explained.

'But you're free during the day?'

She shook her head. 'Sorry. I need to clean my flat and sort out my laundry.'

'Here's the deal,' he said. 'How about I do your housework in the morning, and you give me an hour and a half of your afternoon?'

He was actually offering to clean her flat for her?

She must've spoken aloud, because he smiled. 'Yes. And I'll do it the way you want me to.'

He must really want to spend time with her. 'So what does the afternoon entail?'

'Come with me and find out,' he coaxed.

And he turned out to be as good as his word, cleaning her bathroom and vacuuming her flat and even setting up her ironing board, ready to tackle her laundry pile.

'I can do my own ir—' she began.

'Yes, but you don't have to. Put your feet up and read a magazine.'

She pulled a face. 'I did enough resting when my foot was at its worst. And I feel guilty about you slaving away doing my housework.'

'There's not much difference between doing a bit of

vacuuming and making dinner, you know. And you're pregnant. You need to rest.'

'Rest is a four-letter word,' she pointed out.

He sighed. 'OK. You can do your ironing.'

'Thank you.'

She'd just about finished when he said, 'It's time to go.'

Again, he wouldn't tell her what they were doing until they reached their destination: but then he ushered her into a grand London hotel.

'I thought we could have a Christmas afternoon tea,' he said.

There was a massive Christmas tree in the corner of the room, decorated with red and gold tinsel and baubles; garlands and swags in similar colours decorated the rest of the room. A pianist in the opposite corner in white tie and tails was playing a selection of Christmas songs—though not, to her relief, 'Last Christmas'.

The waiter led them over to their table, which was beautifully set with a white damask tablecloth, bone china cups and saucers, and a real silver tea strainer. Once they'd chosen their tea—English breakfast for Alex and passionfruit and orange for Dani—the waiter brought over a china cake stand with their afternoon tea. 'The sandwiches on the bottom tier are cream cheese and cucumber, turkey and cranberry, and ham and mustard,' he said. 'The middle layer are warm winter spiced scones, wrapped in a napkin to keep them warm, with apricot jam and clotted cream; and on the top there are apple and cinnamon doughnut baubles, mini mince pies, Stollen bites and mini chocolate Yule logs. If there's anything you need, just ask.'

'Thank you,' Alex said.

'This is lovely,' Dani said. It was the sort of thing she would've enjoyed planning as a surprise treat; and it was wonderful to be on the receiving end.

'It's meant to be one of the the the best Christmas afternoon teas in London,' he said.

'I can see why. The bread's perfect,' she said after her first taste of the turkey and cranberry sandwich.

And the scones were even nicer. 'Best ever. I'm definitely going to bring my parents here,' she said. 'My mum would love this.'

'Have you told your parents about the baby?' he asked.

'Not yet,' she said. 'It's something I'd rather do face to face.' She looked at him. 'Have you told yours?'

'I'm holding out until we have a scan photo,' he said.

'That's a good idea. I might do the same.'

'Do you want me to come with you when you tell them?' he asked.

That rather depended on how things were between them. 'Maybe,' she hedged. And should she offer to go with him? But that assumed a level in their relationship that she wasn't sure they'd reached.

'Just let me know. I'll leave it to you,' he said.

So he wasn't being pushy about it. That made her feel a little bit better.

Even so she was quiet when she went over to Hayley's for their planned movie evening. How were she and Alex going to tell people about the baby? And how were people going to react?

'Are you all right?' Hayley asked when she handed Dani a mug of hot chocolate.

'Sure,' Dani fibbed. 'We're really busy at work. You know how it is.'

'You would tell me if something was wrong, wouldn't you?'

Guilt flooded through her. 'Of course,' she said. Nothing was wrong, now—Alex's test results meant that the baby definitely didn't have Huntington's. But if she told Hayley about the situation tonight, she knew her best friend would worry about her, and she wanted Hayley to enjoy her wedding to the full. Dani promised herself that she'd tell Hayley everything when she was back from her honeymoon.

Though she found herself feeling more wistful than usual when they watched the film. The endings of some of the relationships in the story were clearly happy, and others were more ambiguous. How would it all work out between Alex and herself? She still didn't have a clue how he felt towards her, even though he'd spent the weekend making such a huge fuss of her. Was it only because of the baby, or was it for her?

Alex walked into the pub and scanned the room for his best friend. Tom had clearly been watching the doors because he raised his hand from his seat by the bar. Funny, he didn't look any different from when Alex had last seen him, the best part of a year ago. And yet so much had changed in that time.

'Thanks for meeting me tonight,' Alex said when he reached Tom's table. 'Especially as I didn't exactly give you a lot of notice and it's coming up to Christmas.' And especially as he'd been totally unavailable for the last ten months.

'It wasn't that hard to move things round. And it's good to see you, Alex. I've missed you.' Tom gave him a hug. 'So how's it going?'

'It's a bit complicated,' Alex said ruefully. 'Let me buy you another pint and I'll tell you about it.'

When he sat back down at their table, Tom said, 'Explain complicated.'

'Put it this way—how would you feel about being my best man and godfather?' Alex asked.

Tom stared at him, looking shocked. 'Wait, what? Marriage and a baby? When did all this happen?'

Alex filled him in on how Dani had rescued him when he'd been at his lowest point, her unexpected pregnancy, and the fact that she'd just refused to marry him. 'Which was all my fault for not asking her properly,' he admitted. 'I just said to her that we could get married.'

'You said what? You idiot! Why didn't you tell her you were madly in love with her and she'd make you the happiest man in the world if she'd agree to marry you?' Tom shook his head sorrowfully. 'Alex, I'm beginning to think you shouldn't be allowed out without your own personal PR person to tell you what to actually say, and also tell you when to shut up.'

'I could probably do with some personal skills training,' Alex admitted.

'Book a course online. Tonight,' Tom said, rolling his eyes. 'So what happens now?'

'I'm trying to show her that I love her,' Alex said.

'Because I keep getting it wrong when I open my mouth, and actions speak louder than words, right?'

'That depends on what you do,' Tom said.

'If I *can* persuade her to marry me, would you be my best man—and godfather to our baby?' Alex asked.

'I'd be honoured. But only if I meet her first and she actually likes me,' Tom warned.

'Don't you need to see if you like her, too?' Alex asked.

'From what you've told me,' Tom said, 'I already like her. She's good for you.' He paused. 'Have your parents met her yet?'

'No. And I haven't told them about the baby either.'

Tom groaned. 'You really do like living dangerously, don't you?'

'She hasn't told her parents either,' Alex pointed out. 'We've been waiting on the results of my genetic test. Once we've had the dating scan and got photographs for them, we're going to come clean.' He dragged in a breath. 'And I'm pretty sure they're all going to want to know what we're going to do—if we're going to raise the baby together as a family.'

'Is that what you both want?' Tom asked.

'It's what I want. What I hope Dani wants,' Alex said. 'But until I can convince her how I feel about her, I need to keep everything under wraps. Just for a little bit longer.'

'Good luck,' Tom said, 'because I think you're going to need it.'

On the Monday Dani was able to book a scan for the end of the following week. Alex continued to spend the evenings with her, cooking dinner while she had a power nap, and she had to admit that she really appreciated the rest—the hormones were really wiping her out.

He also took her to a candlelit carol service in the middle of the week. Singing Victorian carols in an ancient church was incredibly moving; and it felt natural for Dani to tighten her fingers round his when he held her hand. Afterwards, they walked through Trafalgar Square to get hot chocolate and see the Christmas tree, still hand in hand.

This felt like the way things had been when they'd first started their 'distraction' dates, she thought. Though he still hadn't kissed her or said anything about his feelings. She had absolutely no idea where she stood with him. He must care about her, or he wouldn't be trying to look after her; then again, was he only doing that because she was pregnant and he felt it was his duty to look after her?

Normally, she would've been straight-talking and asked. But they were heading towards Christmas—and last year her world had imploded at Christmas. She really couldn't face a repeat of that.

At the weekend, Alex produced tickets for the Christmas trail at Kew. 'It's meant to be really gorgeous,' he said. 'Everything from a tunnel of lights through to the light show at the Palm House.'

And the trail lived up to the hype, with festive lights and sculptures everywhere. There were old-fashioned fairground rides; although Alex refused to let her go on the helter-skelter, citing her newly healed foot, he agreed to ride with her on the old-fashioned carousel. Dani felt ever so slightly swept off her feet when he helped her onto the white horse with its gold-painted mane; and she liked the fact that, as the horses seated two, Alex climbed on behind her and wrapped his arms round her waist.

Tonight he was making her feel really cherished.

There were fire pits next to stalls of gourmet marshmallows; she picked cinnamon and apple flavour, and Alex toasted them for her.

'This is amazing,' she said. 'I've never done this before.'

'Me, neither,' he said. He gestured to the children holding their parents' hands as they queued up to see Father Christmas. 'This could be us in a few years, bringing our little one.'

So was this thing between them still all about the baby? Or was it about them?

She still didn't have an answer by the end of the evening, even though Alex actually kissed her goodnight, and it made her feel weak at the knees.

Was she getting carried away by the magic of Christmas? Or did they have a future?

The day before Dani's scan appointment, the ultrasound department called her.

'I'm so sorry. The radiographer you're booked in with has gone down with the virus that's doing the rounds, so I'm afraid we'll have to reschedule your scan appointment,' the receptionist told her.

'Thanks for letting me know.' Dani was able to re-book the appointment for just after Christmas, but there was a hard knot of disappointment in her stomach. She'd hoped that going to the scan would finally push Alex into talking about his feelings. It looked as if she was going to have to wait.

She told him about the change that evening when he'd cooked them pasta and garlic bread at his place. 'So it'll be another couple of weeks.'

'Are you OK with that?'

She shrugged. 'You know what it's like, working in a hospital over the winter. People go down with viruses all over the place. It can't be helped.'

But the disappointment must have shown on her face, because he wrapped his arms round her. 'So this means either telling your parents without the photograph or waiting a few more days.'

'I'd rather give them a photograph,' she said.

'OK. I'll go with that, too,' he said.

But he still didn't tell her he loved her.

Then again, she hadn't told him either.

One of them was going to have to say it first. But right now she didn't want to take the risk, in case she was guessing wrongly and he didn't say it back.

On Christmas Eve, Hayley and Sam got married. Dani, as the bridesmaid, couldn't help being slightly teary-eyed as they made their vows; it was good to see them both looking so happy. And it gave her so much hope for the future; last Christmas Eve, she'd felt that love had just stopped existing. This year, it would be different.

She loved the way that Sam's brother had organised a snow machine for the photographs. This was what a real wedding should be like, she thought: full of light and love and laughter.

Alex turned up as one of the evening guests, looking handsome in a formal suit. How ridiculous that it should make her heart skip a beat; she saw him in a suit all the time at work. And yet when he came over to talk to her, her knees went weak. The way he smiled at her, the warmth in his eyes... Was she getting carried away with the wedding atmosphere, or did it mean something?

'You look amazing,' he said. 'That dress really suits you.'

And, being empire line, it hid the fact that she was starting to develop the tiniest, tiniest bump.

'Thank you.' She smiled at him.

'Dance with me?'

She nodded, and of course Maybe Baby would choose that exact moment to play a slower song. What could she do but step forward into his arms and sway with him to the music?

I love you.

Alex almost said the words.

Almost.

But this was Christmas Eve. The first anniversary of the day that Dani's husband had broken her heart. This would be the worst possible time for him to talk about love. And it wasn't the right place either: her best friend's wedding.

So he just held her close and hoped that he'd find the right words to tell her, and the right place to say the words.

Soon.

CHAPTER ELEVEN

ON CHRISTMAS DAY, Dani drove over to her parents' house.

Mandy Owens greeted her with a hug. 'I'm so glad you're home. I mean, after la—' She stopped mid-word, looking horrified.

Dani knew what her mother had just stopped herself saying. 'Mum, honestly, it's OK. You don't have to walk on eggshells or worry about what you say because of what happened last Christmas with Leo. It's a year ago now and I'm fine. I'm over him.' And, thanks to Alex, she really was.

'I just worry about you being lonely, love.'

Dani smiled. 'I'm way too busy to be lonely, Mum.' This time next year, she'd be busier still. Not that she could talk about that yet. So instead, after they'd exchanged presents, she distracted her mum with the shots of Hayley's wedding on her phone.

'And you say she's gone to Iceland for her honeymoon?' Mandy asked.

Dani nodded. 'How romantic is that? Christmas, the Northern Lights, and guaranteed snow.'

And although she really enjoyed spending the day

with her family, with the chatter and the board games and their traditional post-lunch walk in the park, she realised as she drove home that she'd actually missed being with Alex.

Did he feel the same way about her?

Maybe it was time she stopped being such a coward and actually asked him.

She'd do it at the scan, she decided.

As she walked through her front door, her phone pinged to signal an incoming message. She looked at the screen, half expecting it to be a late one from Hayley, but it was from Alex.

Merry Christmas.

So he had been thinking about her, then.

Merry Christmas, she texted back. How was your day?

She knew that, like her, he'd spent his day with his parents.

Good. Yours?

Good, she replied.

I'm glad. See you at the scan on Tuesday?

The scan. She wasn't sure if she was more excited or terrified about it. Everything had been on hold for so long. Would the scan finally be the place where they could move on?

See you Tuesday, she typed.

* * *

On Tuesday morning, Dani met Alex in the hospital reception area at half-past eight.

'Given that the most of the radiography department know both of us, even though we can insist on patient confidentiality,' she said, 'this is when I think we're going to be outed.'

'Would you rather say that I'm just supporting you as your colleague?' he asked.

She damped down the hurt that he'd even asked. 'If you like,' she said, keeping her voice cool.

'Actually, I don't like. At all,' he said. 'I'm going with you because this is my baby.'

'So people are going to know. They're going to ask questions.'

'Bring it on,' he said.

The radiographer called Dani in to the ultrasound suite. 'Dani, it *is* you!'

'Hi, Jessie,' Dani said with a smile.

'I wondered if it was when I saw your name on the list, but then I thought it was probably just someone else with the same name,' Jessie said. 'I had no idea you were expecting.' She looked at Alex and raised her eyebrows. 'OK. Obviously I'll keep full patient confidentiality.'

'Thank you,' he said.

Jessie looked at Dani's notes. 'So you're almost fourteen weeks.'

'I know it's really late for a dating scan,' Dani said, 'but we had a very good reason for leaving it this long.'

'My biological father died from Huntington's,' Alex said, 'and we didn't know if I'd inherited it. We had to wait for my test results to come through to see if we needed to consider CVS for the baby.'

'I assume that your test was all clear, then?' Jessie asked.

'Thankfully, yes,' Alex replied.

'That's good,' Jessie said. 'One less complication to worry about. Well, not that I'd dare try to tell an obstetric consultant and a registrar about when to worry in pregnancy!'

'I did have a scan booked for twelve weeks, but the radiographer I was booked in with went down with that virus that was doing the rounds, and then it was Christmas,' Dani said.

'Well, you're here now and that's what matters,' Jessie said. 'I guess you already know the drill, as you both use the portable scanners in your department or the emergency department, but do either of you have any questions about the procedure?'

Dani shook her head. 'No questions. We just want to see the baby.'

'It's always a lovely moment, seeing a baby on the screen,' Jessie said. 'But when it's your own it's very different. If you didn't bring tissues, I have some.' She gestured to the box by the side of the low bed where Dani was lying. 'I'm warning you now that you'll need them.' She looked at Alex. 'And I mean *both* of you.'

'Thanks,' Dani said.

She bared her stomach and Jessie smoothed radio-conductive gel over her skin, then ran the head of the transceiver across Dani's abdomen.

'And here we are,' Jessie said quietly, turning the screen so they could both see it. 'One baby. There's a nice heartbeat there; I can see ten fingers and ten toes, and the spine looks good.' She did some quick measurements. 'And you're spot on with dates, Dani. The baby's measuring at fourteen weeks.'

Dani could barely take it in; her whole attention was focused on the black and white image on the screen, the heart beating steadily and the baby moving around in the womb.

She'd seen babies plenty of times before on the screen when she'd performed an emergency scan. But Jessie was right: although it was always a lovely moment to see the baby's heart beating, it was completely different when it was your own baby. Visceral. And she was shocked by the tide of fierce, protective love that swept over her.

She glanced up at Alex and realised that his eyes were wet.

So were her own. She hadn't even realised that she was crying.

'I'll give you both a moment,' Jessie said, and left the ultrasound suite.

'Our baby.' Alex's eyes were wide with wonder. 'Dani. There's something I want to say to you.'

'Me first,' she said. Because now was the time to be brave. 'I've realised over the past couple of months that you're not very good with emotional stuff. When you just casually said we could get married, it sounded as if you'd sort of proposed out of duty—that you thought you ought to do it for the baby's sake. But the way you've been with me ever since… It makes me think—hope—that you might feel about me the same way that I feel about you.'

'I hope you feel the same way about me,' he said, 'because I love you, Dani. I know our relationship has been totally upside down, with the baby coming first, and I was trying to hold back because I didn't want to be a burden to you if I ended up testing positive for Huntington's. But then you were so tired, and I wanted to support you, and I found myself falling for you anyway. When we started dating, even though we called it distracting each other from waiting for the test results, I fell for you even more. And I made a complete mess of asking you to marry me. It was too late to tell you then that I loved you because it seemed like an afterthought—and it wasn't, Dani.' He shook his head in apparent frustration. 'It's so stupid how I always know the right thing to say at work, but when it comes to my personal life I make such a hash of it.'

'But then you tried to show me how you felt,' she said. 'You did some really special things for me—that carol concert, taking me to *Mamma Mia*, and toasting marshmallows for me at Kew. It showed me you'd listened to what I said.' She paused. 'I thought you might say something at Hayley's wedding.'

'I wanted to,' he admitted. 'But it was Christmas Eve, the anniversary of a really bad time in your life. Part of me wanted to say something to make you forget that, but part of me didn't want to risk the association.'

'Actually, you were right not to say anything,' she said. 'Christmas Eve wasn't appropriate.'

He dropped down on one knee. 'This probably isn't an appropriate time either—and my best friend says I need my own PR person to tell me when to speak and what to say—but I love you, Dani, and you'd make me the happiest man in the world if you'd agree to marry me.' He took a deep breath. 'Danielle Owens, you make my world a better, brighter place, and I want to spend the rest of my life with you. Make a real family with you. Will you marry me?'

She took his hand and drew him up to his feet. 'I love you, too, Alex. Yes.'

He kissed her then, and it was so tender that she found herself in tears all over again.

'Hey.' He kissed her tears away.

'They're happy tears,' she said.

'Good.' He wrapped his arms round her and kissed her again. 'So how fast do you reckon we can organise an engagement party?'

'That's an easy one,' she said. 'We have New Year coming up. Your flat's bigger than mine. All we need to sort out are drinks and nibbles—which we can buy ready-made from the supermarket—and a playlist of music.'

'What, no pomegranate molasses?' he teased.

She laughed. 'We're going to do something uncomplicated for once.'

'Sounds good to me.' He looked at her. 'So we need to tell our parents. And Hayley and Sam.' He paused. 'Um. I'm assuming Hayley will be your bridesmaid and godmother?'

'If that's all right with you.'

'I'm more than happy.'

'What about your best friend?' she asked. 'Have you started patching things up yet?'

He nodded. 'We've started rebuilding bridges.'

'So I'm guessing he'd be your best man and our baby's godfather?'

'If you're happy with that.'

She smiled. 'I'm happy.'

Jessie knocked on the door and came back in. 'All OK?' she asked.

'All very OK,' Alex and Dani said in unison.

'Excellent. I forgot to ask you—would you like a photograph, and if so how many copies?'

'Six,' she said promptly. 'One each for us, one for both sets of parents, and two for the godparents.'

'And we have an engagement party, a wedding and a christening to plan,' Alex said, holding Dani close. 'This time, we're going to try to get things the right way round…'

EPILOGUE

July

'THIS HAS TO be the most beautiful baby in the history of the universe,' Mandy Owens said, giving her new grandson one last kiss before passing him to Tracey Morgan for a cuddle.

'He's adorable,' Tracey agreed. 'And my daughter-in-law is the cleverest girl in the world.'

Alex and Dani exchanged a glance. Their parents had definitely forgiven them for sitting on the news for the first few months. Mandy had cried when they'd given her a copy of the scan photo, and Sid had then grilled Alex to within an inch of his life, making absolutely sure that Alex wasn't going to hurt Dani the way that Leo had.

Tracey had cried, too, and hugged Dani. 'It's because of you that we have our son back—and now a grandchild to look forward to as well. No more shadows.'

'At the beginning of last year, I think the world was a difficult place for all of us,' Mandy said. 'But now the sun's shining, our kids are happy, and we've got little Harry William Sidney Morgan to look forward to making a fuss over.'

'What, even when his nappy needs changing?' Alex asked with a grin.

'I have a feeling that's going to be our department, Will,' Sid Owens said with a rueful smile.

'Of course it is,' Will Morgan agreed. 'We're modern granddads. And the nappies nowadays are much easier to sort out than they were when our two were young.'

'Unlike the prams,' Sid said, looking mock-disgusted.

Alex laughed. 'I happen to know how much time you two spent researching the best car seat that turns into a buggy and a pram. You loved every second of playing with it in the shop. And I hate to think what his wooden train set's going to be like when he's older.'

'As if we're plotting how many bridges, turntables and sheds we're going to have,' Will teased, and hugged Dani. 'I'm so thrilled and honoured you named him after both his granddads.'

'Seconded,' Sid said.

'Just as, if we have a girl next time, her middle names will be Amanda and Tracey,' Dani said with a smile.

Her mother and Alex's both went pink with pleasure.

'I can't wait to take him to the park,' Will said.

'We need one with a boating lake,' Sid said, tapping the side of his nose.

'And an area where we can launch a rocket—not one of those foot-pump air things but the proper sort with a motor and a parachute,' Will added.

Alex and Dani exchanged a glance, not sure which

made them happier—the fact that their parents all got on well, or the way their fathers were having such fun plotting what they wanted to do with their grandson.

Just then, there was a knock at the door.

'Come in,' Dani said. 'Save us from the granddads and their trains, boats and rockets.'

Hayley and Sam walked in, carrying a bottle of champagne, some plastic glasses and a card. 'Congratulations,' Hayley said, and handed the bottle and glasses to Danielle's father. 'Sid, would you and Will mind…?'

'Of course,' Sid said, and he and Will sorted out the cork and pouring a glass for everyone.

'And once I get a cuddle with my newborn godson,' Hayley added, 'I might just forgive you for originally keeping the news from me for so long, Danielle Morgan.'

Tracey handed the baby to her with a smile. 'He's so like Alex when he was born, Hayley, though I know his eyes will change and be like Dani's.'

'Oh, he's beautiful. Well, little man, welcome to the world.' Hayley cuddled him. 'And, unlike your mum, I don't sit on exciting news for months instead of telling my best friend who's actually more like a sister than a friend. So you can gurgle at your mum and tell her that at Christmas, young Harry, you're going to have a little playmate.'

'Wait—what?' Dani asked. 'You and Sam…?'

'We're three months. I was going to tell you earlier,' Hayley said, beaming, 'except we were a teensy bit busy planning a wedding.'

Will gave her a hug and clapped Sam on the shoulder. 'That was Dani's line when we told you, Haze, and you said that was even more nonsense than waiting until you're past the first trimester to tell the people closest to you. And, as an obstetrician, I might remind you that I'm good at doing maths and counting backwards.'

'OK, so I waited until the first trimester was over. *Next* time, we tell each other the second we've done the test,' Hayley said.

'It's a deal.' Dani hugged her. 'Congratulations, both of you.'

'Thanks.' Sam smiled at her and took the baby from his wife. 'Hello, gorgeous Harry. And don't listen to your mum about trains, boats and rockets. They're great. Your dad and I are going to be right there with you and the granddads. And we're going to teach you and the Bump how to rock-climb and skate and bungee-jump...'

He was greeted with a round of groans from the four women.

'It could be worse,' Alex pointed out. 'Mum, Mandy—has he shown you that video of people doing the forward abseiling?'

'Nightmare,' Dani said. 'Don't even think about scaring them, Sam. We'll stick to skating and trains, OK?'

Sam kissed the baby. 'Your mum's scary. I'd better do what she says. And give you back to your dad, because I think there's a nappy change needed.'

'That would be perfect practice for December,' Dani said with a wink.

'She's right,' Hayley agreed. 'Plus it's godfather duties.'

Sam groaned and accepted a nappy from Alex. 'I can't even claim that I have to get back to work instead, because we came up at the end of our shift.' Deftly, he changed the nappy. 'Right, Harry. Now you smell nice again, you can go back to your mum.'

He handed the baby back to Dani, and accepted a glass of champagne from Will.

'Welcome to Harry,' Alex said, lifting up his glass. 'And congratulations to Hayley and Sam—because babies are the most precious gift of all.'

'The most precious gift of all,' everyone echoed, and lifted their glasses.

* * * * *

If you missed the previous story in the
MIRACLES AT MUSWELL HILL HOSPITAL
duet look out for

CHRISTMAS WITH HER DAREDEVIL DOC

If you enjoyed this story, check out
these other great reads from
Kate Hardy

MUMMY, NURSE... DUCHESS?
THE MIDWIFE'S PREGNANCY MIRACLE
CAPTURING THE SINGLE DAD'S HEART
HER PLAYBOY'S PROPOSAL

All available now!

MILLS & BOON®

MEDICAL ROMANCE™

THE ULTIMATE IN ROMANTIC MEDICAL DRAMA

MILLS & BOON®

EXCLUSIVE EXTRACT

He enticed her into one sizzling night… Now notorious
sheikh Hazin al-Razim is desperate to claim midwife Flo
as his bride!

Read on for a sneak preview of
CHRISTMAS BRIDE FOR THE SHEIKH
the second book in Carol Marinelli's
RUTHLESS ROYAL SHEIHKS *duet*

Hazin lowered his head and their mouths met before he
was even fully seated. His lips were warm and Flo's pouted
to his.

Soft and sensual, his mouth claimed hers.

She had never known a kiss like it, for it sent a river
of shivers through her and the brief bliss of relief faded
for she *had* to taste his tongue, yet Hazin made her wait. His
hands came to her upper arms and he held her steady when
she ached to lean into him.

Then his mouth left hers and she felt its warm drag
against her cheek and the scratch of his jaw as his lips
found her ear. His breath was warm and he told her his
truth. 'I want you so badly.'

For a second she sat, his cheek pressed to hers, his
ragged sexy breathing in her ear and his hands firm on her
arms and Flo closed her eyes in a vague prayer for common
sense to prevail.

It didn't.

Fired on by one kiss, her body crackled like a chip in
hot oil and she offered her response to his indecent request.
'Take me to bed.'

Don't miss the scorching duet from Carol Marinelli:

RUTHLESS ROYAL SHEIKHS
Two royal brothers – bound by duty,
but driven by desire!

A born leader and a playboy prince… But *nothing* is
more important to Ilyas and Hazin al-Razim than
honouring their royal birth right!

Until their searing passion for two beautiful, fiery women
challenges everything they've ever known – and these
sheikhs won't rest until they've claimed them…

Discover the first part, Ilyas's story
CAPTIVE FOR THE SHEIKH'S PLEASURE

Sheikh Ilyas al-Razim won't let *anything* stand in his
way, especially not the waitress daring to think she can
blackmail him! He'll take the impossibly stunning
Maggie Delaney as his hostage… But once her
innocence is proven, dare she surrender to the pleasure
this desert prince promises?

Available from Mills & Boon Modern

And read the second part, Hazin's story
CHRISTMAS BRIDE FOR THE SHEIKH
Available from Mills & Boon Medical Romance
Both available December 2017!
www.millsandboon.co.uk

Join Britain's BIGGEST Romance Book Club

- **EXCLUSIVE offers every month**
- **FREE delivery direct to your door**
- **NEVER MISS a title**

Call Customer Services
0844 844 1358*

or visit
millsandboon.co.uk/bookclub

* This call will cost you 7 pence per minute plus your phone company's price per minute access charge.

KCB4

MILLS & BOON®